I0666651

A New Creation

The Beyond Belief Trilogy

Book One

A New Creation

Jayne Lawson

This book is NOT the inspired Word of God. It is a historical novel based on real people and events which occurred during biblical times as recorded in the Holy Bible. All incidents and dialogue, and all characters with the exception of some well-known historical figures, are products of the author's imagination and are not to be construed as real. Where real-life historical figures appear, the situations, incidents, and dialogues concerning those persons have been embellished with conversations, feelings, and background from the author's imagination.

All Scripture references are taken from the King James Version of the Bible.

All rights reserved solely by the author. The author guarantees all contents are original, except where quoted from the KJV Bible or otherwise noted, and do not infringe upon the legal rights of any other person or work. No part of this publication may be reproduced in any form without the written permission of the author.

Cover illustration by Ryanna Campbell.

Copyright © 2020 by Jayne Lawson
All rights reserved.
ISBN: 978-0-578-67067-6

Acknowledgments

To my husband, John, thank you for making my dream of visiting Israel come true. Your love and support made this book possible.

Thank you, Ryanna, for using your gift of art to draw the cover illustration for me. I love you so much!

Thank you, Jimmy Jr. and Rick DeYoung, for guiding John and me through the footsteps of Jesus as you took us throughout the "Land of the Bible," teaching us and sharing the Word of God, past, present, and future!

Thank you, Pastor Tim Campbell, for sharing so many books from your personal library with me to help in my research of ancient Israel.

Thank you, Jesus, for saving me, loving me, and promising to one day take me home to be with you forever.

A New Creation

Chapter One

"And we know that all things work together for good to them that love God, to them who are the called according to his purpose." Romans 8:28

The desert sun had not been up long as Hadassah made her way along the steep pathway leading from the Sea of Galilee back to her aunt's home. The water in the clay jug the young woman carried on her shoulder sloshed back and forth as she maneuvered her way around several large stones that threatened to send her sprawling if her dark eyes wandered too far from the trail. Pausing for a moment, she balanced the jug with one hand while she hooked a stray lock of black hair behind her ear. Nodding her head in greeting to the younger girls who passed her on their way to Capernaum's largest public well, Hadassah whispered "Shalom" as they scurried by. She envied those girls who didn't have the long trek to the freshwater sea on the city's edge, but because her aunt, Judith Caelinus, insisted that her water be drawn from the largest body of fresh water in the region, Hadassah made the trip to the sea daily.

Judith believed there were magical healing powers in its waters, but Hadassah knew the truth. Water was water. That was it. Nothing magical about it, but she would never say that to her aunt. It was not appropriate; she would never disrespect her father's sister, so she obliged Judith by remaining silent and filling her jugs with water from the huge lake without complaint.

Hadassah picked up her pace, then stifled a small cry as she stubbed her toe on the jagged edge of a rock jutting out from a clump of dried out weeds. "Serves me right for my ill thoughts. Forgive me, Lord," she whispered, not stopping to inspect her injury. Knowing she needed to have the water warmed for her aunt, Hadassah continued swiftly up the road to the home she shared with Judith and Justus Caelinus. She glanced eastward toward the glowing orange orb rising in the cloudless sky, then hastened her steps even more. It would not go well for her if she were late. Judith would not be pleased.

She hurriedly passed by the homes of families she had known since she was a child, turning onto the path that led away from the awakening town. Most of the dwellings in Capernaum were small and unadorned, simply serving as a shelter for the family of a carpenter, fisherman, or other tradesman. Built to house a man and his family, these stone and mud brick houses lined the streets of the Jewish village.

Constructed with a single large room in which to prepare meals and gather with the family in the evening, most were practical and simple. Unless there was a second floor, families usually slept on the flat rooftops of their homes in the cool of the desert night.

In comparison, the Caelinus home stood apart in its grandeur. Surrounded by a large outer wall composed of irregular stones fitted together so tightly they required no mortar, the property was partially occluded from the curious eyes of passersby. Stoic dark-skinned servants clad in leather breastplates over linen tunics flanked the massive wooden gates to the main house. Date palms near the whitewashed portico stood tall and regal, gently swaying from the warm arid winds while providing a bit of shade and protection from the relentless heat of the sun. Ornate statues carved from large marble boulders lined a cobbled walkway to the formal entrance, and drought resistant shrubs and ornamental flowers were symmetrically placed on the columned porch. The house itself was formed of the same type of hewn stone as the walls, but intricate carvings in the outer walls provided a decorative border to the building.

Inside was just as grand. White plastered walls throughout the multi-floored home were adorned with mosaics that mimicked the designs found in the palatial Roman houses. The largest rooms were for individual members of the family, others for guests or entertaining, and the rest for keeping the household functioning. Even the servants had their own living quarters although they were small and furnished sparsely in comparison to the opulent rooms of the master and mistress of the house.

As Hadassah approached the back entrance, she lowered her gaze as she moved past the guards. Although they knew her, and she knew them, not a word passed between the men and the young woman as she entered the well-foliaged courtyard. She walked quickly up the narrow outer staircase to the second floor and entered the house quietly.

Moving along the familiar passageway to Judith's bathing chamber, she entered the room and set the water pot down near the kettle. Picking up a bundle of small sticks, she placed them in the fireplace and lit the kindling with a nearby candle. Soon the fire was burning with enough strength to warm Judith's water. Hadassah poured the clear liquid into the kettle, then hooked the metal container over the dancing flames. Retrieving several small towels from a shelf, she placed them neatly in a hand-woven straw basket near the fire where its warmth would permeate the cloths. On a smooth wooden tray, she arranged five vials of scented oils from which Judith would select the fragrance that appealed to her the most.

"Hadassah? Is my water prepared?"

Hadassah turned toward the bedchamber immediately. Judith's voice was not unkind, yet Hadassah knew she was expected to be prompt about her duties, and despite the gentility in the voice, she knew a negative response would upset her aunt terribly. They were family, but Judith was the mistress of the house, and Hadassah was expected to obey without question.

"Yes, Dodah Judith. It is ready," replied Hadassah, using the Hebrew term of affection for her aunt. As soon as she was bid, Hadassah carried the warmed water into the inner room, then left quickly to retrieve the towels and oils. When she reentered the bedchamber, she set the basket on a small wooden table adjacent to the canopied bed, and the tray of oils on the dressing table.

Judith allowed Hadassah to help her out of her nightclothes, then sat on the edge of her bed as she reached for a towel.

"Ah, you warmed these as well. You are so good to me, Hadassah." She buried her face into the heated cloth. "Would you dampen this for me?" She handed the towel to Hadassah, who dipped it into the warm water, then wrung it out before giving it back to her.

Hadassah stood quietly by the bedside as Judith finished her cleansing ritual. Holding a light blue linen gown, she slipped it over Judith's head and shoulders, securing it with a gold brocade belt around the slim waist of the thin woman.

"The oils, please." Judith waited as Hadassah brought the tray to her.

Judith picked up a tiny glass bottle, inhaled its fragrance, then set it back in the basket. She repeated this with each of the other bottles, then said decisively, "I'd like the lavender today. It's such a soothing scent." She cupped her hand.

Hadassah poured a few drops of the precious oil into her aunt's palm and watched as Judith rubbed the fragrance onto her pale skin. Assured that no more oil would be needed, Hadassah set the vial back into the basket and picked up an ivory comb. Moving to Judith's side, Hadassah began to pull the comb through the long dark hair of the Hebrew woman. A few strands of gray peeked out from among the thinning black tresses, hinting not of Judith's age, but of a long-lasting illness that had tormented her for years. Gently untangling the strands, Hadassah combed and plaited her aunt's hair expertly, pinning it back, allowing an unhindered view of the golden teardrop earrings that Judith loved to wear.

"You have such a gentle touch, Hadassah. I don't know what I'd do without you," smiled Judith as she inspected her reflection in a polished bronze mirror. "My necklace, please."

From a finely entwined chain of gold links hung an ornate silver charm. Shaped like a serpent poised to strike, Judith had purchased it years ago on her first trip to Damascus. Reported to have healing powers, Judith wore it faithfully. Hadassah carefully clasped the pagan piece of jewelry around her aunt's neck.

"Perfect," stated Judith as she gingerly caressed the necklace. "Justus loves this piece."

Justus Caelinus was an important man in Capernaum and that pleased him greatly. Although he could trace his Jewish ancestry, Justus had been born a Roman citizen, never seeing Judea until he had been sent as a young man to the region by the Roman government. Since he had never associated himself with Jewish society, his loyalties were firmly aligned with the Romans, and securing their favor by demonstrating his shrewdness with money as a Judean tax collector was a position he relished. Although this duty was usually assigned to local inhabitants, Justus' placement was a carefully calculated maneuver by Rome to keep firm financial control on the region.

While Justus occasionally embellished the customs due, he usually treated the Jews fairly, but he was still perceived as an outsider. Until he married Judith, that is. While he insisted he only had the best interests of the Jews in his heart, he was still a Roman representative and not trusted by the majority of the Jews in the area. Although he was never openly snubbed, Justus knew that was not acceptance either. He was smart enough to know that it would take more than mere words to endear him to the people from whom he was sent to collect taxes.

After a few weeks in Capernaum, Justus had identified Judith's father as a worshipper of money more than one who worshipped the Hebrew God, and the fact that he had an attractive daughter of marital age did not go unnoticed by the Roman official. Persuading the girl's father to allow Judith to marry a Roman tax collector was easy. The small purse Justus offered the greedy merchant was more than ample to garner the old man's permission to marry Judith. Once wed, the walls of blatant disfavor began to crumble around Justus. The wisdom of marrying a local Jewish girl squelched many whispers of skepticism regarding his motives, especially since Judith's father made no secret that he wholly supported the union, claiming Justus was "really a Jew in his soul." Justus' generosity to the merchant's meager purse had paid off.

From Judith's perspective, her marriage to Justus was a way to escape the drudgery of life as a merchant's daughter and an opportunity to move up in the social status of Capernaum. She embraced without reserve the wealth and opulence that came with Justus' position, never giving her godly heritage a single thought as she eagerly accepted the ways of the Romans and their gods.

"Hadassah, I am finished. You may remove these." Judith gestured to the items Hadassah had brought into the bedchamber, then asked, "Tell me, am I presentable?"

"You are beautiful as always," responded Hadassah as she removed the bathing items.

Judith laughed softly. "You would tell me that even if I were a shriveled old hag, wouldn't you? No matter. When you say that, it satisfies my soul's desire." She stood and walked over to a window. Her blue eyes brightened a bit as she looked out toward the horizon. "It is a lovely morning, is it not? The gods will be benevolent today."

The paleness of her skin and the frailty of her body made Judith appear much older than her actual age. The beauty and enthusiasm for life that had caught Justus' eye so long ago had waned, causing her to constantly beg the Roman gods for a restoration of health and a husband who would not reject her. Her eyes hopeful, she turned abruptly and said, "I must go pray."

Hadassah looked up at her aunt through thick black lashes, saddened for the woman before her. She loved her aunt dearly, and it broke her heart every time Judith bowed down to the idolatrous gods.

Retreating to her personal place of worship, Judith would kneel before a small pagan altar where she would beseech the favor of Diana, the Roman goddess of love. After that, she would pray to Aesculapius, the god to whom was attributed the gift of healing. Having depleted all of her own resources for a cure, Judith's hopes for recovery now rested solely in the gods of Rome.

The illness had robbed her of the pleasures that she had embraced in her first years of marriage. Traveling with Justus to places like Jerusalem, Hebron, or Damascus had thrilled her. There was even a time when Judith had accompanied Justus on one of his annual trips to Rome, but now she usually remained in Capernaum when her husband traveled. On those rare occasions when Justus needed her presence with him in Caesarea to see the games or celebrate a festival, she would go, but it cost her greatly. The fatigue from travel exhausted her and robbed her of any joy from the trip, but she would never refuse Justus. Her fear of being replaced by someone younger, healthier, and more beautiful overcame any discomfort from the chronic disease that plagued her.

As Hadassah tidied her aunt's bedchamber, a gentle breeze blew in through the window and with it, the faint scent of almond blossoms. As she worked, her mind wandered to an earlier time in her own life. Rekindled memories of long ago brought a smile to her lips. She pictured her mother mending garments and speaking of how God had brought His children to the Promised Land from Egypt. The stories of the miracles He had done that resulted in the Egyptian pharaoh allowing the Israelites to leave the foreign land had thrilled her as a young child.

As she worked, she smiled as one of the psalms her mother taught her came to the forefront of her mind. Her softly sung words filled the bedchamber. "I will praise Thee with my whole heart. Before the gods will I sing praise unto Thee. I will worship toward Thy holy temple and praise Thy name for Thy lovingkindness and for Thy truth for Thou hast magnified Thy word above all Thy name."

With a song in her heart, Hadassah placed clean nightclothes under the pillows, then picked up a small woolen blanket near the foot of the bed. Its deep blue yarns were entwined with golden strands creating a woven picture of the stars, sun, and moon, and as Hadassah held the fabric in her hands, the joy within her was replaced by an overwhelming sorrow. Judith's dependence on the stars guided her daily decisions, and ever since her journey to Damascus, where she had purchased the intricate piece of handiwork, she had kept the small tapestry near her. Hadassah grimaced as she folded the idolatrous blanket and set it at the bottom of the bed.

Despite her displeasure with Judith's lack of faith in the Hebrew God, Hadassah was grateful for being allowed to worship the God of her forefathers. Judith never prevented her from going to the synagogue or having her own quiet time to pray to the One in whom her own faith was anchored.

She sighed as she scanned the room. Everything was in its place. Hadassah was meticulous in her cleaning, taking care even in the smallest detail. Satisfied with her tasks, she returned to her own room, allowing her mind to amble back once more to an earlier time when she stood on a small wooden stool alongside her mother, baking bread together. Honoring God through her labors was most important for a woman. Her mother had taught her that, and Hadassah was determined to honor her mother and her God in her service to Judith every day.

She paused by her window and gazed out toward the hillsides surrounding Capernaum. How she wished she could bake one more loaf of bread with her beloved mother! Although her childhood memories were less vivid now, she treasured each one that she could recall. Except one.

Her father, Benjamin, had been a hard worker, and Deborah, her mother, had always stood by his side. On a trip to Tyre, a confrontation with thieves had left many in their traveling party dead or dying as the merchants resisted the marauders. Hadassah's life had been spared due to her mother's quick thinking, but when a family friend found her, she had become a homeless little girl. When she returned to Capernaum, her father's older sister, Judith, had insisted Hadassah come to live with her and her husband.

Justus Caelinus was not thrilled to have a little girl as part of his family, but he relented as long as his wife accepted full responsibility for the child. Unable to have children of her own, Judith saw Hadassah as an answer to her many prayers to the Roman goddess of fertility and an outlet for her maternal desires.

In her first few months of living with Judith, Hadassah had learned much, and even Justus was forced to agree that the young girl had been a blessing to the Caelinus household. Now, more than a decade later, Hadassah's memories of her life before coming to live with Judith were only shadows in her mind. The one thing she managed to hold on to was her faith, and Hadassah was grateful that Judith had never forced the worship of Roman gods upon her.

With her morning work behind her, Hadassah relished the opportunity to have her own personal time with her Lord. She grabbed a shawl, wrapped it around her shoulders, and headed to her favorite quiet place. Entering the courtyard garden, she retreated to a secluded corner and a small stone bench. Here she sat and allowed the serenity of nature to flow over her. Although she could no longer see her mother's face, Hadassah knew the woman who had given her life loved the Lord dearly. Deborah had instilled the importance of daily prayer and worship into her daughter's heart, and Hadassah had remained faithful to her upbringing. Closing her eyes, Hadassah bowed her head and whispered a psalm she had memorized many years ago.

"I will bless the Lord at all times! His praise shall continually be in my mouth. My soul shall make her boast in the Lord; the humble shall hear thereof and be glad. O magnify the Lord with me, and let us exalt His name together. I sought the Lord, and He heard me, and delivered me from all my fears."

She kept her head lowered and allowed the peace of God to envelop her as she quietly meditated on the words she had just offered up in worship. The fragrance of the flowers wafted through the air, and she felt at peace.

Opening her eyes slowly, her gaze fell upon a cluster of blue irises.

The symbol of faith and hope.

Reaching out to gently touch the petals, she murmured softly, "For Thou art my hope, O Lord God: Thou art my trust from my youth. By Thee have I been holden up from the womb: Thou art He that took me out of my mother's bowels: my praise shall be continually of Thee."

As her sweet praises drifted upward to heaven, she humbly prayed, "Do not forget me, O Lord. I am your servant. Help me to do Your will and to trust You as my father and mother did and our forefathers before them." Hadassah hesitated for a moment, then added, "Please help Dodah Judith to forsake all other gods and return to You."

Although she longed to spend more time in the solitude of her beloved garden, Hadassah rose to her feet, smoothing her tunic as she stood. While she had completed her specific tasks for Judith, there were many other needs of the household to which she was responsible. Daily activities were to be handled without a word from the mistress of the house. Hadassah mentally reviewed her duties as she reentered the house and headed toward the kitchen.

Oversee Judith's midday meal preparation.

Replace the flowers in the bedchamber.

Fill the lamps with—

Hadassah's head jerked toward the cooking area as she heard a loud clamoring beyond its door. As she moved toward it, an enraged voice shrieked.

"It must be perfect! Everything must be perfect!"

Hadassah recognized the high-pitched voice of Aelia, the Caelinus' gray-haired housekeeper. Serving the Caelinus family long before Hadassah had arrived, the aged Jewess kept the household running efficiently and seamlessly. No one wanted to be on the receiving end of Aelia's displeasure. Hadassah opened the door to the kitchen just enough to peek in through the crack.

Aelia's nostrils flared, and she vigorously shook one finger as she chastised a young boy who stood wide-eyed and silent in front of the angry old woman. Flinging her hands in the air, Aelia's eyes narrowed as she continued her rampage. "This will not do! Look at this fruit! It is unacceptable! Caelinus' son is coming, and you expect me to serve this? Where does your master get his fruit? From the refuse heaps? No, take this back! And don't return until you have something suitable for serving. Tell him if he cannot do better, I shall take my business elsewhere!"

Aelia turned on her heels and stomped off, leaving the young lad holding a basket of overripe fruit in his shaking hands.

Hadassah quietly closed the door and leaned against it.

Justus' son? Coming here from Rome?

She had met her uncle's only son once when she was a very young girl, and even without knowing anything about Rome's cruel and oppressive nature, Marcus Caelinus had frightened her with his centurion battle dress and weapons of war. Now older and better able to understand the presence of the Roman Empire in her homeland, Hadassah's recalled memories frightened her. Marcus' reputation as a Roman centurion was no secret to anyone in the Caelinus household. He was a fierce man in battle, and now he was coming to Capernaum.

Hadassah's breathing came in short gasps as her hands covered her mouth.

A Roman centurion!

She involuntarily shuddered.

Chapter Two

"And the fourth kingdom shall be strong as iron: forasmuch as iron breaketh in pieces and subdueth all things: and as iron that breaketh all these, shall it break in pieces and bruise." Daniel 2:40

Sebastos was always busy with ships coming and going. Designed by Herod the Great, the man-made harbor at Caesarea made the city a very prosperous seaport, as well as the political center for the Roman province of Judea. Its horseshoe-shaped breakwaters provided protection from the powerful waves of the eastern Mediterranean Sea, making it a popular hub of trade in the region. Merchant ships laden with salt from the Dead Sea or grain from the fertile fields of Egypt frequently made port at Sebastos, selling their cargo to traders to take on their own journeys to the east and north. Occasionally, Roman warships offloaded military troops and equipment, maintaining a strong presence in the invaluable port, displaying the Empire's strength and control. Today was no exception.

The single mast of the *Romulus* caught the sea breeze, which aided the thirty rowers as they propelled the ship through the harbor's narrow entrance. Standing quietly on the oak deck of the vessel, Marcus Caelinus surveyed the activity in the seas around him. As the sun glinted off his silver helmet, Marcus turned his gaze toward the hills surrounding the harbor and the temple of Augustus that overlooked the city of Caesarea. Dedicated to the emperor of Rome, the white-stoned monument stood sentry, welcoming seafarers to Rome's Judean capital. It was the first thing sailors saw as they approached the seaport, and its impressive structure verified that Caesarea was an integral part of the Roman empire.

Even though the ship had been traveling at a good speed, the voyage had been too long for Marcus. Two weeks at sea had taken its toll on the Roman centurion, and he was anxious to be on land. Impatient to disembark, his mood was dark as he scowled, and his steel blue eyes bore into the nervous eyes of the deckhand who interrupted his schedule.

"Centurion, your mount will be brought out as soon as possible once we dock." His voice trembled as he addressed the imposing soldier before him.

Marcus barely acknowledged the comment as the sailor slinked away. Preoccupied with the thought of the task before him, his eyes remained fixed on the landing site as the ship maneuvered to its position at the dock. Ropes from the bow and stern were cast toward the moorings and secured to cypress pilings before the gangplank was lowered.

Expertly moored, the ship groaned to a halt. The sun was nearly overhead, and despite being on the ocean, the heat was rising. Marcus was anxious to be on his way. Unaccustomed to waiting, he strode purposefully toward the ship's cargo ramp ignoring the wary looks from the overworked sailors struggling to reposition sacks of grain and barrels of salt for offloading.

The sharp whinny of a horse came from the ship's hold, and Marcus shielded his probing eyes from the sun as he strained to see into the cavernous bowels of the vessel.

"C'mon, you stubborn beast before I take a whip to you."

Marcus' lips formed a tight line when he saw the harsh yanking of his horse's reins. Fire rose in the centurion's deep-set eyes. Beside the unsuspecting sailor in three strides, Marcus grabbed him by the back of his neck and tossed him unceremoniously on his back.

"If there is any evidence of mistreatment to my horse, you will experience the same ten-fold," warned Marcus angrily before he turned to the animal. He reached out and stroked the dark brown mane of the huge beast until it relaxed under his hand. "Calm your spirit, Ares. I know it's been a long journey," he whispered softly into the twitching ears of his horse. "Let's get off this boat." He led the restless animal down the wooden planks toward the bustling city without another word to the cowering sailor. At the end of the ramp stood a Roman legionnaire who snapped to attention as Marcus approached.

As Marcus stepped onto the crowded dock, the way parted before him as people scurried to get out of the path of the centurion as he guided the snorting steed off the large vessel. He glanced toward the large hippodrome in the distance where crowds of people were moving past its large sandstone walls and into the massive arena.

"Will you be attending the games, Centurion?" asked the soldier who stood watch on the dock.

Marcus shook his head. "I am not here to see the games. My business is with the tribune, after which I plan to leave for Capernaum." He stood quietly for a moment watching the activity around him before effortlessly mounting Ares. "See to the men. I expect all to be as it should be upon my return." His hand was easy on the reins, and when he pulled slightly to the right, Ares turned in the same direction and moved unfazed through the throngs of people.

Marcus rode slowly along the waterfront, ignoring the stares his presence generated. He maneuvered Ares past large warehouses filled with barrels of wine, olive oil, fruit syrups, and garum, a sauce favored by the Romans. The business of trade was bustling, and Rome had rightly recognized Caesarea as an important port of trade for the empire.

He easily guided Ares through the crowds toward the massive Roman theater in the distance, not to see the amphitheater, but to observe the nearby palace of Antipas, the current king of Judea. Built by Herod the Great, father of Antipas, the palace was extravagant in its construction, and its reputation had reached far beyond the Plain of Sharon. Marcus wanted to see it for himself. He halted the big horse as he neared the imposing structure. Squinting his eyes, he surveyed the massive marbled pillars surrounding the palace, then as he slowly guided Ares along, he scrutinized the rest of the building.

Built on a natural promontory that jutted out into the Great Sea, Herod had spared no expense in creating a magnificent palace whose splendor rivaled any other structure in the region, including the Roman temple that stood on the hill above the harbor. Marcus could not help but admire the architecture of the building. Caesarea itself was glorious with its columned promenades and mosaic walkways, but Herod's palace was an impressive monument to Judea's former king.

The man did know how to build.

"Let's go, Ares. Enough of this." Marcus gently nudged the steed's side ignoring the whispered stares from those he passed as he turned the horse around. He sat tall upon the majestic animal, his red linen tunic visible from beneath the ring-mail armor vest, while a cloak of deepest blue draped from his right shoulder to the tail of Ares. Upon his head rested a red-crested silver helmet, its plumed attachment a testament to his rank. Secure to the side of his mount was the oval shield of the Republic, and his straight double-edged sword remained immediately accessible in a silver scabbard hung across his chest. From his thin leather belt, he wore a small dagger easily visible as he rode and ready for use if the need should arise. The medallions attached to his leather chest harness were a silent tribute to his valor in battle.

Heads turned toward Marcus as he rode by, but the curious eyes quickly lowered if he happened to glance their way. Disregarding them, the centurion simply continued on his way down the well-trodden earthen road. Rome was now just a memory as he turned his thoughts toward Judea and its inhabitants.

"Curious people these Jews are, Ares." He spoke as he trotted along, his head moving side-to-side studying his surroundings. "Zealous to a fault. It will be their downfall, no doubt. How foolish are their beliefs. Hoping for their god to send a king to save them. Save them from what? Rome? Rome is their savior, and Caesar is their god. The sooner they accept that, the better it will be for them. Besides, what king could stand against Rome?" He spat on the ground, then said, "Someone must keep them in their place lest their religious zeal be a hindrance to the empire." His lips curled downward. "A pity it has to be me."

His meeting with Pontius Pilate was brief, but necessary, and Marcus was relieved when it was completed. He had his orders, and now he was eager to leave the bustling seaport. Following the Via Maris, the main route from Caesarea Maritima to Damascus, he spurred Ares onward, knowing the ride would be long, but not difficult. The road was well established and would take him directly to Capernaum, but it was still a great distance. Although Ares was well conditioned to long treks, Marcus had no desire to push him unnecessarily. Spending a night under the stars after a few hours of riding was not unusual for Marcus, and he would arrive refreshed the following day. He dug his heels into Ares' side, and the large beast snorted, then cantered through Caesarea and headed toward Capernaum.

* * * * * *

Marcus' first stop was a small Roman garrison near the political border that separated Galilee, the territory of Herod Antipas, from Gaulanitis, the domain of Philip, Antipas' brother. Just east of Capernaum, it was a small outpost, but one of Marcus' duties was to assess and report on the political situation, and he believed there was none better trusted to report the truth than the centurion who monitored the region.

"Marcus! I trust your journey was without incident?" The senior centurion rose and gestured toward a cushioned lounge. A broad smile spread across the elder man's tanned face as his gaze fell upon the younger soldier. "Please sit. Eat. Drink." He gestured to a long wooden table set with platters of fruit, cheese, meat, and bread.

Marcus set his helmet on a side table as he sank into the plush silk pillows spread across a long bench. He reached for a loaf of bread and tore a piece from it. "Your hospitality is greatly appreciated, Cornelius."

"I was pleased when I heard you were coming, and equally as pleased to finally see you," said Cornelius as he grabbed a roasted leg of lamb and took a bite from it. "You've seen the prefect?"

Marcus nodded. "Yes. His demand for an audience was immediate." He picked up a hunk of cheese, inspected it, then bit into it. "It would have been a mistake to keep him waiting."

Cornelius laughed as he chewed. "Yes, it would have been, my friend. When Pilate summons, we must respond." He brought a goblet to his mouth as he swallowed.

Marcus nodded his agreement. "His assessment is that there are small factions rising that could be potential problems for the empire. It is his hope that our presence will be a deterrent to any uprisings."

"A deterrent? Nothing deters these religious fanatics. They talk of a king who will rid the region of Rome and establish their right to this land, and that incites the people into a frenzy." He laughed heartily as he shook his head. "Then we parade around in our cohorts, and the fervor dies down until it starts all over again. Like pesky flies, these Jews need to be swatted away. They are more of an aggravation than a threat. Nothing that Rome cannot control however."

Marcus smirked. "Is there anything Rome cannot control?"

"Not that I am aware of, my friend. And if there is anyone that Pilate suspects is an insurrectionist, he is swiftly dealt with. That sends quite a powerful message to the people."

"Crucifixion will do that."

Cornelius nodded. "Yes, it will, but..." He grinned as he drained the wine in his goblet. "That's the price one pays for peace."

"As long as we're not the ones paying for it."

Cornelius laughed robustly. "Agreed. I remember a time when battles were fought and won for Caesar, and the glory of Rome was displayed throughout the empire. Now, we spend our time in revenue collection, administering judgment on petty Jewish squabbles, and overseeing the infrastructure of this wretched land." Cornelius sighed deeply as he wiped his mouth with his sleeve. He leaned back against the lounge, spreading his long muscular arms on top of it. "With any luck though, I'll be back in Caesarea soon."

Marcus sat up and rested his arms on his legs. "And I will be anywhere but here."

"A shame Caesar does not seek our opinions when it comes to where we are sent. May your stay in this region be short, my friend."

"And yours," concurred Marcus with a grin.

His visit with Cornelius lasted long into the afternoon, and Marcus readily accepted his friend's invitation to stay until the morning. It would be much more comfortable to spend a night in a bed rather than upon the hardened ground of the Galilean wilderness.

Restless in sleep, Marcus woke before the dawn. Sitting upon the side of his bed, he ran his fingers through his thick blonde hair. A sliver of moonlight shone through the small window, and he rose to gaze into the waning darkness of night.

What god did I offend to deserve this?

Marcus knew he still had a long journey ahead of him, and he was anxious to be on his way. Frowning, he forced himself to wait until the sky began to lighten with hues of orange and yellow before finally bidding Cornelius farewell. As he rode out from the garrison, the sun was just beginning to peek over the hills in the eastern sky.

* * * * * *

By the time Marcus reached his father's home, it was long past nightfall. Brightly lit torches cast faint shadows across the outer courtyard of the estate. He raised one eyebrow and scowled as he took in the displayed opulence of the main residence as he rode past it toward the stable. He instantly recognized the all-to-familiar Roman design of the manor illuminated by the flickering torchlight.

Well, now I know where those extra taxes have been going.

As he guided Ares near the stables, the steed's footsteps became muffled as they left the cobbled path and trod down a dirt trail toward a less-than-alert groomsman. Upon hearing Ares snort, the dark-skinned boy turned abruptly. His eyes widened, and his mouth dropped open as the centurion advanced toward him. Quickly dismounting, Marcus led Ares toward the startled young man.

"See to my horse." Marcus commanded. "Give me no reason for displeasure. Do you understand?"

Swallowing hard, the quaking teen nodded his head. "Of course, Master." He gingerly reached for the reins.

Handing him the leather strap, Marcus' hardened look focused on the frightened face of the boy. Youth had no advantage when confronted by a centurion. "Do not disappoint me." The undertone of the threat was not lost on the quivering stable boy, and Marcus' lips tightened as he stroked the side of Ares' face. He towered above the groomsman as he spoke. "Keep a firm hand on him. That will be sufficient to control him. Lay no strap upon him."

"As you command, Master."

Satisfied, Marcus turned and purposefully strode back along the path to the main house. As he neared the entrance, he removed his plumed helmet and entered into the foyer. Small marble statues of Roman gods and goddesses encircled the entry room, and several earthen jugs with flowering plants were set near the windows.

"Marcus, how wonderful to see you!"

He pivoted to face his stepmother. "Judith." He nodded slightly as his eyes noted the pallor of her skin. "You are looking well," he lied.

She smiled and extended her hand. "You honor us with your presence. Your father has been expecting you. I trust your journey was blessed by the gods."

He allowed her to take his hand and lead him into the great room, a large area suitable for entertaining guests. "Blessed? I'd hardly call it that, but it was uneventful."

She ignored his rebuff. "Justus will join us soon. He had unfinished business with which to attend." She gestured to a red cushioned lounge with several plump pillows. "Please, sit, rest." She sat opposite him on an identical reclining sofa. "So tell me, how is Rome?"

Marcus sank into the cushioned seat as he spoke. "Rome is Rome. The efforts in ruling an empire are constant, varied, and often unforgiving." He smiled as he added, "Or were you referring to its social aspects? Perhaps the fashion or latest gossip?"

"No, nothing so trivial as that." She laughed lightly as she shifted her weight.

The insincerity of her feigned laughter did not go unnoticed by Marcus. "Of course not," he commented with a hint of sarcasm. His amused eyes watched her as she averted her gaze from him, and for whatever reason, her discomfort pleased him.

She abruptly changed the subject. "It must have been difficult finding the time to come."

"Finding the time? No, this isn't a social call. I was ordered here."

"Indeed?"

He casually replied, "I have business in the region."

"Business?" Judith leaned toward him as she forced a smile. "Justus has done a superb job here, don't you agree?"

"How could I? I have no way to determine that at this point. I've only just arrived. Suffice to say, I have not heard otherwise...yet."

"I am sure you'll find everything in order."

His narrowed eyes focused on her worried face. "If you are referring to the recent customs collection, it has been adequate."

Judith lowered her eyes as she spoke in support of her husband. "Justus is careful to collect exactly what is due the emperor, Marcus. He is a competent leader and a loyal Roman."

"I have no doubt. He's never been accused of collecting insufficient taxes." He cocked his head slightly as he commented, "I'm sure the Jews would say the same, would they not?"

She shifted her position, looking away from her stepson. "I hope you are not expecting to find anything amiss here in Capernaum, Marcus."

A platter of seasonal fruits and two wine-filled silver goblets were placed on a large olive wood table between Marcus and Judith. He reached out for a cluster of grapes and popped one into his mouth. Shaking his head as he swallowed the sweet fruit, he continued. "Nothing to concern yourself with, I assure you." He bent forward to sip from the cup when he heard the booming voice of his father.

"Where is that son of mine?" Justus Caelinus strode into the room where Marcus and Judith sat. A broad smile spread across his face when he laid eyes upon his only child, and he made haste across the tiled floor to greet him. "Marcus, my son!"

Your son? You had no trouble casting your son aside when his mother died, or have you forgotten that?

Marcus rose to his full height, towering a full head over his father. As Justus wrapped his arms around him, Marcus made no move to reciprocate. He merely waited until Justus released him.

"You seem well." Hands on his hips, Justus nodded his approval as he stepped back and inspected his son.

"I am."

"More recognition, I see." He tapped a finger on the awards on Marcus' leather wrist coverings.

Marcus shrugged, then sat back down. "An occupational necessity."

Justus laughed heartily as he grabbed a plump fig from the platter. He took a big bite, allowing the juices to run down his chin. Wiping his face with the sleeve of his tunic, he sat across from Marcus. "What brings you to Capernaum? The region is at peace, as you see. There have been no fiscal shortages that I am aware of, for if there had been, I would have dealt with them immediately."

"Can't a *son* simply visit his father?"

The bitterness of his reply went unnoticed by Justus, but not by Judith.

Her smile couldn't mask the worry etched on her face. "Of course you can, Marcus. You are welcome any time."

Justus grinned. "Certainly! I am glad you have made time to come! How long will you stay?"

Marcus shrugged. "It all depends on the situation here."

"Situation? What situation?" Justus sat forward, his eyes narrowing as his brow furrowed. "You can't be serious? There is no situation here in Capernaum that would require a legion of soldiers from Rome."

"There has been talk of unrest."

"Unrest? Surely, not here! Perhaps in Jerusalem where the zealots abound, but not here. We are quiet and peaceful as you will find," Justus insisted.

"Yes, Judith mentioned that very same thing. She said you've done an excellent job here, and there was no need for concern."

Justus shot an irritating glance at his wife. "Leave us." His eyes bore into her back as she hastily exited the room. "She speaks without thinking." He turned back to Marcus. "You came alone?"

"I didn't think you could house a legion of men," Marcus stated. "But then I didn't realize your home was so... accommodating." His extended hand swept around the room. "Had I but known, I would have brought my men with me instead of having them quartered at the garrison in Caesarea." His nonchalant grin seemed to placate his father.

Relaxing a bit, a loud chortle came from Justus, and he clapped his hands together. "Just as well! Can you imagine a legion of Roman soldiers here? In Capernaum? They would be bored to tears. No one to fight. No rebellion to squelch."

Marcus eyed his father nonchalantly. "For your sake, I hope it stays that way."

Justus' eyes widened in alarm. "My sake? What have I to do with any rebellion? I merely collect the taxes as required by law."

"Of course, you do."

Justus grabbed a goblet and drained it of its wine. "I can assure you that everything is as it should be." He nervously tapped his fingers against his thigh. "If there were any trouble in Capernaum, I would know, and if I knew, I certainly would alert those to whom I am loyal."

A sarcastic grin appeared on Marcus' face. "Would you now?" He paused, then continued, "I'm curious, *Father,* do you consider yourself a Roman... or a Jew?" He practically spat out the last word.

Justus' face reddened as he opened his mouth to speak. "How dare—"

"Choose your words carefully," cautioned Marcus as he sat back, both arms extended on the cushions behind him. "I am here on behalf of the Emperor."

The not-so-veiled threat was immediately understood, and the fury on Justus' face was replaced with a strained smile. "Marcus, Marcus... we are family. I merely meant how could you doubt my loyalty to our Emperor. Of course, I am Roman." He patted his chest. "My heart is Roman."

"Yet you live in Galilee, and you marry a Jew. It does make one wonder exactly where your loyalties truly do lie," commented Marcus, intentionally baiting his father.

"I can assure you that my loyalties lie with Rome," stated Justus firmly. "If you are here to examine how I conduct the empire's business, you will find that I have cheated Rome of nothing!"

Amused at Justus' discomfort, Marcus finally chuckled. "You think Rome would send a cohort of legionnaires to check on the collections of one *Jewish* tax collector? You have no idea of the complexity of the situation in this region of the world if that is your assessment of my presence."

Justus cleared his throat. "I simply meant your time and talents are far too valuable to waste on someone so insignificant to the empire."

Marcus scowled as he stood. "Stop your feigned humility. It insults me." He turned to leave, then stopped. With a sneering grin on his face, he looked back at Justus. "However, I would be interested in seeing your books before I leave. Just to be sure."

Justus' eyes flashed in anger, but he held his tongue and simply nodded.

As Marcus left the room, the echo of Justus' fists slamming onto the heavy olive wood table reverberated into the hallway. A sardonic grin crept across Marcus' face as he strode to his room, satisfaction filling his soul.

Chapter Three

"For as the heavens are higher than the earth, so are my ways higher than your ways, and my thoughts than your thoughts." Isaiah 55:9

The mid-afternoon breeze lazily blew through the open rooms of the Caelinus house, easing the oppressive heat that seemed to hang in the dry air. Her work finished until the evening. Hadassah took advantage of her free time to walk through the gardens. Graveled pathways meandered through the hearty desert flowers and small shrubs that thrived in the arid climate. Today, Hadassah found respite from the heat beneath a large arbor covered with thick twisted vines. Clusters of ripening grapes hung suspended, tempting all who strolled by to sample the fruit. Large fronds of date palms swayed in the wind as the white blossoms of crocus and saffron on either side of the path danced in the refreshing breeze.

Hadassah relished her time in the garden's peacefulness, and as she sat down in a secluded corner, she slipped her head covering off, unpinned her long black hair, and allowed the desert wind to blow through her dampened tresses. Her eyes closed, and all tension fled her body as the breeze cooled her.

"I don't believe we've met."

The deep masculine voice startled Hadassah, and her eyes flew open as her head jerked upward. In front of her stood the foreboding figure of Marcus Caelinus.

There was no mistaking the authority in his posture. His muscular arms folded across his chest as his steel blue eyes curiously surveyed her. His blond hair, cropped close to his head, was the color of straw streaked by the sun. The only flaw on his clean-shaven face was a small scar on the left cheek. He towered above her, and when she realized she had been staring, she hastily dropped her gaze as she fumbled with her head covering.

"Forgive me," she stammered. She rose and moved to step by him, but his body barred her only way of escape. Pulling her wrap tighter around her, she cast a furtive glance at the graveled pathway. There was nowhere to go, so she was forced to simply stand and wait.

Marcus studied her carefully, then dropped his arms to his side. "I really didn't expect to see anyone out here," he stated. "Please sit back down." He gestured to the bench, but she didn't move. He frowned slightly as he raised an eyebrow. His silence demanded compliance.

Hadassah lowered herself to the bench. Her back was stiff; her hands clasped in her lap, and she kept her eyes downward. The silence was discomforting, but she resisted the urge to flee.

Finally he said, "Who might you be?"

She answered without looking up. "I am Hadassah."

"Hadassah!" His smile was genuine. "I remember you, but I doubt you remember me. I wasn't here very long on my last visit, and it was quite a long time ago. I am Marcus." He waited for her response, but she said nothing. "Are you always this quiet? Some might consider it rude to sit silently beside another when one is attempting conversation."

Mortified by the truth of his accusation, Hadassah tried to explain. "I meant no insult. It's just that..." Her inability to answer unnerved her, and her anxiety elevated to a new high.

He leaned slightly toward her. "Just that... what?"

Her mind struggled for an appropriate response, and when she finally spoke, it was a feeble excuse. "I'm not sure how to address a Roman centurion."

He chuckled lightly. "It's not hard. Just open your mouth and speak. It's really not that difficult."

Her cheeks felt as if they were on fire as she stammered, "No... no... I didn't mean—"

A muted laugh escaped him. "I understand a Roman soldier's presence can sometimes be rather..." He paused as he watched her squirm. "...unsettling."

She couldn't look up at him. Her discomfort was greater than her initial fright, so she kept her head bowed and silently pleaded for God's deliverance.

"You know Hadassah, you have no need to fear me. After all, we're not enemies. In fact, since Judith is your aunt, I suppose you could say we're cousins."

Hadassah's head snapped up as her eyes widened, and her mouth dropped open as she stared at him in stunned disbelief.

Marcus grinned as he raised an eyebrow. "Cousins shouldn't be enemies, should they?" He waited for a moment, but when she remained speechless, he continued in a more playful tone. "I don't suppose you'd ever realized you had a Roman centurion for a cousin, had you?"

Cousins?

His soft chuckle unnerved her, and she struggled to regain her composure. Looking away from him, she chewed on her lower lip as she self-consciously smoothed her tunic.

"The last time I was here…" He studied her flustered demeanor. "You were very young. But that was quite a long time ago. I would think you'd have been married by now."

Uncomfortable with his boldness, Hadassah struggled with how to respond. She resisted the urge to bolt as she tried to defend herself. "I am here because I am needed by my aunt."

"So, you are unmarried by choice? Hmm… yours or my father's?"

Hadassah bluntly explained as her eyes filled with frustrated tears. "I came here when my parents were killed. I was very young, and your father was gracious enough to bring me in."

"My father? Gracious? How noble of him." A faint scowl briefly crossed Marcus' face, but it was replaced almost immediately with a skeptical smile. "He rarely gives anything without expecting something in return. I suppose that something has been your servitude?"

"No! You don't understand. I am not a slave!" she protested. "It is the least I can do to repay them for their kindness to me. I consider it a blessing to be part of this household. I am treated well and want for nothing."

"A blessing? That's an interesting word for it."

"I owe my life to both of them. I could be begging on the streets."

"Then I suppose you are very fortunate to have such a… caring uncle." He pondered her earlier words. "I didn't remember your parents were killed."

Hadassah simply nodded her head.

"How?"

She swallowed hard, not willing to rekindle unbearable memories, but she knew to remain silent would be disrespectful to Marcus. She spoke reluctantly, her voice reflecting great sorrow. "We were going to Tyre. My father had business there, and my family... all of us were making the journey together, but we never made it to the city. Robbers came from the hills and attacked us. My mother hid me in the cleft of a rock by the road and told me to stay quiet and wait for her to return." Her voice trailed off as she closed her eyes momentarily, taking a deep breath. "She never came back."

She wiped away a tear that threatened to fall. "It seemed like forever. Tobias, a friend of my father's, found me. He told me that my parents had been murdered by the robbers. His wife cared for me until we returned home. A few days later Judith came for me, and I have been here ever since."

"How lucky for you that your mother hid you where she did."

She looked up at him and simply stated, "It was not luck. It was God who saved me, and God who brought me here. He has been good to me."

Marcus' brow furrowed, and his insensitive words were vicious. "Good to you? Your God has been *good* to you? He allowed your parents to be murdered. He made you an orphan, and then He placed you here in the role of a servant. I fail to see how that is being 'good' to you."

Hadassah sat stunned.

How can he say those things about God?

She tried to explain. "I could have been killed too... or worse. The Almighty protected me and provided for me. The Scripture tells us 'The Lord is righteous in all his ways, and holy in all his works.' I may not understand why He has allowed some things to happen, but I choose to trust Him in all things."

Marcus shifted in his seat as he shook his head and scowled at her. "Your faith seems to be misplaced."

Hadassah's mouth dropped open slightly as she stared at him.

Misplaced? How can he say that?

She clamped her lips together and willed her rising indignation to abate. Her fingers formed tight fists in her lap, but she said nothing as she turned her head away from him. She heard him rise but didn't move until his footsteps had died away. When they did, she glanced around, relieved to find herself alone.

She stood quickly and hurried to her room. Rushing to her washbasin, she splashed water on her face, dried it, and then moved to her bedside. Shaking from her encounter with Marcus, she fell to her knees. Her heartfelt prayer calmed her trembling body.

"Thank You, O Most High, for keeping me safe. I know You have always protected me and always will. I don't understand why You chose to spare me, but I trust You. You are my refuge and strength. You are my help in time of trouble, and I praise Your holy name." She rested her head on her bed and allowed the peace of God to envelop her as relieved tears fell from her eyes.

How long she knelt at her bedside she didn't know, but the lengthening shadows in her room prompted her to light the oil lamp on her small table. As the wick caught, she heard stirrings in Judith's bedchamber.

"Hadassah? Hadassah, are you there?"

"I am here." She rushed into her aunt's room and saw Judith stretched out on her bed.

"I do not feel well. Please bring me some tea." Judith's long dark hair was loosed and spread out on the pillow. Small beads of perspiration dotted her forehead. Her eyes were closed, and the pallor of her skin alarmed Hadassah.

Hadassah quickly moved to the fireplace and started a small flame to heat the water for the therapeutic tea. She searched through the basket of medicinal herbs until she found those designated to give strength to the body. Expertly, she crushed the tiny plants in a small bowl, then placed them in a clean cloth, tying them securely inside the fabric. Placing the small bundle in a cup, she poured the hot water over the cloth and allowed the essence of the healing herbs to seep through.

Carefully carrying the tea, she sat on the edge of Judith's bed. "Dodah Judith," Hadassah said softly as she offered the drink. "Here is your tea. Drink it carefully; it is hot." She gently held her aunt's head with one hand as she brought the cup to the ailing woman's lips.

Judith sipped the tea slowly, then allowed Hadassah to slip her garments from her weakened body. "Thank you, Hadassah." Her eyes were closed, and her breathing was shallow, but Hadassah knew it was rest that Judith needed more than anything else.

The coming of Marcus had been too much for Judith. Justus had insisted that everything be perfect for the arrival of his son, and now Judith was paying the price for it. Overseeing every aspect, from the meals to the entertainment to the furnishings of the guest room, Judith had called upon every reserve of strength in her physical being to complete the preparations to Justus' satisfaction. Despite Hadassah's tender warnings, Judith had insisted on managing every detail, and now she was exhausted.

"I don't know why the gods do not answer me," she quietly lamented as Hadassah helped her into her nightclothes. "I have prayed for so long, yet they remain silent. Even the stars do not favor me. What have I done wrong? I have tried to be a good wife to Justus. If only I had been able to give him a child..." She sank back into the pillows as Hadassah pulled the celestial blanket over her.

"I will be nearby," assured Hadassah as she turned to leave. "I will hear you if you call."

"Hadassah..." The despair in Judith's voice was heavy. "Would you pray? Would you pray to the Holy One for me? Perhaps He would answer your prayers."

"Of course, Dodah Judith. I always pray for you."

* * * * * *

Rising early the next morning, Hadassah had walked down to the Sea of Galilee and returned home with its water before Judith had awakened. Stopping for a moment at the back of the house, Hadassah's bright eyes followed a dusky green bee-eater as the tiny bird darted in and out among the pink and white blossoms of the colchicum lining the pathway to the back stairs. She set the jug down and watched the bird in its quest to find its morning meal.

"Good morning, Hadassah."

Startled, she stepped back and hit the water jug, threatening to tip it over. Reaching out a hand, she steadied the wobbling vessel as she looked up. Standing at the top of the stairs was Marcus. He wore a white linen tunic that hung to his knees. Thick brown sandals matched the brown leather belt around his waist. Hadassah blinked several times as she looked at him. He looked like one of the marble statues in the foyer of the house, and that made Hadassah uneasy.

"Good morning," she replied softly.

"Judith has you out early."

"She wasn't feeling well last night. I wanted to have her water ready before she woke, so I went to the sea earlier than usual."

"She didn't sleep well?"

"Her sleep was fitful. She woke several times."

"Bad dreams?" He cocked his head awaiting her response.

Hadassah shrugged and shook her head. "Perhaps. I don't really know."

Marcus walked down the stairs, stopping at the bottom step. "You take very good care of her. Such a dutiful niece."

"It is the least I can do."

Marcus smirked. "I suppose it is. Your deity must be very pleased with you."

His sarcasm was not lost on Hadassah, so she hastened to pick up the clay jug and leave the garden. She stepped past him and ascended the stairs. When she reached the top, she heard his footsteps coming up behind her. His near proximity disturbed her, so she quickly entered the house and scurried down the hallway feeling his eyes upon her. It wasn't until she entered Judith's outer bedchamber that she breathed a sigh of relief. She set the water jug down and noticed her fingers trembling. Clasping her hands together, she waited for her rapidly beating heart to slow.

Why does he torment me so?

She tried to focus on her tasks, but the image of Marcus at the top of the stairs continued to invade her thoughts. So preoccupied with what had happened in the garden that the water she was pouring into a small pot spilled over.

"Oh!" Frowning, she grabbed a small cloth to clean the mess. The fire she had started earlier was ready, so she placed the pot over the flames. Glancing over at the room in which her aunt slept, Hadassah was relieved that Judith had not witnessed her misjudgment in pouring the water.

After a quick run to the kitchen, Hadassah returned with a bowl of warm broth flavored with pieces of white fish. In her pocket, she carried several pieces of freshly baked bread. She arranged the food on a small tray, then hastily prepared the morning tea. It would not do to serve Judith food that had grown cold, so she moved efficiently. Finally, she was ready and carried everything into Judith's room.

Removing the window's covering, Hadassah allowed the morning sun to illuminate the room. "Dodah?" Her voice was low, but loud enough to rouse the sleeping woman. "Dodah? It is time to break your fast."

Judith's sleepy eyes fluttered open and focused on the face staring at her. She shook her head.

"No. I am tired, Hadassah. Let me sleep."

"You must eat, Dodah. You need to eat to regain your strength."

Half-heartedly, Judith allowed Hadassah to help her into a sitting position. "My breakfast already?" She inhaled the aroma of the broth that was held before her. "This does smell good." She leaned forward slightly, permitting Hadassah to plump supportive pillows behind her.

"Aelia said she made this especially for you." Hadassah picked up the bowl and held it as Judith ladled a spoonful to her lips.

"It's delicious. You will thank her for me?"

"Of course."

Judith finished her breakfast without much coaxing, and when she had downed what was left of her tea, she spoke. "I hope they are listening today."

Hadassah turned toward Judith with a questioning look on her face. "Who?"

"The gods. I hope they hear me today, Hadassah. I must get better. Please bring me my rose-colored gown and the white shawl. I feel I must go pray to them. Surely, they will hear me today."

Hadassah nodded. She sighed in resignation as she retrieved the articles of clothing that Judith had requested. The memory of what her mother had once taught her from the Holy Scriptures echoed in her mind.

Thou shalt have no other gods before Me.

* * * * * *

"You can tell me, my son. What is the real reason you are here?" inquired Justus as he leaned back against several huge pillows. He drank slowly from an ornate silver goblet, savoring the sweet juice of the pomegranate.

Marcus rose up from his reclining position. Leaning on one elbow, he glanced at his father. The callous use of the familial terms aggravated him, and he had no intention of lessening Justus' anxiety.

"Why so troubled?"

Justus shrugged a shoulder. "If Rome is displeased with my performance, I have a right to know."

"A right to know? You have only the rights the Emperor chooses to bestow upon you." Marcus kept his replies cryptic for simple sport.

Justus huffed as he said, "I cannot correct a wrong if I do not know what it is."

Marcus finally relented. He shook his head as he admitted, "You *are* too suspicious. I am not here to remove you from your post. If anything, you seem to collect an ample, if not excessive, amount of revenue, which..." He inspected a purple fig before taking a bite of it and continuing his explanation. "...would explain this." He extended his arm and swept his palm once more from one side of the room to the other.

Alarmed, Justus feigned innocence in his voice. "What do you mean? Surely, you aren't suggesting ill-gotten gains on my part? I assure you I am fair in my customs collections. Ask anyone."

"I don't need to ask anyone. You are a publican like every other publican. Just remember, as Caesar himself has said, he prefers his sheep shorn, not shaven."

Justus shifted uncomfortably but said nothing.

A lopsided grin appeared on Marcus' face when he saw his father pale. "You have nothing to fear. The emperor is curious as to how viable the talk of rebellion is in this region. Sometimes, the reports received by the Senate are not as forthcoming as an eyewitness account. Don't you agree?"

"Of course," Justus concurred, a bit too quickly. "How long did you say you would be here?"

Marcus shrugged as he leaned toward a platter of assorted nuts and fruits. "I didn't." He grabbed a handful of almonds and tossed a few into his mouth. "I presume I will be here as long as is necessary. Capernaum and Caesarea may be peaceful, but Jerusalem is another story. There is always someone stirring things up in that city. If there are any flames of rebellion there, they must be doused before the Jews ignite a bonfire that would only succeed in irritating Rome while destroying themselves. All this talk about a king rising up against Rome is pure nonsense, but nonsense must be squelched nevertheless."

"You can't be serious, Marcus. Surely the Jews know that to go up against Rome would be an exercise in futility. It would be foolish of anyone to try."

"It is true that anyone who goes against Rome is a fool, but then this world is full of fools. Just walk the Appian Way. Its crosses are never bare." Marcus rubbed the stubble on his chin. "However, there is a faction here that must be brought into submission. This brotherhood of overzealous Jews must be silenced. It only takes a few to incite the weak to bond together when they feel threatened, and that is what Rome wishes to rid itself of."

"You mean those who speak of a *messiah*?" Justus chuckled. "The Jews have been looking for a messiah for centuries." He stood and walked over to the window. "Look out over the land. What do you see? Is there anyone in this land of shepherds and fishermen who remotely looks like a warrior king? One able to confront Rome? Even if Antipas himself were to gather his most loyal men, which I might add are few, even he wouldn't be able to stand against the Roman army. The emperor has nothing to fear."

"I didn't say he was afraid," Marcus corrected. "I would call him cautious."

"Nevertheless, there is no rebellion here. Capernaum is a peaceful place. There has never been anyone of any political or religious significance here, and there never will be. These people are easy to subdue and keep satisfied. There will be no uprising here."

"Then no one has anything to fear, do they?"

Justus cast a wary look back at his son. "No, Marcus. No one at all."

Marcus nonchalantly tossed a grape up into the air and caught it in his mouth. "Tell me about Hadassah."

"Hadassah? What about her?"

"She's been here a long time." It was more a statement than a question.

"I suppose so. Her parents were killed tragically when she was just a child. She needed a place to stay, but... you already know that."

Marcus nodded, and with an ambiguous smile, he admitted, "I do, but her presence here is a curiosity."

"How so? Judith was her only living relative, why wouldn't we care for her?"

"It must have been a great adjustment for you all."

Justus suspiciously eyed his son as he spoke. "Yes, but it was our duty to bring her into our home. She was so young when she first arrived, and Judith cared for her as if she were her own."

A skeptical smile appeared on Marcus' face. "How fortunate for Hadassah to have such a caring... family," he said, emphasizing the last word. He stretched his long legs out in front of himself and leaned back against the thick pillows. "Still, I am curious as to why she remains here."

"What do you mean? Hadassah has been a great comfort to Judith. In many ways."

"I'm sure she has been. But Hadassah is grown now. She is of marrying age, is she not?"

A low snort escaped Justus' lips. "She is here to care for Judith. I am in no rush to marry her off. As long as Judith needs her, she will remain here with us."

"I see," said Marcus. "At least now it makes more sense." As he rose, he swallowed the remainder of the liquid in his goblet.

"What does that mean?"

Marcus bluntly replied, "It means there had to be some gain for you, or Hadassah would be out on the streets begging like all the other orphans. As I recall, there's not much room in that heart of yours for women and children."

"How dare you!"

"Really, *Father?*" His eyes narrowed, and his facial features hardened. "Need I remind you of how little you cared for my mother and me? Not even an appearance at her funeral, as I recall. In fact, there's not much about you that I recall at all during my childhood."

Justus squirmed under Marcus' gaze. "You don't understand—"

"Oh, I understand completely." His words were laced with bitterness.

"I had my work—"

"Your work?" Anger flashed in Marcus' eyes. "What work might that have been?"

Justus rose abruptly. "I don't have to take this from you!" His desire to flee the room was impeded by Marcus, who stood between the older man and the archway to the hall.

"You're speaking to the Emperor's representative," Marcus corrected as he crossed his arms across his chest. "You *do* have to take this from me."

The chilling truth of Marcus' statement destroyed any hint of bravado that Justus possessed. His demeanor humbled instantly, and the brashness in his voice vanished as he stammered his reply. "Marcus, Marcus, you don't understand. It was a busy time... I.... you... your mother..." He fumbled for words.

Disgusted, Marcus spat his words out. "There is nothing you can say that will justify your abandonment of me or my mother, so stop trying. I am here on behalf of the Emperor. This is not a family reunion by any stretch of the imagination." With that, he turned and left Justus standing alone and speechless.

Chapter Four

"And the fame of him went out into every place of the country round about."
Luke 4:37

The eastern Galilean mountains were silhouetted against a sky just beginning to lighten as the rising sun began to erase the blackness of the night. Streaks of pale blue-gray began to appear as Hadassah strolled through the awakening marketplace. She had already purchased several small fish from the boats returning from their night's work, and now she was on her way to the merchants eager to sell their wares. There was still plenty of room in the basket that hung on her arm for a bounty of fresh fruits and vegetables. She lingered near a table that offered artichokes, olives, and leeks, but it was the assortment of spices that caught her eye. She inspected one of the containers of cinnamon, took a whiff of the aromatic spice, then placed it in her basket. A handful of coins passed from her to the shopkeeper before she moved on. Soon, her basket was full, and her shopping was complete. She maneuvered her way through the growing crowd and set out on the road leading away from the center of the town back to her home.

She walked in solitude along the side of the dirt road until she heard the sound of a horse coming up behind her. Shielding her eyes with her hand, she turned and saw Marcus atop Ares, slowing as he approached her.

"Good morning, Hadassah."

He stopped so close that Hadassah felt the breath from Ares' nostrils, and she took a quick step backwards. Marcus sat tall in the saddle of the big animal, and Hadassah noticed how authoritative he appeared even when not in his uniform. She bowed her head slightly, then looked up at him waiting for him to make his reason known for approaching her.

He spoke without dismounting. "I am not surprised to find you at the market so early. You are a very efficient young woman."

Unaccustomed to compliments, Hadassah felt her cheeks warm as she turned her attention to her basket. She rearranged the produce several times.

A small grin appeared on Marcus' face. "I think your vegetables are fine where they are."

Hadassah froze, her hand in midair. Slowly her fingers opened, and she dropped a leek back into the basket. She kept her eyes away from his face.

"I don't suppose you'd like a ride back to the house?"

Before she could stop herself, her head lifted, and she blurted out a loud "No!" She began to stammer. "I... It wouldn't be... I mean..."

A low chortle escaped Marcus' lips. "Relax, Hadassah. I'm sure you'd rather walk. Accepting a ride on the horse of a Roman soldier would be highly inappropriate, would it not? Even if that soldier was a cousin."

His comment mocked her, and she fought to maintain her composure.

"Sometimes propriety just gets in the way." He made a slight clucking sound, and Ares lifted his head. A nudge in its side spurred the large horse to action, and Hadassah indignantly stood in place, watching horse and rider disappear down the road, the tension in her body beginning to fade.

"Hadassah! Hadassah!"

She turned toward the voice and recognized the young woman hurrying toward her.

"Zara? What's wrong?"

A slim woman with long black hair framing a heart-shaped face rapidly approached Hadassah. She cradled a large woven basket full of vegetables in her arms, and when she stopped, her breathing came in short gasps.

"Zara? Are you all right?"

"Yes. Yes, I'm fine. Are you? I saw him! I saw him speaking to you." Lines of worry etched the young woman's brow.

Zara and Hadassah often ran into one another at the water's edge, and over time they had become close friends. Although she was a few years younger, Zara was very protective of Hadassah. "Are you all right?" she asked again, her eyes probing Hadassah's face for reassurance.

"Yes, I am." She took a deep breath, exhaled, then smiled at Zara. "I'm fine. Truly, I am."

"What did he say? That was him, wasn't it? The centurion. It was him."

Hadassah turned to look down the road. There was no sight of Marcus.

Relieved that he was no longer visible, she finally relaxed. "Yes, that was him."

As they fell into step together, Zara asked, "What did he want?"

"He offered me a ride."

Zara stopped abruptly. "A ride?"

Hadassah nodded as she became somber. "He scares me, Zara. Sometimes, I think he is merely toying with me. The way a cat torments a mouse. The play continues until the cat is bored, then..." Hadassah gave Zara a "you-know-what-I-mean" look.

Zara's lips formed a thin line as she shook her head. "These Romans are awful. I wish they were gone. They're nothing but trouble." She kicked away a stone in the road as they resumed walking. "Do you know how long he'll be here?"

"No. Longer than I 'd like, I'm sure."

"Well, maybe I can cheer you up a bit. I have something to tell you." Her previously concerned eyes now sparkled with excitement. "But you must promise not to tell anyone."

Hadassah laughed lightly. "Who would I tell, Zara? Marcus?"

Both girls chuckled as they continued down the road.

"Promise me," insisted Zara.

"Fine. I promise."

"Do you remember I told you about the wedding of Uri's cousin?"

"Yes, you've spoken of it for weeks as I recall," Hadassah playfully reminded her.

"It hasn't been that long!"

"I know," Hadassah laughed. "I'm just teasing you. What about it?"

"That's where it happened. During the celebration, they ran out of wine."

"That's your news?"

"No! They ran out of wine, and the servants went to get more, but there was none to be found. So, one of the guests told them to get some water instead, and they did. They filled six jugs with water, and then..."

"What?"

"A man changed the water into wine!"

Hadassah looked at Zara with questioning eyes. "You mean he made wine using the water? Right there at the wedding?"

"No. I mean, the water in the jugs became wine... instantly." Zara eagerly awaited Hadassah's response.

She just stared at Zara, trying to understand. "What do you mean 'the water became wine instantly'? What are you saying?"

"I'm saying that the man changed the water in the jugs into wine. They put water in the jugs, but when they poured it out, it was wine!" Her voice hushed as she whispered, "It was a miracle!"

Doubt spread across Hadassah's face. "A miracle? Uri saw this?"

"Yes, he did. He said everyone was talking about the wine, so he asked someone where they got it, and then they told him what happened."

"So, Uri didn't actually see this happen. Someone just told him?" Skepticism surrounded Hadassah's words. "This is your miracle?"

"He wouldn't lie. You know he studies with the rabbi—"

"I didn't say he lied, but it sounds more like he misunderstood exactly what happened."

"No, he didn't! It's true! Uri said it was the best wine he ever tasted. Better than the first wine that was served."

Hadassah rolled her eyes and sighed.

"What?"

"Oh nothing. I am sure if Uri said it, then it must be true." The sarcasm in Hadassah's voice challenged Zara.

"It is the truth, Hadassah!" She folded her arms across her chest and pouted as she defended Uri. "I'm telling you, it's true! That man changed the water into wine! All the servants were talking about it, and Uri heard them."

"That's my point, Zara. He *heard* them. He really didn't witness this miracle himself. For all he knows, the wine could've just been brought out from another room."

"I can't believe you don't believe me!" Her tone became indignant. "Uri may not have seen the actual miracle, but he was at the wedding. He talked with the servants who saw it. I'm telling you, it really happened!" Zara stared at Hadassah's unconvinced face.

"Really, Zara? A true miracle? You can't be serious. Miracles from the Almighty have a spiritual purpose. A real purpose. Not changing water to wine so there can be more merriment at a wedding."

"Uri wouldn't lie." Her lower lip jutted forward in an exaggerated pout as her hands rose to her hips.

"Oh, really? Uri has been known to exaggerate at times."

Zara scowled as she looked directly into Hadassah's doubting eyes. "Well, I still believe him."

"That couldn't be because your heart sees only him, could it?" Hadassah lifted an eyebrow. "You don't think you could be a little bit biased?"

Zara clamped her lips together and turned away. Her steps became more forceful, and small clouds of dust rose from the pathway as she stomped along. "Well, I believe him even if you don't. Uri said six jugs of water were changed to wine, so that's what happened. If that wasn't a miracle from God, then how would you explain it?"

"Zara, you really can't believe this, can you? You said yourself that Uri didn't even see this happen. It was probably just a story told by someone who had a bit too much wine in the first place. And who was this guest? Was he a prophet? Because only men of God can perform miracles."

"I don't know. Uri didn't say, but he did tell me not to say anything to anyone, but you and I, well, we *were* best friends..." Her hurt eyes stared straight ahead as they walked.

Hadassah's lips curved downward. "We *are* best friends, Zara. You know that, and you don't have to worry about me telling anyone. Besides, who would I tell? No one would believe it. I don't believe it." She slowed her steps as they neared the fork in the road that led to the Caelinus home.

"Well, I do know one thing. Uri has never lied to me."

Hadassah stifled a groan. "Exaggerated truths are still lies, Zara."

The two girls walked in uncomfortable silence. Zara's shoulders slumped slightly, and her woeful eyes stared at the ground as she ambled alongside her friend.

Guilt pierced Hadassah's heart as she realized her lack of belief had hurt Zara. She stopped and took a deep breath, then turned and offered an apology. "I'm sorry, Zara. You are right. It could be true, couldn't it? And wouldn't that be wonderful?"

Lifting her head, Zara's eyes brightened as she readily forgave Hadassah. A grateful smile spread across her face. "You won't tell anyone?"

"Not a soul," promised Hadassah as she turned down the road toward the Caelinus house.

* * * * * *

Although autumn was approaching, the days were still hot and dry, but not as oppressive as the midsummer months had been. Judith had welcomed the drop in temperature, even though it was minute, and now she felt well enough to accompany Justus into Caesarea to stay a few days by the shore of the Great Sea.

Remaining in Capernaum to watch over the household, Hadassah had little to do once her morning duties were completed. She often visited the garden, relishing the serenity and closeness to God that she felt when surrounded by the flowers, breathing in their sweet fragrances, and listening to the melodic songs of the birds. This day, however, she chose to walk along the shores of the Sea of Galilee. Without a heavy jug of water on her shoulders, her step was light along the water's edge, and the cool breeze coming off the sea brought refreshing relief from the noonday heat. Tiny wavelets lapped at the shore as sunlight glittered in the watery ripples.

Small wooden boats bobbed offshore, ready to set sail when the afternoon faded into evening. Voices of fishermen preparing their nets could be heard; their laughter peppering muffled remarks. A single gull soared high overhead.

As she strolled along, she noticed a lone man standing farther down the shore. Hadassah knew most of the local fishermen, but this one she didn't recognize. His simple unadorned tunic was similar to that of a local tradesman, but his face was unfamiliar. For a moment, he reminded her of Marcus for he stood tall and straight as a man with authority, yet he was clearly not a Roman, much less a centurion. His common garment certainly did not suggest a man of position. She strained to see him more distinctly, but the distance between them was too great for her to see him clearly.

I wonder who he is.

Raising a hand to her forehead, she squinted her eyes and followed his gaze to a group of fishermen preparing nets for the upcoming evening's catch. Her curiosity was piqued as two of the fishermen leapt over the side of their boat and headed toward the unknown man. As she continued to walk toward them, familiarity dawned.

That's Simon and Andrew! They must know him.

Her attention shifted back to the stranger only to see him slowly turn his head toward her. Not wanting to be caught staring, she quickly averted her eyes from him. When she glanced back, not only was the stranger still looking her way, but now Andrew and Simon were turned toward her as well. Smiling, they waved at her. She awkwardly returned the gesture, stopping where she was. A gust of wind blew her loose scarf to the ground, and she stooped to retrieve it. She wrapped it around her head, and then looked once more at the threesome. They were walking together away from the boats. Hadassah cocked her head as she watched them.

I wonder where they're going...

* * * * * *

Although Capernaum was not a huge city, it still had its own synagogue, and Hadassah and Zara often met there to worship together. After the prayers and teaching had concluded, they frequently sat beneath the huge boughs of a gnarled olive tree to share a meal of fruit and flatbread while they discussed what they had heard.

Today was no different. They found a spot near the east side of the synagogue and settled down to eat and chat.

"Sometimes I just don't understand what they're talking about?" Zara stated as she bit into a sweet date.

"Sometimes? Is that all?" Hadassah laughed lightly. "I should think it would be hard to understand something you do not focus on."

"It's hard to focus on someone when you can't see them."

"Maybe you'll be ready to leave on time the next time we come, and we'll be able to be closer to the front," chastised Hadassah impishly. She bit into a dried apricot.

"It wasn't my fault!"

"It never is!" giggled Hadassah as she dug for the almonds deep in her pocket.

Zara tore a piece of bread in half and offered it to Hadassah, then snatched it away before her friend could grab it. "I should eat this all myself!" She laughed gaily, then held out the bread once more.

Taking it from her, Hadassah teased, "You'd become as big as a house. What would Uri think then?"

"He would love me no matter what. By the way, I really was listening most of the time!" Zara insisted. "It was a different rabbi, wasn't it?"

Hadassah's tone became serious. "I think so. I couldn't see him very well, but it just seemed different today."

"Different? How?"

"The reading was different. His words were so... so powerful."

"Powerful? What do you mean?"

Hadassah struggled to explain. "When he read from the Torah..." She bit off a piece of bread and chewed it thoughtfully. Finally, she swallowed, then said, "It was just different. I've never heard the other rabbis speak the way this man did. He was—"

She stopped suddenly when a small crowd at the steps of the synagogue began shouting.

"Rabbi! Tell us more!"

"Please, Rabbi!"

Her eyes sought out the one to whom the people were calling. She sat up straighter, then leaned forward a bit, straining to see what was happening. "I can't see anything."

Zara stood and reached for Hadassah's hand. "Come on! Let's go see what's going on!"

"No, I don't think...." She resisted the tugging on her sleeve, but Zara's persistence won, and Hadassah allowed herself to be pulled to her feet by her friend. Together, they moved closer to the commotion.

"Can you see anything?" whispered Zara as she rose up on her tiptoes.

Hadassah scanned the crowd and recognized several familiar faces, but she saw nothing out of the ordinary. She balanced herself on a rock to gain a few more inches of height. As she continued surveying the area, she saw

Simon and Andrew come out onto the synagogue steps. Her eyes widened as the man to whom the crowd was speaking came into view.

It's him! The man on the beach! He was the one teaching today?

Mesmerized, Hadassah strained to hear what was being said. As the crowd's cries grew louder, any attempt of hearing him was futile, so she simply stood in place, watching and waiting.

"Rabbi, tell us more!"

"When will the messiah come?"

"Where is our king?"

"Rabbi! Rabbi!"

Abruptly, silence fell upon the people as a wild man advanced toward the steps. His arms flailed uncontrollably, and his mouth foamed profusely as he began screaming at the rabbi. The throng stepped away, giving Hadassah a clear view of what was happening.

Words were coming from the crazed man's mouth, but to Hadassah's ears it seemed like multiple voices were screaming at the rabbi. "Leave us alone! What have we to do with you, Yeshua of Nazareth? Have you come to destroy us? I know who you are, the Holy One of God!"

The Holy One of God?

Hadassah shivered, but it was not cold. The hairs on her neck seemed to stand on end, but she couldn't turn away. She had to see! She craned her neck just as the rabbi spoke.

"Hold your peace!" His voice was powerful, but controlled, and its authoritative tone could not be mistaken. The rabbi had spoken, and involuntarily Hadassah held her breath. Her hand flew to her mouth as he continued to speak.

"Come out of him!"

His words were so clear and strong that Hadassah had no trouble hearing them, but she didn't comprehend what was happening.

Who is he talking to?

Her eyes widened as she watched the screaming man collapse to the ground. Then the ear-piercing shrieks went silent. Not another sound came from him! The crowd gathered closer around the motionless man; their curious eyes focused on the still form.

Then he began to stir. First, his bare arms moved to raise his torso. Then he was on both hands and knees, taking deep breaths. Droplets of perspiration fell from his forehead as he shook his head back and forth. Finally, he pulled himself to his feet and stood erect. The people began to push backwards, giving him a wide berth. Gasps of astonishment began to emanate from the onlookers as the once-afflicted man slowly looked around. Gone was the flailing of arms! Gone was the frothing at the mouth! Gone were the tormented shrieks!

He brushed his dampened hair from his brow. Turning toward the synagogue, his now-clear eyes fell upon the man standing quietly on the stone steps. Slowly, he made his way toward the rabbi.

Hadassah stared dumbfounded as the demoniac approached his healer. So many questions filled her mind, but as she watched the scene unfold before her, no answers came. Confusion seemed to fill the air as she heard her own thoughts being verbalized all around her.

"What's happening?"

"Who is he? What doctrine is this?"

"He speaks with such authority! From where does it come?"

"His words... He just commanded the unclean spirits, and they obeyed!"

Her mouth agape, Hadassah stood transfixed as the newly healed man dropped to the ground. She couldn't hear what was said, but she clearly saw the man reach out for the hem of the rabbi's garment. The rabbi leaned over slightly, touched the man's shoulder, and said something to him.

The man grabbed the rabbi's hand and kissed it over and over. Finally, he rose to his feet and began shouting praises to God! Rushing from the grounds of the synagogue toward the town, he passed so close to Hadassah that she could have reached out and touched him. Standing speechless, her bewildered gaze followed him until he disappeared beyond the olive trees, and then she turned back toward the synagogue. As her stunned mind struggled to understand what she had just witnessed, the rabbi turned, and she had an unobstructed view of him. Baffled, she searched his serene face for answers.

How did you—? Who are you?

A myriad of questions continued to assault her mind. She stepped down off the stone upon which she stood and moved to the nearest tree. Leaning against it, she closed her eyes until her thoughts began to make some sense of what she had observed. When she finally opened her eyes, she realized what the only possible answer to her questions could be.

I just saw a miracle from God!

"Hadassah? Hadassah!" Zara grabbed her friend's arm. "Did you see that?"

The spell broken, Hadassah looked deeply into her friend's eyes and nodded.

"Yes! It was…" she looked directly into Zara's face. "It was a miracle!" Then her voice hushed as if she had just uttered a sacred secret. "Did you hear what they called him? 'The Holy One.' Did you hear that, Zara?"

"I did! What do you think it means?"

"I don't know, but—" She stopped when Zara grabbed her hand and pulled her away from the synagogue crowd. "Oh Zara, I just don't know! I can't believe what just happened!"

Not wanting to leave, Hadassah and Zara lingered as long as possible simply reveling in the aftermath of something very special and reflecting on the miraculous event they had witnessed. Finally, Zara uttered what neither wanted to hear.

"C'mon, Hadassah. We have to go. It won't do us well to be late to our duties," Zara cautioned. "If we are, they'll never let us come again."

Hadassah nodded and reluctantly allowed Zara to pull her away from the synagogue's outer court. "You're right of course. It's just that… We witnessed a miracle!" She paused for a moment and looked back at the emptying courtyard before scurrying down the path with Zara. As they half-ran down the road, Hadassah stopped abruptly. She grabbed Zara's shoulders and stared into the surprised eyes of her friend. "Could he have been the man at the wedding?"

Zara's eyes widened as she turned her head back toward the synagogue. "The rabbi?" She looked back at Hadassah. "You think he's the one who changed the water into wine?"

Hadassah shook her head. "I don't know, but if it really happened like Uri said, do you think it could have been him?"

"It must have been him!"

Remorse seized her, and Hadassah looked at Zara through misted eyes. "I'm so sorry I doubted you."

The hug she received from Zara assured her that all was forgiven, and together they hurried down the path toward the town. Stopping for a moment to catch their breath, Hadassah admitted, "I've seen him before."

"Who? The rabbi? Where? He's not from around here. Where have you seen him?"

"At the seashore. He was with Simon and Andrew. I thought he was a fisherman, but now, I'm not so sure." She looked at her friend and softly asked, "Who is he, Zara? Who is this man?"

* * * * * *

Hadassah hummed as she inspected the blue and white blossoms of the irises before cutting the stems with a knife. She couldn't get the synagogue miracle out of her mind as she continued searching for the perfect flowers to set in Judith's bedchamber. So focused on the demoniac's healing, she never heard Marcus come up behind her.

"You sound happy."

Hadassah jumped at the sound of his voice, dropping the blooms she had already cut. She turned around quickly. He was standing no less than two feet from her, and his nearness unsettled her. She knelt quickly, gathering the freshly cut stems.

"I'm sorry. I didn't mean to startle you." He stooped down and helped pick up the flowers she had dropped. "For Judith?" He handed them to her.

"Yes. She takes such pleasure from the irises as do I." She took the blossoms from him as she stood up. "They're my favorite."

Marcus cocked his head and studied her. He said nothing, and Hadassah self-consciously returned to her task.

"You were out yesterday." It was more a statement than a question.

She answered without looking up. "Yes. I went to the synagogue. Judith permits me to attend as much as possible."

"Ah, yes. It was your Sabbath, wasn't it?" He followed her as she moved around the garden. "I'm surprised Judith doesn't go with you. After all, she is Jewish."

"Yes, but she doesn't go with me. She places her faith in... in your gods, not the true God of Israel."

Marcus' eyebrows rose. "The *true* god? And who might that be?"

Hadassah hesitated, but only for a moment as she responded bluntly, "The God of Abraham, Isaac, and Jacob. He is the one true and living God." Only a slight tremor in her voice betrayed her confidence in speaking to him so boldly.

"Really? This is the same god that has allowed your people to fall under Roman rule? Hmmm... doesn't sound too powerful if he allows Caesar to control Israel, does he? As I see it, Caesar himself is the more powerful god."

"Caesar?" Hadassah stared at Marcus, her brow furrowed as she questioned, "But he's just a man. How can he be a god?"

"He's the emperor. Emperors are descendants from the gods," Marcus stated.

"That's what you believe?" Her question was innocent, and Marcus took no offense.

"I suppose I do."

"Do you pray to him?"

"To Caesar? No. I don't pray to anyone."

"Why not?"

"Why should I?"

"I pray for help or guidance, and I praise God through my prayers."

"I prefer to depend upon my own resources when I need help, and I praise my gods through my victories in battle."

Hadassah studied the Roman's face as he spoke, but she saw no mockery in his face.

He really believes that?

She couldn't comprehend a life without God, so she simply stated, "Believe what you will, but I choose to put my faith in the God of my forefathers."

"No matter how misplaced it may be?"

"You wouldn't say that if you'd seen what I saw yesterday." Hadassah reached out to cut another iris.

"What did you see?"

She hesitated, then turned around to face him, emboldened by the truth within her that refused to be kept hostage. It burst forth from the depths of her soul as she announced, "I saw a miracle yesterday, and only God can perform a miracle."

"A miracle?" His eyebrows rose as a skeptical grin spread across his hardened face. "You're sure of that?" The taunting arrogance had returned to his eyes as they challenged her declaration.

Hadassah's instant regret at her outburst caused her to turn her back to him and resume her gardening. She fought to keep her frustration from showing, and then silently chastised herself for her misjudgment of Marcus' reaction.

"It really was a miracle," she insisted softly.

He rubbed his chin and pressed his lips together, suppressing a chuckle. "Well, you'll have to tell me about this so-called miracle since I wasn't there to see it for myself. In fact, I don't think I've ever seen one, so I am most interested in what happened." He sat down on a nearby bench. "Tell me, what was this amazing miracle of yours?"

Hadassah's dark brown eyes narrowed with irritation at his deriding tone, but she drew in a deep breath and willed herself to remain respectful as she pivoted to face him. "If you truly want to know—"

"I do." He crossed his arms over his chest. "Please, enlighten me."

She searched his face for a sign of sincerity, but his expression was stoic as he waited. She looked directly into his eyes as she began. "There was a man possessed—"

"Possessed?" interrupted Marcus. "What do you mean?"

"He was controlled by an evil spirit."

"Really? How do you know this? How do you know this possession was an evil spirit?"

"He was screaming and throwing his arms around."

"I see. Like someone who was perhaps… angry?" Marcus lifted one eyebrow as he waited for her response.

Hadassah shook her head. "No. He was crazed and frothing at the mouth.

Like a sick dog. Then he ran over to the rabbi—"

"The rabbi? Who is this rabbi? Does he have a name?" Marcus leaned forward, both forearms resting on the tops of his thighs.

"Of course he has a name. I think it's Yeshua. At least…"

"At least, what?"

She sighed in exasperation at his continual interruptions. "That's what the sick man called him, so I'm not sure, but I do know the rabbi is a healer. He healed the possessed man."

Marcus ignored her obvious annoyance. "So, he's a rabbi and a healer?"

"Yes."

"And just exactly how did he heal him?"

"He told the spirit to come out of the man, and it did."

Marcus sat back and smirked. "That's it? That's your miracle?"

Taken aback by his casual reply, she tried to explain. "It *was* a miracle. The man was possessed by an evil spirit, and then the rabbi commanded the spirit to leave, and it did."

"I see. And you believed this to be a miracle?"

"Of course, it was." She paused for a moment, then added, "Plus, it called the rabbi, 'the Holy One.' Do you know what that means?"

Marcus shrugged his shoulders. "No, Hadassah, I don't. What does it mean?"

"It means he was sent by God."

"Your *Hebrew* god?" he mocked. "I see. So, he was one of your prophets then?" His guffaw rebuffed her.

She frowned as she shook her head. "No. Not a prophet."

"Then what? A sorcerer?"

She scowled at him. "No! Not a sorcerer." Her frustration was mounting. "I don't know exactly who he is, but I do know that only God can do a miracle, and since it was a miracle, it had to be God."

"Ah, I understand. You think that your healer is a god. Hmm… a man supposed to be a god. Isn't that what you said about Caesar?"

Hadassah felt trapped. "I didn't mean that. I… I believe God sent him."

"Don't you think you could be grasping for something that's not there?" He eyed her carefully. "Couldn't your demoniac just have been a very angry man who lost control momentarily, then when confronted by this rabbi, he came to his senses?"

"You wouldn't think that if you had been there," she said as her exasperation with Marcus grew. "If you had seen him."

"The lunatic?"

"No! The rabbi." The futility of trying to clearly explain what happened upset her greatly, and she just shook her head. "I don't know how to make you understand."

"Maybe I should go with you the next time you go to the synagogue."

She involuntarily gasped as he winked at her. Her startled eyes widened, and she started to speak, but quickly closed her mouth.

Marcus chuckled at her discomfort. "They probably wouldn't take too kindly to a Roman invading their synagogue though, would they?" He watched her lips press tighter together. "Now that would take a miracle! By the way, I admire your self-control."

She spun around quickly and hacked at another bunch of blue irises. "I know you don't believe me, but I know what I saw. It was a miracle."

He moved to stand beside her, his words less confrontational than before. "Hadassah, miracles are designed for the weak and the imaginative. They are built on a foundation of sand and offer nothing more than false hope to those who seek some kind of reassurance that the gods are listening to them."

She turned around defiantly, fire mingled with tears in her eyes. "That's not true! Miracles do happen. Just because you don't believe in them, doesn't mean they don't exist. God is the same today as He has always been. He performed miracles in the days of Moses and the prophets, and if He so desires, He can do them today. In fact—"

Suddenly, she remembered to whom she was speaking, and her hand flew to her mouth, and the fury in her voice vanished. "Forgive me... I meant no disrespect..." Her voice hushed as she lowered her eyes, fearful of what might come, yet knowing in her heart she deserved punishment for her lack of respect for Marcus Caelinus.

"Hadassah..." His voice was low and tender as he tried to relieve her distress. "Look at me." His finger reached out and tilted her chin upward.

She refused to look at him as she braced herself for the reprimand she knew was coming.

"There is nothing to forgive."

His voice sounded sincere, and she timidly glanced upward through eyelashes wet with unshed tears.

"I am not angry with you. In fact, I admire you for stating your mind. I like a woman who can think, and you certainly have proven you can do that. You are free to share whatever is on your mind when you are in my presence."

Hadassah's voice was a relieved whisper. "You are most merciful."

"I've never been called that before." He chuckled as he watched her cheeks redden, then took a step backward. "You should probably get those flowers up to Judith. She wouldn't appreciate them if they were to wilt."

Hadassah nodded, grateful for the opportunity to leave. She quickly made her way back into the house as Marcus watched her ascend the stairs to his stepmother's chambers.

* * * * * *

Hadassah was still shaking by the time she entered Judith's outer room. She grabbed a large earthenware jar, filled it with water from a pitcher, and arranged the irises in it. Carrying the jar into Judith's bedchamber, she set it on a long narrow table by the window where the blossoms were illuminated by the sun's afternoon rays.

Turning, she scanned the room quickly, then stopped with the realization that something was definitely out of place. Judith's outer garments were scattered on the floor on the far side of her bed, but Judith was not there. Hadassah stooped to pick them up as she heard a faint noise.

"Dodah?"

What was that?

She heard it again. A voice, muffled and low.

Dodah?

"Hadassah..."

"Dodah, where are you?" Hadassah rushed to the bathing area. Her eyes darted around the room until they fell on the fallen form of her aunt.

"Dodah!" Rushing over, she dropped to her knees. "Are you hurt? I'll get help!"

"No! No. Please, just help me get back to the bed." She reached a weak hand to her niece's arm. "If I can just get to my bed, I'll be fine."

Although she disagreed with Judith's self-diagnosis, Hadassah would not go against her aunt's wishes. She assisted Judith to her room, helped her change into a clean gown, and made her comfortable in her bed. As soon as Judith drifted off to sleep, Hadassah went back to the bathing area to retrieve the strewn clothes. As she had done many times before, Hadassah spent most of the evening washing the sickness out of Judith's garments and begging God to heal her aunt of this mysterious malady.

* * * * * *

Later that night, Marcus stood alone in the great room of his father's house, warming himself by the central fire pit. His hand closed around his recent message from Pilate, and irritation filled the features of his ruggedly handsome face.

Jerusalem.

He took a deep breath and crushed the paper in his hand. As he exhaled, he tossed his orders into the flames.

Tomorrow I will go to Jerusalem. It's time to put an end to this talk of rebellion.

"You Jews are fools to threaten Rome," he said under his breath. He spat into the fire in disgust.

You don't even realize who it is you're up against. If Rome so desires, you will be wiped from the face of this earth in the twinkling of an eye. You cry out for a king? The only king you need is Caesar.

Marcus turned toward the sound of soft footsteps coming from the inner house.

Hadassah?

He started toward the entryway when he saw a young boy pass through carrying a small oil lamp. Realizing it was not whom he thought it was, Marcus simply watched the lad disappear into a dimly lit corridor. Refocusing on the task at hand, he walked slowly toward his quarters. Dawn would come early, and by then he would be well on his way to the city of Jerusalem.

Chapter Five

"Then said Jesus unto his disciples, If any man will come after me, let him deny himself, and take up his cross, and follow me." Matthew 16:24

Several days had passed since Marcus left for Jerusalem, and Hadassah was relieved that things had returned to normal once again in the Caelinus household. She no longer felt the need to tread lightly as she moved throughout the house or garden. The fear of accidentally running into Marcus had been alleviated by his departure, yet she often caught herself expecting to see him in the courtyard or at the top of the stairs. Remembering that he had left, the knot in her stomach would fade, and her troubled spirit would settle.

Moving quietly through the open passageway of the house, Hadassah made her way to the cooking area. Judith had awakened late after a fitful night of sleep, and now her hunger had made her irritable. Summoning Hadassah with a harsh voice, she had demanded something to ease the discomfort she felt within her abdomen.

"Aelia?" Hadassah stepped through the threshold into the food storage area. "Aelia, are you here?"

The gray-haired old woman stuck her weathered face out from the pantry closet. The flour on her cheeks gave evidence that breadmaking was in progress.

"Yes, Hadassah? What is it you need? Is it Judith?" She wiped her hands on her apron as she approached the young woman.

Hadassah nodded as she smiled, remembering Aelia's protective nature when she had first arrived at the Caelinus household. Aelia had immediately taken Hadassah under her wing, soothing the fears of the small child who had been deprived of her parents in such a horrific way and was now thrust into a foreign household. Many nights Hadassah had cried herself to sleep in the comforting arms of the older woman whom she regarded as a surrogate grandmother.

"Dodah Judith is not feeling well again. She is requesting something for her ills. Do you perhaps have some broth for her?"

Aelia smiled. "Of course. I have a delicious fish broth set aside for just an occasion such as this. A few of my special herbs added to it will ease her discomfort." She moved to the earthen oven and removed a small metallic pot. Ladling a portion of broth into a small stone bowl, she sprinkled some medicinal herbs and spices into it, then set it over the smoldering fire.

Without asking, Hadassah pulled a small wooden stool nearer to Aelia's breadmaking table. Its uneven legs threatened to topple her as she settled herself upon it.

"Aelia," she began, "what do you know about the Messiah?"

"What is it you want to know?" Aelia set the ladle down and moved to the table. She picked up a ball of dough and floured it liberally.

"When will he come?"

"No one knows the answer to that, my child. Only the Eternal can answer that question." She began to work the dough with her spindly fingers.

Hadassah sighed. "He will come though, won't he?"

Aelia wiped her floured hands on her apron, then turned to Hadassah. "The Eternal has promised to send Messiah, and what He has promised, that He will do. You must never lose your faith. He never fails to keep His word, but as to the exact timing, no one knows that. I hope to see the Messiah in my lifetime, but that is not in my hands."

"How will we know him, Aelia?"

"He will fulfill the prophecies of old."

"Prophecies? What prophecies?"

Aelia smiled as she gazed down at the young woman before her. The interest Hadassah had in the Jewish faith pleased her immensely. "I am no scholar, Hadassah, and I am an old woman, but I do remember some of the teachings of my father." She leaned against her table. "He will be like Moses... no, more than a prophet. He will be the Anointed One of God. He will rescue the oppressed and redeem His people Israel." Then she nodded her head knowingly. "We will know him. I am sure of it. The Eternal will not send us our king and keep him hidden from us. When the Messiah comes, all of Israel will know, and it will truly be a time of rejoicing."

Hadassah said nothing as she contemplated Aelia's words.
We will know him.

She stood as Aelia retrieved the warmed bowl of broth. Wrapping it in a thick cloth, Aelia held it out. Hadassah took the steaming soup and inhaled its aroma. "Oh, this smells delicious!"

"Careful with it," cautioned Aelia, a smile of appreciation on her face. "The bowl is quite hot. I wouldn't want you to burn yourself or spill any of the broth."

"I will guard it carefully. I am sure Dodah will be most grateful. Thank you."

Aelia reached out and cupped Hadassah's face in her hands. "You are such a blessing to this household." She kissed her on the forehead.

With a timid smile, Hadassah looked up at the older woman. "You are the one who is a blessing, Aelia. I don't know what I would do without you."

Aelia chuckled under her breath as she turned back toward her baking. "The Eternal One has blessed us both, child. Now scurry along before the soup cools. I have work to do. I can't spend all my time talking to you."

Hadassah grinned at the mock chastisement. "As you wish, Aelia. Thank you for the broth."

She hurried back to Judith who was reclining against her pillows. Setting the bowl down, Hadassah arranged the bedding so that Judith could sit comfortably while eating.

"Aelia had this ready for you. She added some herbs to help with the pain." Hadassah lifted a spoon of the liquid to Judith's lips. "Careful. It is still very hot."

As Judith sipped the broth, she closed her eyes. "So good, Hadassah..."

After finishing the soup, Hadassah wiped Judith's face with a warmed towel. "Are you cold?"

"No. I am comfortable. Please, sit beside me for a moment." There was no harshness to Judith's voice as she patted the blanket.

Sitting at the bedside as she was bidden, Hadassah waited for Judith to speak.

"Do you remember any of the psalms your mother used to sing to you?"

Hadassah's eyes brightened slightly as she responded, "Of course." She thought for a moment, then began, "O God, thou art my God; early will I seek thee: my soul thirsteth for thee, my flesh longeth for thee in a dry and thirsty land where no water is." She lifted her face upward, closed her eyes, and continued. "To see thy power and thy glory, so as I have seen thee in the sanctuary. Because thy lovingkindness is better than life, my lips shall praise thee. Thus will I bless thee while I live; I will lift up my hands in thy name."

When Hadassah opened her eyes, she was stunned to see tears on her aunt's cheeks. The tormented look on Judith's face frightened her, and as Judith wrung her hands together, Hadassah reached out, touching her aunt's shoulder lovingly.

"Dodah, what's wrong?" Hadassah's voice was barely above a whisper as her eyes searched Judith's anguished face.

"Leave me now," she responded without opening her eyes. "I am so tired, Hadassah. I must sleep." She turned over, her back to the young woman, and said no more.

Rising quietly, Hadassah left Judith's side. She stopped in the doorway and glanced back at her aunt. Judith's shoulders were shaking, and Hadassah resisted the impulse to run back and comfort her. Instead, she quietly retreated to her own room where she fell to her knees once again and prayed that God would touch her aunt and restore her to perfect health.

* * * * * *

With Judith not wanting to be disturbed, Hadassah found herself with ample time to stroll the streets of Capernaum and enjoy the sights and sounds of the small village. Her slender fingers played with the coins in her pocket, and she hoped to find a few good bargains.

Stopping to purchase a handful of almonds, Hadassah paid the vendor, then munched on the nuts as she continued her walk. Rounding a corner, she stepped quickly aside to avoid a collision with a group of people rushing past.

"Hurry! This way!" A young woman called out to someone as she ran by. A few more people hurried past Hadassah talking excitedly among themselves. She watched them, her curiosity mounting as others scurried by. The early afternoon marketplace quickly began to empty as shoppers abandoned their tasks and joined the growing throng.

Where are they going?

She strained to hear some of the conversations of the passersby.

"Come! It's the rabbi!"

"Hurry!"

The rabbi? Could they be talking about my rabbi, the Healer?

She hesitated for only a moment, then turned and followed the crowd down the narrow street to a small home. So many people were rushing to enter in that Hadassah doubted there would be room for her. She was content to listen from the outside, but the pressure of those behind her pressed her forward through the open doorway. The small home was nearly wall-to-wall with excited people, but Hadassah managed to wriggle into a small spot in a corner. She leaned against the cool wall and tried to make herself comfortable. The throng of people surrounding her made it nearly impossible to see anything except the backs of the heads of those immediately in front of her.

She remained unnoticed in the corner of the small house, not really knowing what to expect. Nearly every part of the hard dirt floor was covered as more and more people pushed their way in. People were talking all around her, but it was difficult to understand anything anyone was saying. She bit her lower lip and glanced over toward the door.

This was a mistake. I should go.

She tried to move, but it was impossible. The sheer pressure of bodies kept her in place. Holding tightly to her shawl, she shifted her weight and leaned back against the wall. She felt the beginning of a cramp in her back and sighed in resignation at her predicament. She was going nowhere.

Then he spoke, and Hadassah recognized the voice immediately. It was him! It was the Healer! A hush instantly descended upon the crowd as the man they all came to hear spoke of the kingdom of God and repentance of sins. He quoted from the Torah, explaining it so clearly that there was no question in Hadassah's mind as to the meaning of the passages. Mesmerized by his words, Hadassah didn't mind that she couldn't see him; she was just grateful she could hear him. The power in his voice stirred her soul. Had it not been for the bodies pressed so tightly around her, she would have left earlier. Now, she rejoiced for her inability to escape.

As she listened attentively, a tiny sliver of sunlight made her squint her eyes and look upward toward the source. She saw a small portion of the roof's mud-caked tiles had been removed as fingers twisted and turned to grasp more of the clayed branches that stretched across the wooden beams.

Someone is trying to hear from the rooftop! Thank You, Lord, that I have place here to stand and listen.

She shifted her position once more and glanced around. From the corner of her eye, she saw one of the scribes from the synagogue. He was whispering something to a man next to him, and Hadassah saw the second man nod. The scowls on both of their faces clearly disclosed their annoyance with something, but she refused to be distracted. She returned her attention to the rabbi.

She narrowed her eyes once more as the ray of light broadened, and without thinking she brought her hand up as a shield from the brightness. The hole in the roof had been enlarged greatly, and Hadassah was surprised to see several people on the top of the house peering in through the hole.

What are they doing?

She cocked her head slightly when a flattened bedroll began to be lowered through the hole. Her brow furrowed as she tried to make sense from what was happening.

"Make way!" came a call from the roof.

The people began to murmur their dissatisfaction as their eyes moved toward the voices from above. The rabbi had stopped speaking, and the crowd began to move backward, making room for the descending mat. As the mass of bodies pressed against her, she was forced tighter against the wall. She could only see what was happening above her, and she followed the path of the bedroll. Attached to each corner, ropes controlled the descent. When it neared eye level, Hadassah gasped when she saw what it held.

It's a man! What is happening? Why is he being lowered? Who is he?

She tried to stand on her tiptoes to see, but when the mat fell below the level of the heads in front of her, she could see nothing more.

The room had stilled. No one spoke; no one moved. Hadassah strained to hear what was being said. The unmistakable tone of the rabbi's voice filled the room.

"Son, your sins are forgiven."

What? His sins are forgiven? What does he mean by that?

Before she could unravel her own thoughts, she heard his voice again, but now there was an edge to his words.

"Why do you think such evil in your hearts?"

Me? Is he talking to me? I'm sorry! I would never–

From the corner of her eye, she saw the scribe struggle to turn, but he could not. Like her, he was trapped where he stood. While every head in the room was turned toward the rabbi, the scribe and his companion had turned away as if they had been caught in some despicable act.

Is it them?

She looked forward again, waiting for something... anything to happen. No one moved; no one spoke. Then she heard it. Way before she felt it, she heard the wind as it blew through the house, and then the rabbi spoke again.

"Which is easier to say, 'Your sins are forgiven' or to say, 'Arise and walk?' But that you may know that the Son of man has power on earth to forgive sins..."

Hadassah held her breath expectantly.

"I say unto you, arise, take up your bed, and go into your house."

A collective gasp went through the room, and although she didn't believe she could be pressed any more into the wall, the crowd seemed to squash her against it even more.

"Glory to God!" The voice came from above, and Hadassah looked up. Four triumphant faces peered down from the hole, cheering loudly.

Suddenly, the people began praising God, clapping their hands, and lifting their voices in jubilant rejoicing. The whole house seemed to shake with their adulations.

What's happening?

In frustration, Hadassah craned her neck to see something... anything. She tried to push her way forward, but it was impossible to move.

"What's happening?" she called out to others standing near her.

"He's walking!"

"The rabbi healed him! He's walking!"

"All praise to God Almighty!"

The throng began to move outside, and finally Hadassah could see the reason for the rejoicing. The paralytic man stood without any assistance, his bed rolled up and tucked under his arm. He was weeping, and his hands were held heavenward as he praised God.

"I have trusted in your mercy; my heart shall rejoice in your salvation!"

Others happily joined in. The shouting was almost deafening, and many had fallen to their knees praising God.

"Amazing!"

"Never have I seen such a thing!"

"Praise the Lord!"

"Blessed be the name of the Lord!"

Hadassah now had a clear view of the rabbi. He sat quietly, watching the celebration as it moved from inside to outside. She noticed nothing extraordinary about him, yet there was something about him that was so different from anyone she had ever known.

Who are you?

As he stood, four other men rose. Hadassah immediately recognized Simon and Andrew, but the other two she knew by face only; she had seen them often with the other fishermen. They were all talking excitedly among themselves. As the rabbi moved to leave the room, he stopped for just a moment and glanced at Hadassah. He smiled, and Hadassah shyly smiled back. As he exited the house with the four men, she waited until she could freely move, then rushed out to follow them as they headed back toward the center of town.

When the road forked, Hadassah expected them to head toward the marketplace, but the rabbi took the way leading out of Capernaum. Hadassah knew she couldn't accompany them, so she just stood at the crossroads and watched the men walk away. As the rabbi neared the end of the road, he stopped at the receipt of custom house. Hadassah knew the building well; it was where Justus did much of his work. There was a small line of men waiting to pay tribute.

Hadassah watched as the rabbi leaned over and spoke to the publican.

She squinted her eyes as she observed the interaction. When the tax collector stood up, recognition came.

That's Levi! I've seen him before with Justus.

Although there were several men still waiting to pay their taxes, Levi came out from behind the collection table and walked away with the rabbi leaving the taxpayers calling out after him.

Where's he going? He can't just leave his work!

Hadassah tilted her head, watching until they had disappeared around a bend. When she could see them no longer, she turned and slowly headed toward the marketplace. The image of the bedridden man jumping for joy was seared in her mind, and she knew without a doubt she had witnessed another miracle, but that didn't answer the most pressing question she had.

Rabbi, who are you?

* * * * * *

"I cannot believe it!" The outrage in Justus' voice echoed through the hallways. "He left! Just like that, he left!" He threw his goblet against the wall barely missing Judith's head. Wine splattered everywhere as the cup clattered to the floor.

Startled, Judith motioned to a servant to retrieve the goblet and clean the mess Justus had created. "Perhaps he'll return tomorrow." Her voice lacked conviction.

Justus sneered. "Let Levi dare show his face to me. He will most certainly regret leaving his post without so much as a word to me." He shook an angry fist in the air.

"You have no idea why he left?"

He turned to face his wife. The fury in his words was unmistakable. "How would I know? I wasn't there! When I see him, he will rue the day he failed at his duty. I will make sure of that!" Justus turned his head and spat on the ground. "And with revenue to collect! He just abandons his station! Unbelievable!"

Judith watched in silence as Justus continued his ranting. Finally, he stormed out of the great room, and Judith rose from her seat. Unsteady on her feet, she put a hand against the wall to balance herself, then slowly made her way down the hallway.

* * * * * *

The early evening breeze blew from the Great Sea bringing the Caelinus household a welcome respite from the heat. Hadassah moved about quietly as she tended to her nightly duties. She had already prepared Judith's bedchamber for sleep, but the mistress of the house was restless and not yet ready to settle in for the night.

"Hadassah, come and sit with me." Judith held a goblet of freshly squeezed pomegranate juice in one hand.

Hadassah lowered herself to the floor in front of her aunt.

"No. Sit here. By me." She indicated the bed next to her.

Surprised, Hadassah rose and then sat next to Judith.

"You remind me so much of my brother's wife. I see Deborah's compassion in your eyes. I hear her voice when you speak." Judith's smile faded somewhat when she added, "I see her faith in you." She sat without speaking for a few minutes, then finally said in resignation, "Hadassah, I have a confession to make. I am not well, and it... it terrifies me."

Hadassah reached out for Judith's hand. "What are you afraid of, Dodah?"

"Look at me, Hadassah. I am old beyond my years. My skin has no color. I am weak and frail. I fear... death."

Hadassah shook her head defiantly. "No, Dodah. You will get well."

Judith looked at her niece through loving eyes. "You don't understand, Hadassah. It is much worse now. My days of wellness are far outnumbered by those of illness. I believe I haven't many days left."

"Aelia surely has something to increase your strength." She rose quickly. "I shall go and–"

"No, my dear sweet Hadassah." Judith reached out a trembling hand and pulled her niece back down to the bed. She caressed Hadassah's cheek and smiled feebly. "So much like your mother..."

Suddenly, Judith closed her eyes tightly and sobbed into her hands. "What will become of me? I am a woman without hope."

A look of compassion accompanied Hadassah's words as she softly said, "There is hope, Dodah. There is always hope." Tenderly, her fingers wiped away the tears on Judith's cheek. "I know of someone who may be able to help you."

Judith's eyes fluttered open as a fatalistic laugh escaped her lips. "Help me? No one can help me, Hadassah. I have been seen by the best healers. I have taken more medicines than I can count. I have made many offerings to the gods. I have bargained and pleaded with them, yet they remain silent. There is no one who can help me now."

Hadassah took a deep breath, then said quietly, "I know of a man."

A cynical look spread over Judith's face. "A man?"

"Yes. I have seen him myself. He heals people."

Judith's brow furrowed in disbelief. "What do you mean 'He heals people'? Is this man a physician?"

"No. He is a rabbi, and I've seen him heal people...twice."

Judith shook her head. "A rabbi? I cannot speak to a rabbi."

"Why not?" A look of puzzlement crossed Hadassah's face.

"Years ago, I turned my back on the God of our people. He will not hear my prayers now."

Hadassah shook her head rejecting Judith's statement. "No, Dodah. God always hears the prayers of a repentant heart. The Scriptures tell us that the Lord is good and ready to forgive all who call upon His name."

Judith made no reply. Her silence encouraged Hadassah to continue.

"If you just heard him speak, you would believe. We could go together to the synagogue when he returns to Capernaum."

"The synagogue? I cannot go there. What would people say? What would Justus say? I am more a Roman than a Jewess, and I must remain true to Rome, not for my sake, but for his." Judith's voice was unconvincing.

"That is not true, Dodah. You are Jewish. You are a child of Abraham as much as I am. You have every right to go to the synagogue," argued Hadassah. "Surely, no one would judge you for that."

Judith shook her head. "No. It would be an affront to Justus. I cannot do that to him. I am the wife of a Roman citizen."

Hadassah's lips formed a thin line as she contemplated what to do. Finally, she spoke. "The rabbi often speaks to the multitudes that gather near the sea. We could go there. There's so many people there that no one would take notice of you, and it wouldn't be going against Justus."

Judith's voice wavered. "I don't know if it would be right. I could never deceive my husband."

Hadassah's plea was heartfelt. "I would never encourage you to defy your husband, Dodah, but if there is a chance, even a small one, that the rabbi could free you of this plague, Justus would surely be agreeable to that, would he not?"

Judith turned toward Hadassah, and for the first time, there was a hint of hope in her voice. "I don't know..."

"I cannot imagine such a good man as Justus not wanting the very best for you. He cares for you deeply, Dodah. I know he does."

Judith's lips pressed together tightly, and she held firm to Hadassah's hand. Finally, she slowly nodded her head. "Tell me about this rabbi of yours."

Hadassah's entire face lit up as she began to recount her experiences. "The first time was at the synagogue. I sat in the back and listened as he shared from the Torah. Dodah, it was so powerful! Almost as if the Eternal Himself was speaking! I didn't understand everything he said, but what I did understand moved me deeply! And afterwards, he healed a man!

"The rabbi stood on the steps, and a man possessed by an evil spirit came running up to him shrieking and flailing his arms. The rabbi commanded the spirit to come out of the man, and it did! Just like that!" She snapped her fingers. "And the evil spirit called the rabbi, 'the Holy One.' Can you imagine that, Dodah? The Holy One! It truly was a miracle! A miracle from God Himself! Then the possessed man praised God just like everyone else after the healing. He didn't scream anymore; he didn't throw himself on the ground and writhe around. He was perfectly normal!"

Judith listened with rapt attention. "Are you sure he was made whole?"

"Completely. I have seen him since then in the marketplace. He is just like you or me." Hadassah's eyes sparkled with excitement. "And then there was the man who couldn't walk. His friends brought him on a mat to the rabbi, and then the rabbi healed him just by telling him to get up and walk! And then the man stood up, picked up his mat, and walked on his own!"

"You saw this?" Disbelief covered Judith's pale face. "How could these things happen?"

Hadassah's reply was filled with confidence. "Dodah, I know it's hard to believe, but it really happened. I saw it with my own eyes! I know it was God. This man... this rabbi... he is from God. He has to be. When he speaks, it is with such power and authority. I know he could heal you."

Anguish twisted the features on Judith's face. "How can I go to him, Hadassah? I am no longer a true daughter of Zion. I have forsaken the God of my forefathers. He would never have mercy on me."

As tears fell from Judith's eyes, Hadassah tried to reassure her. "God loves us all, Dodah. His love for you has never changed. The Scriptures tell us that He loves us with an everlasting love and wants to forgive us. Remember the Psalmist? He wrote 'He hath not dealt with us after our sins; nor rewarded us according to our iniquities. For as the heaven is high above the earth, so great is His mercy toward them that fear Him.' Dodah, I know if you just call upon Him, He will forgive you and heal you."

Abruptly, Judith turned from her niece, burying her face in her pillows. "Please go Hadassah. I must be alone."

Reluctantly rising from the bed, Hadassah did as she was bid. She sighed deeply as she left Judith's bedroom, stopping in the arched doorway to look back at her aunt. The sound of her Judith's weeping echoed in the room, and Hadassah's heart was close to breaking.

Chapter Six

"For Zion's sake will I not hold my peace, and for Jerusalem's sake I will not rest, until the righteousness thereof go forth as brightness, and the salvation thereof as a lamp that burneth." Isaiah 62:1

Marcus rode through Jerusalem with little fanfare. Accompanied by less than twenty legionnaires, his procession did not go unnoticed, but it also did not give way to cause for alarm among the inhabitants of the holy city. Even the Jewish men who harbored disdain for Rome and all of its influences paid little attention to the centurion and his small band of men. They were used to seeing evidence of Rome everywhere, whether in flesh and blood or in engraved abominations such as coins or emblems. Desensitized to the presence of Rome, life continued as usual within the walls of the ancient city, but like a simmering pot, eventually things would come to a boil and explode. Fighting would ensue until the Romans extinguished the flames of rebellion, and then the cycle would repeat itself.

Marcus raised a fist into the air, and the soldiers halted their steeds behind him. He glanced around, and seeing nothing unusual, he tapped his heels into the muscular sides of Ares. The horse immediately began to trot through the cobbled streets making a clip-clop sound with each step.

"Hardly seems as though these people are capable of organizing a revolt," stated Gaius, as he maneuvered his horse beside Marcus. The young Roman had ridden with Marcus for many years, and the two of them had forged a friendship tested by both time and battle. Gaius' title of centurion was newly bestowed, and when his men were assigned to the same region as that of Marcus, he saw an opportunity to glean more from the seasoned soldier for whom he had much respect.

"Never underestimate an enemy, Gaius. It only takes a few to incite rebellion," cautioned Marcus as he continued his surveillance of the populace.

Merchants were calling out to passersby to inspect their goods, and

Marcus noted tables of fresh vegetables and fruits as well as fabrics, small pieces of furniture, and even cages that held doves or pigeons. He halted by a table laden with figs, dates, and pomegranates.

Catching the eye of the seller, Marcus flipped a small silver coin in his direction. Much like a frog darting its tongue out to snatch its morning meal, the merchant quickly reached out and grabbed the coin in mid-air, not caring what image was upon it. With a toothless grin, he held up a basket of newly harvested dates and allowed Marcus to inspect the ripened fruit nestled within it.

"The best in all of Jerusalem, Centurion. Or perhaps a juicy fig?" He held up a large plate piled high with the purple fruit.

With a quick nod of his head, Marcus reached down and plucked two figs from the platter. Biting into one, Marcus savored the sweetness, and as he rode on, he heard the cries resume from the merchant enticing others to buy his produce.

The bright colors of the soldiers were a sharp contrast to the more subtle shades of the Jews milling around the marketplace. This made it quite easy for Marcus to differentiate between the locals and foreigners as he surveyed the early morning shoppers. For most male Jews, the simlāh, a heavy woolen coat-like garment covered the kethōneth, the linen undergarment, which was held in place by some sort of belt. The simlāh was also large enough to conceal a weapon, and simply because the garment had the religious fringes to remind the Jews of God's commandments, it didn't mean the wearer was a pacifist. Marcus kept a sharp eye for any suspicious movements in the crowd.

Despite being in the city for several months, Marcus' senses remained heightened whenever he rode through the busy streets. His right hand cautiously moved to the hilt of his sword when his eye caught a subtle, yet discomforting movement ahead of him. His steely eyes met the angry gaze of a young man whose fingers held tightly to a jagged stone barely visible in the folds of his simlāh. Marcus' grip tightened around the handle of his blade.

You come up against me with a rock? You are such a fool.

As he neared the potential attacker, another man placed his hand on the arm of the seething Jew and whispered into his ear. The rock fell to the ground as the man spat resentfully onto the dirt. Marcus relaxed his grip, but his hardened eyes never left the face of the potential assailant until he had ridden past.

"Apparently, he was not ready to meet his God," murmured Gaius with a low chuckle.

Marcus nodded. "Not today, anyway."

They rode further on until Herod's temple came into view. Marcus reined Ares to a stop and gazed up the slope of Mount Moriah. Perched above the city, the magnificent temple stood like a beacon, and its architecture never ceased to impress Marcus.

Like the palace in Caesarea, the structure was an impressive monument to its builder. White marbled columns, one entire stone for each pillar, stood twenty-five cubits high supporting the engraved cedar roofs over the portico. Double colonnades surrounded the temple, and a golden eagle decorated the main gate of the western wall.

"It may be a Jewish temple, but Rome is still needed to protect it," Gaius stated, nodding toward the winged symbol of the Roman Empire. "They don't even realize Rome is their protector and savior."

Marcus nodded. "It would do them well to accept that. Instead, there is constant talk of rebellion. I don't think I will ever understand these Jews." Shaking his head, Marcus sighed as he said with a smirk, "Let us hope their long-awaited messiah doesn't show up tonight. I'm tired. I need nourishment and rest."

Gaius laughed. "If he did, it wouldn't take long to squash his troops. A bunch of bearded zealots against the finest Rome has to offer? Hardly worth the effort, if you ask me."

"Caesar thinks it's worth the effort, or we wouldn't be here," Marcus reminded. "We do have our orders, Gaius."

"Of course. Maintain the peace, no matter the cost."

Marcus tugged on the reins, and Ares turned away from the front of the great temple. With the raising of his hand, Gaius and the rest of the soldiers followed Marcus as they made their way toward Antonia, the Roman fortress.

* * * * * *

Marcus bolted upright in his bunk. The pounding of his heart seemed nearly as loud as the pounding on his door. Throwing the thin coverlet off of himself, he swung his legs over the bed and stood up, straightening his tunic. Only a sliver of moonlight provided any light in the small room.

"Come!" he shouted angrily as he ran his fingers through the loose hair on his brow.

The door opened, and a timid servant hesitantly stepped into the room. He held a small oil lamp near his face. "There is trouble, Centurion. The prefect demands your presence."

Marcus opened his mouth to speak, but before he could respond, the servant had disappeared into the night leaving him standing in the darkness.

It took Marcus only minutes to make himself presentable to his superior, and as he purposefully walked through the halls of the fortress, Gaius met him.

"I hate being wakened from a good dream," lamented Gaius as he fell into step with Marcus.

"It's never a good sign to be summoned before dawn," grumbled Marcus. Their footsteps echoed through the empty corridor.

Gaius nodded. "I suppose the zealots were active during the night, and now we have to pay the price for their insurrection."

Marcus nodded as he spoke harshly. "Pity the man who runs afoul of me today."

As they entered the Praetorium, they were greeted by the nod of another centurion waiting for Pontius Pilate.

Marcus sighed deeply, irritated that his sleep had been interrupted, and that he would most likely have to head out into the streets without a morning meal. He was not in the mood to be satiated by one or two figs.

When the prefect arrived, all three men snapped to attention.

Angry eyes moved from centurion to centurion as Pilate stomped around them in fury. "I do not care what it takes, but this ends now! Roman lives were taken during the night! Find out who is responsible and bring them before me! Do you understand? Failure to do so will be regarded as incompetence in your duties!"

He didn't wait for any acknowledgement from the centurions, but simply turned brusquely and stormed out of the judgment hall.

"Well, that's a great way to start our day," stated Gaius dourly.

"So much for the city of peace," responded Marcus dryly.

* * * * * *

As the sky began to glow with the pink and blue hues of the dawn, Marcus and Gaius moved through the now quiet streets of Jerusalem by foot, sending their men out in small groups to search for the rebels. Choosing to be ambulatory rather than ride their steeds, they strode purposefully along, ever watchful of the activity around them. The previous night had stunned the Roman legionnaires when a flurry of random attacks had kept the details separated and more vulnerable, resulting in the deaths of several soldiers. Marcus' orders to his own men had been direct, demanding swift and immediate reprisals against any suspected perpetrators. Now the centurions and their men were on high alert whether on foot or horseback.

It was a bold move by Marcus to walk through the marketplace without a more protective detail, but over the past few months of his tenure here, he had found the volatility of Jerusalem always seemed to wane with the rising of the sun. Now as merchants were once again preparing their tables for the morning crowds, and a few early risers were already meandering through the marketplace, Marcus and Gaius walked without incident. They were given a wide berth as they seemingly strolled nonchalantly through the streets. Their eyes never lingered on a specific area, but continually scanned their surroundings for any questionable activity, and they were prepared to draw their weapons in an instant.

This morning, business commenced as expected, and the soldiers made their way unmolested through the city. While no one stepped up to have any social interaction with the two men, there was also no overt animosity toward their presence. It was as if the violence of the previous night had never happened.

"Seems quiet, doesn't it?" asked Gaius as he surveyed the area in front of them.

Marcus nodded. "For the most part." He glanced upward as his eye caught the quick closure of a shutter. "The light of day always sends the rats scattering."

As the sun rose higher in the sky, the people began to fill the city streets, and it wasn't as easy to navigate without bumping into others who were scurrying about their own business. The Jews were quick to move out of the path of the two centurions, but Marcus and Gaius remained watchful as they walked.

As they neared the sheep market, they paused beneath one of the five porticos near the medicinal pools of Bethesda. Gaius cast a furtive glance at the infirmed lying around the perimeter of the pool nearest them.

With a tilt of his head, Marcus indicated the path to the pool area.

"You really want to go in there?" Gaius asked. The scowl that accompanied his wrinkled nose indicated his displeasure at the thought.

"Once around, then we leave," affirmed Marcus.

They maneuvered their way around the pool, ignoring the stench that often accompanies severe sicknesses. Some ailments were obvious, while others suffered from maladies that couldn't be seen outwardly. Many were impotent in some way, helpless to meet their own needs, and desperate for the compassion of another human being. Most simply lay on the stone pavement around the pool in silence... waiting.

Marcus and Gaius either stepped over those blocking the path or pushed them out of the way with their feet. No one resisted; some merely groaned, while a few weakly pled for mercy.

As they neared one man lying on a mat, he extended a thin emaciated arm toward them and cried out, "Please help me. I have no man to help me." His weakened voice accentuated the severity of his condition.

A look of disgust covered Gaius' face. "Help you what, old man?"

"I have no one to help me to the pool when the waters move. Please—"

"We are not your servants. Help yourself." Marcus roughly pushed the man aside with his foot and continued walking toward the gate at the far end of the pool area.

"I hear they believe one of these pools has healing powers," commented

Gaius when they reached the portico.

"Healing powers?"

"Yes. Supposedly if the waters are troubled, that indicates one of their gods—"

"They only have one," interrupted Marcus as he leaned against one of the limestone columns supporting the porch.

"One? One what?"

"God. The Jews only have one God," he clarified.

Gaius nodded. "Right. I forgot. Rather restrictive, don't you think?"

"I guess they believe he can do everything. No need for a god of this or that if yours can do it all," stated Marcus.

Gaius tipped his head toward the sick around the pool. "I guess he's not very good at healing, or there wouldn't be so many of them in there."

Marcus smirked as he nodded his head. "Maybe he's just too busy for them." A light chuckle escaped his lips as he moved slightly, allowing a man to pass into the pool area. "Better to be one of many gods in an empire, than one god in a place like this."

Gaius agreed. "Perhaps we—" He stopped speaking as his gaze followed the man who had just walked by them. "What's he doing?"

Marcus turned to see to whom Gaius was referring. "Just talking to that old man over there. Same one who spoke to us. Probably asking him to help him into the 'healing' waters." Marcus chuckled as he turned back toward the city street.

Gaius crossed his arms over his chest as he laughed. "Maybe we should have thrown him in the pool as an example of Roman compassion." As he continued to watch the interaction between the two men, his mocking laugh faded.

"Marcus..."

Standing transfixed by the scene before him, Gaius reached over toward Marcus. Tapping him on the shoulder, Gaius said, "Marcus, he's standing."

"Who?"

"The man who couldn't move. The one you pushed aside. He's getting up."

"What?"

Marcus pivoted just in time to see the frail man stoop to pick up his tattered bedroll, then stand upright without assistance. An exclamation of praise could be heard as the once-helpless man embraced the taller man standing by him.

Both Marcus and Gaius stared as the sick man, now made whole, rushed by them into the city streets. They watched him until he disappeared among the people.

Skeptical, Marcus turned to Gaius. "Are you sure that was the same man?"

"I'd stake my life on it."

"Where is the man he was talking to? I want to speak with him." Marcus' brow furrowed as he turned back toward the pool. He scanned the area, but the mystery man was nowhere to be seen.

Gaius' eyes darted back and forth through the now-growing crowd. Murmurs of a miraculous healing punctuated the air. Gaius reached out and grabbed the arm of a bystander.

"Did you see anyone leave here?"

"I saw no one, Centurion."

Gaius rushed outside the gate to the city street leaving Marcus to question some of those still waiting by the pool.

Moving to the vacated spot of the healed man, Marcus stooped beside another ailing man and looked him directly in the face. "Did you see the man who was here earlier, speaking with the sick man on the mat next to you?"

"Yes, Centurion. I saw the Healer," came the reply.

Marcus froze.

The Healer? Could this be the same man to whom Hadassah had referred?

"Do you know who he is? Did you see where he went?"

When the man shook his head, Marcus stood up and scanned the area once more. Loud shouting voices averted his attention to a narrow street just past the pool, and he sprinted toward the commotion. Rounding the corner, he came face to face with an angry mob confronting several Roman soldiers.

"I would rather die than be enslaved by your kind!" The zealot pulled a large curved knife from beneath the folds of his simlāh. The threatening wave of his blade generated a combined Roman response as swords were immediately brandished.

"You dogs occupy our land! You take what is given to us rightfully by God! Strike me down and more will rise up! We will rid our land of the Roman plight!" He made a lunge at the Roman nearest to him, but the swift blade of the same legionnaire silenced the zealot permanently. The mob quickly scattered, leaving the Romans standing over the still body of the attacker.

"That's one who won't bother us again." Marcus' voice was filled with disdain as he spat on the body. The incident at the pool was forgotten as he turned brusquely and walked away.

* * * * * *

Three days later, Marcus found himself standing once again in the great hall, but this time it was not his turn to stand before the prefect awaiting orders. Marcus had been assigned the unfortunate duty to stand in attendance during the judgment of criminal offenses against Rome. While his role in the adjudications was not strenuous, it was tedious to a man who preferred action to negotiation, and Marcus was not one who relished standing idle. However, he was a soldier, and as always, he followed his orders without question.

He stood stoically to one side of the prefect as, one by one, men were brought in, accused, and sentenced. Most crimes were petty. Thievery, rioters, insolence toward some official, but occasionally a more serious charge would be brought to the prefect, and he would rule according to Roman law. The majority were spared the death sentence, but those who had chosen what were considered capital crimes against the empire were given the ultimate punishment that Rome could dispense – crucifixion.

Rome's most heinous form of capital punishment, crucifixion was a brutal way to die, and while Marcus was in no way sympathetic with murderers or traitors, he found no satisfaction in watching a man die on a wooden cross. Initially beaten raw with whips embedded with pieces of rock and bone, the convicted man would then be forced to carry his own crossbeam to the site of the execution. Here, as in Rome, the preferred places of crucifixion were along the busiest roadways so that the people could witness the punishment for those who dared rise up against the empire. In Jerusalem, the southern roads from Bethany and Jericho were prime sites for crucifixions as they were heavily traveled, plus crosses could be elevated on the side of the Mount of Olives for all to see whether traversing the roads or remaining in the city. Unlike Rome however, the corpses were not left on the crosses for extended lengths of time since the Torah, the Jewish religious writings, required any Jew executed by crucifixion to be buried before sundown.

Death by crucifixion was horrific. Large spikes, hammered through the wrists and ankles, secured the condemned to the cross, even when the heavy beams were lifted and dropped into place. Weakened by the scourging, many were nearly dead by the time the long nails were driven through their flesh. Once raised, the guilty simply hung in agony, waiting for death. The effort to breathe was excruciating as the malefactor struggled to push or pull himself up to allow air to move into his lungs. Death usually came from suffocation, which was slow and torturous, sometimes taking days for a man to die. Occasionally, it would be necessary for a soldier to break the long bones of the criminal's legs to expedite the dying process.

There was no doubt the day would see several Jewish zealots sentenced to die this way. It had taken Marcus and his men only a few days to round up those responsible for spilling Roman blood, and the prefect insisted on immediate justice. Undoubtedly, Pilate hoped the public executions would deter any further uprisings, and if not, the crucifixions would continue.

As the sun moved lower in the afternoon sky, Marcus looked straight ahead, hoping the adjudications were nearing an end, and he could take his leave of the judgment hall. While he wasn't physically tired, the hours of non-activity exhausted him, and the thought of wildly riding Ares with no particular destination in mind was very attractive. His random thoughts were interrupted when the prefect rose from his chair.

"Tell me, Marcus, what do you think of Jerusalem? It is your first time here, is it not?"

Surprised at being addressed, Marcus turned his gaze toward his superior.

Pilate walked over to a basin and dipped his hands into its tepid water. He splashed some of it on his face, wiped his hands on a linen towel, then ambled over to a window on the western side of the hall.

Marcus' thoughts quickly coalesced as he considered the appropriate response, but before he could reply, the prefect spoke once more.

"I much prefer Caesarea, but the nature of times requires my presence here more often than not. It is not a position I relish. I thought perhaps—"

Hearing footsteps from the entry, both Marcus and Pilate turned around as the latest concern was brought for judgment. Dressed completely in white with large blue fringes on the border of his outer garment, Marcus recognized the traditional garb of a Pharisee, a representative of one of Jerusalem's religious sects. Although seeming quite small in stature next to his escort, the Pharisee walked boldly forward. Just peeking out from beneath his sleeves was his phylactery, a leather pouch strapped to his arm that held a small scroll of religious passages.

Marcus raised an eyebrow as the Jew approached the bench of the tribune.

What does a Pharisee need from Rome? They have their own religious council.

Sensing no danger from him, Marcus relaxed slightly, but kept a wary eye on the complainant.

"How can I assist you?" asked Pilate as he perused the man before him.

"I am here to request Rome's intervention on a most grievous matter."

"I gathered that." The Roman governor yawned loudly. "That would be why I am here. Do not be redundant. State your request."

"Forgive me, Prefect. Perhaps you have heard of this man... this Yeshua of Nazareth?"

"Enlighten me."

"He consistently breaks our laws. He must be stopped. Brought to justice."

"For what crime?"

"He dishonors the Sabbath. As you know—"

"Do not presume what I know."

"I would not do so, Prefect. I meant to say that this Yeshua encourages our people to break God's laws. He must be stopped!"

"God's laws? This is a religious matter, not a Roman one. Take it to your Sanhedrin," Marcus stated calmly.

The Pharisee turned toward Pilate. "He broke the law! You cannot sit and do nothing! It is your duty to administer justice!"

The angry demand irritated Pilate, and he tolerated the pious Jew no more. Marcus' superior officer rose to his full height, towering above the Pharisee. His steel gaze bore into the face of the self-righteous Jew, and as he spoke, the smaller man took a step backward.

"Do not suppose to tell me my duty. My obligation is to Caesar, not to the Jews." His voice was on the edge of fury. "You tread on dangerous ground, *Pharisee*." He spoke with such disgust that the Jew stood in stunned silence. "Need I make myself clearer?" Pilate's hardened eyes narrowed as he waited for the answer.

"I meant no disrespect." Bowing his head meekly, the Pharisee's voice trembled slightly as the Roman governor sat back down. "It is just that Yeshua... this self-proclaimed rabbi... has broken our law. There are claims that he heals the sick, incites men—"

"Incites men?" The prefect leaned forward attentively. "To what?"

"On one particular occasion, Yeshua instructed a man to carry his mat on the Sabbath. The Torah is very clear that we do no work on the Sabbath, yet this Yeshua does that very thing!"

Pilate stared incredulously at the Pharisee for a brief moment before bellowing, "You cannot be serious! You bring before Rome a man who bids someone to *carry a mat?* That is your crime?" His face reddened. "I should have *you* flogged for bringing such a ridiculous charge to me and wasting my time." As the prefect's voice escalated, the Pharisee seemed to shrink in stature. "This is not Rome's concern!" He angrily waved his hands in the air, dismissing the stunned Jew. "Take it to your priests and their council!"

"But Prefect—"

"We are finished here!"

The Pharisee knew it was useless to continue, and dejection was in his posture as he slinked out of the judgment hall.

Marcus felt no pity for the man.

Such petty grievances. Would they have us crucify a man simply because he carried a mat on the wrong day?

And then Marcus remembered.

Carried a mat? The man at Bethesda carried a mat. When was that?

Yesterday? No, it was two days ago... the Jewish Sabbath! The Pharisee said his name. What was it? Yosef? Yael? Yeshua! Yes, that was it! He called him Yeshua.

"I have had enough," stated the governor curtly as he rose to his feet. Marcus snapped to attention.

"Can you imagine such absurdity? First, they want to punish a man for the 'reprehensible' act of healing the sick. Then they accuse him of the 'appalling' crime of instructing a man to carry a mat." Pilate's mocking laugh filled the Praetorium. "And they wonder how Rome could occupy this region so easily." He grabbed his goblet and in one gulp emptied it of its contents. "We are done here." Without another word, Pilate strode past the centurion and headed for the large double wooden doors leading to the outer courtyard.

Marcus saluted and waited for his superior to leave before relaxing. Once alone, he straightened the leather wristlets he wore, adjusted his helmet, and walked the expanse of the room to the rear exit. As he left the Praetorium, he strode purposefully toward the stables. Ares would be waiting. No doubt the steed was as antsy as he was for a brisk evening ride.

As he waited for his horse to be saddled, he allowed his mind to wander to the earlier confrontation with the Pharisee and then to the medicinal pools of Bethesda.

Who is this Yeshua?

* * * * * *

Thousands of stars glittered like diamonds in the night sky, and although the moon was only mid-way through its monthly cycle, its brightness transformed the Judean wilderness into a barren ghostly-gray landscape. Marcus kicked his heels into Ares' sides, and the horse increased its pace as they exited Jerusalem through the gate by which temple sheep would be brought into the city for sacrifice.

Night rides could be somewhat precarious in rugged terrain, but the moon's illumination was enough that Marcus could easily navigate the path upon which he rode. Normally, a lone traveler would be a good target for the thieves who abounded in the nearby hills, but Marcus kept in the open and maintained constant surveillance around him. Although he was not in his full uniform, his weapons remained ready at his side. The double-edged sword was secure in its place, and the smaller dagger hung in the strap across his chest. His hand was light on the reins as Ares moved effortlessly along the ancient roads surrounding Jerusalem, facilitating a quick retrieval of the blade if needed. Lastly, if he perceived himself to be outnumbered, Marcus had the utmost confidence that Ares could outrun any animal in the entire Roman province, so he rode without much concern about his personal safety.

The desert wind upon his face was warm, but not uncomfortably so. The solitude was comforting, and the lack of responsibility was liberating, providing Marcus with the respite he needed from the last few days' obligations. Off in the distance, small campfires flickered on the hillsides as shepherds guarded flocks of sheep throughout the night. He pulled Ares to a stop as the distant howl of a wolf penetrated the night air.

He allowed his mind to wander until it meandered back to Bethesda's mysterious Healer. He tried to recall the facial features of the man, but their passing of one another had been fleeting, and Marcus had not taken enough time focusing on the stranger's appearance to recall it now. Annoyed with his inability to visualize the Healer, he tried to empty his mind of anything, but it was impossible. As soon as the memories of the day faded, another vision materialized in his head.

Hadassah.

Her image surprised him, but he did not try to suppress it. While he could recall the fragrance of her hair, the joy of life in her laughter, and even the fiery discussions they shared in the garden, he found that the months apart had also dimmed his recollection of her face. Frustrated that his memory of her was also fading, he scowled as he yanked on Ares' reins. The horse protested with a snort, then turned to the left and began the trek back to Jerusalem.

Marcus glanced to the north beyond the walled city. A strong desire to speak with Hadassah tugged within him. He now wanted to know what she knew about this Yeshua. He wanted to know if Yeshua really was the same man that Hadassah had spoken of with such reverence, but not so much that he would forsake his duty here. His obligation was to Rome, and Rome wanted him in Jerusalem. He knew in his heart that outright rebellion was coming, and that would keep him here indefinitely.

Resolved to his fate, he turned his head back toward the old city and nudged the steed's sides once more. For the first time, Marcus wished himself back in the garden at his father's estate facing the fire in Hadassah's eyes as she fought so strongly for her beliefs. Now, he had no idea when or if he would be returning to Capernaum, or if he would ever again see the young Jewish woman who somehow crept into his thoughts when he least expected it.

Chapter Seven

"The LORD openeth the eyes of the blind: the LORD raiseth them that are bowed down: the LORD loveth the righteous:" Psalm 146:8

Passover was a very busy time in Jerusalem. It was a time when all of Israel remembered how God delivered them from the oppressive bondage of an Egyptian pharaoh; a time when God raised up one of their own to lead them from their captivity to the Promised Land, and a time when God demonstrated His supremacy above all others by way of ten unimaginable plagues.

From places as far north as Sidon and Tyre, throngs of pilgrims made the journey to the holy city to remember how God heard the cries of His children and delivered them from captivity. Some came from southern cities like Hebron and En Gedi, while some traveled from lands so distant their names were rarely heard in the region.

This sudden influx of Jews increased the population of Jerusalem to nearly six times its normal size, creating an unpredictable mass of humanity that the Roman legionnaires were expected to keep under control. At night, campfires could be seen all along the hillsides surrounding the city as fatigued travelers set up temporary dwellings for the feast days. Merchants lined the streets with their wares, hoping to entice weary travelers to stop and inspect their commodities. Those brazen enough to sample the goods without paying were often chased down by the locals. Rarely did the legionnaires get involved in such petty crimes in Jerusalem.

Marcus sat high upon Ares as his men broke off into groups of eight, each its own squad. As a commanding officer, the responsibility of delegating each band of men to its specified destination fell upon him, and with the marked increase of foot traffic came the need for more vigilance by the legionnaires. Urging Ares to move forward, he began his own surveillance of the crowds. People milled around shoulder to shoulder, and it took a keen eye to discern normal chaos from covert conspiracies aimed at malicious or riotous activity.

He made his way slowly down a main street, scanning side to side. Despite seeing nothing suspicious, he remained alert, keeping one hand on his weapon at all times. Occasionally, his gaze met unfriendly eyes, but no aggressive overtures were made toward him as he rode. The bleating of lambs and goats seemed to float above the crowds, and occasionally a stray animal would cross in front of Ares, barely missing the massive hooves.

"Stop thief!"

Marcus turned toward the shouting in time to see a cloaked figure dart around a corner and disappear into the crowd. He kept Ares still as several young men gave chase into the marketplace.

"Centurion! Do something!" demanded the victim. "He stole my grapes!"

Marcus raised an eyebrow as he assessed the merchant before him. "Your grapes, eh?"

"Yes! He's a thief! He should be beaten within an inch of his life!"

"An inch of his life? For a bunch of grapes?" Marcus suppressed a laugh. "Fine, bring me this thief, and I will personally take him to the prefect and tell him that you make demands of Rome for justice. Your name?"

The merchant hesitated as his eyes narrowed in frustrated anger. In feigned humility, he bowed his head. "Forgive me, Centurion. Rome has far too many other important issues than to concern itself with one beggar stealing food." He backed away from Marcus, never looking up again.

Through a sarcastic smile, Marcus said, "As you wish." He then made a clucking sound, and Ares continued his slow walk down the street leaving the disgruntled merchant behind.

As Marcus rode along the eastern wall of the city, he continually surveyed the area around him. Approaching the Golden Gate, he looked ahead to a procession moving along the way out of the city. Curious onlookers lined the road, and Marcus sat up a bit taller to see the attraction as he pulled back slightly on the reins. Ares came to a halt, uncaring about the commotion ahead of them.

Roman soldiers were prodding a condemned man down the road. He was bloodied from a beating, and he struggled to carry the heavy wooden crossbeam laid upon his shoulders. When he stumbled, the crowd jeered as soldiers forced the already dying man to his feet and pushed him toward the city gate leading to Mount Olivet. Those who plotted against Rome would think twice before committing their crimes as they witnessed the judgment doled out to those who dared rise up against Caesar. Although Marcus found the death penalty unnecessarily cruel, he could not deny its effectiveness in deterring criminal behavior. What he couldn't understand was the unpalatable attraction that drew crowds to witness the inhumane form of punishment. With a kick of his heels into the horse's sides, Marcus turned Ares and headed away from the funeral march.

* * * * * *

"Marcus, tell me more about this Passover," said Gaius as he reclined against a large cushion on a lounge. He took a large bite from the roasted lamb that had been set before the two men.

Marcus wiped his mouth with the sleeve of his tunic before responding. "There's not much to tell. From what I understand, it's a time when the Jews commemorate leaving Egypt."

"That's it? All this..." He swept his hand in an arc in the general direction of the Jewish temple. "Because they left Egypt?"

"Supposedly it was a rather spectacular exit," stated Marcus as he lifted a goblet to his lips. He drank deeply, then returned the vessel to the table. "The Jews were slaves in Egypt for hundreds of years. Their prophet beseeched the Pharaoh of Egypt to grant them permission to leave the land, so they could return here to their homeland. Their request was denied, but this prophet kept demanding they be set free. From what I understand, the Jewish God performed some so-called miracles, and eventually the Pharaoh agreed."

"What kind of miracles?"

Marcus shrugged. "I don't know. I don't really give much thought to childhood tales." He inspected a plump date, then took a bite from it.

"I heard that they sacrifice lambs—"

"They always sacrifice lambs," interrupted Marcus. "It's how they make atonement for their sins."

"By killing lambs? How does that work?"

"No idea. I think the lamb has to be flawless."

Gaius' brow wrinkled as he pondered Marcus' explanation. "Flawless? What makes a lamb flawless? Fat and tasty like this one?"

Marcus shook his head as he chuckled. "I don't know. I've heard that a lamb with any kind of blemish is unacceptable for slaughter. They even have a special field where they raise the sheep intended for sacrifice at the temple."

"So, they raise perfect sheep just to kill them?"

"I told you the Jews were a peculiar people. After they kill the lambs, they feast for another seven days."

"Eating all those lambs?" Gaius broke a hunk of bread from the loaf and dipped it in a bowl of broth. "What is the feast for?"

Marcus shrugged his shoulders and shook his head. "Who knows? I can't keep up with all their feasts and days of remembrances. What I do know is that when Jerusalem gets this crowded, there is the potential for chaos. The zealots look for any reason to incite the people to rebel." Marcus wiped his mouth and hands, then tossed the napkin onto the table. "And we are here to make sure that doesn't happen."

Gaius studied his friend's face, then asked, "So you didn't celebrate any of this?"

"Me?" Marcus' eyes widened as he questioned his friend.

"Isn't your father Jewish?"

Marcus' laugh had an edge of contempt. "Justus is Jewish when it's convenient. His Jewish heritage is admitted only when it is beneficial to his purse."

Gaius' eyebrows rose slightly. "You weren't raised in their ways?"

A snort of disgust accompanied Marcus' reply. "Hardly. I can never recall a time when any Jewish tradition was observed in our household, nor have I ever met anyone in our family with Jewish blood in their veins. My mother was Roman, and she embraced every aspect of Roman life, including the worship of the gods of Rome. My father was in Rome, so he did the same. He did whatever he deemed necessary to please those in power over him, and that most certainly did not include observing Jewish customs. It was only when he was sent to Judea, he suddenly proclaimed he was one of them, but it was only from his desire to be accepted by the Jews, the very people he shunned all his life, and I assure you that the only reason he did that was for financial gain. Even his marriage to Judith was a calculated plan of acceptance by those he forsook years ago."

"Really?"

Marcus snickered. "What better way to be accepted by the Jews than to marry one of their own?"

"I suppose one does what one must do, eh?" Gaius laughed. "In the name of Caesar, of course."

Marcus chuckled. "Of course."

* * * * * *

The following day, Marcus' responsibilities included patrolling the temple area to ensure no eruptions of violence occurred on the mount. With three squads assigned to him, Marcus simply walked purposefully about, overseeing his men and maintaining an undeniable Roman presence on the grounds. Everywhere he looked, small clusters of rabbinical students huddled at the feet of their teachers as the Torah was taught. Each group seemed identical to the next with the exception of the age of the students.

Marcus stood and observed one group of young boys no older than ten as the rabbi held a writing tablet and poured honey onto it. As the teacher handed the tablet to one of the boys, he bent over and looked into the lad's eyes and said, "May you never forget that the words of God are like honey."

Marcus shook his head and scowled.

Honey? More like vinegar...

He walked along the western exposure of the temple, continually scanning the activity around him. Although the lessons were being conducted in every direction, it was a small gathering just beyond the massive structure itself that caught Marcus' attention. Narrowing his eyes, he moved with determination, focusing on those congregated around a very familiar Pharisee. It took Marcus only a moment to recognize the priest as the same one who had approached Pilate. He stopped, crossed his arms over his chest, and listened to the teaching coming from the lips of the Jewish rabbi.

"Our Deliverer will soon come! The Eternal One will do as He has promised our forefathers. As He delivered us from the hands of the Pharaoh of Egypt, so shall He save us from the stranglehold of the Roman empire. Our Messiah, our King, it is he who will judge righteousness! He will put an end to the wickedness that surrounds us… the heresy… the sin!"

The rabbi's face reddened as his voice escalated, and those around him seemed spellbound as they listened without uttering a sound. "The Lord himself will raise unto David a righteous Branch, and a King shall reign and prosper, and shall execute judgment and justice in the earth!"

Marcus tensed and attentively eyed others who stood within range of the rabbi's voice. The words that resonated through the crowd were capable of igniting a spark that would result in a fiery furnace of violence, and Marcus knew he would not be able to extinguish it on his own. A quick surveillance of the area around him confirmed what he was confident he would see. His men had the area surrounded and stood ready to act should things explode. Their presence was stabilizing, and there were no overt signs of rebellion in the Jewish men who had gathered near the zealous Pharisee. They simply stood at the periphery of the study group, nodding their heads as they listened to the words of the charismatic religious leader. Each soldier's hand was poised to retrieve his sword if necessary, but no need arose.

The Pharisee's voice grew in volume and passion. "As the prophet Moses said, 'The Lord thy God will turn thy captivity, and have compassion upon thee, and will return and gather thee from all the nations, whither the Lord thy God hath scattered thee.' It is written that the Messiah will gather His people from the four corners of the earth, and He will rule over the land Israel as promised to our father Abraham. From that time forward, there will be peace in Jerusalem and the world without the oppression of the Gentiles." The rabbi dramatically bowed his head and began a prayer that Marcus had heard repeatedly as he had walked along the portico.

Finally allowing himself to relax, Marcus removed his hand from the hilt of his sword but remained standing in place until the prayer was completed and the men and students began to disperse. Only then did he continue his walk. Turning along the busy southern wall, he reached the Huldah Gate and paused on the steps to scan the groups of people exiting and entering the temple grounds.

"Alms, please..."

Glancing over his shoulder, Marcus found himself looking into the unseeing eyes of a destitute beggar perched against the stone wall. The clouded gray eyes stared beyond Marcus as his emaciated hand extended outward.

"Please, have mercy..." As he brushed Marcus' tunic, his tattered sleeve fell back exposing an arm with a long jagged scar hardened with age.

Marcus swatted the arm away, ignoring the man's pleading. He turned his back to the beggar and remained standing on the monumental staircase that led from the southern streets of the city to the temple mount.

"Alms, please—"

"Quiet old man!" snapped Marcus. The authoritative tone in his voice silenced the beggar as startled bystanders quickly turned their heads away from the centurion as they headed toward the ritual purification baths.

The blind man said no more, but kept his bony arm extended.

Marcus ignored the glares from the Jews as they moved past him. Being accosted by a blind beggar irked him greatly, and he had no intention of giving anything to the sightless man. Marcus simply stood in place and observed the activities around him.

Most of the worshippers were fairly direct in where they were going. The majority headed for the Royal Stoa, the area where animals could be purchased for the temple sacrifices or money could be exchanged. Marcus fell into step behind a man leading a lamb into the temple complex. After walking back through the gate, the man moved toward the priests who examined the animals, while Marcus strolled into the Gentile court. Stalls had been erected throughout the courtyard, and vendors were constantly barking their wares to the crowd. Normally, the moneychangers were cloistered in the Stoa, but due to Passover and the thousands of worshippers who made the pilgrimage to Jerusalem, it was necessary to for them to set up in the area normally reserved for non-Jews who desired to visit Herod's temple.

The cacophony of bleating lambs and blaring voices of impatient Jews was deafening, and Marcus moved near the periphery of the courtyard as he surveyed the chaos around him. As he strode along the southern exposure of the mount, a shrill voice rose above the din.

"I can see! I can see!"

Marcus jerked his head around and saw a disheveled beggar running along the portico. Voices seemed to diminish in volume as heads turned toward the crazed man leaping across the courtyard.

"I can see!" he repeated. "Praise to the Most High! I can see!"

Comments echoed all around him as the man continued to jump and shout over and over, "I can see!"

Marcus squinted his eyes, following the exuberant man across the grounds. The familiarity of the shouting man made Marcus pause. Suddenly, he knew!

That's the beggar at the gate! His eyes... they were sightless! I saw him! He was blind! How is this possible?

Marcus stood speechless watching and listening to the commotion around the man.

"It's a miracle!"

"I know him! He's been blind since he was a young child!"

"Praise be to the Almighty!"

How could this be?

He hastened toward the growing crowd.

"Make way!" Marcus commanded.

The people parted immediately, and Marcus marched up to the now-sighted man.

"Show me your arm," demanded Marcus as he grabbed the beggar by his ragged clothes.

Despite the roughness with which Marcus took hold of the man, the joy on the beggar's face never wavered. Marcus pushed the sleeve back and beheld the scar.

"It was the Master! He healed me! They said he was coming. I called out to him, and he came up to me!" Tears fell from his newly healed eyes. Their clarity could not be mistaken. The murky cloudiness Marcus had seen earlier in the blind beggar's eyes was gone.

Marcus' face twisted in anger as he shook the man. "Who? Who came up to you?"

"The Nazarene! He asked what I wanted, and I told him I wanted to see, and then... then he healed me! I can see, Centurion! I can see!"

Marcus leaned in, his face nearly nose-to-nose with the beggar. "The Nazarene? Who is this Nazarene?"

"They say his name is Yeshua, and he is..." He reached his bony hands upward and set them boldly upon Marcus' shoulders as he reverently whispered, "He is from God, Centurion." And then more loudly, "He is of God!"

Marcus felt as though he had been slapped in the face. "Where? Where did this happen?" Marcus kept his voice low, but there was an intensity in his words.

"There." He pointed toward the Huldah Gate. "He was there."

Marcus shoved the beggar away, pivoted, and pushed his way through the throng to the gate. Bursting through it, his eyes darted from side to side, but he did not see the one for whom he sought. His lips pressed together tightly as he shook his head in frustration.

Who are you, Yeshua of Nazareth?

* * * * * *

The blasts of the shofar echoed through Jerusalem. The paschal lamb was being slaughtered in the temple, and the Levites would soon sing the Hallel, a recitation of Psalms passed down through the ages.

Marcus paced in the Antonia Fortress. Somewhere in Jerusalem, Yeshua was with his followers celebrating the Passover. The frustration of not knowing the truth about the so-called rabbi who could do miracles was mounting within him, and he couldn't sit still. Compelled to action, but not knowing exactly what to do, he grabbed his cloak and headed out into the night.

He wore nothing that identified him as a centurion, but his blond hair and beardless face left no question as to his ancestry. He knew that could make him a target, but he trusted his instincts. Still, he wore a worn leather scabbard across his chest that held a razor-sharp dagger. He would be ready in the event a close encounter would necessitate self-defense. The fact that his behavior was reckless did not occur to him until much later.

The desert breeze was warm, gently caressing the palms, and their fronds rustled faintly. Marcus walked with determination through the near-empty streets knowing it was highly unlikely that he would see any miracles or have an encounter with the Nazarene, but he needed a release for the vexation that mounted within him.

As he rounded a corner, a sudden movement in the shadows caught his eye. He slowed his steps as he scrutinized the darkened passageway that veered to his right. His hand slowly moved to the scabbard, and he withdrew the dagger cautiously.

"Come out in the name of Caesar." His voice demanded a response, but there was none. He waited silently, keeping his eyes fixed on the blackness of the side street, and his ears strained to hear any movement. His blade was firmly in his hand now, and he was primed to fight if necessary.

"I said, come out now before I come in. For if I do, I will hunt you down like the dog you are and slay you where you cower," threatened Marcus.

It was only a matter of moments before the shuffling of feet could be heard and a form emerged from the night's cover. Angry eyes were visible beneath a dark hood that covered the head of the discovered individual.

Marcus stood his ground; his muscles tensed as the man stepped forward. A curved silver knife peeked out from the folds of the simlāh, and the threat between the two men suddenly became very real.

"Don't be a fool," warned Marcus, his eyes narrowing as he focused on the face of his enemy. The short thin beard testified of a manhood that had newly arrived, while the livid eyes that stared back at him still belonged to a teen whose fury continued to be stoked by an immature fervor.

"How dare you call me a fool!" hissed the young man. He yanked the ancient knife from his belt and waved it menacingly at Marcus. "You have no right to be here, Roman!"

Marcus had no desire to kill a boy. "Put it down."

"Or what? I am not afraid of you." He spat on the ground at the feet of Marcus. "Your kind should go back to Rome where you belong."

Marcus took a deep breath and exhaled. "You are but a child. Go home to your mother."

All sense of reason left the teen, and he lunged at Marcus, swinging the miniature scythe wildly.

Marcus easily stepped aside, avoiding the thrust. He turned quickly, and the enraged teen came at him again. This time, Marcus caught the cheek of his opponent with the tip of his dagger, hoping to dissuade another attack.

The teen reeled backward, his knife tumbling to the ground. Reaching a hand to his face, he felt the stickiness of blood on his fingers. He struggled to remain standing, his feet slipping out from under him more than once. Fumbling around for his weapon, he was defenseless and now fear replaced the hatred in his earlier expression when he saw Marcus towering over him.

Marcus took a step toward him with his dagger in full view. "You attack me; you attack Rome. You attack Rome; and you bring death upon yourself. I warned you."

Marcus never knew what hit him, but one moment he was poised to teach the Jewish teen a lesson, and the next, he was opening his eyes and staring into the face of Gaius.

"Marcus? Marcus? Are you all right?" Gaius knelt beside his friend as other legionnaires gave chase to the two hooded men who had been standing over the centurion.

Marcus rubbed the back of his head, feeling a large lump growing beneath his fingers.

"Yes... I think so. What happened?" He pulled himself to an upright position.

"I rounded the corner just in time to see someone drop that stone on your head." Gaius nodded his head toward a large rock on the road. "He took off running with the other one. Hopefully, they'll catch them." He helped Marcus to his feet. "What are you doing out here like this?"

Marcus rose and winced as he stood to his full height. "I needed to walk."

"You needed to walk? What are you trying to do? Tempt the fates?"

Marcus said nothing; the scolding was well deserved. He had let his guard down with the teen and would have paid the ultimate price had Gaius not come along.

"I thought it was supposed to be quiet during Passover," said Gaius as he scanned the area in which they stood.

"I thought so too, but who knows with these Jews. Everything about them is a mystery." Marcus wiped the dirt off his tunic. He looked around the ground and spied his dagger. Stooping down to retrieve it, he replaced it into his scabbard.

Gaius frowned as he fell into step beside Marcus. "When we catch them, they'll have a taste of Roman justice." He tapped the handle of his sword.

"Stand in line."

Gaius chuckled lightly. "The gods favored you tonight as they always do, my friend. I know of no one who has slipped through death's fingers as often as you."

Marcus' grin was forced. "Perhaps." He became solemn as they neared the temple mount. "I have only myself to blame. I left alone. I had no armor or sword. I was on a fool's mission."

"And what was that mission?"

"To clear my head."

"From what?"

Marcus hesitated and took a deep breath before finally confessing what plagued his thoughts. "The Nazarene."

"The Nazarene?" Gaius' eyebrows rose slightly. "What disturbs you about him?"

"There's too much about him that can't be explained." His eyes narrowed. "I want answers, Gaius."

"Answers? I'll give you answers, my friend. His followers spread rumors about him to gather support for a rebellion that is doomed before it's begun. These Jews seek a leader, and he's just another fanatic stupid enough to try and be one. He will fade into the dust like all the rest."

Marcus lowered his voice. "Like all the rest? Hardly. How do you explain the healings? The blind man today. The lame man at the pool." He paused for a moment, then added, "There are claims of other healings as well." He stared into the night as he spoke with determination. "This man cannot be ignored, and if I have to follow it through on my own, I will."

"What do you propose to do?"

"I don't know," Marcus stated. "But one way or another, I will find him and get my answers."

Chapter Eight

"But I say unto you which hear, Love your enemies, do good to them which hate you," Luke 6:27

Several weeks had passed since Hadassah had shared with Judith about the miracles of the Healer. Passover and the Feast of Unleavened Bread had come and gone, and her aunt had said no more about their conversation. Hadassah was reluctant to press Judith any further regarding meeting with the man whose reputation was spreading throughout the region, but she refused to believe there was nothing more to be done for her aunt. Determined to act on Judith's behalf, she chose to seek out the one called Yeshua on her own and beg for his help.

The morning sun was barely peeking over the eastern mountains of Galilee when she set out. A pale orange hue began to permeate the cloudless sky, promising another day of unrelenting heat. Hadassah hurried along the shores of the Sea of Galilee, scanning the small wooden boats that had returned from a night of fishing.

"Hello!" she called out to a group of fishermen heaving their woven nets onto the shore for cleaning and mending.

Upon recognizing her, one man smiled and waved. "Hadassah! What brings you out so early?"

"Josiah! I am searching for Andrew," she explained as she neared him. "Do you know where he might be?"

He shook his head. "No, I'm sorry. I haven't seen him for several days. He and Simon spend most of their time with the Teacher."

"The Teacher? The rabbi? The one who heals?"

"Yes. They are rarely here these days, but this morning they passed by heading in that direction." He pointed to the northeast.

Hadassah's eyes brightened. "Thank you! Thank you so much!"

"Of course, Hadassah. May the Eternal One bless you."

"And you as well, Josiah."

She scurried up the path leading away from the fishermen and headed toward the northern shores of the Sea of Galilee. Soon she crossed the crest of a small hill and saw a multitude of people, many clustered in small groups. She raised a hand to her forehead, scanning the area. The sounds of conversation mingled with laughter rose to meet her ears, and her own excitement mounted as she descended into the crowds.

He has to be here!

Her soft leather sandals created tiny dust clouds with each step. So absorbed in her thoughts, she did not hear her name being called. It wasn't until she was almost at the bottom of the first knoll that she realized someone was shouting her name. Turning, she saw Zara rushing toward her.

"Zara! What are you doing here?" Worry crossed her face as her friend ran to catch up to her.

A broad smile crossed Zara's face as she neared Hadassah. "I came to hear the rabbi! Uri said he comes here often to teach." Her breathing came in short gasps, and she put both hands on her hips as she bent forward to catch her breath. She raised a hand to sweep the damp hair off her forehead. "I was hoping I'd see you here! Come, let's find a place near the front!" Her bright brown eyes sparkled with life.

"So, it is him? It's Yeshua?"

"Yes! Come on!" stated Zara as she reached her hand out, grabbing the sleeve of Hadassah's muslin tunic.

"You're sure?" she asked before she allowed Zara to pull her along.

"Yes, I'm sure! Come on!" Zara cocked her head and scowled when she felt resistance to her tug. "Are we going to stand here all day in the sun, or are we going to see the rabbi?" She crossed her arms in front of herself and stuck out her lower lip. "You keep saying you want to find Yeshua! What are you waiting for?"

As if she'd just been awakened, Hadassah blinked several times, then replied with a huge smile, "Of course! Let's go!" She reached out and took hold of Zara's hand, eliciting a wide grin on the face of her friend.

"I knew you'd go with me!"

As they hurried down the path, Hadassah glanced at the others who were half-walking, half-running to the shore of Galilee. They were a tossed salad representation of humanity. Some were old, some young. Some were laughing and moving easily despite the increasing number of travelers. Others struggled along, requiring assistance to move forward with the multitude. Fathers carried their children on their shoulders, and young ones held tightly to the hands of their mothers as they were pulled along. Bumped and prodded, Hadassah stumbled and lost her grip on Zara's hand.

"Zara? Zara!"

Frantically, Hadassah scanned the massive group before her as she was carried along. As anxiety mounted within her, she could not do anything but continue onward. This crowd moved as one with a dedicated purpose.

A young woman next to her apologized quickly when she bumped into Hadassah. "Forgive me! I'm just so excited to see Yeshua!" Her sparkling blue eyes reflected the anticipatory joy in her voice. "I have waited for so long to see him!"

Hadassah opened her mouth to respond, but before she could utter a word, the woman had scurried off, leaving Hadassah to abruptly realize the implications of the words she had just heard.

He really is here! Yeshua! I'm going to see Yeshua!

Suddenly, it no longer mattered that she could not see Zara. It did not matter that she had been walking all morning up and down the roads on a search that had seemed to be fruitless. Hadassah's spirit now soared! She was going to see the Healer! She was going to see Yeshua!

Finally, the momentum of the crowd slowed, and people began to mill around, hunting for places to sit on the hillside. Hadassah found a small patch of grass where she hoped she would have an unrestricted view of Yeshua. She quickly looked around for Zara, but her seeking eyes froze when she saw Yeshua moving toward an area where a few large boulders formed a natural sitting area near the shoreline of the sea.

He walked with a small group of men, and when he sat on one of the large stones, they dropped to the ground at his feet. Yeshua faced the throng sitting on the hillside and looked up at the faces that anxiously waited to hear the rabbi.

"Hadassah! There you are!"

She didn't want to take her eyes off of Yeshua, but she turned quickly to see Zara plop herself on the grass beside her.

"I'm sorry I lost you. When I realized you weren't with me, I looked back, but I couldn't see you. It was impossible to retrace my steps," apologized Zara. "But I knew you'd be close to the front."

Hadassah had returned her gaze to Yeshua. "I know. I couldn't see you either. I prayed you'd find me." She reached out and gave a squeeze to Zara's hand. "This was such a wonderful idea. I'm so glad you're here."

Like Hadassah, Zara's eyes were now fixed on Yeshua. "Me, too. You know, I've heard some say that he's the one."

Hadassah cast her a questioning look. "The one?"

Zara lowered her voice and leaned in toward her friend, so that only Hadassah could hear her utter the words, "The Messiah."

Hadassah slowly turned her head back toward Yeshua as her gaze took in more than just what she saw. She sat mesmerized at the possibility that the one for whom all Israel had waited, the one promised by the Almighty for centuries was sitting just beyond her, and Aelia's words came back to her.

We will know him.

Whether it was the wind that carried his voice or the natural shape of the land around them, Hadassah didn't know, but when he spoke, she heard him plainly just as if he were sitting right next to her. She listened with a new intensity in her soul.

The Messiah! Is it you, Yeshua?

A fierce hunger for his words possessed her, and she shut out everything around her as her attention focused solely on Yeshua.

"Blessed are they which do hunger and thirst after righteousness, for they shall be filled..."

Are you the One we've been waiting for?

"Blessed are the merciful, for they shall obtain mercy..."

Our Deliverer?

"Blessed are the pure in heart, for they shall see God..."

Our King?

She suddenly found it hard to breathe; her unblinking eyes were fixed on Yeshua. Her heart beat so rapidly within her that she felt it would burst from her chest.

"Blessed are the peacemakers, for they shall be called the children of God..."

The Holy One?

"Blessed are they which are persecuted for righteousness' sake, for theirs is the kingdom of heaven..."

Enthralled by the possibility that she could actually be in the presence of Israel's Messiah, Hadassah intensely studied the man who captivated the crowd. Although he wore common garments, surrounded himself with people just like her, and sat casually on the rocks as he spoke, there truly was something about him that was different, and that mystified her.

Hadassah had always thought the Messiah would be a majestic king, perched on a fine horse with servants attending to his every need. Yeshua was nothing like that. He was more like someone she would see in the marketplace or in the fields. Yet, there was no denying the power in his words. He spoke with such authority that Hadassah knew he had to be more than just a man... more than a teacher... more than a rabbi. He was different. Like her, hundreds of others sat still and focused, unwilling to move lest a word go unheard.

"It's been said he is from Nazareth," whispered Zara, breaking the spell.

Surprised, Hadassah turned to Zara. "Nazareth?"

Zara nodded, never removing her gaze from Yeshua. "I know. What good comes from there, huh? Well, that's what I've heard."

Hadassah's thoughtful eyes narrowed.

Surely the Messiah wouldn't come from Nazareth?

She turned back to Yeshua.

"But I say unto you which hear, love your enemies, bless them that curse you, do good to them which hate you, and pray for them which despitefully use you and persecute you."

Love my enemies? What is he talking about? The Romans? I'm supposed to love the Romans? And pray for them?

Her gaze lowered, and her brow furrowed as she struggled to understand the meaning behind the words that seemed so contrary to what she felt within her. She shifted her weight and leaned forward slightly as she tried to refocus on what she was hearing.

"But when you pray, use not vain repetitions as the heathen do. For they think that they shall be heard for their much speaking. Be not therefore like them for your Father knows what things you have need of before you ask him."

As Yeshua lifted his hands and face toward heaven, his powerful words rode the wind. Her eyes reverently closed; her breathing deepened, and her heart filled with awe as his example of prayer quickened her soul.

"Our Father which art in heaven, hallowed be thy name. Thy kingdom come, thy will be done in earth as it is in heaven. Give us this day our daily bread, and forgive us our debts as we forgive our debtors. And lead us not into temptation, but deliver us from evil. For thine is the kingdom and the power and the glory, forever."

* * * * * *

"That was amazing!" exclaimed Zara as they began the trek back to the village. They walked slowly, keeping pace with the multitude that followed Yeshua, who was somewhere ahead of them.

"Yes, it was," agreed Hadassah, although her voice lacked conviction.

Zara cast a quick look at her friend. "What's wrong?"

"Did you hear him say to love your enemies?"

"Yes, but I don't think he really meant that. I mean, do you believe he wants us to love the Romans?" asked Zara as she walked beside her friend.

"I don't really know, but he did say it."

Zara frowned as she kicked a stone aside. "I don't think the Messiah would tell us to do that. After all, he's coming to be our king, not to join forces with the Romans."

"But he said it clearly. I mean, sometimes he does speak in ways I don't completely understand, but that was pretty clear," rebutted Hadassah.

Zara shrugged her shoulders. "Maybe he's not the Messiah."

"How can you say that? After all he's done!"

"It just doesn't make sense to me," Zara admitted. "When the Messiah comes, he will be our king, and kings don't befriend their enemies. If anything, he'll probably kill all the Romans."

"What?" Anger flashed in Hadassah's eyes. She stopped abruptly and glared at Zara.

"What?" Zara cast a quizzical glance at her friend. "What did I say?"

Hadassah continued strongly. "In case you've forgotten, my uncle and aunt are Romans. Marcus is a Roman, and even as much as he frustrates me, I wouldn't want him to be killed. He's never done anything to me. And even though he's our enemy, I don't wish him dead."

"I'm sorry. I didn't mean to upset you," apologized Zara. "But they're not all like Marcus. Besides just because he hasn't done anything to you, doesn't mean he hasn't some something to someone else. The Romans are really awful, and you know I'm right. I don't think I'd be shedding any tears if the Messiah got rid of them all. Except your aunt and uncle, and Marcus," she hastily added.

Hadassah's frustration mounted. "You know, some of our people are just as brutal."

"Maybe, but I think the Romans are the worst. I've heard they crucify thousands just because they're not Romans."

"I don't think that's completely true, Zara."

"Uri told me. He said that the Romans would crucify every Jew if they had the chance. That's why we need the Messiah to come. To get rid of all of them." Her voice was defiant and very reflective of Uri's opinions.

Hadassah's lips tightened, and she fought to hold her tongue.

They walked in silence until finally, Zara spoke. "Do you think you'll see Marcus again?"

Hadassah shrugged her shoulders. "I don't know."

"He's still in Jerusalem?"

"I think so."

"When will he return?"

"I don't know that he will."

Zara saw sadness in Hadassah's downcast eyes. "I'm sorry. I really didn't mean to upset you."

"Let's not speak of it anymore, okay?"

Zara nodded, and they said no more about Marcus or the Romans.

As they trailed behind the rabbi and his closest followers, Hadassah suddenly remembered her initial reason for seeking out Yeshua.

Dodah!

"Zara, I must speak to Yeshua! Come on!" She quickened her pace, maneuvering her way through the throng to get as close to Yeshua as she could. When only a few feet behind him, Hadassah stopped wriggling her way through the people, and kept a respectable distance as she strained to see through the men surrounding him.

Maybe if I see Andrew, I can ask him if there's a way to–

Suddenly, the crowd seemed to detach itself from Yeshua, and Hadassah had an unrestricted view of the rabbi. Instantly she froze as words of warning rang out.

"He's unclean! Move away!"

What? Where?

Her head snapped back and forth as she desperately sought the whereabouts of the unclean man.

"Unclean! Get away from the Master! Get back to your own kind!"

Hadassah tried to step further back as she struggled to retreat into the crowd, but the wall of people behind her prevented any movement. Fear enveloped her when she saw the approaching leper.

Wrapped in filthy rags and unkempt in appearance, he walked boldly toward Yeshua. Hadassah was well aware of the dangers of leprosy, and she cringed, trying to shrink back into the crowd.

A leper! Please stay away! Don't come over here!

She squirmed and pressed herself back as much as she could, all social amenities forgotten as she tried to distance herself from the leprous man.

Yeshua raised a hand toward the people, and silence fell immediately like a curtain that is drawn to shut out the light. Collectively, the crowd became motionless as they watched the leper boldly move nearer to the rabbi.

"Lord," pleaded the diseased man, "If you will it, you can make me clean."

The desperation in his voice touched Hadassah's heart, but she knew there was no hope for him, and she wished he would simply leave. The leper's disheveled appearance and discolored bulbous skin repulsed her, but she was unable to tear her eyes away from him.

That poor man. He asks the impossible of the rabbi—

Her thoughts came to an abrupt halt as she watched Yeshua stretch out his hand to touch the leper.

No! No! Don't touch him! He's unclean!

She wanted to scream out to Yeshua, to warn him, to stop him, but no sound came from her opened mouth. Instead, she stood mutely, watching the leper reach out to Yeshua. Then she heard the rabbi's words.

"I will. Be clean."

The leper slowly lifted his arms high and rotated them in the sunlight. His skin was now smooth and unblemished! The patchy pallor was gone! The sloughing tissue had disappeared! An audible gasp filled the street, and as the man turned, Hadassah stared unbelievingly. The leper's face was unmarked, and as he wept and praised the Lord, she could see no visible sign of the contagious disease that had ostracized him from Jewish society.

Hadassah blinked rapidly to stem the tears that filled her astonished eyes as her hands rose to cover her mouth. "Praise be to the Eternal," she whispered reverently, and then with anguished soul, she lamented, "How could I have doubted... O God, forgive me!"

Hushed voices became louder as euphoric praises began to emanate from the crowd. Words such as "miracle," "God's anointed," and "Messiah" began to circulate freely among the onlookers.

She stood mesmerized as Yeshua instructed the man to go show himself to the priest and give the required offering.

"Looks like we got our miracle," whispered Zara. She linked her arm through Hadassah's, pulling her back as the crowd closed in around Yeshua.

Quietly weeping, Hadassah allowed herself to be withdrawn from the group.

Alarmed at the tears on Hadassah's face, Zara replied, "What's wrong? Are you okay? Hadassah, what's the matter?"

"How could I have ever doubted, Zara?" Remorse filled her reddened eyes. "How could I?" She moved her gaze to Yeshua. "I've got to talk to him, Zara. I just have to."

"Talk to Yeshua? Now? We can't even get close to him. He's way ahead of us. Besides everyone's trying to get to him, and we've got to get back. It's nearly time for the evening meal. We can't be out after dark."

"But—"

"No 'buts,' Hadassah. I'm sorry. I really am, but you'll have to wait for another time. You'll get another chance. I know you will."

Despite Zara's encouraging words, Hadassah's heart was heavy. She had doubted Yeshua and that shamed her greatly. Why would he even talk with her now? And then, she heard her own words echoing truth in her heart.

For Thou Lord art good, and ready to forgive, and plenteous in mercy unto all them that call upon Thee.

* * * * * *

The torches were lit around the perimeter of the Caelinus house when Hadassah arrived. She hurried to her room and threw her simlāh on her bed. Quickly washing the dust from her face, she changed into a clean linen tunic. Running a comb through her thick hair, she pulled it back at the sides and secured it away from her face. Satisfied that she was presentable, she headed toward the main room, knowing her aunt and uncle would be there for the final meal of the day. She mentally prepared an excuse for her tardiness.

As she made her way through the house, she heard an unfamiliar man's voice coming from the entryway. She rounded the corner to see Justus scowling at his guest. Unseen by either man, she moved into the shadows and waited for the right opportunity to slip past the men without interrupting their conversation.

"I tell you the truth, Justus! The servant lives! I saw it with my own eyes!"

"You saw what? A living servant? That is hardly unusual."

"But he was near death, Justus. There was no hope for him. That's why Cornelius went to the rabbi. He went on behalf of this slave."

"Cornelius? The centurion?"

"Yes, surely you remember him. He is the one—"

"I know who he is, you idiot." Justus rubbed his chin as he reflected on the man who helped build the town's synagogue. "It was his servant?"

"Yes."

"And you saw him? This dying servant? You can verify it?"

"No, of course not. I could not... would not... defile myself. If he should die in my presence—"

"I thought not." Justus made a clucking sound as he shook his head. "So all you bring me is hearsay. Come to me when you have facts, otherwise you simply waste my time. All this talk about this rabbi bores me." He waved his hand in a dismissive gesture.

Hadassah's head jerked up, and her eyes followed Justus as he escorted his guest to the outer courtyard.

Rabbi? Is he talking about Yeshua?

She strained to hear more, but their voices were no longer audible. Quietly, she made her way into the great room and sat beside Judith. "I overheard Justus talking to someone. What is it about?"

Judith turned to her niece and whispered nonchalantly, "I don't know. I really wasn't listening." Beads of perspiration dotted her pale face as she cooled herself with a feathered fan. "I hope they finish soon. It's time for our meal. Have you had a nice day?"

Hadassah nodded, then said softly, "I was with the rabbi today. You know, the one I was speaking to you about. The same one who healed the lame man. He was in Capernaum today."

Judith frowned at Hadassah. "I remember, but I also recall telling you that I was not interested in seeing him, so we do not need to speak of this man again."

"But Dodah, he healed a—"

"I said no more, Hadassah! If you insist on bringing him up every time you see me, I will forbid you to see him again. Do you understand?" Judith ignored the young woman's defeated eyes and continued to fan herself as Justus reentered the room. She turned her gaze away from Hadassah and smiled at her husband.

"That man is a babbling idiot," he stated as he sat opposite the women. He nodded at the servants in attendance, and they began to serve the meal.

Fresh bread was set before the family along with a large pot of vegetables bathed in a thick broth. Justus ripped a piece of bread from the loaf and dipped it into the stew. Thick brown liquid fell upon the table as he brought the dripping bread to his mouth.

"I tell you I am weary of these rumors. First, this supposed healing of a leper, then Cornelius' slave. I find it tedious and—"

"What did you say? Someone was healed from *leprosy*?" Judith's hand froze in mid-air over the pot, and the bread she held fell into the warm stew. She stared at her husband, her eyes widened and unmoving.

He rolled his own eyes in disgust. "Of course not." Oblivious to Judith's astonishment, he chewed loudly, swallowed, then reached for more bread. "It is merely a rumor, an attempt to trick these gullible Jews to rise up against Rome. Healing a leper?" He turned his head and spat on the ground. "That's impossible."

Hadassah's head was bent low as she softly murmured, "Naaman was healed."

Justus spoke as he chewed. "Fables, Hadassah. Stories of old that no longer have any merit for us. If they were true, every leper need only dip himself in the Jordan seven times, eh? I don't see that happening."

Judith cast a furtive glance at her niece, then turned her attention back to her husband.

Justus shrugged his shoulders as he drained his goblet. Setting it down, he replied to his wife, "Supposedly, this... this rabbi touched a leper, and the disease was gone. Ridiculous, I tell you! Who in their right mind would even go near a leper, let alone touch one? Pure stupidity if you ask me."

"Who was this... this healer?" Judith asked hesitantly as her eyes moved from her husband to her niece.

"Some Nazarene. Can you believe that?" He chuckled as he shoved the sopping bread into his mouth. "That alone discredits the story. What good comes from Nazareth?"

The rest of the meal progressed as usual with Justus monopolizing the conversation. At its conclusion, he simply stood and left, while Hadassah and Judith remained at the table.

Hadassah struggled to keep her emotions under control as she finally had the opportunity to speak freely to her aunt. Her voice was a tense whisper. "It's not a fable, Dodah. I saw it!"

Judith's head jerked toward Hadassah, but this time there was no reprimand in her look. "The leper? You saw this leper healed?" Judith's questioning eyes widened once more as Hadassah nodded.

"Yes, Dodah. I was as far from him as we are from the doorway. I saw it all! It's true! We did all move away from him, but not the rabbi. He stood right there and reached out his hand to the man. Then, he set it on the man's shoulder. And then, he spoke. That's all he did! He just said a few words, and the leper was healed! Just words, Dodah!" She glanced around the room for assurance they were alone. Her voice remained low. "He can heal you, too. I know it!" Hadassah grabbed her aunt's hand in her own and pleaded, "You must go to him. You must! I'll take you!"

"Not now, Hadassah." Judith quickly scanned the large room. Her whispered voice was shaking. "We must not speak of this now."

Hadassah nodded in understanding as her now hopeful eyes met the troubled ones of her aunt. For the first time, she was optimistic that Judith would seek out Yeshua, and if she did, Hadassah knew he could heal her.

O Most High, please have mercy upon my dodah. Take her to Yeshua.

Chapter Nine

"Who hath ears to hear, let him hear." Matthew 13:9

The light of the full moon shimmered on the still waters of the Sea of Galilee as Marcus rode Ares along its shores. Wavelets lapped at the water's edge, and off in the distance, silhouettes of fishing boats slowly made their way across the large lake. A warm breeze fanned the plume on Marcus' helmet as he guided the horse along the well-worn path toward Capernaum.

I wonder if Hadassah drew water from here today.

It had been months since he had seen her, yet she still crept into his dreams on occasion. He closed his eyes, and for a moment, he could see her dipping her jug into the water, the gentle breeze blowing her dark hair away from her face. He smiled as he recalled the fire in her eyes when he had questioned her about her beloved Healer.

Ares snorted, and Marcus opened his eyes just in time to see a small fox scurry away from the hooves of the stallion. He gently tapped his heels against the horse's side and pulled the rein to the left creating a wide berth between Ares and the now curious creature that watched cautiously from a small boulder near the edge of the freshwater lake.

He had thought of Hadassah frequently during his time in the old city. Tired of his sedentary assignment, his mind often wandered as he stood in position for hours on end. It hadn't taken much for him to be reminded of Hadassah. A scent of lavender wafting on the wind, the lilt of a young woman's laughter in the marketplace, or the blooms of irises adorning the sills of opened windows could bring her to the forefront of his mind. Now he was returning to his father's home for a brief respite from his duties in Jerusalem, and he was eager to reach the Caelinus estate to see Hadassah. Even though he expected to be confronted by her deeply held beliefs, the vision of the young Jewess spurred him on.

Finally nearing his father's stables, he glanced up at the main house. Torches around the courtyard had long been extinguished, and there were no lamps to welcome him home. Marcus sighed when he realized the probability of anyone being awake at this hour was very small. Dismounting, he gave charge of Ares to the groomsman, then walked up the pathway to the house. He slowly climbed the stairs to the entry. Presuming his room would be as he had left it, he saw no need to alert anyone to his arrival. Morning would be soon enough to greet his father.

"Marcus?"

He turned abruptly toward the well-known voice and saw Hadassah standing on the landing below him. The unexpected encounter surprised him, and he stood speechless as her questioning eyes awaited a response.

Holding a small oil lamp, her face was illuminated, and Marcus simply stared at her as she looked up at him.

"Marcus?"

He blinked twice, then composed himself. "I didn't expect anyone to be roaming the halls at this hour."

"I couldn't sleep," admitted Hadassah as she pulled her flaxen shawl tighter around her shoulders. "I didn't know you were returning. I thought you were still in Jerusalem."

He removed his helmet as he replied, "I am in Jerusalem indefinitely, but I needed to come to Caesarea, so I thought I would stop here before heading into the city."

She nodded as she looked up at him through her thick lashes. "I hope your journey went well. I am sure that your room is prepared. If it is not to your liking, please let me know, and I will attend to it immediately."

"I trust it will be fine." When she didn't move, he cocked his head slightly as he studied her face. "You have something more to say?"

"It is really none of my business," she admitted.

"Perhaps." He eyed her curiously. "Speak freely. I promise I won't get angry."

"You can't make the promise."

"Oh, I can. I just can't promise I'll keep it." His mouth curved slightly.

"Spoken like a true warrior." A faint smile appeared on her face.

For the first time, he allowed himself to laugh. "Even the bravest warrior knows it is foolish to speak falsehoods to a discerning woman. What would you like to ask me?"

She hesitated, and her smile disappeared as she bluntly asked, "Are you my enemy?"

His brow furrowed as he questioned, "Your enemy?"

"You're not, are you?" It was almost a plea.

"I don't think of myself as your enemy, Hadassah." He stepped down to her level slowly, so as not to frighten her. "Why are you asking me this? What's happened?"

She shook her head. "Nothing. I've just heard things, and I can't believe you'd be here to destroy my people."

Marcus sighed. "Hadassah, if we wanted to destroy you, don't you think you'd be destroyed by now? We're here to keep the peace and protect you. This place is part of the Roman empire. It is my duty to protect it from all who rise up against Rome. Sometimes, those individuals do come from within, and those we have to deal with, but I am not your enemy. I promise you that."

She nodded in understanding. "Will you be here long?"

How long will I be here? How long would you like for me to be here?

He started to lift his hand toward her face, then dropped it quickly to his side. Clearing his throat, he finally spoke. "Not too long. Less than a fortnight. It seems Rome needs a solid presence in Jerusalem right now, so I was sent to Caesarea to see to the relocation of more men."

Hadassah's dark eyes caught the waning moonlight, and flecks of gold seemed to shimmer in them as she looked up at him. Marcus found himself becoming lost in them.

"Is it dangerous?"

The spell broken; Marcus blinked twice. "What?"

"I asked if Jerusalem was really so dangerous that it requires so many soldiers to keep peace."

He shook his head. "Not really. A show of military might is simply a peaceful way of squelching any hints of rebellion. When a legion of Roman soldiers marches through a city, the insurgents tend to fade into the underbrush. Well, most of them." He raised an eyebrow and grinned. "Are you worried about me?"

Heat rose in her cheeks, but she stood her ground. Indignant, she crossed her arms over her shawl as she retorted, "Hardly. I am more concerned about my friends who travel there. Besides, it was my understanding that Roman centurions are quite capable of taking care of themselves, are they not?"

Amused at her reaction, he smirked, "Yes, they are."

"Then there is no need for me to worry. Goodnight, Marcus." She slid past him, pushed the heavy door open, and entered without looking back.

Marcus watched her until she disappeared behind the door. His eyes lingered on the closed door through which Hadassah had just walked. He drew his lips into a tight line as he exhaled long and slow.

Oh, how I've missed you, Hadassah!

Stepping up to the same door, he hesitated for just a moment, then opened it. The hallway was empty. Disappointment pricked at his heart until he pushed the emotion back into the recesses of his mind. Dropping his gaze to the floor, he watched a small beetle scurry across his sandaled foot before it disappeared into a tiny crack in the wall.

"Goodnight, Hadassah," he whispered as he headed to his room.

* * * * * *

The old familiar feeling of uncertainty had returned to the pit of Hadassah's stomach and with it was the image of Marcus at the top of the stairs. He had stood regally, and with the moonlight glinting off his armor, his presence was ominous to say the least. As she closed the door to her room behind her, she leaned against it and shut her eyes tightly, forcing the picture of Marcus out of her mind. Finally, she relaxed and slowly opened her eyes. The knot she felt within her had faded.

In the dimness of her room, Hadassah changed into her nightclothes. She walked over to a small wooden table and added some olive oil to a clay lamp whose flickering flame cast shadows that danced along the wall. She picked up her shawl, carefully folded it, and set it on the back of a chair. Moving to her bed, she pulled the blanket back, but then turned and padded over to the window. The view was breathtaking, and for a moment, she lost herself in the thousands of glittering stars in the night sky. A gentle breeze caressed her face as she rested her forearms on the window's edge. Her mind drifted to Yeshua and the people he had healed. In her mind's eye, she saw the demoniac, the lame man, and the leper once more, and questions permeated her thoughts as she lifted her eyes to the heavens. She longed for answers.

The Messiah... is it really you? Our people have been waiting so long for you. Who else could do all the things that you do? You must be him. There's no other explanation.

As the rhythmic chirping of crickets blended with the rustling of palm branches, the distant memory of her mother's voice spoke of the Lord's promise. "And in that day shall the deaf hear the words of the book, and the eyes of the blind shall see out of obscurity, and out of darkness. The meek also shall increase their joy in the Lord, and the poor among men shall rejoice in the Holy One of Israel." Her eyes filled with hopeful tears.

Could Yeshua really be the Messiah... the Holy One?

* * * * * *

When Marcus entered and sat down for breakfast, the only one who wasn't surprised to see him was Hadassah. Judith said nothing, but her surprised eyes betrayed her calm exterior. Justus' hand stopped midway to his mouth, and it was only a quick recovery that prevented him from spilling a goblet of fresh apricot juice.

"Marcus? I was not expecting you," he stammered as he set the cup back down.

"It was late when I arrived. I chose not to disturb you." Marcus reached for the bread, then slathered it well with honey and slices of fig. "I'm here to see to the relocation of my men to Jerusalem. You needn't be alarmed." He took a large bite from his bread. "I won't be here too long."

"Nonsense," stuttered Justus. "You are always welcome. Rome is always welcome."

His father's attempt to placate a perceived threat irritated Marcus, but he held his tongue. He glanced over at Hadassah, who sat quietly eating a slice of walnut and almond cake. She hadn't looked at him since he sat down.

"Good morning, Hadassah," he said pointedly.

She glanced up through her dark lashes. "Good morning, Marcus. Had we known of your coming, we would have greeted you properly. I trust your journey went well?"

Amused, he stifled a chuckle. "Yes, it went very well as a matter of fact. The night was cool, and the moonlight provided just enough light so the darkness did not impede my trip. It was quite peaceful actually, and when I arrived here, hardly anyone was up and about."

Hadassah kept her eyes lowered, and her lips tightened as she picked at her meal. He found her feigned nonchalance charming, and it was difficult to direct his conversation to his father, but he believed to keep himself in her favor he should do so, and her favor was something he very much wanted.

When she excused herself from the table, Marcus resisted the impulse to follow her. Instead, he remained seated and pretended to listen as Justus droned on and on about his achievements in the town of Capernaum. Finally, unable to continue with the deception, Marcus excused himself, leaving his father staring at him as he made an abrupt exit.

Knowing how often Hadassah went to the garden, Marcus headed for the courtyard. As he moved past the grape arbor, he reached out and snapped a branch laden with the plump fruit. He had eaten half the cluster before he reached the center of the courtyard. When he approached the stone bench where she often sat, he sighed deeply with a frown. She wasn't there. The depth of disappointment he felt surprised him.

Get hold of yourself, Marcus. She's just a Jewess. She means nothing to you.

He sighed in resignation.

Yeah, keep telling yourself that.

Turning to leave, he stopped when he heard someone singing. The voice was sweet and soothing, and the melody seemed to float on the air. He knew immediately that it was Hadassah. He wanted to call out to her, but he knew she would stop, and that he didn't want, so he simply stood and listened.

"O sing unto the Lord a new song: sing unto the Lord, all the earth. Sing unto the Lord, bless his name; shew forth his salvation from day to day—"

She rounded the path and nearly bumped into Marcus. "Oh!"

"You sing nicely," he commented, then added quickly, "I probably should have made myself known."

"Yes, you should have." Her arms crossed in front of her, and she stared at him with pursed lips.

"But then you would have stopped singing."

"Yes, I would have."

"So that's why I kept silent. I wanted to hear you sing."

She held her stance, but her scowl was slowly replaced with a hint of a smile. "I suppose I could forgive you."

"Forgive me? I didn't ask for forgiveness."

"Well, you should have."

"For what? Is it a crime in Capernaum to listen to someone singing?" He sat down on the bench. "You know, you're quite a bit different than when I last was here."

"Different? What do you mean?"

He scratched his chin. "Well, for one, I don't recall you being quite so... so bold when speaking with me. Perhaps I am not as frightening as I once was?"

"Perhaps."

He laughed loudly. "Please, sit here. I promise I'll behave myself."

"I trust that isn't one of those promises you might find difficult to keep?" she teased.

"I knew that would come back to haunt me." He held up his hands as if surrendering. "I will do my best to keep my word."

She lowered herself to the bench, careful to keep a respectable distance between them.

"You were very quiet this morning. Did you not sleep well last night?" asked Marcus.

"It took a while before I could fall asleep, and then Judith needed me during the night, but I am rested enough. As for this morning, it would have been rude of me to intrude on the conversation between you and your father." She tilted her head slightly as she waited for his response.

Marcus raised an eyebrow. "Very considerate of you." His eyes lingered on her face as the sunlight streamed through the arbor and illuminated her from behind. An aura of light surrounded her, making her appear like a vision.

She could rival any of Rome's goddesses.

"Marcus?"

He shook his head to dissipate his mental fog. "Yes?"

"Are you all right?"

"Yes." He realized he had been staring at her. "I'm sorry. Just preoccupied. In fact, I wanted to speak with you regarding a serious matter if you have the time."

"I do."

"What do you know about this... this Healer of yours?"

"Yeshua? What is it you want to know?"

He shook his head noncommittally. "Nothing specific. Just curious. You've mentioned him a few times. I wondered if you knew anything about him besides these so-called miracles you told me about."

She shook her head slightly and lowered her gaze as she spoke. "I really don't know much about him. I know he sometimes teaches at the synagogue. And he's from Nazareth."

"Nazareth?"

She nodded, looking up at him. "Yes. You know of it?"

"I've heard of the place. Maybe I'll ride out there sometime. Care to join me if I do?" He winked at her as a grin appeared on his face.

She felt the blush rise in her cheeks, but her retort had more bite in it than embarrassment. "Your lack of propriety is not flattering. In fact, it is not a quality I would expect from a respectable Roman centurion."

His amused eyes were accompanied by a broad smile as he slightly bowed his head. "I am surprised you find me respectable. But..." He winked, "The invitation stands."

Although she kept herself from smiling, she could do nothing to hide the sparkle in her eyes. "Perhaps I misspoke. Nevertheless, I will decline. Now, if you'll please excuse me. I must go." She stood abruptly and exited through the arbor that he had come through earlier.

His eyes followed her until she was out of sight. A half-contented sigh escaped his lips.

Hadassah, you are the most intriguing woman I have ever met.

* * * * * *

Marcus sat with his arms across his chest. A scowl was fixed on his face as he listened to Cornelius, his longtime friend and fellow centurion.

"I speak only the truth, Marcus. I know it is difficult to accept. I struggled also, but I heard things... things told to me by reputable men. Men who swore on their lives that their testimony was true.

"Daniel has worked for my family for as long as I can remember. His loyalty is without question. Years ago, when I offered him his freedom, he chose to remain here with me and my family. He is like a father to me, and when he became ill..." Cornelius paced the floor as he spoke. "When he became ill, I prayed for his recovery, but it did not happen."

"You summoned physicians for him?"

"Of course. When no one in Capernaum could help, I paid enormous fees for the best in Caesarea, but even they had no answers for what ailed him. He was wasting away before my eyes." Cornelius stopped by the window and gazed outward, his back to Marcus.

"I had heard many things about this man... this teacher. I wanted to see for myself." He turned to face his friend, holding his hands out in front of himself. "Marcus, I *saw* him heal a leper!"

As he lifted an eyebrow, Marcus' blue eyes reflected skepticism. "Cornelius, he couldn't have been a leper. Nothing cures leprosy. You know it. I know it."

"Marcus, I know his family. He had been leprous for so long that they mourned him as dead. He had been banished to the leper colony. But that day, he approached the teacher as a leper, but left as a man whole. I saw him! His skin was spotless! Even the priests have declared him clean. I have no doubt at all that he had been miraculously healed." Cornelius paused for a moment. He swallowed hard, then continued. "I went to him personally."

"The leper?"

"No. The teacher." His voice trembled as he confessed his deed. "I begged him to heal Daniel. I knew he could do it. I just knew it. I told him he needn't come to my house. I wouldn't dare ask him to defile himself by entering the home of a Gentile. He would be unclean according to their laws, and I knew he only needed to speak healing, and it would be done. That's what he did for the leper. Just words. He spoke them, and the leper was healed. I knew he could do the same for Daniel."

He looked directly at Marcus, then said, "And he did it. I will never forget the words he spoke to me. He said. 'Go your way, and as you have believed, *so* be it done unto you.' That's all it took, Marcus! And now, Daniel lives!" Cornelius nearly collapsed on a cushioned bench opposite Marcus as if a huge weight had been lifted off his soul. "It's true. I swear it. You must believe me!"

Marcus' steely eyes narrowed as he contemplated the enormity of Cornelius' confession. "You have told no one else of this?"

Cornelius shook his head. "No one but my family is aware of what happened, and I have ordered their silence in order to maintain control."

"Keep it so. If these Jews find out that their precious rabbi is reaching out to Gentiles here, there may be trouble. It's enough that I must deal with the zealots in Jerusalem. Tell no one."

"Of course, Marcus."

"Good. Now, where is this Daniel? I want to speak with him."

* * * * * *

Marcus sat high upon Ares as he rode into the village of Nazareth. Olive groves covered the hillsides, and Marcus could see several people working the presses. Wearing his uniform, he caught the eye of nearly everyone as he rode quietly down the dusty street. Riding past a small sandstone house, he nodded at an elderly woman sitting on a wooden bench, her hands weaving colored threads into a nearly finished piece of fabric. Her suspicious eyes squinted as they took in the fair-skinned soldier sitting imposingly atop the majestic animal.

There was no breeze to provide any respite from the dry heat, and despite Ares being used to riding long hours without water, Marcus chose to rest at the public well. He rode up, stopping in front of a group of young women near the well. The laughter of one abruptly ceased when she made eye contact with Marcus. The others turned their heads, then silence befell them all.

"Might you spare some water for my horse?" He dismounted quickly, waiting for an answer.

Hesitantly, one of the maidens stepped toward him with her jug. Water sloshed out of it as she poured it into a trough. She said nothing as she moved backward.

Marcus nodded his thanks, then spoke. "Do any of you know Yeshua... the teacher?"

The girls glanced nervously at one another.

"I know of him," stated the one who watered Ares. "But he's not here. He left quite a while ago. Almost two years. Right, Hannah?" She turned her head toward one of the others.

"I don't know." She refused to make eye contact with her friend or Marcus.

"I see. Perhaps you could tell me where I could find someone who does know him. Maybe his family?" His hard gaze never left the face of the one who seemed to be the leader.

"His brother and mother live over there." She pointed to a cluster of homes. "The carpenter's house." She shook her head. "But I told you. Yeshua hasn't been seen here for a long time."

Marcus lifted himself up onto Ares' saddle. "Thank you. I appreciate the water and the information."

His sandaled feet tapped into the horse's side, and Ares began walking away from the well. Marcus smiled to himself as he heard the excited chatter of the young women resume as he left them behind.

They'll have much to share at the evening meal tonight!

He rounded the bend and saw several shops on both sides of the broadening street. The stone structures had walls plastered with mud and straw, and most had roofs composed of wooden beams and tree branches covered with a thick layer of clay. A few had two levels, but the majority were single story dwellings.

The clopping of Ares' hooves against the earthen road resulted in several heads turning his way. Eyes that opened wide upon seeing Marcus quickly narrowed and looked away as he neared. Mothers hurried their children inside their homes, and craftsmen returned to their work without raising their heads.

Marcus brought Ares to a stop by a home that had long planks of wood leaning against a side wall. Several small tables were stacked next to the planks with a few chairs piled upon each other.

He raised an eyebrow as he perused the perimeter of the small courtyard. Before he had a chance to dismount, a young bearded man came from behind the house carrying a long beam on his shoulder. He stopped immediately when he saw Marcus.

"Shalom." He set the beam down and looked up at Marcus. "You're looking for furniture?"

A sardonic grin spread across Marcus' face. The idea of a Roman centurion purchasing house furniture from a Jewish carpenter amused him and a slight chuckle escaped his lips.

"No. No furniture today. I seek information. I am looking for the family of the rabbi. Have I come to the right place?"

The carpenter studied Marcus before speaking. "If you're referring to Yeshua, you are at the right house. You are speaking with his brother. I am Yaakov."

"Where is your brother?"

Yaakov shrugged. "Who knows? He wanders the land teaching anyone willing to listen to him from what I am told."

"He doesn't live here?"

"Here? No," answered Yaakov with slight disdain in his voice. "He is somewhat … nomadic in nature. He has chosen to reject the occupation of our father and embrace the role of a *rabbi*." He practically spat the word out of his mouth.

"You don't approve?"

Yaakov crossed his arms and narrowed his eyes as he glared at Marcus. "My brother has never been taught by a rabbi. He is delusional to think himself at the same level as one who has spent a lifetime studying the Torah. As for those who follow him… well, they are just as delusional as he is."

"You've heard of the supposed miracles he's done?"

Yaakov scoffed at Marcus' question. "Miracles? You can't be serious! My brother is a carpenter's son as I am. We don't do miracles. We build furniture. Only God does miracles, and I tell you, Centurion, my brother is not God." He picked up the beam once more and settled it on his shoulder. "Was there anything else?"

Marcus regarded Yaakov thoughtfully, then shook his head. "No. I appreciate your candor."

So even your family doubts you. You are a man without a home. What keeps you going, Yeshua? What are you trying to prove?

He tugged lightly on Ares' rein. The horse immediately turned and trotted back down the road, leaving behind small clouds of dust that floated silently back to the ground.

Marcus left Nazareth frustrated and dissatisfied. Although he had spent most of the afternoon speaking to other Nazarenes about the itinerant rabbi, the information garnered was scant and very similar to that which Yaakov had already provided. Now as the first stars of the evening appeared, fatigue crept into his tired muscles, and he made the decision to spend the night in the desert rather than complete the long ride back to his father's house.

Spending the night out of doors was not a hardship for Marcus, and his makeshift camp was more than adequate for his needs. His years of military service had often necessitated establishing an outside shelter for the night, and he was fully equipped to do so again. He carried ample grain for Ares as well as water for both of them, and his own hunger was easily managed with the provisions he was accustomed to carrying when traveling. Finding a flat section of dirt, he cleared the area of any debris and laid his cloak down. Weapons close by, he made himself comfortable and closed his eyes. Sleep came quickly, and he slept soundly until the break of day.

As the dawn sky began to lighten, Marcus arose. Fully rested, the journey to the Caelinus estate would be easy for both him and his horse. After Ares had finished his morning barley, Marcus saddled him, hoisted himself upon Ares' back and started the ride home. As the sun began to peek over the Galilean hills, he could see flocks of sheep on the distant pastures as he traveled northward.

The hours passed by quickly, and Marcus covered a great distance before his first stop. By noon, the desert heat was rising quickly, and Marcus sought refuge beneath a lone fig tree. Halting his horse under its spreading branches, the palmate leaves shaded them both as Ares took advantage of the respite and nibbled on a few stems of thin grass. Off in the distance, the waters of the freshwater sea shimmered in the golden rays of a sun as yellow as the Judean fields of wild mustard. A few feeding sheep still could be seen on the hillsides, but most of them had found shadier places in which to graze. Marcus reached into a small bag tied around his waist. Pulling out a dried apricot, he inspected the shriveled fruit, then took a bite from it. He chewed it slowly as he tried to make sense of what he had learned about the Nazarene.

Who are you, Yeshua? And what is it about you that captivates so many, yet not your own brother?

A warm breeze teased the few strands of blonde hair peeking out from under Marcus' helmet as he sat contemplating the mysterious Jewish teacher. He spat on the ground, frustrated that he had relatively little information about him. Finally, he mounted Ares. The horse lifted its head, then reluctantly began to trot. Marcus steered Ares toward the Sea of Galilee. It would be cooler along its shores.

As he rode along, he cocked his head when he thought he heard something. Continuing along, the sounds were unmistakable. He was hearing what could only be chatter between individuals! Carried by the wind, he was unable to discern the muffled words or determine the size of the group, but he knew without a doubt that he was hearing several conversations, and this realization heightened his senses.

Who is out here? Thieves? Soldiers? Zealots?

He slowed Ares to a walk, cautious of what might lay ahead. Squinting his eyes, he scanned each side of the dirt road before him. Automatically, his hand moved to the hilt of his double-edged sword as he advanced along, listening acutely for a clue as to the location of those speaking.

Perhaps just shepherds, but just in case...

Unsure of what lay ahead, Marcus carefully continued forward until the road forked. Bringing Ares to a halt, he studied his choices. To the left, he would head toward his father's house and away from the voices. To the right, he would ride closer to the water's edge, and perhaps identify the source of what he was hearing. However, not knowing if they would be friend or foe made Marcus hesitate, not out of fear, but prudence. He was alone, and while he could easily defend himself against a few, a horde of zealous rebels might not have an outcome to his advantage. Still, he was a centurion of Rome, and it was his duty to investigate anything suspicious. He turned Ares to the right, trusting in the horse's ability to outrun anything in this region if the need arose.

Marcus gently nudged Ares, and they slowly continued forward. Attentively listening and looking for anything unusual, his warrior skills were on alert, unwilling to be caught unaware and vulnerable. The voices grew louder, and it seemed as though there were more than just a few responsible for the clamor. As he rounded a bend, his eyes widened, and he yanked on the reins bringing Ares to a sudden stop.

There were hundreds, maybe thousands of men, women, and even children gathered on a grassy knoll, filling the air with conversation and... laughter. The massive crowd baffled him.

Why are they all here? This is no uprising. These are families, not warriors...

He scanned the area from one side to the other, hoping for a clue as to the unusual assemblage of common people. His hand remained tight on his sword as his gaze swept the crowd. In the distance by the water's edge, the movement of a small group of men caught his attention, and Marcus focused on them. Although aware of a few wary glances his way, Marcus ignored them and kept his eyes on the men at the shore. They seemed to be the focal point of the throng. One man vainly tried to direct the crowd farther back on to the hillside, while a few others were in the water pulling a small fishing vessel to the shore. As soon as the boat was beached, Marcus saw another man step into it. Facing the crowd, the mystery man began to speak, and the crowd hushed.

Marcus leaned forward slightly as he sat atop Ares, his probing eyes fixed on the one who stood tall in the wooden boat. Although the distance between him and the man was great, Marcus had no problem hearing the man speak. It was if the words floated on the wind, and that Marcus found fascinating.

"Behold, a sower went forth to sow…"

As he listened, realization came to Marcus.

Yeshua.

"Some seeds fell by the wayside…"

Marcus guided Ares to a secluded spot where he could remain in the saddle and still watch and hear.

"Some fell among thorns, and the thorns sprung up, and choked them. But other fell into good ground, and brought forth fruit…"

He speaks of planting?

Marcus glanced around him. The people sat riveted to the speaker. Even the children were quiet.

This is what attracts them to him?

Marcus listened intently, trying to make sense of what he was hearing, but he had difficulty reconciling the fact that the man speaking was the same one who healed the lame man at Bethesda or the blind man in Jerusalem. He shook his head disbelievingly.

What point is he trying to make? He certainly isn't a threat to Rome unless he's planning on pelting us with seeds.

Regardless of his skepticism, Marcus remained until late afternoon. Although he wanted to arrive at his father's house before nightfall, he also wanted to hear everything Yeshua had to say and perhaps even speak to him personally. Like so many around him, Marcus was fascinated, but not with what he heard as much as he was by the man himself. As soon as Yeshua stepped from the boat, the people rushed him. The devotion of the crowd puzzled Marcus, and he marveled that they followed such an insignificant person en masse, not even giving the centurion a second glance as they hurried by.

Having a personal audience with Yeshua would be impossible. Marcus knew he could never get through the people without using force, and he was not willing to do that. He kept Ares still as the multitudes moved on, and it wasn't until only a few stragglers were left, that he gave a tug on the reins, turning Ares back to the road to Capernaum. His mind kept reviewing what he had witnessed.

He speaks in riddles... bizarre stories that are so random, so unconnected, yet the people flock to him. Like moths drawn inexplicably to a flame. Why? What do they see in him? What does Hadassah see in him?

Chapter Ten

"Create in me a clean heart, O God; and renew a right spirit within me." Psalm 51:10

Judith and Hadassah made their way through the mass of humanity that had journeyed to hear Yeshua speak. It had taken a great deal of persuasion from Hadassah to convince Judith to travel the distance to hear the rabbi, but once she had relented, Judith knew it was the right decision. She knew Justus would not be pleased to know that she had gone to hear the teachings of the rabbi of whom so many rumors were spoken, but she also knew that on this day Justus had business in Caesarea and would not return until well after the evening meal. He would never know.

The internal struggle was real for Judith. Not only were her allegiances divided between the gods of the Romans and the God of Israel, but she also harbored a great fear of this Healer of whom Hadassah spoke so confidently. If he truly was of God, he would know of Judith's infidelity to the God of her own people.

What if Hadassah is right? What if he can heal, but he chooses not to heal me? What if he rejects me the same way I rejected the God of my forefathers? What is to become of me?

"Dodah, are you all right?"

Judith's thoughts were interrupted by Hadassah's query. She focused on her niece's concerned face. "You are so sweet to worry so much about me. I am fine." She tried to sound convincing and sighed in relief when Hadassah simply smiled at her and continued leading the way to Yeshua.

Judith stepped carefully as she followed her niece, maneuvering around others who had already found a place to sit and hear the popular rabbi. As she walked, she reflected on the blessing that Hadassah had been to her.

When Hadassah was a child, she had filled such a need in Judith's life. Being a faithful wife and mother was all that Judith really wanted, but when she was unable to bear a child, her despondency nearly drove her mad until Hadassah arrived. True, the circumstances were tragic, but she had believed the gods had favored her by providing her with a child she could call her own!

Through the years, she had raised Hadassah the way she believed her brother would have wanted. She had done her best to see that Hadassah was raised according to Jewish custom, and she had enlisted the aid of Aelia in teaching the young girl the stories of their faith. Judith believed that in order to one day find a good Jewish man for Hadassah, the child must be raised according to Jewish tradition. A worshipper of the Roman gods would never find a suitable husband in Israel.

Judith had been stunned when Justus decreed that Hadassah would not marry, stating that the agreement had been for Hadassah to care for her aunt until God saw fit to restore Judith's health. At first Judith had argued with Justus, but when her niece became of age, Judith's health had declined so greatly that she relied more and more on Hadassah. Reluctantly, Judith agreed to have Hadassah remain in the Caelinus household to provide the care she now needed. She prayed she would never be a burden to Justus, and with Hadassah by her side, she never would be.

As they moved forward, more and more groups of families and friends crowded along the shoreline of the Sea of Galilee in anticipation of hearing Yeshua. Under the watchful eye of their mothers, young children scurried around, chasing one another, enjoying the opportunity to play, while the older siblings searched for comfortable spots from which a family could sit and listen.

Hadassah and Judith were among the fortunate who found a place to sit that was partially shaded. The thick gray-green leaves of the large aloe plant afforded only a little protection from the sun, but it would be greatly appreciated as the day wore on.

"Do you think this will be close enough, Hadassah?" Judith lowered herself to the ground.

Hadassah turned to her aunt and saw fatigue on Judith's face. "Yes, Dodah. It will be fine. We don't need to be closer. We'll be able to hear everything from here. Besides, the shore is rocky, and it would be too uncomfortable for you."

Judith smiled gratefully as she looked around her. "There are a lot of people here." She adjusted a head covering as she surveyed the multitudes around them.

"There always are. I guess when word got around about the healings that Yeshua does, everyone wanted to see for themselves." Hadassah sat down beside her aunt. "Are you really okay, Dodah?"

"Yes, just a little apprehensive, I suppose."

"You don't need to be. I promise— Look, Dodah! There he is!" Hadassah pointed to a group of men walking along the shore.

Raising her hand to her forehead, Judith shielded her searching eyes. It was easy to find the men to whom Hadassah referred because several onlookers rose to their feet and ran over to them. Judith frowned as she studied the rabbi and his entourage. She had expected someone more priestly in appearance. Yeshua was clad only in a kethōneth, an off-white tunic over which hung a brown simlāh. Without a sash, the simlāh hung loosely and moved freely as he walked. His head was without a covering, and his wavy black hair was just above his shoulders. His rugged face was framed by his dark hair and a closely cropped beard. There was nothing about him that indicated he was anything more than a common fisherman or farmer.

Yeshua moved neared the water's edge as more people crowded around him. His associates worked diligently, yet ineffectively, to keep the people from pressing in on him. Even as far back as the women were sitting, those who were previously seated now rose to move closer to him.

"He's going to be pushed into the sea if those people don't move back," commented Judith. Dissatisfaction punctuated her comment.

Hadassah agreed. "If they'd just sit down, they could hear him speak. They need to give him room."

"He's not quite what I expected," stated Judith bluntly. "He doesn't look any different than anyone else. I thought he'd at least be dressed like a rabbi. In fact, he looks quite poor. From Nazareth, you said?"

"Yes, but he's a wonderful teacher." Hadassah's eyes were fixed upon him. "Wait until you hear him speak, Dodah. You will be amazed."

Yeshua stopped near the water's edge and pointed toward a cluster of wooden boats. Three other men immediately headed out into the water to a nearby fishing boat anchored by the shore. Together, they moved it closer to

Yeshua and held it still as the rabbi stepped into it.

"What's he doing? Is he going away?" Judith asked anxiously. "Is he leaving?"

Hadassah shrugged her shoulders as a confused frown formed on her face. "I don't know. I hope not." She kept her gaze on Yeshua and his followers.

The men shoved the boat a few yards out into the water until the rabbi motioned for them to cease pushing it. Several others approached to help steady the boat as Yeshua began to speak.

Realizing he was merely using the boat as a platform from which to speak, Judith allowed herself to relax next to Hadassah and simply listened to the powerful words coming from the mouth of Yeshua. Hadassah was right. His words were easily heard, and they captivated her. She was fixated on him. Everything around her faded from view.

"Behold, a sower went forth to sow..."

Judith leaned forward a bit, and even when the breeze blew her hair across her face, her hopeful eyes remained focused on Yeshua.

"Some seeds fell by the wayside..."

Judith stared straight ahead as his words penetrated her soul.

"Some fell upon stony places..."

My heart has been as stone...

Standing in the boat, Yeshua seemed like any other fisherman, but Judith began to understand he was far from ordinary.

"Some fell among thorns..."

The thorns of foreign gods choked away all I once believed...

"Other fell into good ground and brought forth fruit..."

"Deborah, the fruit of your faith sits by me...

Judith's mind was spinning with disconnected thoughts. His words pricked at her heart, and then she knew. She knew that God had sent him, and now would be her last opportunity to repent. She tried to make sense of what Yeshua was saying and what she was feeling inside. Closing her eyes tightly, her body shook as fear enveloped her.

Finally opening her eyes, she looked back at the man she firmly believed had been sent by God, the God of the Hebrews, the God of her people. She had heard about his miracles. She had listened to him speak. But now, her despair only seemed to deepen.

What a fool I have been! I have rejected the God of my forefathers. There is no hope for me!

How long they sat and heard the words of Yeshua, Judith did not know. The shadows had lengthened, and there was still no respite from the heat, yet no one had left. Restless and discomforted, she shifted her weight.

"Hadassah?"

She turned to her aunt. "Yes?"

"I'm sorry. I don't feel well. Maybe it's the heat..." Judith's face had a pallor that was not there earlier.

Alarmed, Hadassah helped Judith to her feet and gathered their things. "Are you strong enough to walk home, or shall I have someone take us?"

Judith uttered weakly. "If you help me, and we go slowly, I believe I can walk."

"If you are sure."

"I'd like to try."

Hadassah gently supported Judith, and together they meandered through the seated throng to the main road.

"Whenever you need to rest, tell me," instructed Hadassah as they headed toward Capernaum. Worry washed over her concerned face as she assisted Judith along. It was a long way back to their home.

They walked only a short distance before Judith was unable to go on. Hadassah guided her to a large boulder upon which she could lean and rest.

"Wait here, Dodah. I will go and get help."

Hadassah hurried off to a nearby house and returned within minutes leading a donkey behind her. Her eyes opened in alarm to see Judith slumped over, sitting on the ground.

"Dodah! Dodah!" She dropped to her knees beside Judith, reaching out to touch her aunt's face.

Judith whispered, "Do not fear, Hadassah. I am merely tired. It was easier to sit and rest, than stand." Her smile was weak, and it brought no comfort to Hadassah.

After placing her head covering on the animal's back, Hadassah helped Judith onto the donkey.

"Are you comfortable, Dodah?" Hadassah's worried eyes scanned Judith's face for reassurance.

"I am." Her hand reached out and touched Hadassah's cheek. Her weakened voice was barely audible, but she managed to whisper, "What would I do without you?"

Hadassah began to guide the little donkey down the road. She carefully avoided anything that might cause the animal to stumble. Keeping a wary eye on Judith, she made her way toward home.

Later that night, after she had helped Judith into bed, she sat quietly in her room. Fatigue made it difficult to attend to her own nightly care, but she pushed herself to wash the dust from her hair and face, but not before a few tears trickled down her cheeks.

She sighed deeply as she changed into her nightclothes. Sitting on her bed, she extinguished the small lamp on her bedside and slid her feet under her lightweight blanket. As tired as she was, sleep eluded her. She had expected so much more from the day, and she couldn't squelch the disappointment she felt inside. As she began to lose hope that Judith would ever be healed, a still small voice that she recognized immediately spoke to her hurting heart.

Be of good courage, and He shall strengthen your heart, all ye that hope in the Lord.

* * * * * *

Sometime during the night, the skies opened up. Rain poured from the heavens as thunder rumbled through the darkness. Flashes of lightning cut through the black veil of night, silhouetting the distant mountains on the far side of the Sea of Galilee.

When one monstrous bolt hit nearby, its crackling shattered the solitude of her sleep. Hadassah bolted upright in bed! Another flash, another roll of thunder, but now she heard something else.

What was that?

As her mind emerged from the fog of sleep, she heard it again!
Someone was weeping! Dodah!

She quickly rose, wrapped herself with the blanket, and padded softly to Judith's bedchamber. She peered into the darkness. When another bolt of lightning briefly illuminated the room, Hadassah could easily see the sobbing form of her aunt on the bed.

Hurrying over, she sat beside Judith and reached a hand to her shoulder.

"Dodah," she said softly. "What's wrong? Why are you crying? Are you hurting?"

Judith was facing the wall and answered without turning. "There is no hope for me, Hadassah! I am doomed!" Her entire body shook as she wept bitterly.

"No hope? What do you mean?" Hadassah struggled to make some sense of Judith's declaration.

"Didn't you hear him today?" She finally turned toward her niece. "It is my heart that is the stone!" Her face was ashen, and her reddened eyes overflowed with tears.

"What? What do you mean?" Hadassah clutched her aunt's hand.

Judith trembled as she spoke. "He said the seeds had fallen on stony ground. That stony ground is my heart, and the seeds are his words of truth. I know it! I have not let them grow because I refused to let them take root in my heart. I have denied the God of my forefathers, and now I am lost! There is no hope for me, Hadassah!"

That cannot be true! God wouldn't send someone to us just to tell us we had no hope for redemption!

Hadassah shook her head vehemently. "No, Dodah! That cannot be true! Yeshua brings us messages of hope, not doom. In the synagogue, he speaks of God's love and his kingdom to come. He speaks of repentance. He has said that God forgives those who repent of their sins. No one is without hope, Dodah. No one."

Although Judith had turned back toward the wall, the young woman leaned over and wrapped her arms around her aunt. "You must believe, Dodah. You must not lose hope. Yeshua also spoke of seed that found their way to good ground, remember? That is your heart now! It is fertile soil for his words to take root and grow! There is hope for you, Dodah, but you must forsake the gods of the Romans. They are only idols. Return to the God of our forefathers. He loves you, Dodah, and he waits for you to come back to Him."

Judith could not speak; her sobs racked her body as she cried. Finally, there were no more tears to shed. Exhausted, Judith turned to look into the face of her devoted niece.

"Pray to God for me, Hadassah. Beg Him to give me another chance," she whispered in desperation.

"I will, Dodah. I will. I promise, but you must pray, too. He longs to hear from you. He holds his arms open, waiting for your return. He is longsuffering, full of mercy. Please Dodah, call on him. He will not refuse you."

"Oh, Hadassah!" Judith turned away once more, but Hadassah remained. She sat rubbing Judith's back until her aunt's breathing became deep and rhythmic, acknowledging that sleep had finally arrived. Slowly rising, Hadassah returned to her own room contemplating Judith's words. Unable to sleep herself, she knelt by her bed and prayed.

"Almighty God, please help Dodah. Speak to her heart. Let her know that You still love her. That she can find forgiveness from You. Open her eyes to your truth. Give her the strength she needs to renounce the sinful Roman idols and return to You. And then, O Almighty God, somehow help us get to Yeshua. I know he can heal her. Please—"

A flash of light and the accompanying boom of thunder startled her again, and she jumped to her feet. She hastened over to the window and looked out into the night. The storm was vicious, and although she couldn't see it in the darkness, she knew the Sea of Galilee would be rough, maybe even deadly. She thought of the fishing vessels out on the angry water, and momentarily, she was distracted from her aunt's troubles. Knowing her friends would be tossed mercilessly, she whispered another prayer for those she knew would be fervently working to keep their boats under control and stay the hand of death.

Returning to her bed, she pulled the blanket up to her chin and rested her head on the pillow. Several tears trickled down to the bed sheets. She wanted so badly to trust God, but the storm continued to rage all around her, both within and without. Fear of what might never be threatened to engulf her as sleep eluded her.

* * * * * *

Judith had remained in bed for several days, and Hadassah was deeply concerned. She hovered over her aunt bringing warm broth, medicinal herbs, and anything else that she could think of to aid her aunt's discomfort, but she feared this was not only a physical ailment that needed healing. Still, she always made sure Judith had a clean gown and a fresh bed as the dreaded illness returned with a vengeance.

This morning, Hadassah had risen later than usual due to yet another late night with Judith. After completing her personal morning activities, she walked into Judith's bedchamber with fresh towels and linens only to find her aunt's bed empty.

"Dodah?" She set her things on a table and scanned the room. Nothing looked unusual, but an uneasiness stirred within Hadassah.

"Dodah, are you here?"

Receiving no answer, she hurried to the great room. No one was there, so she moved quickly throughout the house.

Where could she be?

"Dodah? Where are you?" Her panic-filled voice received no response. "Dodah?"

She rushed down the hall, turned a corner, and slammed into the solid form of Marcus, knocking a half-eaten apple out of his hand.

Flustered, her eyes widened as she realized what she had down. "Marcus! I am so sorry. I... I..." She bent down to retrieve the fruit.

"It's fine. Are you all right? What is it that has you in such haste?"

She rose up before him, apple in hand. Frantically, she explained, "I can't find Judith! I've looked everywhere! Her bedroom. The main room. Everywhere in the house. I don't know where she could be!"

"Calm down. She's around somewhere—"

"But where, Marcus? I've got to find her!" cried Hadassah. Panic rose in her voice as her eyes darted back and forth beyond Marcus.

"Why? Is she in harm's way?"

"She's sick. Very, very sick, and she's not in her room. She wouldn't leave without telling me." Hadassah's body trembled as she spoke.

"If she's that sick, maybe she went to find a doctor?" he offered.

"No, doctors cannot help her. She's tried. She's so weak, Marcus. Where could she have gone? Please... please help me find her," she pleaded.

He placed his hands on her shoulders. "You have to settle down. I'll help you, but you need to be able to help me, and you can't do that if you're hysterical. Take some deep breaths."

Hadassah looked into his eyes and nodded as she obeyed his words. She forced herself to breathe slowly.

"Maybe she went somewhere with my father," he suggested.

Hadassah shook her head vehemently. "No, she wouldn't go anywhere without me. You don't understand. She's really sick. She wouldn't have had the strength. Where would she have gone anyway?"

"Have you checked the courtyard. Maybe she went there. It's quiet, peaceful."

"Yes, yes! Let's go there."

She allowed Marcus to lead her to the garden, but when they arrived, the only thing that greeted them were the bees buzzing among the blossoms.

"She's not here!" Hadassah cried woefully.

Marcus thought for a moment. "The stables?"

Although she couldn't fathom Judith on a horse, she followed Marcus along the path toward the stable.

"You're sure she said nothing about going out today?" he asked.

"No, nothing. She's been in bed for the last few days, ever since we went to hear Yeshua."

Marcus stopped abruptly and turned to her. "Yeshua? Your Healer? You went to hear him?"

"Yes. He was speaking in Galilee, and we went to hear him. I was so happy she wanted to go, but now, I think it was too much for her." Guilt enveloped her face, and her condemning voice dropped to a near-whisper. "What if something has happened to her? It's all my fault. If I hadn't been so insistent–"

"It's not your fault," he stated strongly. "Judith is a grown woman. She's not a child. She is perfectly capable of making her own decisions about whether or not to stay home."

"But she's been so sick. If she was going to go out, she would have said something to me."

"You are not her mother, Hadassah. You had best remember who is really in charge. She may be your aunt, but she is still the mistress of this house. She doesn't need your permission to go out."

Feeling chastised, she nodded without a word. Tiny tears coursed down her cheeks.

Marcus saw her wipe them away, and his voice softened. "We'll find her, Hadassah. If she's that sick, she wouldn't have gone far without someone knowing."

She said nothing, but her eyes reflected the fear she felt for Judith. As they walked to the stables, she silently prayed that God would protect her aunt.

"Stay here." Marcus disappeared into the groomsman's quarters leaving Hadassah waiting outside.

Nervously chewing her lower lip, she wrung her hands until Marcus reappeared. His look told her that Judith was not there.

As soon as their eyes met, he said, "She's not here, but she was. She had the groomsman take her to the marketplace, and then told him that she would return this evening. She left early this morning, alone."

"He left her there? Why? Why did she go to the marketplace? I always shop for her. She never goes there. Does he know when she is returning? Why didn't he stay with her?"

He shook his head. "He said she told him to leave. She would make her own arrangements to return home." Hadassah's worried face tugged at him, and he finally sighed, "She wouldn't have left without telling you if she was still sick. She must have felt better."

"No, Marcus. She could not have recovered that quickly. It doesn't work like that. What if she can't come home? What if she so sick, she can't–"

"Hadassah—"

"What if—"

"Hadassah—"

"Maybe—"

"Hadassah!"

The harshness of his voice stunned her into silence. She turned to face him; her eyes glistening with unshed tears. Marcus' natural commanding presence overwhelmed her, and when she opened her mouth to speak, no words came.

"Let's go find her," he stated.

"Find her?"

"Yes." His eyes narrowed. "If she's as sick as you say, she'll need help to get back home."

"Thank you, Marcus. I know you are busy, and I shouldn't have bothered you with this. You surely have more important things to do, but—"

"Yes, but it will be easier for me to take you to Judith than to deal with your hysteria while you wait here for her."

"Hysteria?" Her head snapped up as she padded along behind him.

"Did I say that?"

She heard a low chuckle escape him as he walked over to the stalls, and she felt relieved when she realized he was teasing her. Gratitude filled her misty eyes. "I am grateful to you, Marcus. Truly I am." Sincerity accompanied her words.

Compassion replaced the authoritative tone in his voice as they walked to the stall in which Ares stood. "She's your aunt. You care for her, and she is my father's wife, so I have some stake in this."

"I know, but she is a grown woman as you said. Do you really think I should go to her? Maybe I should just wait."

He laughed lightly under his breath. "I find you so intriguing, Hadassah. One minute, you worry yourself sick over Judith, and the next, you are prepared to ignore everything and carry on as if all is as it should be."

Warmth rose in her cheeks, and she lowered her head. "I'm sorry to be such a bother, but maybe you're right—"

"I'm what?" Marcus stopped and turned to her. "What did you say?" He winked at her, and a faint smile appeared on her face.

"I meant to say that maybe I was wrong," she corrected.

Marcus grinned. "Maybe you were, but nevertheless, we are heading into town to find Judith. Would you prefer to ride or walk? Ares could easily support the two of us, you know."

Her lips clamped together as she crossed her arms in front of her. "I cannot ride with you on that horse."

He watched her curiously as she stood defiantly before him. "Ah, there's the Hadassah I remember. Tell me, who are you afraid of? Me or Ares?" Smiling to himself, he turned and stroked the horse's neck before alleviating her discomfort. "We can certainly get to the center of town quicker than walking if we ride, and if Judith is too sick to walk home, we'll have a way to bring her back."

"You can ride, and I can walk beside you," Hadassah suggested.

He led Ares out of the stall, bringing the huge animal to a halt next to Hadassah.

"Come." Marcus motioned for Hadassah to move nearer.

Knowing to disobey was unacceptable, she stepped over to him, and when he grabbed her waist and lifted her up on to Ares' back, a small gasp escaped her lips.

"I'll lead him. You enjoy the ride. No impropriety here." He winked at her again, and she reddened once more.

Chapter Eleven

"But without faith it is impossible to please him: for he that cometh to God must believe that he is, and that he is a rewarder of them that diligently seek him."
Hebrews 11:6

By the time Marcus and Hadassah reached the center of Capernaum, it was early afternoon. A huge crowd was moving as a single unit down the center of the main street.

"Do you see her anywhere?" she asked, her hand on her forehead as she scanned the area.

He shook his head. "No. This isn't going to be easy. There are a lot of people in the streets."

"I wonder what's happening?" she said, straining to see the attraction.

"I'm not sure. But I'm learning that whenever I encounter a large group of people, your Yeshua is often at the center of it."

He led her through the street slowly as he maneuvered in and out among the people. However, unless they pushed their way through the multitude, their search would take time. He secured Ares to a small sapling, then helped Hadassah to the ground.

"You picked the wrong day not to wear your uniform," lamented Hadassah. "If you had, the people would definitely part to let you through."

"Maybe I should simply lift you up and let you stand on my shoulders," he said with a mischievous grin.

She opened her mouth to respond, but he turned away from her to look down the street.

He reached out and tapped the shoulder of an older gray-haired man who tottered by them. "Tell me, what is happening?" He gestured toward the crowd.

"It's the Teacher. The Teacher is here."

Hadassah's eyes widened as she tugged at Marcus's sleeve. "It's Yeshua! He's talking about Yeshua!"

"I got that," Marcus stated curtly.

"We've got to get closer," she insisted.

Marcus felt his patience slipping with her. "I know, Hadassah." He lowered his voice. "Do you mind if I handle this?"

Embarrassed at her own assertiveness, she whispered, "I'm sorry," and lowered her head submissively.

He turned back to the man. "You're speaking of the rabbi? The one who heals?"

"Yes, yes! The rabbi is here!"

Marcus shook his head as he scanned the crowd. "We're not getting through that. If Judith is here, it's going to take one of your miracles to find her."

"Please, Marcus, we've got to try." Her plea touched something in him, and an exasperated sigh escaped him.

"Yes, we do." Pressing his lips together in a thin line, his hand moved to her back, and he pushed her gently toward the crowd. "Let's follow them a bit. Maybe we'll see her."

Hadassah knew that Marcus did not care for Yeshua, but she knew he would keep his word and help her find Judith even if it meant following the rabbi and his followers through the entire town. "Maybe you'll get a chance to hear Yeshua speak."

He gave her a knowing smile. "I've already heard him speak."

"You've already heard him?" Hadassah's questioning eyes searched his face.

"Yes." He offered no further information as they joined the crowd.

Suddenly, the people stopped, and the voice of Yeshua was unmistakable. "Who touched me?"

Hadassah looked up at Marcus and whispered, "That's him! I know his voice! That's Yeshua!"

"Yes, I know. Your miracle worker often asks ridiculous questions," scowled Marcus as he strained to see what was happening.

"Ridiculous questions? What do you mean?"

"There are hundreds of people in this mob. We are standing shoulder to shoulder, and he wants to know who touched him? It could be anyone."

"Can you see him?"

"No. No, I can't."

Then, as if an unseen hand had reached down and parted the crowd, a small gap appeared, and both Hadassah and Marcus could clearly see Yeshua and those around him.

"Look! That's Simon and Andrew! I know them! They're always with him," she explained as she pointed out the two fishermen who stopped beside the rabbi.

Yeshua turned slightly and scanned the crowd.

"Somebody has touched me, for I perceive that virtue is gone out of me." The power in his voice stilled everyone except...

Judith!

"It was I, Master." Her voice trembled as she spoke. Clutching her cloak tightly around her, she timidly shuffled forward and fell at Yeshua's feet.

Hadassah gasped as her hand flew to cover her mouth, and Marcus stiffened as he watched, unsure of what to do.

Hadassah started to bolt forward, but Marcus' firm hold on her arm kept her in place. His intense glare focused on Judith cowering on the ground in front of Yeshua. The fingers of his other hand closed around the dagger hidden in the folds of his garment as he waited and watched. Regardless of how he felt about his father, he would never allow anyone to hurt his stepmother.

"Please, let me go to her," she begged Marcus in a hushed voice as she tried to loosen his grip on her.

"No. Not yet." Poised to move to Judith's side if needed, he stood tensely as he kept his gaze focused on her and Yeshua.

Judith's voice trembled as if awaiting a deserved punishment. "I knew if I but touched your garment, I would be healed."

Yeshua reached a hand down to Judith and rested it on her head. Then he spoke with the voice of authority, yet compassion. "Daughter, be of good comfort. Your faith has made you whole. Go in peace and be whole of thy plague."

Judith began to sob. Her thin body shook as tears cascaded down her cheeks. Casting her grateful eyes upward, she reached up for his hand.

Taking it into her own, she kissed it again and again. Finally releasing it, Judith remained on the ground, quietly weeping tears of gratitude as Yeshua continued along the road.

Hadassah turned toward Marcus, but before she had a chance to speak, a young boy pushed her aside as he ran toward Yeshua. "Sir!"

Yeshua stopped once more and turned toward the lad as did those next to him.

The boy ignored Yeshua and bowed in front of one of the other men.

"He is of my household," said the man beside Yeshua. He turned to the lad. "What is it?"

Bent over with his hands on his thighs, the boy struggled to catch his breath as he spoke. "Your daughter... is dead," he stated between his gasps. "Trouble not... the Master."

The man's face contorted in agony, and an anguished cry came from him. He staggered and reached out to anyone to steady himself.

Murmurs ran through the crowd at the sorrowful news.

"How sad!"

"Poor Jairus! His daughter has died!"

Immediately, Yeshua reached out both hands and placed them on the man's shoulders. He looked directly into the grieving man's eyes. "Fear not. Believe only, and she shall be made whole."

Lifting grief-stricken eyes, the man stared at Yeshua for the longest time. Finally, he nodded his head, but the heartbroken look remained on his face. Shoulders slumped, Jairus remained at Yeshua's side as they resumed walking down the street away from Marcus and Hadassah.

Reluctantly taking her eyes from Yeshua, Hadassah looked first at Marcus, then back toward her aunt. "Dodah!" She ran to her and dropped to the ground draping her arms around her sobbing aunt.

"Dodah, are you alright? Let me help you up."

A group of people began to surround Hadassah and Judith, bombarding them with questions, and Hadassah feared they would be trampled. She shielded Judith from the curious onlookers, but it wasn't until the large frame of the Roman centurion pushed through the crowd and stepped to her side that she felt safe. Reluctantly, the people relented, and Marcus easily escorted the women away from the insensitive throng.

He maneuvered them near a secluded wall, then turned his back to them. His stance was a silent warning to anyone daring to come near the two women, and his protective position gave Hadassah and Judith the privacy they needed.

"Dodah, what are you doing here? Are you all right?" Concern etched deep lines on Hadassah's brow as her eyes searched for signs of anything that would give her a clue as to her aunt's status.

The listless look in Judith's eyes was gone. Instead, tears fell from eyes that sparkled as she spoke. "I am beyond all right, dear Hadassah!" She paused and looked directly into her niece's probing eyes. "I am healed!" she exclaimed. "I am healed!"

Hadassah's mouth dropped open as she struggled to comprehend Judith's words. "Healed? What do you mean?"

"He healed me, Hadassah! Yeshua healed me! I knew I could never confront him directly. How could I? I had abandoned the God of Israel. I had no right to ask anything of him, but I thought... I thought if I could just touch his garment." She paused, closing her eyes in remembrance. Her voice was a reverential whisper. "If I could just touch his simlāh, I knew... I knew I would be healed. So, I managed to get close behind him, and when he slowed just enough, I reached out and... and I touched him. Just barely, but..." Her eyes shone as she continued, "I felt it!"

"Felt what, Dodah?"

"His strength, Hadassah. It flowed through me, and I knew! At that moment I knew I was healed!" Her smile was radiant. "And then he stopped and asked who touched him, and I was so scared. I fell to my knees before him and confessed that it was I who touched him."

She raised her head and a smile spread across her face. "And then he called me a 'Daughter.' Do you know what that means, Hadassah?"

Mutely, Hadassah shook her head.

Judith threw her arms around her niece and held her close. "It means I am forgiven, and I am restored. The Holy One of God called me a daughter! A daughter! I am a daughter of Zion once again!" The joy in her voice was unmistakable. "I am forgiven! I feel as though I have been born again!"

* * * * * *

Unable to comprehend Judith's proclamation of healing by Yeshua, Marcus remained silent as he led the women back to the Caelinus home. Judith babbled on about how she had been afraid to speak to Yeshua, but as she followed him, the urge to touch Him was overwhelming. It had taken every bit of courage within her to creep up behind him and reach out just to touch the hem of his garment.

Skepticism waxed strong in Marcus' spirit, but he held his tongue. Fortunately, being in the lead, neither woman could see him as he occasionally rolled his eyes at Judith's declarations.

Healed? By touching his clothes? She speaks madness! Garments do not heal. She is delusional.

Trained to listen astutely regardless of his personal feelings, he contemplated every word that Judith spoke. His logical mind could not reconcile what she was saying with what he knew to be fact, yet Hadassah seemed to readily embrace everything Judith said as undeniable truth.

Confusion was not something with which a centurion was familiar, and the frustration of not feeling free to question Judith for clarification added to his rising irritation.

I will get answers. Maybe not now, but I will get them.

* * * * * *

"Hadassah, I wish to speak with you." The harsh voice left no doubt as to the mood of Marcus.

She had come to the garden to meditate and pray, but he had shattered the serenity of the moment. The smile on her face vanished when she turned and saw the hardened look in his eyes. "What's wrong?" She sought his face for clarification. "Have I done something to anger you?"

Marcus sat next to her on the stone bench. "No." His reply was unconvincing, and it caused a shiver to run through her. "I am perplexed, and I need answers."

"What do you want to know?" She tried to remain relaxed and consciously clasped her hands in her lap, while forcing a faint smile.

"The other day when Judith was supposedly healed, from what exactly was it that she suffered?"

Color rose in Hadassah's cheeks. "I cannot speak of that with you," she stammered.

The irritation in his eyes matched that in his question, "Why not?"

"It's somewhat... delicate." Uncomfortable, she averted her eyes from him.

"Delicate? Explain yourself."

"It's something that is usually only spoken of between women." Her distress went unnoticed by him. "And even then, only with family."

He scratched his chin as his eyes narrowed. "You need to put propriety aside and answer my question."

Alarmed, Hadassah simply murmured, "I...I cannot. It is not my place."

"Your place?"

Embarrassed, she tried to discreetly explain. "It is a matter for women. It is not spoken of to men."

"I want to know how she was healed and of what. It is my responsibility to determine the authenticity of such a claim," he lied.

"Authenticity? What do you mean?"

"Do not question me." The sternness in his response startled her.

Her eyes reflected confusion as she answered. "I'm sorry. I meant no disrespect, but I am not comfortable sharing such intimate information with a man."

"Then I shall ask Judith."

"No!" She immediately softened her tone. "It would surely embarrass her. Please, Marcus."

He raised an eyebrow, and the austerity of his look softened slightly.

Hadassah pleaded with him. "It would be so distressful for her to discuss this with you. More than you could imagine."

Dissatisfied, he folded his arms across his chest. "I want answers, Hadassah. From you or her, it matters not who, but I want them now."

An uncomfortable silence permeated the air as Marcus stood waiting. He cocked his head as he studied Hadassah's lowered head. "Perhaps there was nothing that needed to be healed in the first place," he challenged.

Hadassah gasped as she jerked her head upward. "How can you say that? You know how sick she's been."

"No, I don't. I only know what you've told me."

Hadassah shook her head in disbelief. "I have not lied to you, Marcus. Judith has been unable to leave her room for days at a time. Surely, you've noticed how pale her skin has become. Why would she carry out such a ruse? What would be the reason?"

"You tell me."

"I don't understand what you mean. I have been with Judith nearly all my life caring for her. Ask anyone in the household. Ask Aelia. Judith was truly sick. She had sought help from as far away as Damascus, yet nothing proved helpful. It was Yeshua who cured her. You were there! How could you deny what happened?"

Hadassah rose to her feet, hurt that Marcus would doubt her. "You saw it, Marcus. You saw Judith."

"I saw nothing," he stated bluntly, "except a woman groveling at the feet of an itinerant teacher making a fool of herself."

Hadassah stood in shocked silence as Marcus continued his accusations.

"Did it ever occur to you that maybe it's a simple case of mind over matter? That you've simply chosen to believe in a charlatan?"

"What? No! Yeshua is no charlatan. I saw the demoniac healed, and I saw the leper healed." She paused, then emphasized each word, "And I saw Judith healed." Pain filled her eyes as she surrendered to Marcus' demand for an explanation.

"Judith has been afflicted with this illness for a long time. She has been unable to bear children due to a condition the doctors have not been able to identify or cure. In fact, they haven't even been able to slow down its course despite the money she has spent trying to do so." Her eyes half closed in sorrow as she betrayed Judith's trust.

"And to make matters worse, according to our law, she would be deemed unclean if anyone knew about her illness, including her husband, so we never spoke of it to anyone, including your father, although he may know." She sighed deeply as she sat back down on the bench. "She would have been shunned by Jewish society."

Her voice was nearly a whisper when she added, "It doesn't really matter whether you believe it or not, but Judith has been completely and *miraculously* healed. And if you chose not to believe, well then, you are the fool."

His head jerked back as if she had slapped him. His angry eyes bore into hers, and he pressed his lips together as his breathing deepened. Tight fists formed at his side.

Hadassah's entire body was trembling, and her heart pounded furiously within her as she faced him.

"You would be wise to consider how you speak to me," warned Marcus.

"Forgive me," she began, suddenly finding courage. "I thought I was free to speak my mind in your presence. I must have misunderstood you. You wanted the truth, and I have given it to you. Is there anything else you require of me?" Her words were void of emotion, and she simply waited for the punishment she was certain would come. This time, she did not lower her eyes, but met him gaze for gaze.

His lips formed a tight line as he studied her defiant form. If anything, a centurion was self-disciplined in every situation. His training had taught him to never take his eyes off his opponent, but his gaze lost some of its hostility as he stood before her.

"We are not finished with this conversation, Hadassah." He hesitated for only a moment, then turned and left her alone in the garden.

As soon as he disappeared from sight, Hadassah took a deep breath and exhaled slowly. She blinked back the tears that threatened to spill over as she slowly rose from the stone bench. Her knees weakened, and she grabbed the nearby arbor for stability.

I wish you had never come here, Marcus Caelinus! Go back to Rome!

* * * * * *

Kneeling at the water's edge, Hadassah noticed her reflection in the water of the Sea of Galilee. Wisps of dark hair framed a face that was troubled, and the frown she saw was indicative of the spirit within her. She tipped her jug into the sea and allowed the cool water to flow into it.

"I thought I'd find you here."

She froze with her hands on her jug when she noticed Marcus' reflection in the stillness of the lake.

"Judith still likes her water drawn from here, I see." The statement was brusque and confrontational. "Healing properties, I believe? Oh, but she doesn't need that anymore, does she?"

Hadassah stood, lifting the jug to her shoulder. She moved past him without uttering a word.

"I'd like to have a conversation with you before I leave—"

She stopped, her back to him. "I didn't think we had anything more to discuss."

"I think we do."

She turned to face him. "Very well."

"You don't make things easy, Hadassah."

"I apologize."

He scowled at her insincerity, but he overlooked it. "I am a centurion. I am used to having my orders followed without question. I am used to getting answers when I ask questions. And I am not used to impertinent women. I was very harsh with you, and I am truly sorry for that."

"Are you?"

Marcus winced at her accusation, willing himself to maintain his composure. "While I don't agree with you regarding your precious Yeshua, I see no reason for us to be at odds with one another."

"Really?" She turned to face him. "You've attacked everyone I care about. Isn't that reason enough? You mock your father. You think Judith is a liar. You accuse me of trying to deceive you, and you said Yeshua was a... what was it? Oh yes, a charlatan. And you don't see any reason why we should be at odds with one another?" Hadassah made a clucking sound as she turned away from him. "I thought you were smarter than that, Marcus."

He stood dumbfounded as she headed up the path. He watched her disappear around a bend, and then followed, quickly catching up to her. He fell into step behind her.

"I have asked about Yeshua."

She did not stop but continued on and spoke without turning around. "I hope you found answers from someone you can trust."

He grimaced at her words. "I did. I went to his home."

"His home? In Nazareth?"

Now, I have your attention. Well, Hadassah, prepare to hear the truth about your precious Yeshua.

"Yes. It was a very revealing visit," he began smugly. "Did you know that until two years ago, your Yeshua was just a carpenter, nothing more. He never studied under a Jewish rabbi. He never studied the healing arts. And now, he just wanders the countryside speaking to whoever wishes to listen to him. He has no home to call his own. In fact, his own family doesn't even believe he is who he says he is."

Marcus watched her carefully as he continued. "And answer me this. Why would your God send such an insignificant man as this to be your king? Wouldn't he send someone more regal? A man in whom there would be no doubt that he is ordained from the heavens? Yeshua is no one of importance, and certainly not worthy of your loyalty or adoration."

Her lower lip began to tremble, and her eyes filled with angry tears. She shook her head disbelievingly. "I heard him speak words that could only have come from God. I saw him do miracles only God could do—" As unfettered tears fell, she picked up her pace. "You know nothing of what you speak." Raising the jug to her shoulder, she hurried along the path leaving Marcus to simply stare at her back as she left him behind.

* * * * * *

Marcus slowly pulled a stiff brush along Ares' sleek gray coat one final time before tossing it into a nearby bucket. He dumped a healthy portion of barley into the horse's feeder, then stepped outside the stall. He had ridden the horse hard, and now he was just as exhausted as the Andalusian stallion.

The sun was low in the sky when he finally made his way up the path to the house's courtyard. It was an indirect way to his room, but he was hoping to run into Hadassah. Passing under the vine-covered arbor, he entered the quiet garden, but saw no one. Disappointment was his only companion.

He sighed deeply. Before he left for Jerusalem, he had hoped to see Hadassah one more time. Departing after a disagreement was not how he wanted to remember her, but now it seemed like that would be the last memory he would have of her.

He sat down on the stone bench as the shadows lengthened around him, and the light faded. Resting his arms on his legs, his mind drifted to their last conversation.

She needed to know the truth. Better for her to know now that Yeshua is a fraud than to find out later.

He felt no satisfaction in his personal justification of what he had revealed to Hadassah. Instead, he felt his own frustrations mounting as an unexplainable desolation dominated his last night in Capernaum.

Chapter Twelve

"As soon as Jesus heard the word that was spoken, he saith unto the ruler of the synagogue, Be not afraid, only believe." Mark 5:36

Exiting through the front gates of the Caelinus estate, Hadassah made her way along the dirt road toward the green knolls to the east. The early morning cloud cover had dissipated, and the heat was already beginning to rise, but her walk was still comfortable as she carried a small bundle under her arm. Coming to a fork in the road, she took the less traveled path toward an ancient grove of olive trees. Their thick trunks and twisted branches were a testament to their age.

As she rounded a bend in the path, she heard her name called out. Looking ahead, she saw her friend standing beneath one of the ancient trees.

"Zara!" Hadassah hurried toward her, embracing her warmly. "I'm sorry I took so long to get here. Are you hungry? I brought some dried apricots, nut bread and a couple of apples."

Zara's bright eyes sparkled in the sunlight. "Yes! Any figs in there?" She peeked into Hadassah's wrapped offering and pulled out the ripened treasure. "You think of everything!" She bit the juicy fig in half. "Come, sit here. I have much to tell you." Her smile broadened as she plopped down on the ground. She chewed and swallowed the last of the sweet purple fruit, then wiped her hands on the apron covering her cotton tunic.

"I saw Uri yesterday—"

"That's your news?" Hadassah teased. "I thought you had something important to tell me." She bit into an apple.

Zara stuck her tongue out at Hadassah, then looked away and tried to sound casual. "I just thought you might like to know the latest news about the rabbi."

"The rabbi? Is it another miracle? Tell me!" Hadassah leaned forward expectantly.

"Oh, I didn't think you'd be interested," taunted Zara good-naturedly as she inspected her hands.

Hadassah laughed. "Okay, okay! You win! You know I'm interested. Tell me what Uri told you… please!"

Zara giggled. "Do you remember that storm we had a week or so ago? All that thunder and lightning?"

"Oh yes, I remember. It was so hard to sleep that night. Why?"

"Well, Uri told me that he and several others were fishing that night out on the sea. He said they were tossed about so much that he feared they might lose the boats, and all would be lost."

"I remember praying for those on the water. I was scared for them."

"Uri said that Andrew told him that in the midst of the storm Yeshua was in their boat sleeping. Can you imagine that? Everyone thought they were going to die, and he was sleeping!" Zara's speech became more animated as she went on. "Anyway, Andrew said they woke him up because they were so scared, and he stood up and told the storm to stop, and it did!"

"What do you mean? He *told* the storm to stop?"

"I mean exactly that. Yeshua stood up in the boat, commanded the storm to stop, and it did! Uri said that Andrew told him the water became calm *immediately*! Like glass! The words were barely out of Yeshua's mouth! Then the clouds parted, and the moon appeared! He swore that's what Andrew said!" Zara's excitement couldn't be contained. "Can you believe that?"

Hadassah felt such relief. She knew Marcus had been wrong! Yeshua was from God. He had to be!

"Oh, Zara, you don't know how badly I needed to hear that," confessed Hadassah, relief flooding her face.

For the first time, Zara noticed the sadness in Hadassah's eyes had lifted. "I know something has been troubling you."

Hadassah's shoulders slumped as she leaned back against the tree trunk and recounted the events of her recent conversations with Marcus. "Ever since Judith was healed, things have been difficult between us. And now, Marcus is leaving."

"That's a good thing, right?"

"It's a very good thing, but I hate to have this rift between us. But he's so adamant about Yeshua being a nobody."

"A nobody? That's ridiculous! Yeshua is our Messiah, no matter what Marcus thinks. Besides, who really cares what the Romans think? They're heathens." Zara's opinionated comments left no doubt of her feelings about Marcus and those who occupied their land.

Hadassah glanced away from Zara as she spoke. "Marcus doesn't believe Yeshua's from God. He thinks he's a fraud."

Zara clucked her tongue, then shrugged, "What did you expect? Marcus is a Roman. An enemy of our people, and Yeshua, he's one of us. That makes Marcus an enemy of Yeshua. Of course, he doesn't believe in him."

Hadassah thought about Zara's words. "I never thought about it like that. I guess they are enemies, except..."

"Except what?"

"I still remember that Yeshua said we were supposed to love our enemies."

"We can't love everyone, Hadassah. Some people are just unlovable." Zara reached out and gave a squeeze to her friend's hand. "Listen, Marcus won't be here forever. Soon he'll be gone, and it won't matter one way or another."

Hadassah nodded her head, but her heart was not convinced. She remained silent as she stared off into the distance.

As Zara munched on some almonds, she studied her friend's face before hesitantly asking, "Hadassah, you don't have feelings for Marcus, do you?"

Hadassah's words mirrored her shocked expression. "Feelings? For Marcus? No! Not at all! No! There is nothing between us," she insisted. "It would be wrong. He is not of our faith. He is against everything that I love. He is a heathen... a Roman... a Gentile! He is...." Her last words were an agonized admission. "... an enemy."

Zara bit her lower lip as she studied Hadassah's anguished face. Wisely, she directed the subject to something more pleasant. "Let's talk of other things." She forced a smile. "We need to finish our lunch. After all, we both have work to get back to, right?"

* * * * * *

As much as Hadassah hoped Marcus had already left for Jerusalem, part of her wanted him to still be at home. She wanted to speak with him but didn't know what she would say if she saw him. As she hurried along, she wrestled with whether or not to inform him about the storm Yeshua calmed, but in her heart, she knew Marcus would scoff at her words, and she didn't know if her heart could take it. She trusted she would know what to do when she saw him. Rushing through the gates, she entered the house and looked for him.

Where is he? Surely, he would have said goodbye...

She thought back to their last conversation, and she realized that it was she who had walked away. It was she who had left him standing by the sea. It was she who had rudely terminated their discussion, and now she doubted he would even want to see her, much less speak with her. Nevertheless, her heart would not allow her to abandon her search.

She headed for the courtyard, but it was empty upon her arrival. Greeted only by the fragrant blossoms swaying gently in the breeze, she stopped to think where else Marcus might possibly be.

Marcus, where are you?

Unable to think of where to look, she sadly ascended the stairs to the main house. As she walked through the hallway, her head was lowered, and she nearly ran into Aelia.

"Hadassah, you need to watch where your steps take you," the older woman scolded. When Hadassah looked up, Aelia saw concern in the young woman's eyes and her graveled voice softened. "What is troubling you, little one?"

"I was hoping to see Marcus before he left for Jerusalem. I needed to speak with him, but I fear he has gone. You haven't seen him, have you?" Hadassah asked.

Aelia shook her head. "No, but then I rarely see anyone in this place. I spend too much time cooking." A knowing smile crossed her face. "If it is meant for you to see him before he leaves, you will."

Hadassah nodded. "I suppose, but—"

"There are no "buts" where the Almighty is concerned."

Hadassah pursed her lips and said with resignation, "I know. 'Trust in the

Lord with all thine heart.' I wish I knew how to do that."

"Do it by faith, my child." And with that, the old woman walked away, leaving Hadassah standing alone.

Hadassah couldn't keep an affectionate smile from appearing on her lips as she walked toward the great room. As she neared it, she heard several voices in a very heated discussion. She knew it was not right to eavesdrop on a conversation to which she was not part of, but when she turned away, she heard Marcus' voice. She stopped and listened.

He's still here! I will be able to make things right between us!

As she waited in the hallway, she became troubled over his words.

"You are speaking nonsense," insisted Marcus. His voice was agitated and loud.

"I agree," concurred Justus.

Then a third man spoke. "I tell you the truth. I swear it."

Hadassah didn't recognize the voice.

"She was dead, but now she lives."

Who are they talking about?

Hadassah heard Marcus' voice escalate.

"You are a fool! No one can resurrect someone from the dead. Your audacity to even speak this madness amazes me."

"I swear to you, Centurion, I speak only the truth."

"You do realize that lying to Rome is a capital crime?" The veiled threat in Marcus' voice was quite clear.

The hardness in his words startled Hadassah, and she knew she should not be listening, but she remained where she was, hearing everything that was said.

"It is no lie, I assure you. The rabbi, he came with three of his followers. He came into the room where we were all mourning the child. Then he spoke. He said that our grief was for no reason as the girl was merely sleeping. But I tell you, she was not sleeping! She was dead! There was no doubt, Justus." Desperation was in his voice. "You must believe me!"

Marcus challenged the man. "Believe what? Your lies?"

"I swear to you I am not lying!"

"So enlighten me. What supposedly happened after he arrived?"

"We didn't believe him. In fact, some of us even laughed at him. Under our breath of course, but he was saying unbelievable things. Impossible things. But despite the contempt we felt for him, when he spoke again, we all did as he bade. We left the room. The only ones who stayed were Jairus and his wife, and the three men who arrived with the rabbi. The next thing we saw was the girl... alive!"

It was Justus who spoke next. "Eli, you saw her *alive*?"

"Yes. She walked out of the room—"

"Are you certain she was dead?" interrupted Justus.

"Of course! I told you we all saw that she was dead. You can ask anyone."

"We're not asking 'anyone.' We are asking you," stated Marcus harshly.

"I swear I speak the truth, Centurion. She was dead. I'd stake my life on it."

"You are doing just that," declared Marcus ominously.

Hadassah shivered at the coldness in Marcus' statement.

There was a time of silence, and then Marcus' voice echoed through the corridor.

"You said the rabbi bade you leave the room, so it would be accurate to say that you didn't actually see the healing, wouldn't it?"

"Yes, but the rabbi told us to leave the room."

"And why do you think he did that?" sneered Marcus.

"I don't know."

"So you couldn't see the deception, that's why," Marcus hissed. "And tell me, what did this Jairus say about it?"

"Nothing. He said nothing. Almost as if..."

"As if... what? She was never really dead? As if it were all some grand illusion to fool the people? And now you come here with this fabricated story about raising someone from the dead? I've heard enough! You will speak of this to no one. Do you hear me? No one! If you do, you will experience the justice of Rome by my hand. Am I clear?"

A quaking voice responded. "Of course, Centurion. I will tell no one."

Marcus' voice boomed. "Leave us!"

As scurrying footsteps faded away, a chill ran down Hadassah's back. *Jairus? I've heard that name before. Who is he?*

She struggled to associate the name with a face, and then it came to her.

He was the man with Yeshua when Judith was healed! His daughter had just died. That has to be who he's talking about!

When Marcus spoke again, she refocused her attention to his voice.

"It's time to do something about this *rabbi*," spewed Marcus vehemently. "He is becoming more than just a simple annoyance. When news of this supposed resurrection is added to all the other contrived miracles, the people will be even more incited to rebel!" He slammed his fist on a table. "Yeshua is becoming a very serious problem for Rome."

"Surely you can't mean that, Marcus. You said yourself that he's just a carpenter," Justus argued. "How could he be such a problem?"

"You can't be that stupid as to think this man cannot incite rebellion." Disgust accompanied Marcus' stinging words. "You know nothing. I will leave for Jerusalem at sunrise. It is time to end this!"

It suddenly became quiet, and Hadassah held her breath expectantly.

"Marcus, wait!"

Footsteps came her way, and Hadassah froze in fear, pressing herself deeper into the shadows. She could almost feel the pounding of his steps as he approached her hiding place. She desperately prayed.

Please don't let him find me!

Suddenly, the sound of his steps stopped, then seemed to fade away. She allowed herself to exhale. She whispered a prayer of thanksgiving, then quickly crept from her spot and silently retreated into the hallway and back to her room. When she closed the door, she fell against it. As she reflected on Marcus' hate-filled comments, her body shuddered involuntarily.

What does he mean 'It's time to end this?' What's he going to do to Yeshua?

* * * * * *

Streaks of pale pink appeared in the sky as the darkness of night faded into dawn. Finding sleep elusive, Hadassah rose early seeking a place to quietly pray to her God. Wrapping her simlāh around her shoulders, she stepped out onto the open walkway of the upper floor. From here, she could easily see the courtyard garden below. Droplets of dew glistened on unopened blossoms as the morning light began to bathe the awakening flowers in its warmth. As she had expected, the enclosure was empty. Closing her eyes, she rested her arms on the short wall along the walkway and tilted her head back, basking in the first rays of sunlight as they kissed her cheeks.

O God, thou art my God; early will I seek thee: my soul thirsteth for thee, my flesh longeth for thee in a dry and thirsty land, where no water is—

A clip-clopping sound interrupted the tranquility of her time with God, and she reluctantly opened her eyes. Turning toward the sound, she saw the familiar crested helmet and red cloak as Marcus rode toward the gates of the estate.

Oh, Marcus, why? Why can't you believe?

The fear within her was overwhelming as she watched him riding atop Ares. Knowing how Marcus felt about Yeshua scared her, but she felt helpless to do anything about it. Downcast, she groaned within herself as an emptiness threatened to engulf her. Unable to watch him without hurting inside, she turned away and reentered the house, never seeing Marcus stop and turn his head one last time toward her window.

Chapter Thirteen

"I am the living bread which came down from heaven: if any man eat of this bread, he shall live for ever: and the bread that I will give is my flesh, which I will give for the life of the world." John 6:51

"Look who's back from a long night of fishing!" Zara's eyes sparkled as she and her companion walked up to Hadassah.

"Shalom, Hadassah."

"Uri! I haven't seen you since you returned from Jerusalem! I suppose you've been busy with a certain someone!" laughed Hadassah.

"I will not deny that I have monopolized his time since he's been back," said Zara proudly. "And frankly, I'm glad he's finally back. Jerusalem is not safe. Look, he leaves me only to come back with this." She raised a finger to touch a small pink scar on Uri's cheek.

He shrugged. "It is really nothing. Just roughhousing that got out of hand. I guess I was too stupid to know when to duck." He shot a lopsided grin to the women.

"All the more reason to stay close to me," affirmed Zara. "Uri, tell Hadassah what you told me about Yeshua." Her eyes twinkled with delight. "Tell her, Uri. Tell her about Yeshua!"

"Yeshua? What about him?" asked Hadassah, her curiosity aroused.

"You may find this hard to believe, Hadassah, but I promise you, it's all true," he began. "We were all moving as one. The crowd was great in size. Too many to number." He slowed his steps so the women could keep up with him. "With Passover so near, many of us were making the pilgrimage to Jerusalem. But whatever the reason, the multitude was great... men, women, children... We all stopped to hear him speak." His eager eyes scanned the shoreline of the Sea of Galilee as they neared its waters, and he gestured to the far side of the sea.

"It was over there. As I said, we were all eager to hear Yeshua speak, so when he stopped, everyone quickly found a place to sit. Of course, we all hoped it would be more than a time of rest, and it was! He began to share his thoughts with us, and it was like feasting at a banquet table! So much was put before us! He spoke of things I have never heard before, and when those with diseases approached him, He healed them all!" Uri's excitement was uncontainable, and his pace increased as he neared the area where fishing boats had come into shore.

"So much time passed, but no one rose to leave. There we all sat." He paused for a moment, a faraway look in his eyes. "It was nearing the time of the noonday meal. We should have been farther along where we could have purchased food, but we had tarried, listening to Yeshua's words. By now, many were hungry, including me, but anything I had brought, I had eaten long ago. It was the same for nearly everyone. So you know what Yeshua did?" He turned to Hadassah. "He fed us! All of us. Yes, he fed us all! We had fish, bread, enough to satisfy every person there! How, you ask? I'll tell you how.

"I thought nothing of it until Andrew came by to collect anything that had not been consumed. I gathered the remnants from those around me, and as I put them into his basket, already nearly full, I might add, I asked him from where all this food had come, and he looked at me with a strange grin on his face."

Uri became more animated, gesturing with his arms as he spoke with greater enthusiasm. "He motioned for me to come nearer to him. When I did, Andrew told me that the Master had provided the food. I had walked near enough to Yeshua to know he carried nothing with him, so I wondered where he had gotten enough food to feed thousands. I must have looked somewhat perplexed, so Andrew leaned close and said that the Master fed us all from a boy's lunch."

Hadassah's brow furrowed as she came to a stop. "A boy's lunch? What do you mean?"

"I mean Yeshua took one boy's lunch and fed us all. *One* lunch." Uri continued with a dramatic flair, sweeping a hand in an arc in front of him. "The entire throng! Thousands of us! We were all fed with a few loaves of bread and a couple of fish from that lunch! That's what Andrew said, and now they were collecting all the leftover pieces. I don't know what they were going to do with them, but I saw several of the men return to Yeshua with full baskets!"

Zara looked at Hadassah. "There's more, too! Tell her, Uri!"

He laughed at her childlike enthusiasm. "I will, my sweet Zara."

"There's more?" Hadassah's eyes glistened in anticipation as she glanced over at the tall young man.

"Indeed–" He stopped abruptly, as he narrowed his eyes and looked toward the fishing boats. "Over there! There he is!"

Hadassah scanned the crowd in the vicinity of where Uri's tanned finger indicated. She shielded her eyes from the hot midday sun and squinted her eyes.

"I don't see him, Uri," stated Zara as she strained to see Yeshua. "Are you sure?"

"Yes, Zara! Look! There! Near the shoreline! See him?"

People were clustered around a group of fishermen, and Hadassah finally saw Yeshua in the midst of them. He was still a good distance away, but she knew him immediately. There was no doubt in her mind. It was him! Her heart began to beat faster, and she hastened her step to keep up with Uri.

"Please tell me, Uri. What is the rest that you have to share?" pleaded Hadassah as they hurried closer to the gathering.

Uri grinned at her and nodded. "Well, after he fed us, the fishermen took their boats and left, but Yeshua stayed behind with us. I don't know why. Maybe he was tired, or maybe he just wanted to be with us. For whatever reason, he stayed. So all the boats left. But then, the next morning when we awoke, he was gone. Now remember, *all* the boats had left the previous night. Yeshua had no boat with which to cross the sea."

His hushed voice made Hadassah lean closer to him. "Some heard the fishermen say he joined them on their boat later that night by..." He waited until he had her total attention. "... *walking to them on the water.*"

Hadassah came to a sudden halt, and her mouth dropped open as she stared at Uri in disbelief.

He stopped and turned to her, nodding smugly. "That's right. You heard me, and I promise you I am not lying. Yeshua walked on the water to their boat, and then the men brought him to this side of the sea."

"That's impossible!" protested Hadassah.

"I know," agreed Uri. "Unless..."

"Unless... you're God," finished Hadassah slowly, allowing her eyes to settle on the man standing by the shore of Galilee.

* * * * * *

They found a place in the middle of the crowd where they could sit and easily see Yeshua. Animated conversations surrounded them, and Hadassah heard the word "miracle" repeated again and again.

Suddenly, a man stood up and shouted toward Yeshua. "Rabbi, tell us, how did you get here?"

Yeshua turned and faced the standing man. A hush fell over the multitude, and even Hadassah leaned forward to hear the answer.

"You seek me not because you saw the miracles, but because you did eat of the loaves and were filled. Labor not for the meat which perishes, but for that meat which endures unto everlasting life, which the Son of man shall give unto you, for him has God the Father sealed."

"What shall we do that we might work the works of God?"

"Our fathers did eat manna in the desert..."

Hadassah heard whisperings all around her as questions were asked again and again of the rabbi.

Yeshua's voice resonated through the air. "Verily, I say unto you, Moses gave you not that bread from heaven, but my Father gives you the true bread from heaven. For the bread of God is he which comes down from heaven and gives life unto the world."

Several voices rang out.

"We want this bread!"

"Rabbi, give us this bread!"

Hadassah's gaze was fixated on Yeshua. Everyone else seemed to fade from her view as she waited in anticipation.

Yes! I want this bread, too!

When he finally spoke, his words stunned her.

"I am the bread of life. He that comes to me shall never hunger, and he that believes on me shall never thirst." Yeshua paused for a moment as murmurs arose from the people.

"What does he mean, Uri?" whispered Zara.

Uri just shook his head, his wrinkled brow conveying the same question in his own mind. "I don't know. He often speaks in ways that are difficult to understand."

A hush descended upon the throng as Yeshua began to speak again. "But I said unto you, that you also have seen me and believe not. All that the Father gives me shall come to me, and him that comes to me I will in no wise cast out.

"For I came down from heaven, not to do my own will, but the will of Him that sent me. And this is the Father's will which has sent me, that of all which he has given me I should lose nothing, but should raise it up again at the last day. And this is the will of Him that sent me, that every one which sees the Son, and believes on Him, may have everlasting life, and I will raise him up at the last day."

Hadassah glanced up at Uri. His eyes were stayed on Yeshua, even though the rabbi was now sitting, conversing with those nearest him, his words no longer for all to hear. Uri abruptly rose, leaving the women behind as he sprinted to the water's edge.

"Where is he going?" asked Hadassah.

Zara just shook her head.

The two women sat quietly, contemplating what they had heard. All around them, conversations sprang up, but the content was the same.

"Is this not Yeshua, the son of Yosef?"

"We know his parents, don't we?"

"How is it that he says, 'I came from heaven'?"

Her brow furrowed as she listened to more and more comments of doubt, and her own heart wrestled with the words she had heard Yeshua speak.

Is he saying that he is the Son of God?

Hadassah's train of thought was interrupted when Uri returned. "I knew it! He is the one! Yeshua will lead us to victory over those Roman dogs. We won't rest until every one of them is dead and gone. Israel will be free!"

Hadassah turned to him. His dark eyes burned with a passion she had never seen in him before, and it unsettled her.

"What are you talking about? Did he say that to you?" she asked, afraid of the answer. She struggled to reconcile the man who spoke of peace and love with Uri's words of hate.

"Not in so many words," admitted the young man, his eager eyes still fixed on Yeshua. "But believe me, he will rise up soon enough, and when he does, all the world will take notice. Our king has come!"

"But Yeshua doesn't speak of war," protested Hadassah as she returned her sights to the man at the water's edge.

"Not overtly, of course. It would be too dangerous for him. But in due time, he will show the world that he is our Messiah, and Israel will be returned to its people once again." Uri was confident in his assessment, and the satisfaction that radiated from his face troubled Hadassah, but she held her tongue.

Could Yeshua really be our Messiah?

* * * * * *

The days had passed quickly, and although Judith's care no longer filled her hours, Hadassah still kept herself busy. She filled her free time with other duties that lessened the workload for others, primarily because it kept her from thinking about Uri and Marcus. As she worked, her thoughts were now occupied with Yeshua's teachings and the possibility that he could be exactly who he said he was.

If Yeshua is our Messiah, surely, he will free us from the Romans. Surely, he will deliver us. That is what the prophets have told us. He will establish his throne forever, that's what the Scriptures say, but what of the Romans? What will happen to them? What will happen to Marcus?

Finished with her midday chores, she was relaxing in the garden when Zara entered and rushed over to her. Collapsing to the bench upon which Hadassah sat, tears streamed down the young woman's face as she sobbed into the skirt of Hadassah's tunic.

"Zara, what's wrong?" Hadassah wrapped her arm around her friend's shaking shoulders and pulled her nearer.

"He's going to Jerusalem!" Zara wailed as tears coursed down her cheeks.

"Who?" Hadassah brushed a lock of hair from Zara's forehead. "Uri?"

"Yes." Her sobs continued as she twisted the ends of her shawl in her hands. "He's leaving after Shabbat. Oh, Hadassah, what will I do?"

The seventh day of the Jewish week, Shabbat was a day of rest and abstention from any type of work, including long distance travel. Therefore, according to what Zara said, Uri would be gone in forty-eight hours.

"Again? Why is he going to Jerusalem this time?"

"He won't admit the real reason, well, not to me anyway." Zara's lower lip trembled as she spoke in a whisper. "But I know, Hadassah. I know, and I'm afraid he'll never come back to me!"

"Why wouldn't he come back, Zara? He cares for you."

"Ever since that day we saw Yeshua, he's been so different. All he talks about is Yeshua destroying Rome and establishing his kingdom. He wants to be part of it, and that's why he's going! I just know it!" she wailed.

"I'm sorry. I don't understand."

Zara shook her head forlornly as she explained. "Hadassah, he wants to be part of the fight. Everything he talks about centers on rebelling and overthrowing the Romans."

"Doesn't every young Jewish man say that? It never comes to anything. It's just talk."

Zara glanced around them before she spoke, then in a tortured voice, she said in hushed tones, "It's different now. When he talks about forcing the Romans out of Israel, his eyes burn with a passion I've never seen before. He's so full of hatred! That's all he talks about. It scares me, Hadassah. And now he told me he's leaving!"

Hadassah pulled back a bit and looked at Zara for an explanation. "It would be impossible to defeat the Romans. He cannot be serious."

"He says there are lots who think the same way he does. He speaks only of how the Romans have no right to be here. How this is our land, and we should take it back no matter the cost! Even if it means all-out war!"

Hadassah shuddered as she grasped what Zara was saying.

War?

"Oh, Hadassah, what am I going to do? He won't listen to me. He said if I cared about him at all, I would understand and support him." Zara dropped her face into her hands and wept bitterly. "He's leaving with a group of friends who are as fanatical as he."

"Friends? What friends?"

"Others who are willing to go to Jerusalem and fight for Israel, I suppose. Uri said lots of the followers are urging Yeshua to lead all of Judea to freedom as its king." Zara dabbed her eyes with her apron.

"But Yeshua never speaks of war. He only speaks of peace."

"I know. But Uri said fighting is the only way, and all his friends agree. Uri said it's only a matter of time before Yeshua sees that his leadership is all that is needed to end the Roman occupation."

"He can't believe that!"

"With his entire being," replied Zara bitterly. Her countenance remained despondent, but no more tears fell as she shrugged her shoulders. "Uri says all it will take is for Yeshua to make his declaration at the right time, and they all are urging him to do so in Jerusalem. Uri said the prophets wrote that God would send us a king to deliver us, and everyone believes that king is Yeshua."

"But Yeshua has never spoken of himself as a king."

"Uri says it's because too many Roman ears are listening. He says Yeshua must speak of overthrowing Rome only in private, or he risks arrest."

"And Uri has actually heard him say that?"

Zara shook her head. "I don't know. He's not part of those closest to Yeshua, but he has friends who are confident the announcement will be soon."

"I don't understand. Yeshua speaks of love, not war. His messages never support open rebellion. Surely, Uri knows that?"

"He believes that Yeshua will rise up and lead the Jews to victory over Rome once the rebellion begins."

"I cannot imagine Yeshua leading an army into battle. He's not a military leader, not like Marcus anyway."

"Uri sure thinks he can be. In fact, that's why he's leaving. He's so convinced that it scares me."

"What do you mean?" Apprehension rose in Hadassah when she saw the fearful look in Zara's eyes. "Is there more?"

"He said he and his friends would do whatever it takes."

"Whatever it takes? What does that mean?"

Zara wailed, "It means I will be a widow before I am ever a bride!" She dropped her head into her hands and sobbed uncontrollably.

Hadassah's mouth parted slightly, but no words came out. The only sounds that could be heard were Zara's crying and the breeze blowing through the swaying palms. She pulled her distraught friend to her. "I'm so sorry, Zara. Surely, this will all pass. Uri will come to his senses. He has to." Her unconvincing voice faded in the wind.

* * * * * *

Shabbat was usually a joyous time for Hadassah when she set aside all the concerns of daily living and focused on her Jewish heritage and the many blessings the Lord had bestowed upon her. Judith had understood her niece's desire to honor God in this weekly observance, and although she herself did not hold to the Jewish traditions of the day of rest, she allowed Hadassah to finish her duties early in order to adhere to the traditions of their people.

Hadassah had already bathed herself, and now she slipped her sadin over her head. The linen underdress, like the rest of her Shabbat wardrobe, had belonged to her mother, and Hadassah cherished the garments. She ran her hands down the fabric, allowing it to fall into place. Reaching into her small closet, she retrieved her most treasured garment, her mother's flaxen kethōneth. Embroidered with green and lavender threads at the hem and sleeve ends, it had long lost her mother's perfumed scent, but Hadassah still brought it up to her face and inhaled deeply.

Wearing her mother's clothing kept the memory of her family alive in her heart, and she cherished every opportunity she had to wear the precious garment. Donning the kethōneth, she smoothed its fabric over the sadin. Shabbat was always a time when the Jews wore their finest apparel as they honored God, and although Hadassah couldn't prepare the Shabbat feasts or attend all the synagogue services, she could dress to please the Lord as she celebrated the day in her room.

Shortly before sunset, Hadassah lit two candles in her room, which represented the two components of Shabbat: zachor and shamor, remembering and observing. These were required of the Jews each week, and Hadassah did her best to follow the commandments, and therefore she covered her eyes from the tiny flames until she had uttered the prayer of her forefathers.

"Blessed are you, Lord, our God, sovereign of the universe, who has sanctified us with His commandments and commanded us to light the lights of Shabbat."

Following zachor, the command to remember, Hadassah quietly sat and thought about the times the Lord had delivered the Jewish people. First, the Hebrews were led from Egypt by Moses. Second, He had saved them from annihilation through the actions of the beautiful Jewess queen, Esther, and there was the time when the Jews were brought back from Babylonian captivity to Jerusalem by Nehemiah to rebuild their holy city.

"Blessed are you, Lord, our God, King of the Universe, for by your hand we were delivered of the oppression by the Egyptians and brought back to our land. By your mighty hand, we were brought back from captivity to the holy city."

Unable to follow shamor, the observance of the Shabbat laws, in their entirety, Hadassah did her best to do what she could. Forbidden to labor during the period of Shabbat, she had completed all the tasks necessary for Judith to be comfortable until the following evening when the first three stars appeared in the sky signifying the ending of Shabbat and the return of normal daily activities.

As the sun sank below the horizon and the shadows began to form, Hadassah retreated to her special place of solitude in the garden courtyard to pray. Lowering herself to her knees by a bench in a secluded corner, she bowed her head.

"Hear, O Israel, the Lord is our God, the Lord is One," she began to recite the shema, the evening prayer. "Blessed be the Name of His glorious kingdom for ever and ever..."

* * * * * *

"Uri left this morning."

Startled, Hadassah looked up from filling her water jug into Zara's puffy red eyes. "Zara! I didn't hear you." She rose from the rocky shore and embraced her friend. She stepped back and looked at Zara's forlorn face. "I'm so sorry. Did he say anything to you before he left?"

Zara's downcast eyes reflected the despair in her heart. "He said he was called by the Almighty to fight this battle and free us from Roman oppression. I think he's going to Jerusalem to fight with the Sicarii. He didn't say that, but I know that's where he's going."

Hadassah's eyes widened, and she stood speechless.

The Sicarii? Surely Uri wouldn't be a part of them. They think nothing of using violence and bloodshed to achieve their goals.

Zara began to weep. "He said it is the duty of every true Jews to rise up and rid Israel of Roman rule. He said everyone who stands with Rome should be wiped off the face of this earth. I know I will never see him again, Hadassah. I just know it."

"Anyone who stands with Rome? That could be Jews as well as Romans!" Hadassah shuddered involuntarily. "He can't mean that!"

"He means it. His head is filled with such hatred for Rome. All he wants to do is rid Israel of them all. No matter what the cost."

"Doesn't he realize the cost could be the lives of our own people?" Her fears were slowly being replaced with anger. "These zealots are fools to think they can stand up against Rome."

"What can I do? I pleaded with him, but to no avail. I have prayed until I can pray no more." She looked at Hadassah miserably. "And you know what the worst thing is? Even if something happens to him, I'll probably never know. He just won't ever return." She paused and then asked fearfully, "Do you think he ever really cared for me?"

"Of course, he cares for you, Zara." She frowned. Her words sounded so hollow. "We must continue to pray that Uri will come to his senses."

Zara took a deep breath. "I heard the zealots were very active in Jerusalem. Many are crucified for all to see." She burst forth in another bout of crying, burying her face in her hands.

Hadassah winced. She had never witnessed a crucifixion, and she hoped she never would. The cruelest of punishments, she had refused to think it would ever touch her life. She could not imagine Uri nailed to a cross. He was so young and had his whole life ahead of him, and most of all, he was betrothed to Zara. They were planning a future together.

"He will return, Zara. His love for you will bring him home." Hadassah pulled her friend into her arms and held her until the weeping subsided. All the while, she couldn't force the doubts from her mind.

What will we do if Uri doesn't come home

Chapter Fourteen

"Jesus saith unto her, Said I not unto thee, that, if thou wouldest believe, thou shouldest see the glory of God?" John 11:40

There was no denying the physical change in Judith, but Hadassah also saw a spiritual change as well. Judith was now a woman who had finally found peace with the true God. She had destroyed the tiny idols that had stood watch over her bedchamber for years, and Hadassah had rejoiced when the celestial blanket had disappeared. When Judith joined her niece for worship at the synagogue, Hadassah had nearly cried. Free from the fatigue and despondency of her past illness, Judith was eager to do things of which she had been denied for so long, so when she received notification of a wedding celebration in Bethany from Leah, Justus' distant cousin, she immediately made plans to attend. She insisted that Hadassah accompany her, and Justus, glad to be relieved of the obligation, had no objections.

Hadassah had never been far from Capernaum, and this upcoming trip thrilled her. She had spent days packing and repacking until she was finally convinced she had everything that she or Judith would need, including a plethora of medicinal herbs and teas in the event sickness might plague them while traveling.

The day of their departure greeted them with clear blue skies and warm temperatures. A faint breeze promised a comfortable morning of travel, and Hadassah was excited to leave shortly after sunrise. Since he was not accompanying them, Justus had made the arrangements for the women to travel with a large caravan to guarantee safety as well as comfort during the journey. Hadassah had no worries as they said their goodbyes, and she eagerly joined the other travelers on their way to Jerusalem.

They started out toward the southern end of the Sea of Tiberias, but due to racial tensions between the Samaritans and the Jews, the caravan had to cross east over the Jordan River for the most secure route to Jerusalem, the Jericho Road. As they made their way toward Decapolis, bypassing the region known as Samaria, they stopped briefly at a freshwater spring to water the animals and nourish the travelers.

Hadassah pulled out a sack of almonds, a block of goat cheese, and a loaf of bread.

"Dodah, some cheese?"

Judith took a chunk of the semi-soft cheese from Hadassah along with a large piece of bread. "It's amazing how much better a meal is when you are in the fresh air!"

Hadassah laughed as she munched on a handful of almonds. "I agree. Here, take some water." She held a small bottle out.

"Thank you," said Judith as she sipped the cool liquid. "This is nice."

Hadassah nodded. "We are so blessed, Dodah. The weather is perfect. We have good traveling companions, and it seems as though we have made excellent time."

"Indeed we have," agreed Judith. "Even though we have several days of travel ahead of us, I believe it will be quite a pleasant journey."

"The Almighty is with us, Dodah. We have nothing to fear."

"You are such an encouragement to me, my sweet Hadassah."

Although Passover was still a few weeks away, the Jericho Road had a greater number of travelers than usual. Some were traders, while others were making an early pilgrimage to the holy city. Hadassah and Judith were just two among many, but there was a common bond among the travelers, so it was as if a big family was making the trip together.

Each day was the same. During the morning, makeshift tents were disassembled and packed away, the animals were fed and watered, and the people broke their fasts with bread, fruit and cheese. In the early afternoon, there was a brief rest to care for the animals and take the midday meal. A couple more hours of travel passed until it was time to set up camp for the night. New friends were made as people gathered together for the evening meal and shared what they had brought with all who sat down to break bread, no matter their final destination or their point of origin.

Hadassah was surprised at how well Judith was traveling now. Although they had planned two weeks for the journey, the caravan made good time and Judith and Hadassah arrived at Bethany ten days after leaving

Capernaum. Located on the eastern slope of the Mount of Olives, a mile or so from the summit, Bethany was a small village, but it was here that Justus' paternal family had lived for generations.

"It's been so long since I've been here," commented Judith as her eyes took in the tiny hamlet. "I can't believe Leah's daughter is getting married. It seems like only yesterday that I met Leah. I was newly married myself, unsure of my place in the family, and Leah hugged me and welcomed me into her home without any reservation." Judith laughed lightly. "She said she was so happy that Justus had found himself a… oh, how did she put it? Oh, yes… a wife of proper heritage."

"Proper heritage?" Hadassah's quizzical look prompted an explanation from her aunt.

"Justus' first wife was completely Roman. I guess this side of the family didn't really approve, but he moved to Rome, so…" She shrugged her shoulders, then sighed. "I suppose I was a disappointment as well. After we married, I wanted to be a good wife, so I… I embraced the religion of Rome to please Justus." Her blue eyes reflected remorse. "Not the proper heritage that was expected."

Hadassah reached out and took her aunt's hand. "But you are a daughter of Zion, Dodah, and you are of the proper heritage now."

* * * * * *

It had been years since Judith and Leah had seen one another, making their reunion so much the sweeter. As the older women discussed the merits of the upcoming marriage and the days of celebration to come, Hadassah busied herself by unpacking their belongings and settling into their room.

Participation in the festivities of a marriage was new to Hadassah. Although many of her friends had married in Capernaum, she had never been a part of the extended celebration due to Judith's need for her to always be close at hand. Now, she savored every part of the wedding festivities, especially helping prepare the meals for the families and friends of the betrothed couple.

The day of the wedding feast filled the air with excitement as the final preparations for the celebratory meal were made. Platters of fresh fish were set upon a long table next to heaping bowls of broad beans, chickpeas, and lentils. Smaller bowls of assorted fruits and nuts were placed within easy reach of every guest. The aroma of baking bread wafted from the oven through the entire house.

The food preparation had been ongoing through the week, and Hadassah had enjoyed helping in whatever capacity she was asked. She proved to be a great help to the women in charge of the meals.

"Hadassah, I praise the Holy One for bringing you to us," stated Martha, one of the women preparing the dough for several more loaves of bread.

Smiling, Hadassah said, "It is a small thing that I can do for the hospitality that my aunt and I have been shown. It is good to be useful."

"Yes, serving others is a joy for me, and I see it is the same for you. And what more joyous occasion than a wedding!" Martha's eyes sparkled with delight.

"It is wonderful, isn't it?" agreed Hadassah. "Such a blessed event!"

"Tell me, have you a beloved?" asked Martha as she shaped the raw loaf on a baking stone.

Hadassah's face reddened as she pounded a fist into her own ball of bread dough. "No. There is no one."

The older woman smiled knowingly. "I only wish my brother were younger and in better health. I would introduce you to him!"

Hadassah felt the heat rise in her cheeks as she stretched and pulled her dough. She struggled to find words to explain her situation. "I chose to care for my aunt—"

"Hadassah," began Martha as she turned to the young woman. "You must never feel the need to apologize for who you are. I meant no offense, and I am sorry to have embarrassed you. Serving others is an honor that many do not understand."

Hadassah looked up into Martha's loving eyes.

"We bless the Lord through our service. Your devotion to your family delights Him, and when it is time for you to marry, He will send the right man. Until then, do not be ashamed of who you are, for you are the child of the Almighty, and that is a reason to rejoice."

A smile of gratitude crept onto Hadassah's face, and impulsively she hugged Martha.

"Thank you for your kind words. I cannot tell you how you have ministered to my heart."

Martha reached out and tucked a loose tendril of black hair behind Hadassah's ear. "Let us get back to work, my child. There is a hungry group we need to feed."

With a lighter spirit, Hadassah joyfully immersed herself in the cooking, and at the day's end, she slept with a contented heart, looking forward to working beside Martha again the next day.

* * * * * *

The following day, the cooking resumed early. There were many to feed as the celebration still had several days to go. Even though the sun had barely begun its daily trek across the sky when Hadassah arrived, the kitchen was bustling with activity. Platters were being filled with figs, dates and apricots. Bowls of almonds and honey were set out, along with trays of broiled whitefish.

Hadassah took her place beside one of the girls baking bread and began to knead a ball of dough as she scanned the room.

"Martha is not here?" she asked as she folded the dough over on itself.

"No. Her brother, Lazarus, is very ill. She stayed with her sister to care for him. He is not expected to... to be with us for much longer."

Hadassah worked quickly, and when all the loaves were ready for the baking, she rushed to her room, washed her face and hands, and grabbed her shawl. Finding Judith, she asked and received her aunt's permission to seek out Martha and help her family in any way possible.

The scene at Martha's home was a sharp contrast to the house she had just left. There were no sounds of rejoicing. There were no fragrant aromas of delicious foods being prepared. There was an air of expectancy, but one that was not desired.

Hadassah hesitated at the doorway, then entered, passing a young woman silently weeping.

"Shalom," whispered Hadassah as she entered the house. Looking around, she spied Martha carrying a tray of cheeses and bread to a table. Strain was etched all over the older woman's face. Hadassah hurried over to her.

"Let me have that," stated Hadassah taking the tray. She set it on a wooden table in the center of the room.

Martha's reddened eyes broke Hadassah's heart, and she simply reached out to take the older woman's hands in her own. "I am here," she said softly. "Tell me what to do."

"He is so sick, Hadassah. We've sent for the Master, but he has not come. If he were here..." She began to weep.

Impulsively, Hadassah wrapped her arms around the older woman until the tears subsided. Before she could offer any words of comfort, the quiet patter of footsteps approached them.

"Martha?" The voice was soft and low, almost hesitant.

Hadassah turned her head and beheld a woman who could have been a younger version of Martha. Dark hair framed a heart-shaped face, and sorrowful brown eyes were misty with unshed tears. Martha turned and reached for the other woman's hand.

"Mary, this is the young woman I spoke of. Judith's niece." Martha dabbed at her tear-swollen eyes with a small napkin. "Hadassah, this is my sister, Mary. She—"

"Forgive me, but we must not tarry. You must come now, my sister," urged Mary, her eyes saying what her heart could not voice.

Martha stared into Mary's grief-stricken eyes and gasped. "No! Not yet! Not now! The Master has not yet arrived!" Together, the sisters rushed to the bedchamber where their brother lay, leaving Hadassah standing alone in the hallway.

She quietly moved into the cooking area and automatically began to finish the preparations for the midday meal. Efficient as always, Martha's kitchen was easy to navigate, and Hadassah found everything she required to attend to the physical needs of the family during their official time of mourning. The aroma of vegetable stew and fresh bread soon filled the house. Satisfied with the prepared meal, Hadassah employed the assistance of a young girl to help tidy the home as mourners would be arriving as soon as Lazarus' passing was made known.

Making sure the oil lamps were filled and the home was made ready for those who would come to pay their respects to Martha and Mary, Hadassah expertly assigned work to those desiring to help out. Floors were swept, curtains were drawn, and incense was set out, ready to be lit when needed.

Hadassah walked through the home one final time, checking to be sure everything was as it should be for the final goodbye to the beloved brother of her new friends. As she neared the bedchamber of Lazarus, sounds of weeping mingled with heartbroken voices could be heard beyond the closed door.

"If only he had been here, Mary, our brother would still be alive," moaned Martha.

"I know," stated Mary, her own voice heavy with anguish. "I'm sure if he could have been here, he would have been."

"Why?" cried Martha. "Why didn't he come? He could have saved him." Inconsolable weeping echoed into the hallway.

"Martha, you know he loved Lazarus like a brother. If it were possible…"

"Oh, Mary!" she wailed. "He is gone! Our brother is gone!" Once more, the muffled sobbing of intense loss was all that could be heard.

Tears filled her own eyes as Hadassah leaned back against the wall across from Lazarus' room and prayed that God would comfort the sisters as only He could do.

O God, whoever this friend is of theirs, please send him soon. He may not be able to help Lazarus now, but he may be able to offer comfort to Martha and Mary in this time of need.

* * * * * *

Judith had supported Hadassah's desire to provide comfort to Martha and Mary, so after her daily responsibilities to the bride's family were completed, Hadassah hurried over to the sisters' home to help them through their grieving.

It had been four days since Lazarus had been wrapped in linens, prepared with aromatic spices and fragrant herbs, and placed in his tomb. The house was quiet when Hadassah arrived, and as she entered, Martha was wrapping a light blue shawl around her shoulders.

"Shalom, Martha," Hadassah said softly as she greeted her friend.

Martha's forlorn smile met Hadassah's concerned look, and she reached out and patted her hand lovingly. "What would we have done without you, Hadassah? You have done so much for us, and we are so undeserving."

"I pray I have been a small bit of comfort to you and your sister."

"Indeed, you have. You have blessed us beyond measure. It was the Lord who sent you to us."

Hadassah lowered her eyes. The unexpected praise humbled her, and she was grateful she had been a help to Martha and her sister. "Your words are kind." She raised her head. "You are leaving?"

"I am going to meet the Master. We were told he was coming. Mary has chosen to stay, but I... I must go to him. I just can't sit here and wait."

Hadassah nodded in understanding. "Have you eaten?"

Martha shook her head slightly as she adjusted the shawl around her shoulders. "No. I find I have had little appetite these past few days."

"You must keep up your strength. Let me get you something to take with you." Without waiting for permission, Hadassah rose and softly padded into the kitchen.

When she returned to the main room with a small bundle of bread and fruit, Martha was no longer there.

"Martha?" Hadassah walked back toward the sleeping area. Hesitantly, she tapped on the door. There was no response.

She's gone to meet her friend.

Hadassah tucked the bread and fruit into her apron pocket.

She needs to eat. If I hurry, I can catch up with her.

Wrapping herself in a dark shawl, she left the quiet house. The tombs were on the eastern slope of the Mount of Olives, not too far from Bethany itself, and it was an easy walk, but a lengthy one. Far in the distance, she could hear the wails of the mourners. Their groanings seemed to hang suspended in the air like a thick fog blanketing everything.

As she made her way along the path, she rounded a bend just in time to see Martha fall at the feet of a man. Hadassah stopped and waited, not wanting to intrude on the sad reunion. Her gaze slowly lifted from the stooped figure of her friend to the face of the one for whom they had vainly waited. Her mouth dropped open at the sight of him as he reached out to the grieving woman.

Yeshua? It's you?

As she stood trying to make sense of what she was seeing, Martha's agonized words reached her ears.

"You gave sight to the blind! You healed the lame! Why couldn't you have come to save Lazarus? He loved you!" sobbed Martha. "Lord, if you had been here, my brother would not have died."

Martha's words were spoken from a broken heart. Her head was bowed, and her words were laced with intense sorrow as her sobbing resumed. Her entire body seemed to collapse as her broken spirit whispered, "But I know, that even now, whatsoever you ask of God, God will give it to you."

Please say something to comfort her.

Then Yeshua spoke. His words were few, but powerful. "Your brother shall rise again."

Hadassah's spirit groaned within her as she heard Martha acknowledge his words.

"I know that he shall rise again in the resurrection at the last day."

A tender gesture, Yeshua reached a hand to the grieving woman's shoulder. "Martha, I am the resurrection and the life. He that believes in me, though he were dead, yet shall he live. And whosoever lives and believes in me shall never die. Do you believe this?"

Martha's response was softly spoken, yet Hadassah heard it clearly. "Yea, Lord. I believe that you are the Christ, the Son of God, which should come into the world."

The Son of God?

Hadassah knew eavesdropping on their conversation was wrong, but she couldn't pull herself away. Her compulsion to hear their words intensified, and she strained to hear their voices clearly, while hoping she would be unnoticed.

So focused on Yeshua, Hadassah did not realize that Mary had passed her until she saw the bereaved woman bow down beside her sister at the feet of the rabbi.

"Lord," Mary quietly echoed her sister. "If you had been here, my brother would not have died."

Yeshua's eyes closed and deep anguish filled his features. His voice was laden with grief. "Where have you laid him?"

Martha pointed toward the tomb. "Lord, come and see."

As he walked by, Hadassah saw tears on his cheeks. Walking a respectable distance behind the trio, she heard the mourners whispering as she passed them.

"Could not this man, which opened the eyes of the blind, have caused that even this man should not have died?"

Yes! He could have saved Lazarus. Martha knew it, and so did Mary. No wonder their hearts are broken. Yeshua could have saved their brother.

She solemnly moved toward the tomb to join those who came to honor a cherished brother and a loyal friend.

Yeshua stopped directly in front of the massive rock obstructing the entrance to Lazarus' tomb. Martha and Mary stood behind him as they waited for him to finish his private mourning. When he turned to speak, his words shocked everyone who heard him.

"Take you away the stone."

An audible gasp filled the air as those who stood within range of hearing his command were stunned in disbelief. Eyes snapped open wide as heads turned toward Yeshua.

Martha spoke first, her words nearly apologetic as she gently reminded him. "Lord, by this time he stinks, for he has been dead four days."

Yeshua looked at her and spoke tenderly, helping her remember. "Said I not unto you that if you would believe, you should see the glory of God?"

As if chastised, Martha lowered her gaze, then turned to those by the gravesite. She nodded, and four men moved up to the huge boulder that covered the tomb's entrance. Grunted efforts finally succeeded in rolling the stone off to one side, and when the men backed away from the tomb, only silence filled the air. The wind had ceased; the birds had stopped their singing. Not one sound of mourning was uttered, and all eyes were riveted on Yeshua.

Finally, he lifted his eyes toward heaven and prayed aloud. "Father, I thank you that you have heard me. And I know that you hear me always, but because of the people which stand by, I said it that they may believe that you have sent me."

Although it was warm, Hadassah shivered involuntarily. She couldn't take her eyes off Yeshua. As he lowered his gaze to the open sepulchre, she held her breath in anticipation.

The Yeshua spoke. "Lazarus, come forth!"

His words were like rolling thunder, and Hadassah could almost feel the power in them. She strained to see if anything was happening. Narrowing her eyes, she leaned forward and peered into the darkness of the tomb. Nothing.

And then she heard it.

A faint shuffling sound came from within. Yeshua remained unmoved, waiting patiently as others shifted their bodies for a better line of sight. Their questioning eyes moved from the man standing before the sepulchre to one another, then back to the tomb. The stirrings became louder, and it seemed as though something or someone was moving inside the burial chamber.

Suddenly, the faint image of a man materialized deep inside the tomb. As the sounds of labored movement increased, the image became more defined. From within the shadows of the tomb, bound hand and foot with grave clothes, hobbled the once-dead brother of Martha and Mary.

Lazarus was alive!

Time seemed to stand still. No one moved; no one spoke. Everyone stood spellbound at the sight of the "dead" man standing in the sepulchre's opening. Martha and Mary stood speechless as they beheld the brother they had recently buried now standing alive in front of them. Before they could utter a word, Yeshua spoke.

"Loose him and let him go," he said as he calmly stepped aside.

Hadassah staggered backward away from the tomb as Mary and Martha rushed to Lazarus' side, yanking the strips of cloth from him. Standing in shocked silence, Hadassah struggled to comprehend what she was witnessing.

He's alive? Lazarus is alive?

Suddenly, shouts of jubilation erupted from those around the tomb as everyone gathered were now rejoicing in the fact that Lazarus was indeed alive! Their cries of mourning were replaced with exuberant praises, and Hadassah finally realized that what she had been wrestling with for so long had at last been resolved. She now knew the truth of Yeshua's identity! She lifted her voice in praise with the others!

It's true! Everything about Yeshua is true! He is the Son of God! Our Messiah has come!

Chapter Fifteen

"Saying, Blessed be the King that cometh in the name of the Lord: peace in heaven, and glory in the highest." Luke 19:38

Judith sat speechless as she listened to Hadassah recount the resurrection of Lazarus.

"And then Yeshua called out for him to come out of the tomb, and he did! Dodah, Lazarus had been dead for four days! He was in that grave. I saw them roll that stone away. I saw Lazarus stumble out, and when they removed the grave clothes, he didn't look at all like a dead man. He was just like you or me! He wasn't a spirit. He was alive! He was whole! I saw him embracing his sisters! I heard him speak! It was not a trick. It was real!"

Hadassah's hands waved about in the air as she talked, sparing no detail of the witnessed miracle. "I promise you, Dodah, everything I am telling you is true. Yeshua is the Son of God! I know it now! He raised a man from the dead! I saw it all!"

Her niece's animated demeanor made Judith laugh as she reached for Hadassah's hands. "How could I not believe you, Hadassah? The joy on your face speaks for you. There is not one bit of doubt in my heart." She closed her eyes for a moment, then opened them as she took a deep breath. "I believe all that you have told me, including..." Judith paused as a broad smile spread across her face. "Including the identity of our dear Yeshua! He must be the Son of the Most High! He is the One for whom we have waited! Yeshua is our Messiah!"

"Oh Dodah, how could we have not known? No one could have done all that he has if he was not God's Anointed One." Her voice broke as she fell into her aunt's arms. The joyous cries of both women rose far beyond the walls of their room into the courts of heaven.

"We have waited so long, Dodah. It's so hard to believe our Deliverer has finally come."

"To save us," confirmed Judith. "He is here to save us from the oppression of the Romans. We will finally have our land and our king."

"Our king..." Hadassah echoed in a reverent whisper.

* * * * * *

News of Lazarus' resurrection had spread quickly throughout the small town and beyond. People had flocked to the home of Martha and Mary to see this living miracle and the one responsible for it, but although Lazarus was there, Yeshua had left, disappointing many. Still many of the Jews who had heard of the miracle had joined with Hadassah and Judith in their belief of Yeshua as the One whom God had sent to free their people from Roman tyranny and occupation.

Later that day as Hadassah was gathering their belongings for the journey back to Capernaum, Judith entered the room and sat down opposite her niece.

"What would you think about observing the Passover in Jerusalem this year?"

Hadassah lifted her eyes to her aunt. "The Passover? In Jerusalem?"

"Well, I thought since we were already here," Judith began, "and Passover is less than three weeks from now. I thought we could stay and celebrate it in Jerusalem. It has been so long since I've been to the holy city. We might even see Yeshua there. Maybe even another miracle? What do you think?"

Hadassah set the bundle of clothing down and knelt on the floor in front of her aunt. She was unable to hide her excitement. "That would be wonderful! To be in the holy city for Passover is something I have dreamed of. And to see Yeshua again would be... well, it would be beyond words, but..."

"But what?"

"Where will we stay? How can we remember the Passover as the Lord intends if we are not in our own home?"

Judith smiled. "Although it has been a long time since I have seen them, your grandfather's brother, your Dod Gabriel, his family still lives in Jerusalem. I know they would welcome us. There is always a place for family, especially those who come to the holy city to celebrate the Passover, plus there are many acquaintances of Justus in Jerusalem. We have no need to worry; it will be easy to find lodging with one of them if need be. Passover is a time for all to come together and remember our deliverance, especially now."

"Oh, Dodah! That would be perfect!"

Judith's heart rejoiced at the happiness her declaration had given Hadassah. "I hoped it would please you. You have done so much for me. I wanted to do something to show you how much I appreciate you. How much I love you." She reached out and stroked Hadassah's long hair. "Your mother would be so very proud of you, as am I. You have been my truest joy in life. My own, yet not my own."

"You are mother to me as if I had come from within you, Dodah. I could not have asked for someone more loving and caring than you have been to me. My mother would have been very proud of you as well."

Judith brushed a tear from her eye and took a deep breath, satisfied with the outcome of their conversation. "So, it is settled. We shall go to Jerusalem for the Passover. I shall send word to Justus, and then we will be on our way."

* * * * * *

The road from Bethany to Jerusalem was always busy, but even more so now with thousands of pilgrims traveling to the city for Passover. Merchants, traders, and a host of others journeying from Jericho joined Judith and Hadassah as they traveled from the southeast slope of the Mount of Olives toward the City of David. The distance between Bethany and Jerusalem could be traveled in less than two hours, and even with several rest stops, the women descended the western slope by the early afternoon.

As they neared the Kidron Valley, Hadassah lifted her eyes and beheld the Jewish temple in the distance. Crowning Mount Moriah, Herod's masterpiece was spectacular to behold! She drew in her breath sharply, and her audible gasp startled Judith, who whipped her head around toward her niece.

"Are you all right, Hadassah?" She reached a steadying hand out to her.

Nodding quickly, Hadassah said, "Oh yes, Dodah! I'm fine! It's just that I've never seen such a beautiful building. It shines like... like nothing I've ever seen before!"

Judith turned back toward Jerusalem and looked up at the monumental building that gleamed brilliantly in the sunlight. "It's like pure gold, isn't it? I am sure it will be even more glorious when we are closer. Let's rest here a moment."

As they shared a midday meal of smoked fish, olives and flatbread, they sat in awe staring at the temple. In all its glory, it stood majestically atop the most sacred piece of land in all of Israel. Believed by many of the Jews to be the very site of God's creation, it was here on this mountain that Abraham, the father of the Jewish people, had prepared to sacrifice his son Isaac in obedience to the God who had called him to this land. It was here that David decreed the city as the capital of his kingdom. And now, it was here that God's dwelling place had finally found a permanent home.

Commissioned by the Lord himself, King David's son, Solomon, built the first Jewish temple. After its destruction by the Babylonians, it was rebuilt by Zerubbabel and the Jews who had returned from captivity. However, it was the additional work commissioned by Herod the Great that transformed the temple into the magnificent structure that rose above Jerusalem now, and for the first-time visitor to the city, it was breathtaking to behold. Gazing upon the holiest of sites for the Jewish people stirred Hadassah's soul, and her excitement overcame her reverence for it.

"I cannot believe I am going to see Jerusalem! To walk the same streets as our forefathers! I never dreamed this day would come, Dodah!" declared Hadassah, her eyes sparkling. She stood to her feet, resisting the impulse to rush down the slope. "I cannot wait to enter through those gates!" She clasped her hands together and clutched them to her chest.

Judith rose to stand with her. She placed her arm around Hadassah's shoulders and drew her closely to her side. Her eyes remained on the city. "I haven't been here in a long time," she sighed wistfully. "It was before I married Justus. I came with my grandfather..." Her eyes held a faraway look.

"Three times a year, he would make the journey to celebrate the Feast days. It was written in the Torah, and he said it was his duty to God to come to Jerusalem to worship." She paused for a moment as if she had just wakened from a long dream, and then smiled. "Your father and I didn't really understand the significance of it all. It was just a glorious family outing to us in those days." Looking around, she pointed to an area where travelers passed before walking across the double-tiered bridge to the eastern gate of the city. "We must go that way."

"Why?"

"To be counted. It's for the Temple tax, I believe, but it's only the men that are truly counted, but we all must pass through. It will only take a moment, and then we will go our way. Come." Judith led Hadassah down the path.

As they neared the city, the Roman sites for crucifixion on the slopes of Mt. Olivet came into view. In plain sight of anyone heading into Jerusalem from Jericho, the rugged crosses stood as silent reminders of Roman justice. Here would hang those who dared to challenge the emperor or his representatives. The few lifeless bodies still hanging on the crosses were in the process of being taken down. It was nearly sunset, and Jewish custom was to remove the dead prior to nightfall.

Hadassah averted her eyes from the crosses as the bile rose in her throat. She unconsciously squeezed Judith's forearm as she held on to her aunt, the weakness in her legs threatening her stability as she walked. Judith said nothing to Hadassah, but simply patted her niece's hand as they moved quickly past the dead and dying toward the city gates.

"How could anyone do that to someone?" whispered Hadassah. "It's worse than the crimes themselves."

"That is exactly what the Romans want us to remember. Submission to their laws from fear of punishment," Judith replied softly.

"It's... it's horrible!" stammered Hadassah as her eyes followed a raven that lit on the outstretched arm of one of the condemned. Suddenly, she rushed away from the road to a secluded spot behind a huge olive tree. Her stomach revolted, and she was forced to empty its contents.

Judith hurried over and then waited with water for Hadassah to rinse her mouth and a clean cloth to wipe her face.

"Oh Dodah, I am so sorry," Hadassah apologized as she cleaned her face with the towel her aunt offered.

Judith lovingly brushed the hair away from her niece's forehead. "Crucifixion is a difficult thing to witness for anyone. It is cruel and brutal. You need not apologize. Let us hurry past."

Hadassah simply nodded and quickly followed after Judith as the road turned toward the gate. Walking together over the bridge, they left behind the dead and dying and headed toward the eastern gates of Zion, the holy city of God.

* * * * * *

True to Judith's words, they were welcomed with open arms to the family home of Hadassah's great uncle, Gabriel. His wife, Milcah, fussed around both of them, ushering them into the central room before disappearing into the cooking area.

"This is a miracle!" Milcah gushed as she reentered the room with a platter of grapes, figs, cheeses, and nuts. "Eat! You must eat! Your journey must have been long especially with so many coming to the holy city." She held out the dish, not setting it down until both women had taken a handful of almonds and some fruit. "And you," she turned to Hadassah as she set the plate on the table in front of them. "You are your mother's daughter! So beautiful!" She extended a plump finger and drew it down Hadassah's cheek.

"You knew my mother?" Hadassah sat forward expectantly.

"I only met her once, it was before you were born. I remember your father adored her. They could hardly wait for your birth."

"She is so much like Deborah," stated Judith proudly. "Not only in appearance, but they have the same heart. So loving and giving."

Faint memories in Hadassah's mind became a bit brighter as she listened to the stories of her mother. She reached out and squeezed Judith's hand while whispering, "Thank you for keeping my mother alive in my heart. How could I ever have survived without your love?"

To that, Judith could only gratefully nod her head as she wiped her own tears away.

"Enough! Enough!" chuckled Gabriel. "You will flood my house with your tears! I am blessed to have my nieces with us for this special time. This is a time to share with family, to reconnect with those we love." They spent the rest of the afternoon sharing stories of where life had taken them.

After Milcah had shown them where they would stay, Judith chose to rest, but Hadassah was eager to see Jerusalem. Venturing out into the bustling city, Hadassah was thrilled by its sights and sounds. She meandered through the ancient streets, passing merchants selling anything from spices and woven cloths to vegetables, fruits and nuts, and even flowers. Simply walking along the narrow streets thrilled her.

As she strolled along, she stopped every now and then to inspect the goods, but found nothing she needed, yet everything she wanted! Her eyes widened in delight as her fingers felt the fine woven linens on display, yet she refused to squander the few coins she had in her pockets.

"Hadassah? Is that you?"

Spinning around, she spied the one who called her name.

"Uri?"

His dark hair was much longer than she remembered, and his beard had grown out as well. Dressed all in black, his countenance was as hard as his gaze upon her. His sinister appearance unsettled her, but she forced a smile.

"What are you doing here? Is Zara with you?" His suspicious eyes darted from side to side as he spoke to her.

"I am here with my aunt for the Passover. Zara is not here with me. When I tell her I saw you, she will be so grieved that she did not come, but she will rejoice that I found you well," commented Hadassah. She tried to be pleasant, but her discomfort made it difficult. "Will you be returning to Capernaum soon? I know she misses you terribly."

For a moment, Uri's hardened eyes softened. "I do not know when I will return. It was good to see you, Hadassah. May the Eternal One bless you and your family, and please tell Zara that... that I think of her often."

"Uri!" A harsh voice beckoned from down the street. "It's time!"

Uri turned his head, nodded, and waved his hand. When he looked back at Hadassah, his eyes were no longer warm, and when he said goodbye, the hollowness of his farewell alarmed her.

"Goodbye, Uri," she whispered as he disappeared into the crowded street. She stood transfixed, staring at the place where she last saw him, hoping he would reappear, but he did not.

I will be a widow before I am ever a bride.

Zara's words echoed in Hadassah's mind, and she was suddenly very frightened for him.

She slowly moved toward a food stand, resisting the urge to follow Uri. Instead, she forced herself to stop and examine the leeks piled high on one corner of a wooden table. Turning the vegetable over and over in her hands, she set it back down when she realized she wasn't really looking at it.

Uri couldn't possibly be going to—

"Stop, thief! Stop!!"

Hadassah turned around just as two hooded men sprinted past her, shoving themselves through shoppers who fell against tables and barrels. Vegetables and fruits scattered everywhere, spices and oils spilled, and angry merchants shook their fists, calling out curses upon the fleeing perpetrators.

With shocked eyes, Hadassah stepped back as a pair of legionnaires raced by her, seconds behind the thieves. Kicking aside anything or anyone in their way, the soldiers' brandished weapons glinted in the sunlight as they ran. Hadassah shuddered to think of the outcome of the chase. As soon as the soldiers disappeared down the road, she stooped to help an old woman pick up the strewn produce.

"You are most kind," stated the woman, her aged hands shaking.

Hadassah tried to calm her own fears as she spoke. "Does this happen often?"

"More than not," admitted the woman. "Those without respect for the laws of God are more bold than ever these days. My Simon, he usually is here with me, but today he had obligations. I bade him go. I told him that I would be kept safe in the hands of the Almighty One." She looked up at Hadassah. "And I was."

At this, Hadassah could smile easily. "Yes, we both were."

It wasn't long before the table had been restocked with almost all of the food that had been displaced, and when she was ready to take her leave, the old woman insisted that Hadassah take a bundle of vegetables and fruit with her.

Her steps were heavy, and she walked a bit slower, finding it difficult to enjoy her stroll with Uri on her mind. Her spirit remained troubled regarding their conversation and the events she had witnessed. A myriad of questions flooded her mind, but she knew only Uri could provide the answers.

What am I going to tell Zara?

* * * * * *

The next few days passed quickly for Hadassah. She and Judith had joined Milcah in shopping for the upcoming meals, and their time together rekindled a familial bond that neither time nor distance could sever. Stories of her grandfather as a boy delighted Hadassah, and she relished the times when she could sit at the feet of Gabriel as he recounted their childhood antics.

It was only when she was alone that a melancholy spirit settled over her. Unable to shake the memory of her encounter with Uri, she often walked through the densely packed streets of Jerusalem hoping to run into Uri once more and convince him to return to Capernaum with her and Judith. As she vainly searched, visions of Uri fighting a Roman soldier or worse invaded her mind, and it tormented her.

She knew she would not share anything about Uri with Judith, not that it would have made any difference to their stay. Judith did not know Uri, and she barely knew Zara. The chance encounter with the zealot would not matter at all to her aunt.

Today, after she had gone to the marketplace to buy fresh fruit, she continued to roam about the city. As she passed the southern steps of the temple mount, she hesitated for only a moment before walking up the steps through the Huldah Gate and onto the grounds of the great temple. She made her way through the hordes of worshippers milling about the outer courtyards and headed toward the Court of Women. Her worries about Uri faded away as she ascended fourteen stone steps, crossed a terrace, and went up another five steps to reach the grounds of the temple. Stopping at the gold and silver-plated gate marking the entrance to the court, her eyes widened in awe as she stared at the massive temple. Beyond the Court of Women, she saw the steps leading to the Gate of Nicanor and the Court of

Israel, and from where she stood, she had a direct line of vision to the huge olive wood doors of the inner temple wherein sat the Holy of Holies. Suddenly, she was overwhelmed with emotions. Reverential amazement engulfed her.

I am standing at the Temple! This is His dwelling place! The presence of the Eternal One! God is here!

Her wonder at the impressive temple brought her so near to tears that she struggled to maintain her composure. Finding nowhere to simply sit and take everything in, she reluctantly left the Court of Women and headed down the stairs into the area reserved for the Gentiles. Her head was swimming, and her heart raced within her as she realized she was standing on the spot where King Solomon had built the first temple so many years before. She knew that within its massive walls, beyond where she could ever go, was the place where God Himself dwelt among His people. Reaching out to steady herself on the wall, she took several slow deep breaths. She raised her eyes to the gleaming marble columns, and at that moment, she wanted to be in the presence of God forever. Time seemed to stop, and how long she stood there, she did not know.

As the morning faded into the afternoon, she reluctantly descended the temple steps back into the city. As she made her way along, she was surprised to see so many headed toward Jerusalem's eastern gate. The crowd almost moved as one, and Hadassah stepped back quickly, pressing herself against a wall as men, women, and children hurried by. Excitement peppered their speech, and Hadassah watched wide-eyed as the procession moved in front of her. Some carried large palm fronds; some carried their garments over their sleeves, but all were heading toward the city gate. She strained to hear anything that would give her a clue as to what was the cause of the commotion.

Where are they all going? What's that? Did I hear them say something about a king? Who could it be?

Summoning her courage, she fell into step beside a young woman who carried a small baby in her arms.

"Where are you all going?" she asked as she hastened her step to keep up.

The woman's face was radiant. "To see the king! We are going to see the king!" She kept walking as she spoke. "He's finally come! Our king has come!"

Puzzled, Hadassah opened her mouth to ask another question, but the woman melted into the throng. Carried along by the crowd's momentum, Hadassah finally found refuge from the current of humanity by sidestepping into a small alcove. Her brow furrowed as she tried to make sense of what was happening.

Our king? We don't have a king. To whom is she referring?

As she leaned against the building, one word from the crowd began to emanate, capturing her attention, and making everything clear.

Messiah!

She heard it again and again. The woman had said they were going to see the king! The one who promised to save Israel from foreign oppression! She couldn't just watch them pass by. If it were true, if it was the Messiah they were going to see, she knew it had to be Yeshua! And if it was Yeshua, she would not give up an opportunity to see him again!

She rejoined the throng as they rushed out of the city. Passing through the eastern gate of Jerusalem, the people lined both sides of the bridge that spanned the Kidron Valley. Laying down their palm branches, cloaks, and shawls, their excitement mounted as each moment passed. Soon cheers and shouts began to be heard from the far end of the bridge near the Mount of Olives. Louder and louder, their adulations resonated all around her.

Hadassah tried to see what was happening, but the distance was too great, and the people were too many for her to get a clear view. She was at the rear of the horde, and thus forced to stand close to the Golden gate, but she leaned forward as best she could to see if it truly was Yeshua who was the cause of celebration. Squinting her eyes, she scanned the long span of the bridge. Too often someone obscured her view, and she would change her position for a better glimpse of what was happening.

Roughly bumped aside, she stumbled, losing sight of the far end of the bridge. Scowling, she huffed as she regained her balance. Standing on her tiptoes did nothing for her view, so she purposefully squirmed her way to the front line of onlookers. She could hear the clip-clop of an animal coming closer as the cheers escalated, and her pushing became more aggressive.

I have to see! Let me through!

Twisting through the crowd, she managed to wriggle her way to a small opening in the front line of cheering onlookers. Her eyes brightened, and her smile broadened as she beheld the man atop the young donkey.

It is Yeshua!!

Sitting on the small animal, Yeshua smiled and waved at everyone he passed. Branches were being waved back and forth as praises to God exploded from the onlookers.

"Hosanna to the Son of David!"

"Blessed is He who comes in the name of the Lord!"

"Hosanna in the highest!"

Hadassah's voice chorused with the multitude. "Blessed is He who comes in the name of the Lord!" Joyous tears fell unhindered down her cheeks, and she waved her hands frantically as she called out her praises to Yeshua as he drew nearer.

Yeshua! Yeshua! I'm here! I'm here!

"Hosanna to the Son of David!"

As he passed, jubilation filled her soul. She could not have loved him more at that moment. She clapped and screamed with the crowd, and as she watched him disappear through the gate into Jerusalem, her heart soared. All around her, people were crying and praising the name of the Lord. Hadassah believed without a doubt that Yeshua was the answer for which her forefathers had prayed. The Messiah had come! It was true! Yeshua was the Messiah!

As the crowd shifted to follow him into the city, Hadassah allowed herself to be carried along with them. Moving as one, they headed toward the great temple, gathering more onlookers as they moved through the already congested streets that the time of Passover always created.

Hadassah happily scurried along with the multitude. Nearing the temple, the cacophony of animal sounds mingled with the shouts of buyers and sellers grew louder, almost deafening, but she reveled in the clamor. Enchanting smells of cinnamon, clove, and other spices wafted by, and Hadassah found the aromas almost intoxicating. She breathed in deeply, savoring the exotic fragrances as she passed through the marketplace. She slowed her pace, pausing to lift her eyes once more to the majestic temple, but then lowering them to seek out Yeshua.

The presence of the Almighty is here! He is here in the very person of Yeshua! Praise to the Lord!

She yearned to be as close to him as possible. Determined to make her way through the crowd, she quickly meandered through the masses. The cries of the poor assaulted her ears, and she struggled to move toward the temple without stepping on one of the beggars sitting near the gate.

There are so many of them! That poor woman. Her clothes... they're so tattered!

As she moved over them, a still, small voice tugged at her heart.

Blessed are the poor in spirit, for theirs is the kingdom of heaven.

She stopped and turned back. Her gaze fell on an old woman sitting alone in the shadows. Reaching her hand into a pocket, she fingered the few coins she had remaining from the market. Hesitating only a moment, she withdrew the money and stooped by the begging woman.

"This is for you," smiled Hadassah warmly. She placed the coins in the woman's trembling hand.

Long, tapered fingers closed quickly over the silver, and grateful eyes looked deeply into Hadassah's, but the woman spoke no words. Hadassah stood and started to walk away, then suddenly stopped.

Blessed are ye that hunger now, for ye shall be filled.

She turned back toward the beggar woman. Once again, their eyes met, and Hadassah remembered the bundle of food she had in her pocket. Pulling it out, she unwrapped it and looked at the fresh produce. It would make a good meal for someone. She quickly recovered it, then held it out for the old woman. Bony fingers closed over the food, then quickly hid the treasure within the folds of a tattered garment.

Hadassah stood to leave.

But love ye your enemies, and do good, and lend, hoping for nothing again; and your reward shall be great, and ye shall be the children of the Highest.

Impulsively, she removed her linen shawl and placed it around the woman's thin shoulders. As she walked away, she heard the old woman resume her cries to other passersby. Hadassah smiled to herself as she continued her quest to find Yeshua.

As she neared the outer courtyard, shouts and screams rose up, mingled with the frantic cries of animals! Hysterical shrieks filled the air accompanied by the rush of wings as a flock of doves took flight. Apprehension rose in her, and Hadassah's eyes darted all around her as people began running past her. Fear gripped her heart, and before she could retreat to a place of safety, she was shoved mercilessly against the stones of the courtyard gate.

A small cry escaped her as her arm scraped against the rock, tearing the skin. A stray goat bleated pathetically as it ran past her, and she tried desperately to see a way out of the courtyard.

What's happening?

"He's crazy!"

"Stop him!"

Hadassah didn't know where to run. Bumped and pushed again and again, she turned her face to the wall for protection as she felt herself being crushed against the rough stones.

Please, Almighty One, help me!

Fearing she would stumble and then be trampled, Hadassah cried out as a strong hand grabbed her arm and yanked her out of the chaotic mass of people.

"No!" she protested, struggling to be free.

"Hadassah!"

Her head jerked upward as she recognized the deep voice that spoke her name.

Marcus!

"Make way!" he shouted as he pulled her away from the crowded gate to a less congested area.

"What are you doing here?" he demanded brusquely as he released his hold on her. His probing eyes bore into hers, then quickly softened as he asked, "Are you hurt?"

"No. I don't think so. Judith and I... we're here for the Passover." Her voice shook as she spoke. "What's happening?"

Marcus took a deep breath, and then answered angrily. "Your Yeshua is what's happening." His lips were tight, and he shook his head slightly as he perused the growing mob. "He tossed over the moneychangers' tables, scattering coins everywhere. The people scattered like sheep without a shepherd. Running, screaming."

Hadassah shook her head. "Yeshua? Are you sure? He would never do that."

Marcus frowned as he raised an eyebrow. "It was Yeshua. Of that, I am certain, and now you have seen what happened because of him." He crossed his arms across his chest. "The goats and sheep got loose, as did the birds. People clamored for the money on the ground in a frenzy to grab a few coins. Basically, your Yeshua incited a riot." His angry eyes surveyed the pandemonium around them.

"But he wouldn't do that!" She stated, still refusing to believe what she heard.

Marcus' lips curved downward as his eyes narrowed. "Really?" He raised an eyebrow as he uncrossed his arms, placing one hand on the hilt of his sword. He spoke without looking at her, careful to keep a sharp eye on the turmoil. "He was calling it... let me see if I can use his words....'a place of prayer and not a den of thieves,' which created this... this fervor through the people. He flung tables over, Hadassah. That's not exactly promoting peaceful behavior."

"Why would he do that?" She was desperate for a plausible explanation.

"You're asking *me* to explain *your* teacher?" Marcus scoffed. He kept a keen eye out for troublemakers even though the crowd was beginning to thin, and his soldiers were restoring order to the courtyard.

Hadassah's brow furrowed as she stood mutely, struggling to comprehend Yeshua's actions.

"I have to get back to my men. Will you be all right?"

She nodded without looking up.

When he started to walk away, Hadassah looked up and called out to him. "Marcus?"

He stopped and turned.

"What will happen to him? To Yeshua? Will you arrest him?" She feared the answer as she waited for him to speak.

He gave her a condescending half-smile. "I wish I could, Hadassah, but for now your Yeshua is safe. He is surrounded by those who idolize him. If I were to take him from here, there would be an even greater revolt, and I don't need that," he scowled. "Listen to them." He paused, and together they could still hear the cries of adulation emanating from the temple grounds.

"Hosanna to the Son of David!"

"Hosanna in the highest!"

"He is an embarrassment to your priests. Yet in their frustration, even they know it is their problem, not ours. Fortunately for him, your Yeshua did not break a Roman law this time, therefore I have no reason to detain him, but..." he reaffirmed, "the day will come when he will go too far, and when he does, I will be right there, and mark my words, he will pay for what he's done."

"What he's done? Tell me, what has he done, Marcus?" she challenged.

Marcus cocked his head as he studied her. "I know he means a lot to you, Hadassah, but be careful in whom you place your trust. You look at him, but you do not see the truth for what it is. Your eyes are blinded by a futile hope of a so-called messiah. You see only what you want to see."

"Me? I could say the same for you."

He shook his head, then simply said, "He is a dangerous man, Hadassah. Be careful who you choose to follow."

"Marcus, you don't understand–"

"No, Hadassah. It is you who does not understand. You and your people." His last words were spoken as if they were gall, yet his gaze softened as his eyes lingered on her face. "Give my best to Judith." And then, he turned and walked away.

"Oh, Marcus," she whispered as she watched him disappear into the crowd.

Chapter Sixteen

"All we like sheep have gone astray; we have turned every one to his own way; and the LORD hath laid on him the iniquity of us all." Isaiah 53:6

Trying to maintain peace in the city of Jerusalem during the onset of Passover week was not as difficult as Marcus had envisioned, especially since the temple incident with Yeshua. While there had been occasions that warranted his intervention, arrests were often made quickly and easily. It was nearly impossible for the unsavory members of Jewish society to stand up against the Roman legionnaires, and because of this, only the most brazen tried, and they were quickly rounded up and incarcerated or worse.

Marcus had a hearty distaste for policing the city. He preferred the battlefield, but he would never question his orders. It was his duty to serve in whatever capacity he was called. Tonight, he would be patrolling the streets with his men once more, and he anticipated a quiet shift as the Jews readied themselves for their day of remembrance.

Dispatching his men to various regions of Jerusalem, Marcus chose to sit astride Ares and ride, knowing this would enable him to cover more of the city than if he traveled on foot.

As he rode, he noted the recent changes in the city. Streets had been repaired, inns were well lighted as pilgrims continued to arrive, special ovens had been set up for the roasting of the lambs, and of course, the temple was prepared to accept the sacrifices that would be brought by the people.

Marcus turned his head as he heard the sound of approaching hoof-beats behind him.

"Gaius," began Marcus, recognizing his friend. "I didn't expect to see you tonight. I thought you were leaving for Jericho."

Gaius reigned in his horse and brought it next to Ares. "I was, but I was reassigned to stay with you, my friend. You must need help," he joked.

Marcus laughed. "That I do! I need someone to keep me awake.

Apparently, the Jews are too busy cleaning their houses and preparing their lambs to cause any trouble tonight."

"It's nice to know the rebels are so pious," sneered Gaius.

Marcus gestured to an area with the ovens. "Amazing, isn't it? This whole place will be filled with people roasting their lambs in a few days, and then everything will disappear, and things will return to normal."

"Well, they are a peculiar people. Did you know they were saying that this Yeshua is now their king? They claim he's healed the blind and the lame."

"Yes, I heard."

"You don't believe it, do you?"

Marcus glanced at his friend. "What I cannot believe is how these people flock to him. He's basically a nobody who has nothing to offer anyone."

Gaius nodded his head in agreement. "He's an odd one, that's for sure. Went kind of crazy the other day at the temple."

Marcus chuckled. "Yes, he did. The priests were not too pleased either. They were livid but couldn't do a thing. He has so much support from the people that the priests can't touch him without inciting a riot. And then we'd have to step in, and... well, that would be quite unpleasant for the Jews."

Gaius' laughter echoed in the empty street. "I had one priest come up to me demanding that I do something. I asked him what he'd like me to do, and he wanted me to take Yeshua before the tribunal."

"For what? Tipping over a couple of tables?" Marcus snickered. "If that's the worst thing that this Yeshua does, he'll soon be forgotten by everyone. That would suit me just fine."

* * * * * *

It was nearly dawn when Marcus settled into his bed. He locked his fingers together behind his head and sank down into his pillow, but sleep eluded him. Every time he closed his eyes, he saw Yeshua. Yeshua at the Sea of Galilee; Yeshua at the temple; Yeshua at the city gates.

He lay in bed reviewing everything he could remember about the Jewish carpenter, but nothing was coming together for him. He had not been an eyewitness to most of the so-called miracles, but he had been present when

Judith had supposedly been healed. Of course, he had not been privy to her exact condition prior to the healing, but he had to admit that she was a different woman than the one he had previously known.

He had heard the Nazarene speak, mesmerizing all who had come to hear him, but his words had made no sense at all to Marcus. He had sought out Yeshua's family whose reactions to his inquiries were unexpected.

When he finally drifted off to sleep, he tossed and turned, and by dawn he gave up the fight and rose to face the day.

He stepped out into the corridor and nodded as two legionnaires passed. The lack of sleep created a foul mood in Marcus, and he frowned as he heard shouts coming from the judgment hall. Turning abruptly, he headed toward the commotion.

"Something must be done!"

Marcus entered the Praetorium and stood silently watching Pontius Pilate address a member of the Jewish Sanhedrin.

"What is it you would have me do?" The Roman governor reclined back in his chair and waited, clearly unhappy with the presence of the Pharisee.

"He is causing disturbances, and those disturbances should concern you." Sweat beaded on the forehead of the priest as he became more animated in his petition. "Don't you see what is happening?"

"And what is that?"

"He speaks of treason against Caesar."

"Caesar? In what way has he committed treason?" Pilate yawned loudly.

"He is being called a king, and we both know there is no other king than Caesar."

A loud guffaw burst forth from the governor. "You amuse me. Your claim implies that you are loyal to Caesar, yet we both know your laws would condemn you for bowing down to someone other than your Jewish God. Is this not true? If not, perhaps I should have *you* bound with chains for refusing to acknowledge Caesar as a god."

A small smile crept up on Marcus' face, but he stood without moving as the pious rabbi stomped out of the hall.

"Jerusalem... I am beginning to loathe this city and its people." Pilate walked over to a window and peered out. "What is it with this... this Yeshua?

Why is he such a threat to these Jews?"

"They say he performs miracles," stated Marcus matter-of-factly.

Pilate turned. "Yes, I have heard. Makes the blind to see. Causes the lame to walk. So, I've been told. Fabricated stories, no doubt."

"Yes," agreed Marcus, "but fabricated stories can inspire people to follow when they seek a savior."

"You think I should arrest him?"

Marcus shook his head. "I don't see that he has committed any crime against Rome, but we do need to watch him."

"His arrest would appease these religious fanatics and relieve me of having to deal with them."

Marcus chuckled. "You seem to deal with them without much difficulty."

"Spoken like a loyal Roman, but I appreciate your flattery." He turned back to the window. "Something will have to be done about this Yeshua, and soon." He paused for a moment, then added, "You are a good man, Marcus. I'd like you to be the one."

"The one?"

Pilate nodded. "Yes. The one to handle this situation."

Although he was surprised at the directive, Marcus' emotions did not betray him; he stood ramrod straight and simply stated, "As you command."

* * * * * *

"Problems?" asked Gaius as he caught up with Marcus in the halls of the Antonia Fortress.

"No, not really. Pilate believes it's inevitable that Yeshua will be taken into Roman custody." His steps slowed as they rounded a corner, and he looked up and down the halls before stopping. "He'd like me to handle it."

Gaius' brow furrowed. "And that troubles you?"

"It concerns me."

"Why? It doesn't bother you when we arrest other insurrectionists."

Marcus' lips tightened as his head shook slightly. "No, but Yeshua's no overt insurrectionist. His arrest, well, it could be problematic."

Gaius raised an eyebrow. "How so? He's just another Jewish radical, right?

When he becomes a threat, arrest him."

"That's the problem. He's really not a threat," confessed Marcus. "Not in the sense of someone who's seeking to overthrow Rome. The only thing he's overthrown is a couple of tables. Believe me, I've been watching him. Hoping actually that he would do something against Rome, so I could arrest him, but he's too smart for that. Even when he speaks, he doesn't talk about rebellion. He speaks of the kingdom of his god. And the people, well, they adore him all the more."

"So, what's your plan?"

"At the moment, all I can do is wait, but sooner or later, Yeshua will make a mistake. It could be a wrong word. It could be something more overt. Either way, I will be ready, but I am concerned as to the timing."

"The timing?"

"Yeshua is beloved by so many. If we bring him to Pilate, the people could use his arrest as an excuse for rebellion. There are already more Jews in Jerusalem than any other time of the year. There could be serious ramifications if he is arrested now."

"So, you think we should do nothing?"

"I'm merely saying I hope it doesn't become a military problem yet. He's just a former carpenter from an insignificant village who wanders the countryside. His ideas are curious, to say the least, and his miracles, well, they are questionable."

Gaius scratched his chin, then shrugged his shoulders. "So? He's a nobody, really. Besides, even if the people revolt, how can they possibly stand against Rome? We would squash them like a bug beneath our sandals. You've seen how easy it is to subdue those who try."

"True."

"Ever wonder why the priests dislike him so much?"

Marcus shrugged. "Who knows why they think the way they do. He's one of their own, yet they act as if he's the enemy, not us." He sighed deeply. "Well, it's of no consequence to me one way or another. I have my orders, and I fully intend to carry them out."

Gaius slapped him on the back and said with a grin, "To the glory of Rome, my friend. To the glory of Rome."

* * * * * *

"You can't be serious!"

Marcus turned toward Hadassah. Her fiery eyes bore into him as he tried to explain. "You need to realize I had my orders."

"Orders? You had your orders?" The fury in her voice rose as she screamed at him. "You don't know what you're doing! He's our Messiah! He was sent from God! How could you? I hate you, Marcus! I hate you!"

"Hadassah..."

She turned and stomped away as he stood helpless to stop her. Her footsteps echoed in the hall until they faded away into the night. He wanted to run after her, to explain how he had no choice, but his legs wouldn't obey his desire.

As he stood, he could hear the voices of a multitude. They were getting louder. Marcus whipped his head around. The sounds were growing. Then he saw them. The faces of so many! Some he vaguely recognized, but most were unfamiliar to him.

"Who are you?" Marcus called out as more and more people filled the hallway on both sides of him. Soon he was completely surrounded.

"He gave my sight back to me!"

"I can walk again because of him!"

"He healed my daughter!"

So many voices accosted him that he could no longer make out what was being said except one word... *Yeshua*! Everywhere he turned, more people were rushing toward him, and now they were all proclaiming Yeshua as their king.

He couldn't fight them off as they surrounded him with their cries. He struggled to move, but the crowd was pressing in on him. Frantically, he pushed against them, searching for a way of escape, but he found none. Reaching for his sword, he found the scabbard empty! He called out for help, but no one came. Instead, the accusations against him rose to a deafening volume. Defenseless, he covered his head as fists came down upon him, and he groaned as he waited for the inevitable.

* * * * * *

Marcus bolted upright in bed. Beads of perspiration dotted his face, and it took a moment for him to orient himself to his location. He was breathing hard, and his heart pounded within his chest.

It was a dream!

He swung his legs over the side of his bed and dropped his head into his hands. The reality that his problem was multifaceted troubled him, but one particular aspect distressed him greatly.

"Why does she torment me so?" His hands formed tight fists as his eyes narrowed. "What do I care what Hadassah thinks one way or the other? She's just another misguided Jew," he rationalized, but his words were hollow. He had wanted to seek her out ever since he had rescued her from the temple mob, but he had resisted the impulse. Remembering their final time together in Capernaum made him hesitant to go to her. Now, she haunted his dreams.

Knowing sleep would elude him once more, he rose. Splashing water on his face, he dressed quickly, crossed the parade grounds of the fortress, and climbed to the top of the eastern wall. Here he found solitude in the early hours of the dawn. The sun's rays were just beginning to melt the darkness of night into a pinkish-blue hue. He glanced at a small stone statue of Mars nestled in a tiny alcove hewn out of the wall.

"Keeping guard, are you?" queried Marcus, his eyes returning to look over the Kidron Valley. "So, tell me what to tell her. She will despise me if I lay a hand on her precious Yeshua, yet I cannot go against my orders. And frankly, I don't want to." A retrospective pause brought a new question to his mind.

Why can't she see him for who he really is?

He turned to stare at the Roman idol. "You have ears, but you cannot hear, and eyes yet you cannot see. Why do I waste my time?" Nonetheless, despite his words, he placed a small coin at the base of the idol before walking away.

* * * * * *

"They what?" An angry Pilate wiped his wet hands on a towel, then threw it harshly on the ground. The fury in his eyes caused his aide to hesitate before repeating his news.

"It appears there is no need for us to arrest him. The Jews have done it themselves, and now... they've come here with the Nazarene."

Pilate glared at the young soldier. "I have no desire to adjudicate their religious squabbles. Get rid of them."

"I tried, but they refused. The chief priest insists he must speak with you." He shifted his feet nervously.

Pilate slammed his fist on the table. "I tire of this!"

It was at this moment that Marcus stepped into the room. Having been summoned by Pilate, he stopped just inside the door awaiting permission to enter and approach the governor. He watched Pilate curiously as the Roman leader ranted and raved.

"Do I look like a Jew? Am I a priest? Do I worship as they do? No! Why bring me this rabbi? He– Marcus! Come, come!" Pilate waved him in. The presence of the centurion calmed him somewhat as he spoke. "I am told the Sanhedrin have arrived with the Nazarene."

Marcus' eyes widened. "Why? What has he done?"

"He breathes."

A puzzled look crossed Marcus' face.

Pilate shook his head disgustingly, then explained. "Nothing. He has committed no crime against Rome." He uttered a curse. "These Jews are the bane of my existence."

"I am sure I can persuade them to leave."

Pilate exhaled loudly, then clamped his lips together as he stomped around once more. Finally, he stopped and slammed his fist onto the arm of his judgment seat. "No, it's time to end this! Bring the Jew to me."

Marcus made a move to go, but Pilate ordered him differently. "Stay. I want you here with me." He pointed to his aide. "You go." The frustrated governor offered no explanation as he sat in his chair.

Marcus gave a slight nod and stepped to the side of the room as the far doors to the hall opened. Recognition was immediate, and Marcus' lips pressed tightly together.

It was Yeshua. He walked steadily; his hands bound behind him. His swollen face was purpled with bruises. However, when he stopped before Pilate, his gaze was strong and unfazed.

The leaders of the Sanhedrin remained at the threshold of the doors of the hall, not entering, but too curious to withdraw into the hall.

Pilate leaned forward resting one arm on his knee. His eyes narrowed as he scrutinized the Jew who stood before him, and then he looked beyond Yeshua to the priests peering in through the doors. Disgust filled him, and he spat on the ground.

He rose from his seat, walked past Yeshua, and continued toward the high priests. His footsteps echoed in the hall as he neared the gawking men. Stopping just short of the entryway, he glared at them and bellowed, "What accusation do you bring against this man?"

"Obviously he is a criminal. If he were not a malefactor, we would not have delivered him up unto thee," stated the high priest self-righteously.

"Take him and judge him according to your law," bellowed Pilate angrily as he turned away from them.

"We cannot! It is not lawful for us to put any man to death."

"Death?" Anger seethed in Pilate's next words as he spun around. "Be gone!" he commanded.

Surprised, the Jewish leaders stood unmoving, their eyes opened wide and their mouths gaping.

"Did you not hear me?" He thundered. "I said to leave! And close the doors! Do not make me ask again!"

The priests never said a word; they simply did as they were bid, leaving Yeshua standing alone in the Praetorium.

Pilate took a deep breath and pounded his way back to the front of the hall. He circled Yeshua twice without uttering a word, then took his seat.

He leaned forward, narrowing his eyes as he once more contemplated the man before him. Finally, he asked, "Are you the King of the Jews?" It was a simple question, but it was spoken with great exasperation. He waited for an answer.

Yeshua looked into the eyes of his accuser and simply said, "Did you say this yourself or did others tell you to ask me?"

"Am I a Jew?" His indignant voice rose in volume. "Your own nation and the chief priests have delivered you to me. What have you done?" Pilate's fists clenched as his frustration mounted. He grit his teeth as he demanded once more, "Are you their king?"

"My kingdom is not of this world. If my kingdom were of this word, then would my servants fight that I should not be delivered to the Jews, but now is my kingdom not from hence." His words were unemotional and confident.

Marcus stood amazed at how calmly the rabbi responded to Pilate's inquiries, and how irritated Pilate was becoming.

The governor's voice escalated even more. "Do you not hear how many things they bear witness against you?"

Yeshua stood silent.

Pilate exhaled forcefully. "Are you a king then?"

Yeshua's quiet response filled the room. "You say that I am a king. To this end was I born, and for this cause came I into the world that I should bear witness unto the truth. Everyone that is of the truth hears my voice."

Marcus remained alert but confused as he listened to Yeshua.

What kind of an answer is that? Doesn't he realize that Pilate has the power to have him executed?

Pilate rose to his feet. "What is truth?" With several long strides, he reached the back of the hall and yanked open the doors. He stepped out into the corridor and spied the chief priests huddled together.

As soon as their eyes fell upon Pilate, they separated and waited for the governor to speak.

His booming voice echoed through the hall. "I find in him no fault at all."

The Jews began to murmur among themselves. "But he incites the people, teaching them all throughout the land. Everywhere from Galilee to here!"

Pilate cocked his head. "Galilee? He's a Galilean?" A grim smile crept over his face.

The priests looked at one another, unsure of how to answer the governor, but before they could respond, Pilate spoke once more.

"Take him to Herod. That's his jurisdiction."

"But–"

"I have spoken! Take him to Herod!"

* * * * * *

It was near dawn when Marcus stepped out of the judgment hall. Yeshua had been taken away, and Pilate had retreated to his quarters.

Walking slowly along the parapets of the fortress, Marcus surveyed the city of Jerusalem. As he gazed out over the land, fires dotted the surrounding hillsides, and the flickering flames of oil lamps could be seen in the windows of the few homes where the occupants were stirring.

Today was their day of remembrance. It was the Passover. Over the past few weeks, Marcus had heard the entire story of how the Hebrew God delivered His people from Egyptian bondage through a series of unexplainable plagues. The death of every firstborn was the last plague wherein the Lord sent an angel of death to every household that did not have the blood of the Passover lamb on its doors.

Marcus leaned on the top of the massive stoned wall and looked out toward the pool of Bethesda.

Was it you? That day the lame man was healed. Was it you, Yeshua? And the blind beggar... did you heal him as well? And Judith? Was she really as sick as Hadassah claimed? Did you restore her health? Then there were the rumors of the resurrections... Are you responsible for those? Are you who Hadassah believes you to be?

He shuddered at the brief thought that she could be right, then shook it off as his thoughts pushed him toward the opposite position.

Impossible! He wouldn't have been taken captive if he were really a miracle worker... if he were a god! He would have destroyed those who sought to take him. Besides, all the talk has been about a king coming to deliver these Jews. Yeshua is definitely not a king. He's just the son of a Nazarene carpenter. His following is not an army, but poor fishermen, carpenters, even women... no one capable of leading an uprising.

As he struggled to reconcile the facts he knew to be true with the possibilities of what could have been, a slight movement in the courtyard below caught his eye. He strained to identify the group. He recognized the priestly garments, but who was that in the midst of them? He sighed deeply when he saw the bloodied face.

It was Yeshua. The priests were returning, and they were bringing Yeshua with them. He sighed deeply.

What is going on? Why are they returning?

He made his way back to the Praetorium, entering just as an irate Pilate took his place on the judgment seat. Escorted by two guards, Yeshua was brought in once again to stand before the Roman governor. Marcus took his place near Pilate and waited.

"Again? They have brought you back to me again?" He cursed as he shook his head. He glared at Yeshua, but nothing came from the mouth of the beaten man.

Pilate rose without a word and strode past Yeshua to the far doors. As the guards opened them, he walked into the open, his eyes darting back and forth, seeking the priests.

Accompanied by a large group of supporters, the high priest had a boldness that was absent from his first confrontation with Pilate. He stood his ground when the governor approached him. Behind him were the smug faces of the Jewish dissidents and religious leaders.

Pilate's lips curled in disdain as he spoke. "You have brought this man to me as one that perverted the people. I told you, I have examined him before you, and found no fault in this man regarding those things of which you accused him. Apparently, neither did Herod, for I sent you to him, and nothing worthy of death is of this man."

He paused for a moment, then added, "I will therefore have him chastised, and then released."

"You cannot release him!" exclaimed the high priest. "He must not go free. He must be dealt with for his blasphemy!"

The unrelenting gathering of men began to clamor their agreement.

Pilate shook his head in disbelief. A heavy sigh escaped his lips as he looked up at the large group surrounding the high priest. He turned to go back into the hall, and then abruptly stopped and turned to face the Jews. A sinister smile crept across his face. "Very well. It is your custom that I should release unto you one at the Passover. Shall I release unto you this king of the Jews?"

"No! Not him! NO! Not this man, but Barabbas!"

"Barabbas?" Stunned, Pilate held high his hand, silencing the men. "And what would you have me do with Yeshua?"

"Let him be crucified!"

Angry frustration shrouded Pilate's face. "Crucified? Why?" he demanded. "What evil has he done?"

"Crucify him!" The repeated cries became louder and more intense as they no longer listened to Pilate's words, but mercilessly demanded the death of Yeshua.

"You ask me to crucify your king?" Pilate asked in exasperation.

"We have no king but Caesar!" came the united reply.

Pilate's narrowed eyes swept over the group, and his lips pressed firmly together. He stomped back to the judgment seat; his face contorted with rage. The doors had been left open, and the Jewish leaders stood just beyond the open doorway once more, peering in to the Praetorium.

As the governor took his seat, a young soldier approached him with a note. Grabbing it, Pilate read it, then crumpled the paper in his hand. He turned to Marcus and spoke in a lowered voice. "Tell me, Marcus. Do you fear what you dream?"

Discomfort grew in Marcus as the image of Hadassah rejecting him and his inability to defend himself against a Jewish mob resurfaced in his mind. His words were forced, but he willed them to be convincing. "No, Prefect. Only the weak fear the dreams of the night."

Pilate held up the crushed paper. "This is from my wife. She is foolish. A believer in dreams. She tells me I should have nothing to do with this man. 'I have suffered many things this day in a dream because of him' she says." He smirked as he added, "She is an idiot. I care not for his innocence or his guilt, but I will end this today."

Rising from his seat, he ordered brusquely, "Bring me water." A servant materialized with a basin and pitcher of water. When Pilate extended his hands over the bowl, the water was poured over them, and he symbolically washed his hands, proclaiming loudly, "I am innocent of the blood of this 'just' person."

The high priest shouted from the back of the room, "His blood be on us and on our children!"

Pilate walked over to Marcus and once more spoke so that only the centurion could hear him. "Those pious fools! They would prefer the murderer Barabbas to this man, Yeshua, who has done nothing."

"What is your will, Prefect?" asked Marcus.

Pilate looked up and said decisively. "I cannot allow insurrection. These people are unreasonable and unpredictable. They could easily incite the rest of the Jewish population to rebel. I cannot allow that. If his death will prevent this, so be it." He paced across the floor, then stopped by the window, gazing out over the city. "I must maintain the order."

He turned to Marcus. "Release Barabbas. As for him..." He gave a small nod toward Yeshua. "Have him scourged. Then..." He sighed deeply. "Crucify him." With that, Pilate left the hall.

Marcus looked at Yeshua, then the guards. "Take him."

* * * * * *

Marcus stood off to the side of the parade grounds as the guards secured Yeshua to a post. As they stepped away, they stripped him of his garments, baring his back. Two Roman lictors moved to either side of Yeshua. In their hands, these specially appointed soldiers held short whips of braided leather thongs. Within the strands of leather were jagged rocks, sharp pieces of bone, and even small iron balls whose purpose was to bruise, tear, and rip flesh.

The lictors stood ramrod straight, their eyes fixed on Marcus. At the nod of his head, the beating began. Intending to weaken the victim, the flogging continued mercilessly. Blood poured from the lacerations as the other soldiers jeered and mocked Yeshua, and as Marcus stood overseeing the lashings, Pilate's words echoed in his mind.

I find no fault in this man.

Chapter Seventeen

"But he was wounded for our transgressions, he was bruised for our iniquities: the chastisement of our peace was upon him; and with his stripes we are healed."
Isaiah 53:5

Hadassah took her place at the table and waited quietly. The prior day she had joined in with the cleaning of the house to assure no leaven was present and that had delighted her. Justus and Judith had never formally observed the Passover in their home, so the experiences of the day of preparation were new for her.

As she reflected on the previous day, a smile appeared on her face. She closed her eyes and remembered how her great uncle had made quite a show in searching for the leaven, the symbol of sin. Holding a candlestick high, he peeked into crevices and crannies until finally he proclaimed in a loud voice, "All leaven that is in my possession, that which I have seen and that which I have not seen, be it accounted as the dust of the earth."

Now as the Passover meal was about to begin, Hadassah silently offered a prayer of thanksgiving to the Lord for allowing her to fully participate in this special time of remembrance. When she felt the cushions next to her move, she opened her eyes, meeting her aunt's smile with one of her own. She felt Judith's hand encircle her own, and she felt an overflowing sense of belonging. Belonging to a family and a people. A people especially chosen by God as His own.

Thank You, Almighty One, for allowing me to be here celebrating this Passover with my family. I shall never forget it or your goodness to me.

Milcah's table was beautifully set with the traditional foods of the Passover, and extra pillows had been placed around it to accommodate this year's extra guests. Gabriel would be at its head, and the others would settle around the table waiting for him to begin the commemoration. Candles were lit, casting flickering shadows on the faces of those already seated. In the table's center, the charoseth, with its combination of apples, nuts, wine, cinnamon, and other ingredients, nestled in a large bowl as a reminder of the mortar used by the ancient Israelites to bind their bricks in building the great cities of Egypt. A plate with unleavened bread was next to a small bowl of bitter herbs. Together, they represented the Hebrew children, bitter with their captivity, fleeing Egypt before their bread had the opportunity to rise. The wine cups were in their proper place, and Hadassah knew they stood for the four expressions of redemption as stated in the Torah.

I am the Lord, and I will bring you out from under the burdens of the Egyptians, and I will rid you out of their bondage, and I will redeem you with a stretched out arm, and with great judgments: and I will take you to me for a people...

Hadassah noted the empty place setting. It was the place for the prophet Elijah to sit should he return to the children of Israel this Passover. She cherished the traditions of her people and their faith, and this night was no exception. Although she could not remember celebrating the Passover with her own parents, she knew it was a custom her grandfather had revered. Soon the sun would set, and she would experience the Passover as never before.

* * * * * *

Beaten and bruised, Yeshua was taken to the common hall. Although severely weakened by the scourging, he managed to walk there in his own strength. Surrounded by a band of soldiers, he was stripped of his garments once more as a purple robe was placed upon his shoulders. One of the soldiers roughly pressed a makeshift crown of flexible boughs with long sharp thorns unto Yeshua's head. As the unyielding thorns penetrated his skin, rivulets of blood began to freely flow down his face.

"Hail, King of the Jews!" scoffed one soldier as he exaggerated a grand bow in front of Yeshua.

Another dropped to his knee, removed his helmet and tipped his head. He repeated the mocking phrase of his colleagues. "Hail, O King!"

"Tell us, please, who hit you?" laughed one more as he struck Yeshua from behind.

Marcus stood watch over his men as they continued the ridicule, but he did nothing to stop them.

Let them have their fun while they can. It will soon be over.

A stiff reed struck Yeshua's face as spittle from one of the soldiers dripped from his cheek. Laughter from the mockers echoed in the great hall as they continued to strike him, their own hands reddening with Yeshua's blood.

While Marcus stood witness to the physical abuse as he had done to countless others before, he felt an uneasiness that he could not quell. The discomfort intensified when, for only a brief moment, Yeshua turned his head slightly and met Marcus' gaze. Unable to turn from him, Marcus was troubled by what he saw, or rather what he did not see in the rabbi's sorrowful eyes. Despite all that had transpired, there was no sign of fear in the man before him, and that was inconsistent with what the centurion had experienced in times past.

"Enough," stated Marcus. His voice did not betray the unsettled feeling he had, and the legionnaires immediately ceased their jeering of the Jewish rabbi and stepped back. "Remove the robe." He nodded slightly toward another soldier who moved to retrieve the mocking garment from Yeshua's shoulders.

As the robe was roughly yanked off, the bloodied wounds on Yeshua's back reopened and began to drip freely. The beating had weakened him to a state just short of collapse, but that was of no concern to Marcus. Under his direction, the men shoved Yeshua out of the common hall.

* * * * * *

"Blessed are you, O Lord our God, king of the universe, who has created the fruit of the vine. And you, O Lord our God, have given us festival days for joy, this feast of the unleavened bread, the time of our deliverance in remembrance of the departure from Egypt. Blessed are you, O Lord our God, who has kept us alive, sustained us, and enabled us to enjoy this season."

Hadassah bowed her head as she listened to her great uncle. His words had been recited for hundreds of years, and they stirred her heart as she thought about how God had brought His people out of Egyptian slavery to the land once promised to Abraham, the father of their faith.

After four hundred years in captivity, God had heard the cries of His children. He had sent a series of ten plagues, culminating with the death of the firstborn in every household except the Hebrew homes that had followed the Lord's decree. Those who had applied the blood of a freshly slain lamb to their doorposts were "passed over" by the angel of death and spared the judgment of God upon their firstborn sons. When Pharoah's own son was struck down that night of the first Passover, the grief-stricken Egyptian king relented and finally allowed Moses and the Israelites to leave the land.

Hadassah watched as the first cup of wine was poured, and Gabriel spoke once more.

"I am the Lord, and I will bring you out from under the yoke of the Egyptians."

He picked up his cup of wine, and the rest followed. As he drank from the cup, so did Hadassah and the others at the table.

* * * * * *

The main road leading to the Mount of Olives was always busy, but when a procession of condemned men walked the fateful path, it became exceptionally crowded. Onlookers jeered as criminals were paraded to their crucifixion sites, but because it was Passover, the road was lined with fewer spectators than usual. Those that did not observe the feast day appeared along the death route to shout cruel epithets as Yeshua and two other criminals stumbled along the road that crossed the Kidron Valley.

Yeshua stooped under the weight of the rugged crossbar he bore across his shoulders as he trudged toward the city gate. Prodded by the Roman legionnaires, he painstakingly moved down the road struggling to remain upright. Finally, weakened by the loss of blood and lack of sleep, Yeshua fell. The bystanders hissed their disapproval of the halting of the procession, and Marcus urged his men to keep order as he scanned the sidelines. His gaze fell upon an able-bodied man whose dark eyes were focused on the form of the fallen rabbi.

"You!" He pointed a finger at the man who, unlike those around him, remained silent as he shifted his eyes from Yeshua to the centurion. "State your name."

Squaring his broad muscular shoulders, the man never hesitated as he looked Marcus in the eye. "Simon. I am Simon of Cyrene."

"Take up his crossbeam," ordered Marcus. He sat stoically atop Ares and waited for Simon to move. When the Cyrene went to Yeshua's side, Marcus turned to the soldier nearest the rabbi. He nodded his head, and the soldier yanked Yeshua to his feet and pushed him forward.

Simon strained to lift the wooden beam to his shoulders, but once in place, he fell into step behind Yeshua, slowing to match the footsteps of the condemned man. Ahead of them loomed the city gate and beyond that, the Mount of Olives.

* * * * * *

As the Passover meal neared its end, the family sang the Hallel, the final hymn. The words of the special psalm of David were known to all at the table, and together they sang the traditional songs of the celebration. As the last line faded into the night, a soft knock was heard at the door.

Gabriel's brow furrowed as he moved to answer it. "Who could that be at this hour?" He opened the door quickly to see Moshe, his neighbor, standing at the threshold with a look of alarm on his face. After a few moments of whispering between the two men, Gabriel closed the door and returned to the table. He dropped down to his pillows but did not recline. Trouble etched the features of his weathered face, and the eyes of everyone were focused on the balding man at the head of the table.

Finally, Gabriel raised his distraught eyes, and his gaze went to each face before resting on the face of his great-niece. "I am afraid I have terrible news. Hadassah, your Yeshua is being led to the place of the skulls."

Hadassah's lack of understanding caused her to dart her eyes from her great-uncle to Judith, then back to Gabriel. "I don't understand. The place of the skulls?"

"Yes. It is the place where the temple tax is determined, but it is also the place of Roman crucifixion. Mount Olivet." His voice was somber.

"Crucifixion? Yeshua? Why? What has he done?" Hadassah struggled to keep from rushing out of the room. Her head whirled to her aunt. "Dodah, what does this mean? How can this happen?" Near-hysteria gripped her. Her body began to shake at the reality of what was being said. "There must be a mistake!"

Shock flooded Judith's eyes, and she grasped Milcah's arm. "It can't be! Dod Gabriel, are you sure?"

"Moshe saw it himself. There were several being taken, but he is sure one of them was your Yeshua." The pain on Gabriel's face for his nieces' sufferings was intense. "I am so sorry."

"I must go!" cried Hadassah. She looked around wildly. "I must go! I cannot believe it! I won't believe it until I see it myself!" Her eyes begged for Gabriel's permission.

"Yes, yes, of course," agreed her uncle. "Come, I will take you and Judith myself. Milcah?"

"Go, my husband," urged Milcah. "It is your duty. Take them. I shall pray that Moshe was mistaken."

Within minutes, the three were on their way to the eastern gates of Jerusalem.

* * * * * *

Marcus had been instructed by Pilate to select the site for Yeshua's crucifixion on the eastern slope of the Mount of Olives where it would be visible from Jerusalem. The governor wanted assurance that the priests could see the execution from the city walls. For an able-bodied man, it was an easy trek to the locale, but for the three men already near death from their beatings, it was almost a relief to arrive at the site.

As each man was positioned on the vertical beam of the cross, they offered no resistance. The arms of the condemned were stretched out on the cross bar and held in place by one soldier as another aligned the five-inch long iron spike above the wrist. The large hammer was brought down with such force that the nail easily penetrated the flesh and wood in one blow. Spikes, two inches longer than those for the wrist, were pounded through the feet of those being crucified, and as shock set in from the final assaults on the body, groans of raw agony seemed to echo all around the mountainside.

Several soldiers hoisted the crosses upright until the wooden beams slammed down into the earthen cavities dug specifically for the crosses. Securing them with ropes, the soldiers turned toward Marcus before stepping away from the site. When he nodded his approval, the men retreated to a spot far enough away to engage in games of chance as they awaited the death of the criminals. Several soldiers stood ready to prevent any interaction from those who gathered to witness the crucifixions, although there were far less in number than usual.

Marcus circled the crosses from the rear, visually inspecting the ropes that secured the rugged beams in place. As he came around to the front, his attention was drawn to the voices crying out from the small groups of people gathering on the slope below him.

"He saved others; himself he cannot save! If he be the King of Israel, let him now come down from the cross, and we will believe him!"

Marcus turned to one of the hecklers nearest to him. His probing gaze fell upon the same religious leader who had accused Yeshua before Pilate.

"He trusted in God," cried the high priest. "Let him deliver him now, if he will have him, for he said, I am the Son of God!" With that, he spat on the ground in disgust.

Marcus shook his head at the hypocritical gathering. He knew several of the onlookers that mocked Yeshua now had stood cheering and waving palm branches just one week earlier as Yeshua had ridden into Jerusalem on the back of a donkey.

Wasn't it just a few days ago that you shouted praises to Yeshua as he entered the city? Hailing him as your King? Such frauds!

A scowl formed on his face as he moved past the first criminal, stopping near the center cross upon which Yeshua hung. Looking up, he saw the lips of the condemned rabbi moving. He strained to hear what was being said.

"Father, forgive them for they know not what they do."

Confusion flooded Marcus' mind as he stared at the man upon the cross. *Forgive us? For what?*

Suddenly, Pilate's words returned to the forefront of his mind.

I find no fault in this man.

The discomfort that Marcus suddenly felt compelled him to step quickly past Yeshua's cross. As he did so, he stopped when he heard the bitter voice of one of the other malefactors call out to the rabbi.

"If you... really are... the Christ... save yourself... and us!" Short gasps for air punctuated his speech.

"Don't you... fear God?" The voice of the second malefactor was almost apologetic in its chastisement.

Marcus turned toward the thief who was speaking.

"You've been judged... and us rightly... now we are receiving... the reward of... our deeds... but this man... he has done... nothing amiss..."

His struggle to speak was tortuous to hear, but Marcus continued to listen as the criminal directed his next comments to Yeshua.

"Lord... remember me... when you... come into... your kingdom..."

Yeshua turned his head. His eyes opened slowly as he looked at the man who begged for mercy.

"Truly, I say to you... today you shall be with me... in paradise..."

Marcus stood trying to make sense of what he had heard.

With him in paradise? What is he talking about? Even near death he speaks nonsense.

* * * * * *

As Hadassah, Judith, and Gabriel headed up the western slope of the Mount of Olives, the reality of what was happening was undeniable. Stunned into accepting what she had prayed was untrue, Hadassah hurried ahead of her aunt and great-uncle. As she neared the crosses, her tears fell unfettered down her cheeks when she saw Yeshua suspended high above the ground.

"No!" she screamed as she collapsed on her knees. "Yeshua! No!"

She sobbed with such depth of emotion, clutching her hands to her chest as she rocked back and forth on the ground, refusing to believe what was right before her. She barely felt the arms of Judith envelop her. Their sobs blended together, and the two women, united in their grief, clung to each other and wept until they could cry no more.

Finally, Hadassah forced herself to look at the horrific scene unfolding before her. Three crosses raised high. Three criminals sentenced to die for their crimes against the government. Her eyes overflowed once more with tears as she stared at Yeshua. The hands that once had reached out in compassion to heal a leper were now pierced with iron spikes; the feet that had walked miles to teach the people about God's love were impaled upon the wretched cross; the man who had brought hope to so many was now bruised and beaten, dying as his blood stained the ground below.

When one of the other criminals began to curse and mock Yeshua, Hadassah turned sharply to look at him. Anger flashed in her hurting eyes.

"Stop it! How can you say that to him? Stop it!" Her cries fell on deaf ears, and the agony she felt at her inability to make the man cease his verbal attack on her beloved Yeshua tore through her. Her shoulders sagged under the weight of grief in her soul, and she slumped forward, her hands supporting her as she sobbed uncontrollably.

Again, she lifted her head toward Yeshua.

Please don't die... don't leave us...

She blinked away her tears as she cast a quick glance to the third cross. This man was closer to death than the mocker. He hung silently, his beaten body struggling to breathe. A vague familiarity tugged at Hadassah, and she studied the man's beaten face.

Suddenly, she gasped and fell back, her soiled hands flying to her mouth as a silent cry rose within her.

Uri! No! It can't be!

Then everything went black.

* * * * * *

"Hadassah? Hadassah, can you hear me?"

Tender hands patted Hadassah's pale cheeks as her eyelashes fluttered open. The foggy image before her slowly cleared, and she found herself looking at Judith's worried face.

"Hadassah! Oh, Hadassah!" Judith swept her niece into her arms and held tightly to her. She wept softly as she rocked Hadassah in her embrace. "I was so frightened! I thought I had lost you." Her voice was a relieved whisper as she kissed the top of Hadassah's head. "My sweet Hadassah…"

All around them, the voices of mocking hecklers mingled with the cries of devastated mourners, but it was Hadassah's cries that tore at Judith's heart.

"Oh, Dodah," wailed Hadassah. "How could this happen? I was so sure he was our Messiah! God's anointed One. How could this happen!" She buried her face in Judith's tunic, desperate to shut out everything.

Judith had no words to comfort her niece as darkness began to blot out the rays of the sun. Sensing the unnatural shadows upon her, Judith raised her head, her questioning eyes scanning the skies for a clue to the deepening gloom. She lowered her face into Hadassah's hair as she sat holding the young woman close to her own broken heart. It was unfathomable to Judith that the one who had delivered her from her own personal illness now hung dying from an old rugged cross.

How could this happen? Who will save us now?

Chapter Eighteen

"I am the good shepherd: the good shepherd giveth his life for the sheep."
John 10:11

The earth crunched beneath Marcus' feet as he made his rounds at the crucifixion site. Now that the skies had blackened, Marcus had instructed his men to be alert for any unauthorized movements near the crosses. The eerie stillness of the unexplained blackness troubled Marcus and nothing he could do relieved the uneasiness he felt as he patrolled the area with a lit torch.

He surveyed those nearest as they waited for death to come to those hanging on the crosses. A few priests stood to one side, arms crossed below self-righteous faces, murmuring to one another, waiting for the inevitable. Mourners, most on their knees, were no longer sobbing in loud wails, but crying softly in their own personal agony. The mockers had left. There really was nothing left to see. A small group stood closer to Yeshua, and Marcus had been told the mother of the rabbi was one of them. His eyes settled on the older woman whose serene gaze was fixed on the center cross. Silent tears coursed down her cheeks as she stood, her unblinking eyes grief-stricken.

She shouldn't be here. She should not have to witness this.

When her head turned toward him, their eyes met, only briefly, but in that moment, Marcus saw no hatred in her gaze as he had in the eyes of so many other Jews who saw him only as the heinous executioner. Self-conscious, he looked away. He stepped purposely toward the far side of the crosses, away from the thinning crowd.

Although he was awake and alert, images of his nightmare crept into his mind, and he couldn't shake them. The man in Bethesda, the blind beggar at the gate, and of course... Judith. Marcus couldn't deny the change in his father's wife, and it distorted his view of what he wanted to believe in Yeshua. So consumed by his thoughts, he didn't hear Gaius approach until he was shoulder to shoulder with his friend.

"It's something about this darkness, isn't it?"

Startled, Marcus silently chastised himself for not hearing Gaius' approach. His reply was curt. "Yes, quite odd."

"I don't get it," began the young centurion. "I thought this man was loved by everyone. Wasn't it just last week that the people were praising him as he rode into the city?"

Again, Marcus' response was short and to the point. "Yes, they were."

"Yet earlier they were screaming to have him crucified." Gaius shook his head. "I just don't understand. I thought they believed he was their king... their messiah."

Marcus glanced over to the group that surrounded Yeshua's mother. "Some still do, I suppose."

"Some messiah. You'd think by now they'd realized he was a fraud."

"Why do you say that?"

"Well, if he was what he claimed, wouldn't he be able to come down from that cross? I mean, if he really was a deity, he'd have the power, right?" Gaius raised one eyebrow.

"I suppose he would," concurred Marcus. He glanced over at some of his men gathered on the ground. He watched one toss a trio of tali on the dirt. The sheep knucklebones were often used in gambling games, and when a cheer erupted from the roller, Marcus sighed deeply. "At least they have something to occupy themselves," he stated under his breath.

"I heard they were playing for his clothes."

Marcus turned to Gaius. "Yeshua's clothes?"

"So I heard. Don't know why they'd want them, but..." He shrugged his shoulders. "Who knows? Maybe they'll sell them to one of his followers."

Marcus scowled.

Gaius studied his friend's face. "Something bothering you?"

"I just can't get them out of my head."

"Who?"

"Remember when we first got here? That man on the mat? At the pool in Bethesda?" He waited until Gaius nodded, then continued. "I think that he was there."

"Who? Who was there?"

"Yeshua."

"Yeshua? So what if he was?"

Marcus took a deep breath before confessing his innermost thoughts. "I think he may have been responsible for the healing."

A low chortle escaped Gaius' lips. "You're kidding, right? Don't tell me you're starting to believe the stories about him."

"I didn't say I believed them, but..." Marcus hesitated, then continued. "The other day, at the city gate, I saw this beggar–"

"This place is teeming with beggars."

"Well, this one was blind. I remember him because he practically blocked my path into the city. I saw his face... and his eyes. I remember his eyes. They were the color of goat's milk. All clouded over. Frankly, it was repulsive. I shoved him out of my way and continued on. I thought nothing of it until I saw him later."

"And?"

Marcus stated firmly, "His sight had been restored."

Gaius's eyes narrowed as he studied Marcus. "What do you mean 'restored'?"

"I mean, he could see! I asked him to explain what happened, and he told me that Yeshua had healed him of the blindness."

"It probably was a different beggar. They all look alike. Easy to confuse one with another." Gaius grinned as he crossed his arms over his leather chest plate. "Then again, maybe you had a bit too much to drink."

"I assure you I had no drink, and I tell you it was the same beggar except now his eyes were clear. As clear and blue as an unclouded sky."

"Come on, Marcus. You can't be serious. Do you really think Yeshua is the miracle-worker they say he is?"

Marcus shook his head. "I don't know what he is, or who for that matter. You heard the priests claim he said he was the Son of God."

"Which god?"

"*The* God. You know the Jews believe there's only one, and supposedly Yeshua is His Son, or so he claims."

"Again, I ask you if he truly was the Son of God, why doesn't he come down off that cross?"

"I don't know. It doesn't make sense to me. If I were in his place, that's what I would do, and I'd come down with a vengeance," replied Marcus as he scratched his chin. "Destroy us all... in a heartbeat."

"There's your answer, Marcus," stated Gaius confidently. "He isn't a god. He's just a man like you or me. Everything he supposedly did is just coincidence or trickery. Don't think so much. Your head will ache from it." He laughed as he slapped Marcus on the back. "I have rounds to make."

Marcus watched Gaius walk away, then lifted his eyes to the center cross. The darkness seemed to deepen as he stood at his post, and the disconcerted feeling was unshakeable. He turned back toward the city of Jerusalem. Small campfires still could be seen on the hills around the city, and a few lights could be seen from the homes within, but other than that, the gloom had enveloped everything. Far below him, even the graves on the mountainside were difficult to make out.

He cast a look across the Kidron Valley and noticed that the Jewish temple was also nearly obscured by the blackness. All that he could make out were the huge wooden doors, now opened for Passover. A golden glow coming from within the temple illuminated the entryway. Marcus had been told that the light was from the massive Jewish menorah that burned within it. From his vantage point on the slopes of Olivet, he could easily see the outline of the huge doors and what he presumed must be the massive veil that hid the most sacred section of the temple. He had heard stories of the inner temple, but this was the only time he had seen what was beyond the doors.

He turned his head back toward Yeshua and the two men hanging alongside him. Most of their moanings had ceased; all their efforts were focused on breathing. He watched as one of the thieves struggled to push himself upward to allow room for his lungs to expand. Exhaustion, coupled with the beatings and exposure to the elements, left him so weak that his efforts to breath resulted in feeble gasps.

At that moment, Yeshua cried out.

* * * * * *

Grief-stricken, Hadassah struggled to rise to her feet. Through reddened eyes, she stared at Yeshua. Clasping her hands to her chest, she groaned inwardly as her gaze moved from the center cross to the one on the right.

Uri hung limp, barely moving except to breathe, and even then, it was clear that death was imminent.

"Oh, Uri..." Her whispered voice broke as she wept for her friend. "How could this happen? Zara loved you; you loved her..."

As silent tears coursed down her cheeks, she turned around toward Jerusalem and saw the soft glow of light coming from the inner temple.

"I was so sure," she said woefully. Turning back to the crosses, her eyes settled on Yeshua. "I really believed you were the one, but now... How could you let them crucify you? If you really are our Messiah, how could they do this to you?"

A slight movement off to the side of the crosses caught her eye. She turned her head to see a silhouetted soldier, just as Yeshua's voice filled the air.

"My God! My God! Why have you forsaken me?"

The heartbroken cry from Yeshua cut through Hadassah's soul. The pain of abandonment in his voice echoed on the mountainside, then faded into the blackness. Hadassah clutched her hands to her heart and fell to her knees again, bowing her face low to the ground and sobbing uncontrollably once more.

"Oh, God in heaven, help him, please..." Her desperate plea was a whisper on the wind.

* * * * *

There were only a few left on the hillside witnessing the impending death of those on the crosses as Marcus encircled the site once more. The soldiers had long since tired of their games and were simply standing around waiting for death to come. The darkness seemed to compel everyone to speak in hushed tones, only the arduous breathing of the condemned cut through the chilling air.

Hearing footsteps coming up behind him, Marcus stopped and turned to face one of his legionnaires.

"Centurion, one of them thirsts." He nodded toward the crosses.

"Who?"

"The one in the center. The king of the Jews." Sarcasm laced his reply.

Marcus scowled. "Give him vinegar."

"But he refused it the first time."

A flash of anger erupted in Marcus' eyes. "You dare to question my order?"

Immediately bowing his head, the soldier stammered his apology. "Of course not, Centurion. Forgive me. Vinegar, as you have stated." He backed away quickly, then when a respectable distance from Marcus, he turned and hurried away to his task.

Within minutes, Marcus saw the young soldier approach Yeshua with a vinegar-soaked sponge held high on a hyssop.

"How much longer can you endure?" Marcus wondered aloud as he stared at the dying man. He shook his head in resignation. "If you really are who you claimed to be, why don't you save yourself?" His sigh was deep and introspective. "Evidently, you are as I am. A mere mortal who disfavored the gods, and this is your punishment."

As he spoke the words, he continued to ponder those whose lives had been impacted by the Nazarene. The lame man at Bethesda. The blind beggar in Jerusalem. Judith. Of those three, he was certain, but what of the stories he had been told? Cornelius' servant. What of that? Cornelius was a trusted Roman. He would not have lied, not to Marcus. And those miraculous feedings of which he had heard? What of those? A mere man could not have fed thousands with a boy's lunch. It would be impossible, yet more than one had said that it had happened. And there was the man called Lazarus. And that girl. The rumor was that Yeshua had raised both from the dead.

He raised his eyes up to the sign nailed above Yeshua's head.

King of the Jews. A king rejected by his own people.

Random thoughts bombarded his mind with unanswerable questions.

Who are you, Yeshua?

As he stood intently watching, a small movement of Yeshua's head caught his attention, and he stared at the rabbi. Before he had any time to consider what was happening, Yeshua cried out with a powerful voice.

"It… is… finished!"

Faint at first, then escalating like rolling thunder, a rumble seemed to swell and burst forth from the bowels of the earth as the ground began to convulse beneath Marcus' feet. His eyes darted from side to side as the undulations became stronger. Widening his stance, he crouched down slightly to remain upright as the earth shuddered and groaned. All creation seemed to cry out in agony as the intensity of the quake strengthened. Fearing the crosses might come crashing down, he cast a look toward them, but they held fast as did the bodies that were nailed to them.

Marcus glanced at the men stationed around the crucifixion site. They were bewildered at the natural phenomenon, but as true Roman legionnaires, they stood fast at their posts.

A faint glow caught Marcus' eye, and he looked out over the Kidron valley toward Mount Moriah and the site of the Jewish temple. From his vantage point, the light of the huge menorah seemed to burn brighter, illuminating the thick heavy veil that separated the inner sanctum from the outer sections of the temple. As he watched, it seemed as if everything in his range of vision froze for a moment in time except the veil. It began to separate, rending itself from top to bottom. He stood speechless as he stared at the temple, watching the veil split into two sections, eliminating the barrier between the outer and inner sanctums.

What's going on? Nothing is making any sense!

Confusion flooded his thoughts as Marcus tried to comprehend what was happening. He started to turn back toward the crucifixion site when his eyes skimmed over the ancient Jewish cemetery on the lower slope of the Mount of Olives. He stopped abruptly when he noticed that many of the white limestone graves had been disturbed; smooth slabs of stone had shifted, and the old sepulchres were lying open as if someone had pushed them aside.

Meticulously, he scanned the cemetery grounds for a sign of those responsible, squinting his eyes as the ethereal forms of men seemed to take shape and move among the graves. Rubbing his eyes, he blinked to clear his vision. When he looked again, they were gone.

Get hold of yourself, Marcus. You're beginning to imagine things.

Even though he decided the slabs had been moved by the quake, he rushed down to the nearest graves and closely examined the area, just in case. He peered into an open grave. Nothing. No bones, no body! He checked another. The findings were the same. He turned abruptly and headed back to the crosses, questions swimming in his head.

What is going on?

Slowly, as the darkness lifted from the surrounding countryside, it also began to lift from his mind. A new awareness seeped into the crevices of his consciousness as he turned slowly toward the limp body of Yeshua hanging on the rugged cross, and a new understanding began to dawn.

He was unable to stop the overwhelming possibility of the truth that bombarded his mind as he glanced back at the Jewish temple. He staggered under the weight of the realization of what had happened and the role he had played in the execution of Yeshua. It nearly dropped him to his knees.

"What have I done?" Marcus murmured with a conviction so deep it cut to his marrow. For the first time, he understood what fear felt like, and it terrified him. He raised his eyes once more to the lifeless form of Yeshua and spoke the words that cut through him like a knife. "Truly, this man was the Son of God."

* * * * * *

"Centurion!"

Marcus turned toward the voice. He swallowed hard, then willed his voice to be unemotional. "What is it?

"These men… they claim to have a letter from Pilate." The soldier's breathing was labored as he stopped in front of Marcus holding out a message with Pilate's seal upon it.

Marcus grabbed the paper, broke the seal, and read the words.

"Where are these men?" he asked looking up.

"We are here," came a reply from the shadows. Stepping out from behind the soldier came two men.

"I am Yosef. Yosef of Arimathea, and this is Nicodemus."

Marcus studied the small frame of the Jewish Pharisee before him. "You? You want the body of the rabbi? For what purpose?"

Nicodemus lowered his eyes. "Yes, Centurion. Please... we have brought myrrh and aloes, and the linens for his body... to bury him according to our custom." His plea was almost reverent.

"You sent him to the cross, and now you want his body?"

"We were not part of that conspiracy," his sorrowful voice declared.

"We have a place for his burial. A newly hewn tomb in which to lay him," explained Yosef quietly. "My own."

Marcus said nothing as he stood stoically. His steely gaze focused on the grieved eyes of the Pharisee.

Nicodemus and Yosef stood silently, and for a brief moment, an unspoken understanding passed between them and the centurion. Finally, Marcus nodded his consent. "After my men assure me that he is dead, he will be removed according to your custom... before sunset. You may take him then."

Nodding slightly, the men stepped back and disappeared into the fading darkness.

Marcus' attention was drawn to the soldiers moving around the crosses. He watched as one broke the legs of the criminal on the far cross. The thief was so near death, he uttered no sound as his bones were shattered. Moving toward Yeshua, the soldier hesitated and turned toward Marcus.

"He's already dead."

Marcus made a slight movement of his head toward one of the guards.

"Make sure of it."

The guard nodded, then took his spear and thrust it upward into the body of Yeshua. Blood mingled with water flowed through the wound.

"How could you?"

Immediately recognizing the voice, he spun around. Taken aback by her presence, he stammered, "Hadassah! What are you doing here?"

Her tortured face spoke volumes, and he knew the answer to his own question.

Of course, you're here. Where else would you be?"

She looked him squarely in the eye, and he knew what was coming before she voiced one word.

"How could you do this to him? You know he didn't do anything wrong! You couldn't wait to destroy him, could you?"

The hatred in her eyes for him wounded him deeply, but he held his tongue as she spewed her accusations at him. He could have silenced her, but he didn't. Her condemnation of him was true, and it tore at his soul. He had no words to offer in his defense, nothing to justify his actions. He simply stood and took the blows of her words as she unleashed all of her anger on him.

Chapter Nineteen

"And as they were afraid, and bowed down their faces to the earth, they said unto them, Why seek ye the living among the dead?" Luke 24:5

Hadassah didn't want to believe that Marcus had a part in Yeshua's death, but he had stood before her, and she knew it was true. Her broken heart bore a double burden now, and she didn't know how to ward off the oppressive sorrow that overwhelmed her.

She hastened over to Judith, pouring out her grief.

"Are you sure it was Marcus?"

"Yes, Dodah. I even spoke to him, but...he didn't answer me. He just stood there." Despair accompanied her words as Hadassah's face contorted in anguish. "I can't believe he killed him. How could he do that?"

Judith sighed deeply. "He is a Roman centurion, Hadassah. He must do as he is commanded."

"Even if it's wrong? He killed Yeshua and Uri! I hate him!" Her words choked off, and she lowered her head. "I will never forgive him for this. Never!"

Judith reached out and pulled Hadassah into her arms. "I know this is hurting you deeply, but you must be strong. God is still with us."

Hadassah pulled away from Judith and lifted her forlorn face to her aunt.

"What will we do now, Dodah? I thought he was our messiah."

"As did I." Judith choked back a sob.

Hadassah's eyes moved to the crosses. "Look... they're taking him down now." She watched as the cross was lowered to the ground then turned away. "It's over, isn't it?"

Neither woman heard the approaching footsteps, so when the deep voice interrupted their thoughts, both jumped.

"Hadassah, may I speak with you?"

Judith and Hadassah turned sharply as Marcus neared them. Despite all of his confidence as a Roman warrior, he hesitated to speak when the women faced him. His eyes moved from one to the other, then came to rest on Hadassah's hardened face. He started to move closer to her, but then stopped where he was.

"I wanted to explain." He paused for a moment, turning his head to view the last cross being lowered to the ground. Slowly, he turned back toward them.

"Explain? Explain what, Marcus? An innocent man being put to death?" Hadassah's wrath exploded once more. "A man who only spoke of forgiveness and loving others being crucified? A man who brought healing to those who desperately needed it? No explanation necessary, Marcus! I saw you *kill* Yeshua!"

Her voice boomed as she continued her ranting. She stepped toward him with her fists clenched while Judith simply watched with her arms crossed over her chest.

He stood still, anticipating Hadassah's blows, but they never came. Instead, she continued her verbal attack. In silence, he allowed her to pummel him with accusations that he knew were true. His gaze never wavered from her outraged face.

"You killed a man who did nothing to you or Rome! He was just a teacher and a healer, while you and your cohorts are nothing but... but cowards! He was an innocent man!"

"No. You're wrong, Hadassah—"

"Wrong?" Her fury was mingled with hot tears. "Wrong? How dare you say that! I saw you! I saw—"

"You're not wrong about what you saw. Yes, the crucifixion detail was my responsibility, and I regret that, but Yeshua was not an ordinary man. He was more than all those things you've just stated. I wanted you to know that..." His hesitation was enough to make Hadassah pause and listen. "I believe Yeshua truly was the Son of your God."

Hadassah's mouth dropped open, but no sound came out. Skepticism filled her eyes as they roamed over Marcus' face. Her hands balled up again as she rushed him, and this time she struck him again and again on his chest.

"How dare you say that! How dare you! You don't believe! You never did!"

"Please, hear me out," implored Marcus as he took hold of her arms.

"Let me go!" She struggled against him until he released his hold.

"Please Hadassah..."

"I don't want to ever speak to you again, Marcus!" She pushed away from him and stepped back, increasing the distance between them. "And I most certainly don't want to listen to you!"

Unsure of what to do, he called out to her as she walked away from him.

"Please, Hadassah. Please listen to me for just a few minutes—"

"Listen to you?" Hadassah whirled around; her face distorted with rage. "You must be kidding! You expect me to listen to you? The one who killed Yeshua? You are more a fool than I thought." She glared at him without a hint of compassion in her eyes.

If I don't speak now, I'll never have another chance.

Despite her refusal to listen, Marcus was desperate for her to hear what he had to say. He called out to her as she started to walk away again. "I saw things... And then, Yeshua, he said things...He was calling out to someone, but no one was there. He called him his father, and he asked him...to forgive *us*. He said we didn't know what we were doing."

She turned abruptly once more and furiously shook a finger at him. "You knew exactly what you were doing, and you don't deserve to be forgiven, not now. Not ever!"

The magnitude of her anger silenced him. Marcus' face was grim as he nodded in agreement.

"Maybe you're right." A deep sigh accompanied his acquiescence as she fled his presence. He watched her until she disappeared, and then he whispered his last words to her. "Goodbye, Hadassah."

With a heavy heart, he walked slowly back to the site of Yeshua's death.

* * * * * *

When Hadassah finally looked back, Marcus was gone. She took a deep breath as the tension left her body, but she felt no closure to anything. No answers to her questions. No hope for the future. The ache inside her was intense, and she groaned as she stumbled along the path.

Lifting her eyes heavenward, she whispered, "What do I do now?" A faint breeze swirled around her, and she heard the voice of Yeshua within her.

Love your enemies, bless them that curse you, do good to them that hate you, and pray for them which despitefully use you, and persecute you.

"I can't," she cried out, stubbornly. "How can I love the ones who killed you?"

Fear thou not; for I am with thee: be not dismayed; for I am thy God: I will strengthen thee; yea, I will help thee; yea, I will uphold thee with the right hand of my righteousness.

She glanced up the hill. Most of the people had left the slope of the mountain, but near the crucifixion site she saw the silhouette of one Roman soldier. In her heart, she knew it was Marcus. She shook her head emphatically.

I just can't.

As she walked over to her aunt, Judith extended her hand, and Hadassah clasped it. Judith asked no questions, and Hadassah was too miserable to offer any information as they headed across the Kidron Valley, back to Jerusalem. They walked in silence toward the eastern gate, each consumed by their own grief and lost in their own thoughts.

* * * * * *

Hadassah couldn't escape the overwhelming sadness that encompassed her. In less than twenty-four hours, she had lost nearly everything that had meant anything to her. Yeshua was gone. Uri was gone. And now Marcus was gone.

Despair was her sole companion as she meandered through Jerusalem. Life seemed to go on as usual everywhere she went. While she felt her whole world had ended, the crucifixion of Yeshua and Uri went unnoticed by most of the people. While others were smiling as they mingled one with another, Hadassah had no joy within her, and although it was the Feast of the Unleavened Bread, Hadassah's broken heart refused to celebrate.

She heard merchants hawking their wares; she passed beggars asking for alms, but she ignored them all, unable to see beyond her own grief. Finally, fatigue overtook her, and she found a secluded spot wherein she could sit and rest. She dropped her head into her hands and bitterly wept.

I thought Yeshua was the promised one, our Messiah. I saw him raise Lazarus from the dead. Who else but God could restore life in someone from the grave? He said he was the Son of God, but how could they kill him then?

Questions tormented her until they finally faded away from her consciousness, and the reality of Yeshua's death replaced them. She lifted her head up to the heavens.

"You would have saved him, wouldn't you? If he really had been your son, surely you wouldn't have let him die." Her whispered voice shook slightly as she sought answers from God, but silence was the only response. Dejected, she rose and walked back to her uncle's home.

* * * * * *

It had been three days since Yeshua had been put to death, and even though Hadassah had accepted the reality of the crucifixion, she still felt lost. For the most part, sleep had eluded her. Despite her best efforts, she tossed and turned throughout the nights, unable to find any peace in slumber.

Once again, a new day was dawning, but nothing had changed for Hadassah. Judith had found solace in companionship with Milcah, but Hadassah chose to mourn in solitude. Today, she sat on the rooftop of Gabriel's home as the sun began to rise over the distant hills of Judea. A warm breeze blew the tendrils of her long black hair, but she made no attempt to control the wisps as they fluttered around her face.

She could see into the city streets, the deserted pathways reflective of the emptiness within her heart. As she stared afar, a movement caught her attention. Refocusing, she saw a young woman run down the narrow street and enter a darkened home. Within minutes, the woman reemerged, followed by two men. The trio ran back the way the woman had come and disappeared beyond the city wall.

Hadassah closed her eyes. In her mind she could still see Yeshua and hear his words.

Blessed are they that mourn, for they shall be comforted.

* * * * * *

"You all *slept*?" Marcus exploded when he received the report that his men had fallen asleep while guarding Yeshua's tomb. "You are Roman legionnaires! You do not sleep at your post!" He stood, slamming his fists on the table.

"The rabbi's followers must have come and taken his body during the night when... when the guards slept," stated the soldier nervously. "It has never happened before, Centurion. Perhaps, there was something in our drink–"

Marcus spun around, rage in his eyes. "You actually want that to be the story on record? All eight of you were drugged, and fell into a stupor allowing an ignorant group of fishermen to steal a dead body from a tomb that was guarded by eight of Rome's finest soldiers and secured with the governor's seal? Is that what you want me to report to Pilate?"

"No, Centurion," he lowered his eyes. "I do not, but–"

"But what?" Marcus' voice rose along with his level of anger.

The soldier's voice shook as he vainly tried to find the words to explain his actions. "I... we... we sought refuge and counsel."

"Refuge?" Marcus's eyes burned. "Where?"

The soldier hesitated, but when Marcus stepped toward him, he quickly stammered, "We fled to the priests."

"The Jews? You went to the *Jews*?" Marcus' face reddened.

"What I reported, I was told to tell you–"

"Told? By whom?" Marcus' unforgiving eyes narrowed as he awaited the answer.

The legionnaire lowered his gaze as he confessed, "The priests."

"The priests? You alone have come to report to me, and you cannot even speak your own words? Instead you must use a fabrication given you by Jewish priests?" Marcus stomped over to the stoic man. "Look at me and tell me the truth, soldier!" He stood nose to nose with the remorseful legionnaire.

Fear was etched on the soldier's face as Marcus' cold and unsympathetic eyes bore into him. Nervously, he cleared his throat. "We did not all sleep,

Centurion. It was as we have always done. We slept only in shifts; of that I am sure."

"You have only this one opportunity to explain what happened, and I warn you, if you lie, I will know." The intent was clear; Marcus never made empty threats.

The soldier swallowed hard. "The area was secure. No one else was there. It was still dark, and we were at our posts when the earth began to shake again. Like at the crucifixions. And then there was the light. A brilliant light and within it, there was a form, like that of a man, but... but his face was on fire, like the bolts of Apollo! His clothing was as new snow, white and glowing. He spoke nothing to us. He seemed to descend from the heavenlies and just hovered near the sepulchre.

"Then the stone that barred the entrance of the tomb began to roll, but there was no one moving it! The ropes beneath the seal just seemed to fall off, and the stone moved on its own. It rolled away from the opening and then stopped. Then, this... this god sat upon the stone itself, and we became as statues ourselves. We couldn't move."

Shamefully, he lowered his head. "I remember nothing else. When we woke, all was as it had been except the tomb was no longer sealed shut."

Marcus eyed the soldier suspiciously. "And then what? You saw Yeshua?"

The man's brow furrowed as he shook his head slightly. "Yeshua? No. We saw no one but the golden being, and we..." His head hung in disgrace. "We fled. As soon as the spell was broken, we ran. We all ran."

"To the priests?"

"Yes."

"They said the truth would be our deaths, and we were paid to report the lie." He allowed a handful of coins to fall from his hand onto the table. "The high priest told us he would convince the governor to spare us all." Regret accompanied his confession.

"You know full well the punishment for failing to maintain your post," stated Marcus barely controlling his anger. "Why would you even suspect Pilate would listen to Caiaphas? Confine yourself to your quarters until further notice. And speak of this to no one!"

The legionnaire silently exited the great hall, leaving Marcus to determine if he would bring this before the governor. Roman guards had very strict orders to follow. Each member was responsible for a specific amount of space, and was expected to guard it meticulously, without sitting or leaning while on duty. If sleep overcame the guard, not only would he be beaten and executed, but the other members of his unit would suffer the same fate as well.

Marcus uttered a curse. He did not want to lose any of his men to such an act of stupidity and irresponsibility. Stomping out of the hall, he headed toward the stable. If he had any hope of defending his men, he would need more information.

Within minutes, Ares was saddled and galloping out across the Kidron Valley with Marcus atop him. The ride was not long, and although he rode the horse hard, Ares was not even close to being winded by the time they reached the tomb. Marcus quickly dismounted and walked up to the open tomb leaving the horse to nibble on the small grasses.

The large boulder still bore remnants of the broken seals, and the rope sat off to one side of the opening of the sepulchre. Too huge for one man to move by himself, Marcus realized there had to be several of Yeshua's followers working together to move the massive stone.

He glanced around the grounds, and seeing no one, he stepped inside the tomb. The late morning sun cast enough light for him to easily see that there was definitely no body there. He stooped over the rock slab where Yeshua had once lain, reached out and picked up the linen that had once shrouded the crucified rabbi. He turned it over in his hands as he inspected it. The facial covering was folded near the head of the slab, but he didn't disturb it. Frustrated, Marcus threw the grave clothes on the ground and exited the tomb.

He walked over to the chiseled stone that served to seal the sepulchre. He knelt down to inspect the cords that had been used to move and secure the rock. There were no marks on the rock; only Pilate's seals had been broken, and the ends of the ropes appeared singed.

I underestimated his followers. They are more daring than I thought. To break the seal of Rome is a capital offense.

The sound of footsteps prompted Marcus to rise and pivot around, moving his hand to his scabbard.

Dressed in the traditional garb of the Pharisee, a man walked up the narrow path to the tomb. A vague familiarity stirred in Marcus' mind.

"Who goes there?" he queried as soon as the man was fully visible.

The man stopped abruptly before answering. "It is I, Centurion. Nicodemus. I mean you no harm. I was the one with Yosef at the crucifixion of Yeshua. We procured the body from you. I have come merely to see for myself."

Marcus relaxed, allowing his hand to fall to his side. "See what?"

Nicodemus stepped up to him, looked at the tomb, then back at Marcus. "It is empty?"

Marcus nodded. "Yes."

"Then it is true." The confirmation settled any doubt in the Pharisee's mind.

"What? That one of your people stole the body of Yeshua? Yes, that's true," stated Marcus. His irritated voice went unnoticed by Nicodemus.

"No, Centurion." A knowing smile crept across his face. "Yeshua has risen as he said he would. I... I didn't believe it at first, but Mary was so sure. She told me she came early in the morning to anoint the body. Others were with her. They were met by..." He hesitated.

Marcus' eyes narrowed. "Tell me the name. He has violated Roman law and will be punished accordingly."

A low chuckle escaped the Pharisee's lips. "That you will be unable to do, Centurion, for they were met by an angel of God who told them that Yeshua was not here. That he had risen as he had predicted."

Nicodemus' voice was strong and vibrant as he recalled an earlier conversation with the rabbi. "Yeshua himself told us 'the Son of man must be delivered into the hands of sinful men, and be crucified, and the third day rise again.' And now it has come to pass! Yeshua lives! He is risen as he said!"

"No one can be raised from the dead," protested Marcus.

"No one but the Son of God."

Stunned at Nicodemus' declaration, Marcus stood speechless. The Jew reached out and placed his hands on Marcus' shoulders.

"I, too, had questions, Centurion. Shamefully, I sought Yeshua by night. I feared my own people, yet I had to know the truth. I knew that no man could do the miracles he did except God be with him. He told me that unless a man was born again, it would be impossible for him to see the kingdom of God."

Nicodemus shook his head thoughtfully as he recalled his conversation with Yeshua. A faint smile appeared on his face. "He made no sense to me. I asked him how a man could be born when he is old? Could he enter the second time into his mother's womb and be born once more? And you know what he said to me? He said unless a man was born of water *and* of the Spirit, he could not enter into the kingdom of God."

"You speak nonsense," stated Marcus, shaking his head.

Nicodemus nodded. "I understand your confusion, but these are his words, not mine. 'For God so loved the world that He gave His only begotten Son that whosoever believeth in Him should not perish, but have everlasting life. For God sent not his Son into the world to condemn the world; but that the world through him might be saved.' Those are the words of Yeshua himself."

Nicodemus looked deeply in Marcus' skeptical eyes. "You know I speak the truth. Yeshua truly is the Son of God, sent to deliver His people, but not just His people... Yeshua said '*whosoever* believeth in Him.' That includes you, Centurion. To believe in Yeshua means you will never perish. Instead, you will have everlasting life in the kingdom of God! Through Himself, Yeshua has given hope to a world that desperately needs it. If you but accept Him for who he truly is, Centurion, your life will change. You will be born again, and you will receive God's gift of eternal life."

Marcus shifted his weight. His discomfort was evident, and Nicodemus nodded knowingly.

"Centurion, you know in your soul that Yeshua's body was not stolen. It is as he said it would be. He has risen. It is time to move beyond mere belief that something may have happened. The time has come to accept what we both know happened. Yeshua, the Son of God, has risen! Our Messiah is alive!" He hesitated for a moment, then stated, "I must go. There are those who need to hear this good news, and I am compelled to tell them! I hope and pray you will listen to what you know in your heart is true, Centurion."

Marcus watched Nicodemus amble off, disappearing into the brush below the gravesite. He turned back to the tomb. Its lack of occupancy was a silent testimony to the truth spoken by Nicodemus, yet Marcus struggled to accept the possibility that Yeshua was now alive when once he had been dead.

The Son of man must be delivered into the hands of sinful men, and be crucified, and the third day rise again.

Everything that Marcus had experienced since coming to Judea was spinning in his head. The teachings, the healings, the miracles... Yeshua himself. Now, he stood before an empty tomb mulling over the things Nicodemus had said. Nothing made much sense, but then when it came to Yeshua, nothing usually did make sense.

He needed answers, but he had no idea where to go to get them.

Chapter Twenty

"And they said, Believe on the Lord Jesus Christ, and thou shalt be saved..."
Acts 16:31

The knocking on the door startled Hadassah, and her sleepy eyes snapped open just as Gabriel called out. "Judith! Hadassah! Come quickly!"

Alarmed that her uncle would summon them so early, Hadassah sat upright, grabbed her tunic and slipped it over her head. She gently shook Judith.

"Dodah, wake up. Dod Gabriel calls for us. It sounds important." Her voice was firm, but not so much as to frighten Judith.

As her aunt roused from her sleep, Hadassah called out to her uncle. "We are coming, Dod Gabriel. We will be right there."

"What's wrong, Hadassah?" Judith quickly changed her bedclothes for a fresh tunic, then pulled her hair back, tying it with a long ribbon.

"I don't know, Dodah. I was awakened by his knocking, and then he called for us." Hadassah ran a comb through her thick locks, wound them into a single braid, and pinned it into place at the nape of her neck. She grabbed a shawl and wrapped it around her shoulders, then offered Judith one of her own.

Satisfied they were presentable, the women hurried into the main room. Gabriel and Milcah were there, and their eyes shone brightly. The women were barely into the room before Gabriel enthusiastically announced his news.

"It is a miracle! He lives!" exclaimed Gabriel excitedly.

Judith looked at Hadassah, who returned her puzzled gaze. She then turned to her uncle. "Who lives, Dod Gabriel?"

He could not suppress his delight as he blurted out, "Your Yeshua! He lives!" His eyes were radiant with joy as he clapped his hands together.

"No, Dod, he died. I was there. I saw—"

Gabriel's head shook as he interrupted Judith. "I am not denying his death, my child. What I am telling you is that Yeshua is no longer dead. He has risen! He is alive!"

"What?" Hadassah stared at him incredulously. "What are you saying?" Her head shook in disbelief. "He was crucified! I saw him die!"

"I am saying that Yeshua has risen from the dead! You must believe me! Of course, I haven't seen him myself, but he has been seen by some of his followers, and they are proclaiming that he has risen as he said he would do!" Gabriel announced boldly. "It is a time to rejoice!"

Judith sat shocked, her face pale. "You are positive that's what they said?" Her voice trembled as she spoke. "Are you truly sure?" She clasped her hands together as if in prayer and drew them to her chest.

"Yes! Yes! I am positive, my niece! I would never break your hearts by telling you something I was not assured to be the truth. But this news is a certainty! Yeshua is alive! He is risen from the dead!"

Judith closed her eyes as she lifted her face heavenward. "Praise to the Almighty!" she whispered over and over as tears of joy freely coursed down her cheeks.

Hadassah was not so easily convinced. "Truly, Dod Gabriel? Who did you hear this from? What people?" she asked, unwilling to believe his words.

Milcah reached a hand out to Hadassah, resting it on her forearm. "I heard it from Joanna. I have known her for years. She is not prone to exaggerations or hallucinations. It was early in the morning when she went to the tomb with her friends to anoint the body. When they arrived, they found the entrance to the tomb open, and the body was gone! They supposed the soldiers had taken the body away, but..."

Milcah's eyes shone as she spoke in a hushed whisper. "She said an *angel* was there! He told her that Yeshua was not there for he had risen as he said!" She clapped her hands together several times as her voice escalated in volume. "You must believe, Hadassah. Yeshua lives!"

"He is alive?" Hadassah dared to believe the answer. "He really is alive?" She turned to Judith for confirmation.

"Search your heart, Hadassah! Surely you must feel within you the truth of what they say! Our Yeshua lives!" Judith opened her arms, and when Hadassah fell into them, both women wept for joy.

* * * * * *

By the time Marcus had returned to Antonia's Fortress, his external composure masked the inner conflict he now faced. He knew his men would be punished, most likely executed for their failure at containing the body of Yeshua, but now Marcus believed there would have been nothing they could have done to stop the resurrection of the Son of God. Persuading Pilate to be merciful would be nearly impossible. The governor was well known for many things, but mercy was not one of them.

"Marcus! Where have you been?" Gaius called out as he approached.

"I went to inspect the tomb of the Nazarene."

"So you've heard then?" Gaius raised a brow.

Marcus nodded. "I've heard."

"And the tomb?"

"Empty."

Gaius made a clucking sound. "Pilate will not be pleased."

Marcus sighed deeply. "Nothing pleases Pilate these days."

"So, we'll search for those responsible?"

"If we are ordered to do so, I suppose we will."

A questioning look covered Gaius' face. "*If* we are ordered? I thought you'd be eager to recover the body and prove the zealots wrong."

"I don't believe the zealots took his body," stated Marcus without looking at his friend.

"Then who? The fishermen? I highly doubt that. They scattered like chaff in the wind when he was arrested. I even heard that as soon as he was taken, one of them staunchly refused any association with him. Some followers, eh?" A wiry grin crossed his face.

"Don't underestimate these Jews," Marcus cautioned. "Things aren't always as they appear."

"What does that mean?"

Marcus hesitated as he faced Gaius. "There has been talk that Yeshua prophesied his own resurrection before he died and that now... now that prophecy has come true."

Gaius lifted an eyebrow as a skeptical grin formed on his face. "Really?

You can't believe that."

Marcus said nothing.

Gaius' smile quickly faded. "You don't believe it, do you?"

Again, Marcus did not respond.

Perplexed with Marcus' silence, he asked again, "Do you?"

Marcus's lips tightened as his hardened gaze felt on his friend's face. "We will speak of this at a later time. Right now, I have to meet with the prefect."

He turned and headed down the corridor to face Pilate.

* * * * * *

As expected, Pilate was outraged, but when the priests presented their fabricated story with a hefty amount of coins, his fiery temper was placated, and he merely ordered Marcus to "handle the situation."

Now Marcus rode through the streets of Jerusalem, unsure of what he was actually seeking. His men had been posted at the city gates, watching for any suspicious activity, but Marcus suspected their efforts would be fruitless. Still, he followed his orders, determined to fulfill his duties as a Roman officer to the best of his ability. It wouldn't be the first time he had followed orders in which he himself believed to be pointless.

The city didn't seem as volatile as the days prior to Passover, and for that, Marcus was glad. The increased presence of the Roman military coupled with the crucifixion of Yeshua squelched any hint of insurgency. As he scanned the crowds for familiar faces, he saw no one that he remembered as one of Yeshua's followers. It was almost as if they had never existed... as if the last few days had been completely erased.

Blind beggars sat by the gates; their hands held out for a few coins. Merchants presented their wares while shoppers bargained for the best deals. Rabbis still taught the same small groups of attentive students. The only thing missing was the underlying air of expectancy.

Deciding to search beyond the city, Marcus turned Ares toward the eastern gate. Crossing the Kidron Valley, he rode up the gentle slope of the Mount of Olives, passing the site of Yeshua's death. He headed toward Gethsemane, weaving Ares through the massive olive trees.

As he ambled through the gnarled trees, a small gathering caught his attention. Maybe a dozen or so men sat shaded beneath the ancient branches of one of the old trees. As he neared, no one bothered to turn his way. Slowly riding by, Marcus looked past those seated to the one who was speaking. He sat up a little taller in the saddle.

I know that voice...

He slowed Ares down, and his stunned eyes fixated on the speaker. He halted the horse and leaned to one side for a better view. Dumbfounded, he stared, mesmerized by what he saw. From his vantage point, Marcus had an unobstructed view of the deep reddened sites of the nail piercings as the man lifted his hands heavenward.

Yeshua? It can't be you. I saw you die. It is really you? You're really alive?

Unsure of what to do, Marcus dismounted slowly. His instincts told him he was making himself too vulnerable, but the desire to see and hear Yeshua compelled him to go forward. He had to verify that it really was the same man he had crucified a few days earlier, if only to convince himself that his eyes were not playing tricks on him. He had to know if the man who was once dead, now sat before him, alive and well.

Marcus had struggled to truly accept the fact that Yeshua had been resurrected, but now the evidence was right in front of him. Taking a few steps forward, Marcus' sandaled feet crunched the dried clods of dirt beneath them. He stopped abruptly when the rabbi lifted his head and looked directly at him. If Marcus hadn't been so disciplined, he would have turned and ran. Instead, he stood stoically without uttering a word, his eyes locked with those of Yeshua.

A slight movement to his left caused him to glance away from the rabbi. One of the followers was approaching. Marcus tensed, his fingers closing around his dagger's handle.

"Welcome, Centurion. I'm Andrew. Please, come join us." He gestured to the circle of men sitting around Yeshua.

The longing Marcus felt within him to sit with the group, to listen to the words of Yeshua, to truly understand what had happened was overpowering, but he fought the urge to join them. Marcus looked back at the rabbi and confessed the obvious, "I cannot. I... I am your enemy."

"There are no enemies here, Marcus." Yeshua's voice seemed to float on the wind.

Marcus hesitated. His heart pounded in his chest. He resisted the urge to flee as he scanned the group. His troubled eyes rested on Yeshua.

If you knew who I was, and what I did to you...

Yeshua simply looked at him with eyes full of compassion, understanding, and... forgiveness.

Marcus glanced once more at the group of men, all looking his way. Their nods and smiles overcame his resistance, and hesitantly he removed his helmet as the men made room for him. Lowering himself to the ground, his eyes darted from man to man. Uneasy about his surroundings, his hand remained poised to defend himself if the need arose.

And then Yeshua began to speak.

Everything around Marcus faded into the background. Captivated by what he heard, Marcus' attention was riveted on the words of truth that came from the man who had been crucified just a few days earlier.

All the questions he had since that morning at the tomb seemed inconsequential now. He knew that the man speaking to him was the same man whose death he had witnessed on the Mount of Olives. He knew when the body had been removed from the cross and handed over to the Jews, there had been no life in it. Yet, here he sat, speaking, laughing, and interacting. There was no doubt anymore. All the questions that had flooded Marcus' mind had been answered by one glaring truth.

Yeshua was alive!

As he feasted on the words of life, Marcus could no longer deny the truth of Yeshua's identity and the reality of the rabbi's resurrection. Marcus knew he really was listening to the Son of God, and the words of Nicodemus echoed in his mind.

For God so loved the world that He gave His only begotten Son that whosoever believeth in Him should not perish, but have everlasting life. For God sent not his Son into the world to condemn the world, but that the world through him might be saved.

Marcus was a changed man. Nothing would ever be the same again for the Roman centurion.

* * * * * *

Hadassah sat very still listening to Joanna recount her experience at Yeshua's tomb. Riveted to the story, she hardly blinked at all while the older woman spoke of angels and the incredible realization that Yeshua had truly risen.

"Mary actually spoke to him, but she didn't even know it was him!" Light laughter came from her lips as she continued. "She thought it was a groundskeeper until the moment he said her name. When he said, 'Mary,' she knew it was him!"

"Can we go to him?" asked Hadassah excitedly. "Where is he?"

Joanna shook her head. "I don't know, but I do know he's been seen by several of his followers. Phillip said Yeshua even appeared to them in a locked room! Can you imagine that? They thought he was a spirit at first, but he was just like you or me!" Her voice became a hushed whisper as if revealing a treasured secret. "Yeshua is risen! Just as he told us." She clasped Hadassah's hands in her own as her eyes danced with joy. "He truly is our Messiah!"

Hadassah's eyes sparkled as she squeezed Joanna's fingers. "Oh, I wish I could see him before we leave. Do you think he'll go to the temple? Surely, he'll come to us?"

"I don't know," replied Joanna thoughtfully. "Someone said that he was going toward Galilee."

"Galilee?"

"Yes, but I don't know if that's a certainty. If not here, perhaps you'll see him there. You are leaving for Capernaum later, aren't you?"

Hadassah nodded. "Yes. Many of us are leaving before sunset today." Impulsively, she hugged Joanna. "Thank you so much for sharing your story. I cannot tell you how much it means to me."

Joanna smiled. "Our Messiah has come, Hadassah! Now you must promise me that you will spread the news to others. The world must know that Yeshua, the Son of God, lives!"

Hadassah beamed. "I will! I promise!"

* * * * * *

Later that afternoon as the procession of travelers left the protective walls of Jerusalem, Hadassah walked in silence as she pondered all the recent events to which she had been a witness.

The joy of Yeshua's resurrection was marred by her knowledge of Marcus' involvement in the executions. Bitterness swelled in her heart whenever she thought of Marcus, and she hoped she would not see him again. Even if he was in Capernaum, she had determined that she would not interact with him unless absolutely necessary.

"Hadassah?"

Her train of thought was broken by Judith's voice. She turned to her aunt. "Yes, Dodah?"

As if reading her mind, Judith asked, "You've been very quiet. What troubles you?"

Hadassah's lips tightened. Uncomfortable with the question, she said nothing.

"Hadassah?" Judith reached out and wrapped her fingers around Hadassah's arm stopping her from moving ahead.

Reluctant to wrench her arm from Judith's grasp, Hadassah stopped, but she didn't look at her aunt.

"What's wrong?"

"I'm sorry, Dodah. It's just that..."

"What? What is it?"

"I was thinking of Marcus."

Judith nodded in understanding. "You have not forgiven him."

"How can I?" Hadassah kept her face to the road as she walked.

Judith walked silently beside her for a few moments before responding. "You understand that Marcus had to do what he did. If he had refused, he would have been severely punished, possibly executed himself."

Hadassah pressed her lips together tightly and said nothing.

Judith continued. "You know he is Justus' son. The chances are great that there will be a time when you will see him again."

Hadassah remained silent, and Judith said no more as they walked. Soon the older woman's attention was diverted to other travelers, and she left Hadassah alone to go chat with them.

The more Hadassah walked alone, the heavier her heart became as Yeshua's words echoed in her mind.

Love your enemies.

A scowl appeared on her face as she plodded along.

How can I love Marcus for what he did? How can I forgive him?

Her questions hung in the air unanswered as her burden of guilt grew.

The rest of their time of travel only succeeded in Hadassah's temperament becoming more sullen as she wrestled with her emotions. Forgiving Marcus for his role in the crucifixions was inconceivable to her, yet the words of Yeshua continued to pound inside her head.

Love your enemies.

Her lack of forgiveness toward Marcus gnawed at her with each mile walked, and she allowed her anger to fester.

He not only killed Yeshua, but he killed Uri as well. I can never forgive him!

As her heart hardened toward Marcus, so did her guilt, but she stubbornly refused to allow any measure of love or forgiveness to filter into her soul.

When they finally arrived home, Hadassah immersed herself into her daily activities, and any memory of Marcus was pushed into the shadowed recesses of her consciousness. However, the bitterness and anger always returned whenever she reflected on her time in Jerusalem.

* * * * * *

"I don't understand, Zara," said Hadassah as she sat with her friend. "How can you be so content after all that's happened?"

Zara's brow furrowed as she raised her eyes to meet Hadassah's. "I guess because in my heart I've forgiven Uri."

"Uri? What about Marcus? He killed him!"

Zara shrugged. "Marcus did what he had to do. He didn't force Uri to join with the Sicarii. That was Uri's choice. If I was going to blame someone, it would be Uri, but I believe he loved me, and I know I loved him. Things just didn't turn out the way either one of us expected. Am I angry?" She sighed deeply. "Sometimes. But mostly I mourn what could have been. I can't stay mad at him. I won't remember him that way. I want to remember him when he was here with me." She wiped a tear from her cheek.

"If only Marcus had not—"

"It's not Marcus' fault."

Hadassah's head snapped toward her friend. "Not his fault?" Her voice escalated. "Marcus is the one who stood there, giving orders to crucify Yeshua and Uri. It most certainly was his fault!" She turned away from Zara, her lips pressed into a thin line, arms crossed over her chest.

"Don't blame Marcus, Hadassah." Her saddened eyes narrowed slightly. "Uri made the decision to do what he did. He knew the dangers when he left." Her voice was heavy with sorrow as she continued. "Marcus had no choice but to obey his superiors."

A stubborn scowl appeared on Hadassah's face. "I am so tired of hearing that. You weren't there! You didn't see what he did to them!"

"No, I wasn't. It must have been very hard for you." Zara's words were spoken with compassion as she wiped away another tear that threatened to fall. "But you have to let go of your anger. You know the Scriptures tell us to cease from anger and forsake wrath. It's God's will for us to forgive, and that's what Yeshua said to do, remember?"

Hadassah turned away from Zara as she stated defiantly, "I can't."

"You mean, you won't."

Hadassah's indignant look quickly faded as Zara continued to speak.

"I know I'm not the smartest girl around, but I don't think that we can pick and choose what we want to believe if Yeshua said it. I mean, if we really believe he's the Son of God, aren't we supposed to try to do everything he says?"

Hadassah squirmed in her discomfort, convicted by Zara's words. She lowered her head as her guilt threatened to overwhelm her.

Zara squeezed Hadassah's hand. "I know it's hard, but if Yeshua said it, you must try, right? Besides, I miss the old Hadassah."

Hadassah looked up through tortured eyes. She spoke in anguished tones barely audible. "Oh, Zara, it eats away at me. Sometimes I get so angry I bury my face in my pillow and scream. Sometimes I want to kill him myself! How can I ever forgive Marcus for what he's done?"

Zara said nothing for a time, but when she did, her words were full of wisdom. "The Lord is good, Hadassah, and plenteous in mercy. In the day of our trouble, we are to call on Him, and He will answer us. Ask Him to help you forgive. Ask Him to help you forgive as Yeshua told us we should do."

* * * * * *

It was early morning when Marcus neared Capernaum. He had ridden through most of the night, stopping only to allow Ares to rest. He wanted to tell Hadassah what he had finally realized. He wanted desperately to convince her of his sincerity, but now that he could see his father's house in the distance, he questioned the wisdom of his decision to visit Hadassah. He feared her rejection, but he pressed on.

"C'mon, Ares. Just a little farther. I promise you a huge portion of oats and barley," said Marcus as he leaned forward to stroke the steed's thick neck. Picking up the pace, Ares easily climbed the final bit of the path to the Caelinus estate.

After securing the horse with the groomsman, Marcus strode up the graveled walkway to the main house. The torches flickered around the outside walkways, and candles glowed from within, casting dancing shadows on the walls.

He entered into the great room to find it empty.

"Father? Judith?"

Hasty footsteps came closer until finally a servant appeared. Marcus pivoted to face him.

The servant bowed his head respectfully. "They are not here. They have traveled to Caesarea. We did not know you were coming. We shall prepare your quarters immediately." He bowed once more and retreated into the hall before Marcus had spoken a word.

"Okay," Marcus said to himself. "Now what?" Removing his helmet, he set it down on a table and ran his fingers through his hair. "So much for–"

"Marcus?"

He spun around to see Hadassah standing with a basket full of towels.

"You're here? I thought everyone had gone to Caesarea."

She shook her head. "No. Judith doesn't need my help as in the past, so the choice to go or stay was mine. It was so soon after we returned, I chose to stay. I had no idea you were coming. I'll go prepare your room."

"It's already being attended to."

"Oh," she averted her eyes from him as she spoke. "Will you be here long?"

"No. I have new orders and need to make arrangements for my men."

"New orders?"

"Yes. It will be a long time before I am in this region again, so I came to see my father once more..." He hesitated, then added, "And you. I was hoping I would have an opportunity to speak with you before I left. I was hoping..." Uncomfortable with the situation, he shifted his weight.

"Hoping...?"

He exhaled forcefully as he tried to explain. "Hoping I could apologize to you. Maybe make you understand..." His hands were held open, but he let them fall to his side.

"I do understand, Marcus." She spoke slowly and deliberately as she lifted her eyes to face him directly. "I am glad you're here. While I confess there was a time when I hoped I wouldn't see you, I have been praying for the chance to speak with you as well. I need to ask you for your forgiveness."

"*My* forgiveness? For what?"

"I was wrong for how I spoke to you in Jerusalem, and I am... I am very sorry." Her words were sincere, and she waited for him to respond.

"Can we sit?" He motioned to the great room.

"Of course."

Hadassah sat stiffly on the lounge, and Marcus sat next to her. Taking her hands in his, he held them for a few moments without speaking. The smoothness of her skin was a sharp contrast to the roughness of his own hands, and when she did not pull away, he felt empowered to speak.

"Hadassah, I know you doubted me when I told you that I believed Yeshua was the Son of God, but I want you to know it is the truth. I have learned so much since I saw you last, some of which I learned from Yeshua himself."

Hadassah's eyes widened. "You saw Yeshua?"

"Yes."

"You are positive it was him?"

"Without a doubt. I saw him in the garden beneath the olive trees. I saw..." He swallowed hard. "I saw the nail prints in his hands. He..." His voice broke, but he forced himself to continue. "He invited me to sit with his followers while he spoke with them. I sat for what seemed like hours, and later he walked with me alone. Just the two of us. He spoke to me of things in my life that he had no way of knowing. Things I had told no one. Things I was ashamed of. Things that I had wished I had done differently. He knew it all."

He dropped his head in his hands as he drew in a deep breath. "I was so ashamed, Hadassah."

As he raised his head, Hadassah saw tears brimming in his eyes. She blinked in astonishment as she listened to the raw emotion in Marcus' voice. She did not doubt his sincerity, and it moved her. She saw the pain in his face as he continued.

"I begged him to forgive me..." He shook his head unbelievingly. "And then he did! He forgave me for everything... even for what I'd done to him." He inhaled deeply. "I didn't know if I'd ever see you again, but I prayed I would."

He looked into her eyes. "I wanted you to know that you were right about Yeshua. All of it. Yeshua is the Son of God. I truly regret my actions. Being part of the crucifixion detail was not a choice I had. It was my duty to follow my orders, but–"

"I understand. I truly do. And if it is forgiveness you seek from me, you have it." She spoke truthfully, and her words were a balm to Marcus' burdened soul.

"I wish we had more time."

Hadassah's brow furrowed as she digested Marcus' words. Finally, she asked, "More time? What do you mean?"

"I am being sent to the north. Near Damascus. I may not get to Caesarea again for a long time." Sorrow and regret mingled with his words.

"When do you leave?" she whispered, not wanting to know the answer.

"At sun-up. You will give Justus and Judith my farewells?"

"Of course."

Stay! Don't leave!

He reached out to brush a tendril of her black hair from her cheek. "I really wish I could stay, but that is impossible. I have my orders, and I must attend to my men. Prepare them for the journey."

She said nothing as she regarded his rugged face. The thin scar on his cheek, the stray locks of blond hair on his brow, the compassion in his blue-gray eyes.

"I wish you could stay as well," she finally whispered as he lifted a hand to her face. She closed her eyes and allowed his fingers to caress her soft cheek.

"I will miss you, Hadassah," he said as he stood.

She lifted her face up to him, her lips slightly parted, and she heard him sigh.

Without another word, he picked up his helmet and left her sitting alone. For the first time, Hadassah realized just how much she cared for the Roman centurion, but now it was too late for her, and the ache in her heart would forever be hers to bear alone.

* * * * * *

Hadassah rose early the next morning just as the sun was peeking over the horizon. The shadows of the night had not yet disappeared, and she was hoping to see Marcus one last time before he left. She hastily completed her morning activities, dressed in a clean tunic, and pinned her hair up before scurrying out to the dining area.

Fresh fruit and nuts were sitting on a table, but it was only set for one. She went into the cooking area.

"Good morning, Aelia," she said upon seeing the older woman kneading dough.

"Hadassah, how may I help you?"

"Do you know where Marcus might be?" She waited expectantly for the answer, but it was not the one for which she had hoped.

"He has gone. He left as soon as the sky began to lighten." Aelia quietly studied Hadassah as the young woman's countenance fell and her shoulders sagged. "He left this for you." She handed her a small wrapped bundle that easily fit in the palm of her hand.

Tenderly, Hadassah peeled back the cloth to reveal several tiny brown balls that looked like giant seeds. Puzzled, she looked up at Aelia.

"Those are the bulbs of the blue iris," stated the older woman.

Hadassah nodded as understanding came. "The blue iris," she repeated in a whisper.

"It's a beautiful flower. I presume it's for your garden."

"Yes. Marcus knew they were my favorite."

"Well, he only asked that I give these to you, and tell you that he hoped one day he would return to enjoy the blossoms."

"I had hoped to see him before he left," she admitted sadly as her fingers closed over the flower bulbs.

"Perhaps he will return one day."

Hadassah nodded. "Perhaps." Her voice was unconvincing as she turned to leave the kitchen.

"Do you remember the meaning of this flower?"

Hadassah stopped at the door and looked back at Aelia. "Yes." Her voice caught in her throat as she softly said, "Hope. They symbolize hope." Hadassah caressed the small bulbs, then placed them in her pocket. "Thank you, Aelia. Your words have been a great encouragement to me."

She walked out of the cooking area and made her way to the second-floor landing. A cool breeze tickled the fronds of the potted ferns on each side of the outer deck as a pair of butterflies flitted past. Casting her eyes toward the western horizon, she sighed. Somewhere out there was a Roman centurion who had captured her heart.

"May the God of Abraham, Isaac, and Jacob go with you, Marcus. May He keep you safe, and one day, may He return you to me. That is my hope…" Her whispered words drifted away on the wind as she stood gazing afar.

How long she stood there, she did not know, but she did know that no matter what happened to her or Marcus in this lifetime, one day they would see each other again.

Author's Note

In 2017, my husband and I visited Israel. It was truly the "trip of a lifetime." Visiting places that I had read about in the Bible was more amazing than I could have ever imagined. Coupled with the biblical teaching received by our tour guides, the DeYoung brothers, Jimmy Jr. and Rick, I learned and experienced more than I ever dreamed possible. Three places that touched my heart deeply were the Sea of Galilee, the pool of Bethesda, and the southern steps of the temple mount in Jerusalem. Knowing I was walking in the places where Jesus once walked was overwhelming.

One other place that became very special to me was the western slope of the Mount of Olives. The evidence is overwhelming that this was the site of the crucifixion of Jesus. Unlike some of the more traditional places thought to be the place, this is the only location where the Roman centurion could have seen the opening of the Jewish graves and more importantly, the rending of the temple veil.

I wanted the cover illustration to focus on this place since the centurion was a pivotal character in this story. After seeing a beautiful painting entitled "Crucifixion 2" by Balage Balogh, I knew I wanted something exactly like that for my book. Initially, I didn't know if I could get permission to use his artwork, so I thought I'd ask my 14-year-old granddaughter if she would try to sketch the scene. After showing her Mr. Balogh's art and describing what I wanted, she created a drawing that was perfect. However, her drawing was very similar to the original piece, and I felt I needed permission from Mr. Balogh to use it on my cover. Not only did he grant that, but he graciously gave me permission to include his artwork as well!

I am very proud of my oldest granddaughter, Ryanna Campbell, for her front cover drawing on "A New Creation." The original painting, "Crucifixion 2" by Balage Balogh, can be seen on the back cover of this book, or at his website at Balage Balogh/Archaeology Illustrated.com.

About the Author

This is the fourth novel written by Jayne Lawson, and the first in her second series of Christian romance novels. Unlike the Eastmont series, which is set in contemporary America, the Beyond Belief series takes the reader on a journey into 1st century Israel. When she's not working on the 2nd book of the Beyond Belief series, Jayne enjoys serving the Lord in her church as Sunday school teacher and deaf ministry leader, traveling with her husband of 42 years, and spending time with her grandchildren.

Other Books by Jayne Lawson

<u>Eastmont Series</u>
Reluctant Love
Healing Love
Courageous Love

*****

Rebuilding the Temple
(a spiritual approach to weight loss)

You can also follow Jayne at her blog, www.writingoneagleswings.com

"Let the words of my mouth, and the meditation of my heart,
be acceptable in thy sight, O LORD, my strength, and my redeemer."
Psalm 19:14

www.ingramcontent.com/pod-product-compliance
Lightning Source LLC
Chambersburg PA
CBHW020633260626
47157CB00008B/2720